I0601743

ANGUS SLIDERS

ANGUS SLIDERS

A MAX CALDER SPY-FI MYSTERY

THE BUREAU ARCHIVES TRILOGY
BOOK 2

ALEXANDER BENTLEY

CHARLTON MANOR PUBLISHING

First published in the United States in 2025 by
Alexander Bentley and Charlton Manor Publishing
First Alexander Bentley paperback edition 2025
-oOo-
Copyright © Alexander Bentley 2025

The right of Alexander Bentley to be identified as the Author of the Work has been asserted by him in accordance with the Copyright, Designs and Patents Act, 1988 in the United Kingdom.

All rights reserved. No part of this publication may be reproduced, stored in a retrieval system, or transmitted, in any form or by any means without the prior written permission of the author or the publisher, except for the use of brief quotations in a book review, nor be otherwise circulated in any form of binding or cover other than that in which it is published and without similar condition being imposed on the subsequent purchaser.

This book is a work of fiction. All characters, organizations, and places are fictitious and any resemblance to real persons, organizations, or places is purely coincidental except for known characters or places which are used entirely fictitiously.

Hardback: 979-8-9986383-8-1
Paperback: 979-8-9986383-7-4
eBook: 979-8-9986383-4-3
Kindle Edition: 979-8-9986383-2-9

Library of Congress Control Number: 2025922025

Printed and bound by Kindle Direct Publishing and
Ingram Spark

For Lucinda

OFFICE OF
TEMPORAL ANOMALIES
ORDO IN TEMPORE
AND
STRATEGIC
INTELLIGENCE

The truth is rarely pure and never simple.

OSCAR WILDE

1948

CHAPTER 1
MISSING MEMORIES

The Mirror can't be completely destroyed—and it never forgets. But it can make you forget. Yet again, I didn't realize it at the time. Yet again, I was about to find out.

Lisbon in 1948 was a city perched on the knife-edge between peace and deceit. The war was over, but its ghosts had taken up residence in every hotel along the Avenida da Liberdade, sipping vermouth in the afternoons and pretending they weren't waiting for something to start all over again.

By day, the city glowed like tarnished brass—trams rattling down the hills from Chiado, sailors smoking on the docks, widows dressed in black trailing incense into churches that smelled of damp stone and old sins. The Tagus shimmered like a mirror no one wanted to look into too closely, carrying the shadows of ships bound for South America or nowhere in particular.

At night, Lisbon transformed into a city of contrasts. In Bairro Alto, jazz from the bars clashed with the mournful cry of Fado, that soft Portuguese blues that made even the happy sound guilty. Spies masqueraded as journalists or writers. Diplomats posed as traders. Everyone had a second name and a third story. The neutral air Portugal had prided itself on during the war hadn't dissipated; it had just thickened, becoming something more profitable.

Everywhere, the city hummed with aftershocks—a slow vibration of what had been and what was coming next. People didn't talk about the future here; they waited for it nervously, like a letter that might never arrive. The city smiled by day, lied by night, and awaited the next war to give it meaning again.

The winter months brought chilly weather, slippery cobblestone sidewalks, and foggy windows. Just like most days in November, it was raining again. Though it rarely fell below thirteen degrees, the steady drizzle carried a persistent, tangible chill. More often than not, you stayed inside during the nights—or the evenings, as the sun set over the cafés lining the streets, and the moon slowly rose into the sky, only occasionally visible through a blanket of gray clouds. The chill and damp seeped into everything during the night, permeating the coats and shoes of anyone who found themselves walking the streets, only to dissipate during the day when temperatures reached a more comfortable eighteen degrees.

I, however, was less interested in the cafés and more interested in the bars that lay scattered throughout the city, like weary splotches of paint on a canvas. I had taken to spending my time in the city's oldest taverna. Tendinha do Rossio, nestled in the heart of Rossio, had been there since 1840 and was like a window into a bygone era. It had a charm that was a long way from the Old Crow in Hell's Kitchen I frequented in New York, but I enjoyed it nevertheless. I sat alone at a table, relaxing with a glass of bourbon as I stared out the window. The bar would be closing soon, and I would be forced to leave my spot, don my hat, and make my way home through the darkness and damp. At that sobering thought, I tipped back my glass, drained it, and stood, stretching as I did. I nodded to the bartender, a short, gamy man with whom I'd developed a rapport despite never asking his name, and left the bar, putting on my hat to shield myself from the wet.

The trams creaked along, their painted interiors sparse now, the wood-and-leather scent muted by the damp air. The Estado Novo's grip on the city remained firm, but I didn't care much about it. By now, I'd traversed more regimes than I cared to admit and had grown weary of the continual shifting politics that always seemed to keep me from my work. This was much different from what it had been only a few months prior—back when I had faced off against the Soviets, the Nazis, Emil Krane, and the Bureau itself. My head ached for a second, and I rubbed my temple—what was that, anyway? What had I stopped them from using? I was certain it would have caused irreparable damage to the world. The Mirror flashed into my mind yet again. Memory failure again.

I stepped into the narrow alleyway leading to my apartment entrance. The alley was hardly two men wide, and so I made my way carefully down it, avoiding the piles of crates and shuttered windows that made the path feel even more treacherous. My boots slid against the calçada portuguesa, but I eventually arrived at my door. The building's stucco was peeling, the small green door faded, but it was a good place to go ghost. I pushed my key into the lock, the rusty mechanism turning reluctantly as I opened the door. It was an apartment building that I called home, though not one of the most popular in the city. The cold air was slightly stale as I made my way up to the third-floor landing where my room was located. Here was the same green paint, less faded but still cracked, and my door marked "No. 3."

This was where I spent the rest of my time when I wasn't haunting one of the local bars. It was sparse, but I called it home. A single large window dominated my room, one of its finest assets. Although the entrance to my apartment was from the alleyway, the window overlooked a busier street below. By the window stood my desk, which held an old Remington Model 10 typewriter and papers strewn about. Writing was how I made my living and funded my hobbies. Of course, my hobbies were always shifting, but recently I'd taken up a fascination with radios. In one corner of my apartment, I had built a simple shelving system devoted to holding all sorts of models, years, and styles of radios. Along the furthest wall, my bed—a small cot that I only used for sleep—and a large wall mirror were anchored. Elsewhere in the apartment, in the only other room, my whiskey bottles sat in the kitchen alongside my fridge, which I knew held a healthy supply of food for when I needed it.

Faint tinges of smoke lingered around the room. I occasionally smoked here, though I preferred to open a window when I did. I sighed—a resigned kind of sigh—as I pulled one of the radios off the shelf: a battered Type A MKIII that I'd picked up from a shady vendor in one of the second-hand shops. It'd seen a war and likely more than one owner, but it was my favorite radio at the moment and one that was used by SOE and MI6 agents across Europe during the war. It was very compact and fit neatly into a leather attaché case. Carrying it carefully, I moved it to my desk, where I quickly pushed aside my papers and typewriter, setting it in the very center. Unlatching the window behind me, I slid it open slightly, rigging a length of wire out into the now steadier rain. It had become a habit of mine to search through Lisbon's night air for voices. It was difficult sometimes, but that was what made my latest hobby fun—shortwave wasn't easy, but by selecting the correct night range and sweeping across the skies, I could find some intriguing signals.

Tonight, however, seemed quiet. Nearly an hour later, I'd heard nothing other than the initial hiss from the speaker when I first turned the radio on. I waited, hoping to hear something— I'd caught men in Naples before and even the occasional song floating across the airwaves. The fresh night air gently seeped in through the window as I stared back into the darkness, listening and waiting. I'd done this countless nights before, and so I knew from experience that I'd get something eventually. And then, there it was. I heard the radio crackle to life. It was a woman's voice in English—not the usual Portuguese English I heard from ships, nor any other dialect I recognized. If anything, she sounded almost London-born, but I couldn't be sure. I listened intently, pen poised in the air.

"Attention, stand by. Two-one groups, check one-six. Ready."

I listened carefully; the type of message I heard was something I hadn't encountered in years, but it was unmistakable. Five-letter groups, each clearly using Able-Baker. The cadence, the dialect, the way the message ended—it was as if my second language had suddenly begun to play through the radio. I had been reciting the message in my head, but I finally lowered the pen and began to scribble the message on a small piece of paper. I struggled to remember something this long in one go anymore —especially not a message over the radio like this. It disappointed me that I couldn't.

I had heard stations like this across the radio waves before, but it was usually the Russians, and even then, it was rare. This one wasn't Russian—this one ended with a concise, recognizable British signoff. It wasn't Bureau, either—I knew the Bureau's M.O. for messages, as they preferred to use a network of local agents and encrypted telephone communication when needed. This message had been sent in classic MI6 Section VIII style for agent broadcasts.

However, there was something off about it. Though it was indistinguishable from the classic MI6 broadcasts I'd known so well when I worked for the organization, there was something that just didn't sit right with me. Maybe it was the cadence. Maybe it was the way the message was sent—so easily, so recognizable. Whatever it was, I'd trained my ear for this. Whoever was behind this message was either MI6 or knew the organization well enough to imitate it.

I sat there in silence, my mind whirring. I wanted to take a shot at decoding the message, but my eyes were tired and my head was abuzz with alcohol. Instead, I stood, staring at the message one more time before carefully folding up the piece of paper. I wanted to conceal it, and so I did what I had done many times before and hid it inside the large label in the collar of my trench coat. It was easy to slide it in from the top and use a simple stitch to seal it in. I knew it would be safe there. I glanced out my window, staring down at the street below. Whatever this message was, it had instantly brought a host of old memories, and I felt a wave of caution wash over me.

The street looked empty. A stray cat trotted beneath the glowing ember colors of the streetlamp, but everything else was still. As I continued to watch, however, the streetlights outside flickered once, twice, and then once more. I rubbed my eyes; it was definitely time for bed. Turning from the window, I shuffled toward my bed, rubbing my neck. I glanced around the room once more—at the radio still on my desk, the typewriter next to it, and the old fridge that hummed in the kitchen. But then, in the mirror next to my bed, I saw it. A face was there only for a second, but it glared at me—bluish eyes out of a shadowy figure, almost wispy, almost as if the body was dripping and deteriorating in real time. It was gone the moment I blinked.

Rubbing my eyes again, I stared at the mirror once more, but whatever I had seen was no longer there. I muttered as I sat down on the bed, kicking my boots off and placing them underneath. "Damn. That's something."

I wasn't sure what I had seen, but I'd been around these things long enough to know that whatever I had just experienced wasn't just a fluke, and it wasn't just my imagination. I was sure that nothing I did tonight would change this, and I was too tired to care in any meaningful way. Tomorrow, I would try and figure out what this strange message over the radio meant. Tomorrow, I would try to recall the figure in the mirror and try to remember why it looked so familiar.

I closed my eyes. My thoughts were racing, triggered by MI6, the Mirror, and doppelgängers. Eventually, I drifted into sleep, images of the past resurfacing. The dream always began the same way.

———

Thin air. Too high to breathe. A black ridge of Andes rock cutting the clouds open. The temple squats along the spine of the mountain—stone walls older than names, Nazi crates scattered between broken idols. The night tastes of iron and rain.

I am running, a gun in one hand. Somewhere behind me, Alicia shouts—orders, warnings, maybe both. Ahead, under the collapsed archway, Krane's men are hauling boxes up the steps —the same boxes they burned a city for. I see metal glinting in the torchlight.

Shots crack. Sparks jump off stone. I slide behind a column carved with serpents. I fire twice. One of the men goes down; another drags a crate toward the altar at the center of the temple. The sound of the wind outside becomes a low, pulsing hum— like the mountain's heart learning to beat again.

Alicia appears in the doorway, dust in her hair, her eyes fixed on the crate. "Don't let them open it!" she yells.

Krane turns. Calm. Always calm. "We already have," he replies, kicking the lid open with his boot. Cold blue light spills over everything—torches, statues, faces. The mountain seems to hold its breath.

I aim. Alicia shouts my name. The light jumps higher, flooding the room, burning edges into every shadow. Then the explosion—no fire, just a pressure that shoves the world away. Columns split, stone screams, and for an instant, I see myself across the altar, holding the gun, mirror-still.

Then silence. Dust falling like snow. Alicia gone. Krane gone. The crates empty.

———

I woke in the dark, cold sweat slick on my back, the echo of that light still behind my eyes. The same dream—every night. The same mountain. The same question: What did I lose up there— and why does it still call me?

Eventually, sunlight seeped through the shutters. The room

was hot and airless, the kind of heat that made the paint peel from old plaster. For a few seconds, I didn't know where I was. I glanced in the mirror by my bed. There was nothing—only my own reflection. Then the light shifted, and I saw the familiar cracks in the ceiling and the typewriter near the window. Lisbon. My temporary exile. I'd had this dream before. The Bureau called it trauma. MI6 called it operational residue. I knew what it really was, though. I knew it was memory, bleeding backward. And it wasn't going to stop.

I quickly stood and prepared for the day, getting ready in my usual fashion before I left my apartment. The morning air was fresh but had already begun to warm, and the rain had ceased. Still, I wore my trench coat with the message inside the label. With me, I carried the Type A MKIII in its attaché case, a note-book, and a pen, which I planned to use in an attempt to solve the message I'd heard over the radio, although I doubted I'd be able to. If it were MI6, as I suspected, nothing in the message would be given over easily, and they'd have likely used a sort of one-time pad to secure it. Without that, I highly doubted I'd be able to decipher whatever was hidden within the bursts I'd heard over the radio waves, and yet I wanted to give it a try anyway. For me, this was like the challenge of a cryptic cross-word puzzle.

I boarded one of the trams, holding tight to the attaché case, and glanced around as it rumbled through the streets. There were only a few other passengers, each seemingly preoccupied with their own thoughts. I was too. I normally enjoyed people-watching, but my mind was on something else today. A deep sense of unease had settled in, though I couldn't place it. There was excitement at the task of attempting to decipher the message, but there was also a nagging feeling that I'd forgotten something… I just didn't know what.

This had happened several times since I'd brought down Krane, narrowly escaping the collapsing temple. Several times now, I'd forgotten things. Sometimes, it had been minor—names, places, or things I'd eaten. But other times, I had forgotten whole chunks of my past—even Krane himself—and only remembered later when something jogged my memory.

And that was how I felt now.

The tram stopped near Café Nicola, where I planned to spend my morning. I stepped out into the street, making my way along until the familiar café came into sight. I entered, and a few minutes later, I was nursing a bourbon with a custard tart beside it, my notebook open and the radio in its attaché case on the table in front of me. I didn't want to open it here, but I wanted to keep it close as I worked on the cipher. I scribbled down a few notes, then created a blank grid where I could puzzle through it. I didn't want to write down the message itself—this had been ingrained in me by my many years as a spy—but writing down the potential solutions to the problem helped me think, so I did. I pulled the message from the label in my coat.

Soon, I had a whole page filled with notes, ciphers, and potential solutions. It was a far-fetched attempt, but I had fallen into a boring routine—writing, drinking my paranoia away until I forgot that I kept forgetting, and then repeating the process ad nauseam. My life had been free, but my mind hadn't.

I sighed, stretching as I took a break from the scribbles. Sipping on my bourbon, I glanced out the window. It had started raining again, but this time I was lucky enough to have no reason to leave. I was halfway through a bite of my custard tart when a noise at the door caught my attention. I looked up and saw a beautiful woman with brilliantly auburn hair, her chin sharp, and her red lips matching her hair. She glanced around the bar before her eyes settled on me.

I stared back at her, maintaining eye contact. She walked toward me, her red scarf and trench coat completing her look— her movements gentle, swaying with quiet confidence; I realized I knew her from somewhere. I racked my brain, trying to remember. Where had I seen her before? Had I met her at MI6 when I cracked ciphers for a living? Or at the Bureau? Or maybe before it all, in Glasgow? Although that didn't seem likely. I furrowed my brow, trying to figure out this puzzle before we collided, but she was already at my table. She sat across from me, smiled gently, and looked at me as if she were waiting for me to speak.

"I know you, don't I?" I was still staring at her carefully. "I've been having some issues with remembering things lately. I'm sorry; you'll have to refresh my memory. It seems to have gone missing again. Are you MI6? If you are, you're probably here because of the message."

"What message?"

"Never mind… How do I know you?"

"I'm Artemis," she said, a hint of sadness in her eyes and a sorrowful smile on her lips. "Do you remember Krane?"

I immediately froze.

How the hell had I forgotten her?

Forgetting Krane, that was one thing, but her? My memories came flooding back at once, and I remembered her again. At that moment, I hated myself for forgetting her—I hated myself for forgetting how she'd helped me, how she'd pulled me out of the collapsing temple.

"Remember now?" She was watching my face.

"Damn. Alicia, I'm so sorry," I said, grimacing. "I am mortified. I thought all these damn memory issues would go away when we got rid of the Mirror and Krane along with it."

She dismissed my apology with a wave of her hand, and though she was difficult to read, I thought I saw a hint of tension and foreboding still in her eyes—that she didn't trust me not to forget her again. But I didn't mention it.

She sighed, taking a second to collect her thoughts before continuing. "That's why I'm here, Max. There are reports that the Mirror isn't gone. Or at least… there may be another one."

I was shocked. I sat there, feeling a weight press down on my shoulders. The Mirror. If the Mirror was still active, then that meant that everything we'd done—every sacrifice I had made—

had been in vain. I closed my eyes for a second, leaning back as I contemplated what she'd told me. Mixed emotions simmered at the brim of my mind, like a melting pot too full of various scraps to make complete sense of. On one hand, I didn't want it to be true. But on the other hand, if it was, maybe—just maybe—I had a chance to fix myself. To fix all the breaks and tears the Mirror had left me with, all the memory gaps and the pain.

Opening my eyes, I glanced at Alicia again. She sat there, her eyes carefully searching my face but remained silent. It was clear she wasn't entirely sure how I would react.

"Well... I guess that makes sense given what has been happening to me," I said, nodding. "I've definitely had some memory gaps lately. It hasn't gotten better. What's the intel?"

Alicia leaned forward, lowering her voice even though nobody in the café cared if we spoke. I knew her body language —she had something big, and she was worried. And if Alicia was worried, I was on edge.

"Rosyth," she said. That was all she offered, but the word was enough to bring back haunting memories I'd tried so hard to suppress—the guilt, the anger, and the pain that had all stemmed from that place.

"Rosyth? What about it?" I asked her, tapping the table with my fingers. "It's shut down, no?"

"I'm not so sure. It should be, but—there are rumors going around that there was a breach there a while back. Some disturbance there, covered up almost perfectly. And there are rumors... MI6 involvement."

"These are all rumors," I said carefully, though I knew she had more. "You wouldn't come all this way for rumors."

"Maybe I wanted to see you," she said, half-laughing.

I knew it could have been true, but I pressed on. Normally, I would have joked with her, but my mind was hell-bent on the Mirror's rumored existence. "Maybe, but I know you, Alicia. You always do your research. So what is it that has you so worried?"

"Well," she said, "what I heard from my sources was initially just about missing pieces—Mirror circuits and the like. But then things started happening, and to be careful, I looked into it."

"What things?"

She didn't answer. Instead, she reached into her coat pocket and slid something onto the table. It was a thin, dirty piece of glossy paper. I glanced at it—quickly at first—then did a double-take. The object she had slid across the table was a small photograph, no bigger than my hand, yet unmistakable. Though the corners had been smudged and slightly torn, the surface wrinkled, and the subject blurred and difficult to make out, I recognized him. I recognized the posture and the face—there was no doubt it was me. A slight fear began to stir in my chest as I stared at the photo, a dizzying sense of déjá vu that just wouldn't go away. It was something I'd had nightmares about, though I never wanted to admit it—one of the fears I drank to forget.

Another doppelgänger. And beneath it was the hastily scrawled text "SL-," though I couldn't make out the rest.

"That's you, Max," Alicia said softly.

I nodded. The lump in my throat felt rancid, rising like bile, and I swallowed before I spoke. "Where'd you get this?"

"About fifteen days ago, near Rosyth. Got it through a dockside contact who lifted it off one of the suits who was allegedly reviewing the site."

"Bureau?"

"No idea. I wanted to reach out to you first."

"There have been doppelgängers before," I said, shaking my head. "But walking around the coast of Scotland? Just out there, like that? And who snapped the pic?"

"Not sure. But if there are rumors of MI6 involvement, that likely means they've somehow gotten their hands on Mirror technology."

"Those damn idiots." I glanced around, as if expecting to see MI6 agents peering around the corner, but there was nothing.

"So what now?" Alicia's voice was quiet, but I could tell from her tone that she already knew my answer.

"Well," I said, standing. "The job isn't finished, is it? I thought it was. If it isn't finished, I suppose we have to go to Scotland to find out what is going on. And on the way, we'll take a few guesses at what signals MI6 has been sending."

CHAPTER 2
LISBON LEARNINGS

Leaving Lisbon wasn't a decision I wanted to make. I really wanted to stay. I didn't want to be dragged back into the life that I now half-regretted, a life I had once been addicted to and yet had grown to despise. But I didn't see a choice. If the Mirror was operational again—if someone, somehow, had figured out a way to bring it back into action—then we needed to get to the bottom of it. And if there was another Calder out there, I needed to put him down. Alicia stood next to me in the café, leaning over to grab the radio case I'd left lying on the table, but as she did, she tapped my leg. It was a slight gesture, but just enough to make me glance at her. I watched her eyes travel across the street before darting back to the table. I followed the direction her gaze had drifted, casually, as if simply glancing up for a second to check the weather, and saw what she had spotted.

A man was leaning up against one of the buildings, holding a parcel in his arms, but he seemed to be intently staring at us through the window. He wore a brown hat and was of medium build; his face was slightly heavyset, but his body looked surprisingly solid. I didn't look at him again. Instead, I ushered Alicia toward the door, as if we had finished our meal.

"What about him?" I asked.

"I noticed him when I first got here," she replied in low tones. "He hasn't left."

"That's enough for me."

We threaded our way out of the café onto the wet street and headed toward the tram lines. As we walked, I occasionally glanced at the sides of the street, careful to never glance directly behind us. By watching the reflections in the passing shops and casually pointing out items to Alicia as if I were merely window-shopping, I kept track of the man. He was closing in on us slowly, following carefully only a few yards behind now. Every once in a while, he pretended to loiter near the stalls when we slowed or stopped. Alicia's fingers slowly slipped inside her coat, and I knew that was likely where her pistol was, ready for use at a moment's notice.

I breathed steadily, calming myself. My body felt older now —it had since our run-in with Krane and the Mirror—and I had to remind myself that my experience should be enough, even if I was slower now. I glanced at the windows again, noting how the man appeared to be walking. I couldn't tell for sure, but from the way he held his hands, I guessed he was left-handed. If that were the case, I knew which side he'd come at us from if he decided to act. Still, he had only trailed us as of yet, so I wasn't entirely sure what he wanted.

We had reached a quieter street, and I glanced at one of the windows again. There were barely any people around—a few bums and a few stray cats, but no crowds. As I watched, however, I heard the man's footsteps quicken—too deliberately, too much of a change from his previous pace.

Then I saw it—the glint, the shimmer of a blade under his coat as he stepped forward.

I didn't think or hesitate. I spun around, grabbing his wrist and slamming his arms into the wall. Beside me, I heard Alicia react, drawing her pistol.

"Ahh, fu—" the man grunted as the knife spun from his grip.

He kicked at me, his boot landing solidly on my chest as I saw him reaching with his right hand beneath his trench coat. Without thinking, I swung my arm out with full force, the side of my hand colliding with the man's temple. I heard a crack as I struck, and he fell backward as I let go of his arm. He crumpled to the ground, his head striking the cement really hard with a sickening thud.

I stepped back, grimacing as I glanced at Alicia. She stared at me, eyebrow raised.

"Sorry about that," I muttered. "Should have probably kept him alive."

She had already bent down and begun rummaging through the man's pockets. "It would have been better to interrogate him for sure. You on edge about something?"

"No. No. Nothing I can't handle." I shivered. The drizzle had begun to cut through my coat.

Moments later, Alicia had pulled the contents of the man's pockets out, stuffed them into her own, and we hurried along one of the side streets. Alicia still carried the radio in her gloved hand, and I was glad it hadn't broken in the fight.

"Where now?" Alicia's voice cut through the quiet as we walked.

"Take a look at his information—anything we can use to identify him," I said gruffly. "We'll head to my apartment before we do anything further."

Our feet splashed in the rivulets of rainwater that ran toward the gutters, slipping through the cracks of the street. Silence enveloped us. It wasn't that I was weary or avoiding her; I just didn't know what to say. I knew that killing the man probably hadn't been the best decision, and I regretted it. Yet part of me wanted it to be justified so that I could absolve myself of any guilt. I'd killed plenty of people, and the man had been trying to kill us—that wasn't what bothered me. What troubled me was how my decision had impacted our ability to glean the information we needed from him. And that was something I truly hated.

By the time we reached my apartment, the fog and rain had thickened even more—so heavy that it seemed to pour over us like a veil, blanching the city in a grayish white. The door creaked as I opened it, and I directed Alicia inside. As I opened the door, however, my body tensed, and I motioned quietly to Alicia. It had been securely locked when I had left the building, and now it opened too easily without my key. I stepped through and froze in my tracks as I glanced around at the room.

The whole place was in disarray. My papers were strewn across the floor. The desk was overturned. The shelves—shelves of radios I'd stored for months—had been ransacked, each radio gutted with its contents piled into a heap.

"Holy…" Alicia's voice came in a whisper.

"Damn it," I said, hurrying over to my typewriter, which seemed to be the only thing that hadn't been touched. I glanced at it. "Hell, they even took the keys out of my typewriter."

"What do you think they were looking for? Or was it only one person?"

"I'm not sure," I muttered, "but I'm damn glad I didn't leave the message I heard on the radio lying around."

Alicia crossed the room, kicking remnants of my items out of the way as she did, glancing around in distaste. "You really kept this place bare."

"Yeah, well—I didn't have much need for personal belongings. No point."

"I suppose. You been holding up okay? …Other than, you know…" Alicia's voice trailed off.

I didn't answer that. "Doesn't seem like whoever did this decided to stay around. I can only guess this is because of your arrival—they couldn't be after the message; I doubt they even know I intercepted it."

She nodded. "He followed me to the café, not you. Which means they probably wanted to keep me from ever giving you that photo."

I knelt to examine my papers. Most had been torn or crumpled. "Whoever it was, they got here too quickly. Someone had my address."

"Terrifying," she replied wryly.

"Well," I said, nodding toward her. "I suppose now's as good a time as any to try and find out what we can about that guy I disposed of."

She nodded and laid out what she'd taken from his body: the man's lighter, half of a cigar, a small hip flask of what appeared to be whiskey, a stub of tickets for a tram route, an empty notebook, and a card. The card, however, was what caught my attention. It was black, sleek, and slightly bent, but the writing on it was still very legible. Avenida Palace.

"Of course. It would be Avenida Palace," I said, standing and straightening my coat. "Shall we head there?"

"Why Avenida Palace?"

"It's a favorite of secret agents, politicians, diplomats, and the like. There are spies from everywhere in that place. I actually wrote about it for one of my jobs… even Manuel Teixeira Gomes stayed there when he was President."

"Then whoever this guy was, he was foreign."

"Yes, most likely," I muttered as I sifted through my items, packing what I needed that had survived. "But it's almost too convenient. Either the place is bait, or it's sloppy work from him. Should never have carried the card with him."

"Either way," Alicia said, "I doubt he expected us to survive the attack. We have to investigate."

I packed a suitcase with my clothes and other precious possessions that had survived. The rain had finally stopped, making it easier to get to the tram that headed toward Avenida Palace. We slipped between shadows until we boarded. I wanted to make sure we weren't being followed, and by the time we'd finished the journey, it was near dusk. Upon arriving at the hotel, which stood prominently above the street in one of Lisbon's most traveled areas, it was undoubtedly a haven for those experienced in spycraft.

The hotel's interior decoration had an exquisite Belle Époque style. The rugs, portieres, and ottoman upholstery were the finest available, with furniture sourced directly from Maple in London. Almost all of the rooms distinguished themselves with their silk lining or leather paper, and the walls in the dining room were overlaid with leafy velvet and oak wainscoting. The hotel's kitchen was considered to be one of Lisbon's finest.

Acknowledged by nobility and favored by secret agents from all four corners of the world, a private orchestra flooded the rooms with music during their famous Saturday balls while the dancing pairs swirled around and spies from everywhere looked for conspiracies.

Inside, the clerks barely raised their eyes as we entered. I ignored them, walking next to Alicia as we threaded our way through the hallways, as if we were already familiar with the building. Along the way, I examined the card again, finding the digits "214" penciled on the reverse side in small letters. It must have been a room number, and so we made our way there, where we encountered our first challenge—the room was unsurprisingly tightly locked.

I cracked my knuckles, then bent down, pulling a pick from my pocket—this was something I was good at. Alicia smirked behind me as she kept watch.

Minutes later, I had the door open, and it swung inward. Alicia had her pistol out in a second, and we slipped inside, making sure to lock it behind us as our eyes adjusted to the dimly lit area. The room was plain, though professional. The curtains were closed, and with only one look around, I could tell that whoever the man had been, he hadn't bothered to fully move in—or had carried very little when he checked in. There was no umbrella, no scattered clothes—nothing.

"Damn. OK. We should search the place." I didn't wait for Alicia's nod of agreement. I yanked open the cabinet drawers nearest to where I stood.

The first drawer was empty, but I had expected as much. If

there was any information, it would have been hidden carefully within the room, ensuring nothing would be found from a surface-level search if it were cleaned or broken into. Then again, the man trailing us hadn't exactly seemed professional, so I thought it best to check anyway. Alicia walked toward the furthest side of the room, nearest to the closed curtains, and began to search the room as well. I glanced around—where would a man of this caliber, who clearly lacked competence yet had enough finesse not to leave his items lying about, hide something?

He carried a hotel card as if almost broadcasting his hideout, followed us without proper cover or distance, and even tried to make his attack while there was a risk of being caught. This wasn't a man who had worked for an organization as long as we had, and if he kept anything in the room, he must have hidden it in the same manner that he planned his attack; not very well.

I crouched near the table beside the bed, running my fingers along the wooden underside. There was nothing taped here. As I crouched, however, my eyes were set on the mattress. It was too carefully tucked and bulged slightly in one area. I slid my hands beneath the edge and lifted it upward—and there, beneath the mattress, was a folder. Alicia turned and walked toward me as I slid the folder out from beneath the mattress, opening it and thumbing through the contents.

"Got something here," I said as she joined me.

"Anything good?"

"Well, for starters—this." I had my hands on it instantly, and I recognized what it was. The small sheet was no larger than an ace of spades, covered in rows of five-digit numbers, printed neatly across the surface. There was no identifier stamped on it —but I wasn't surprised. The instruction in the corner, however, caught my eye. It read simply, "BURN AFTER USE," which confirmed my suspicions.

"Hell," Alicia said, eyeing it. "What are the chances this is the one you'd be looking for?"

"Well, I've still got the cipher in my coat. But we can test it later. There are other papers in the folder as well."

As I spoke, I pulled out several more papers, each one a newspaper clipping, photo, or clandestine note. Though they were characteristically empty and devoid of any signatures, each one was in some way related to her. It was her face in the photos and her code name mentioned in the writings.

"Artemis leaving for Lisbon, departed via boat. Trace her there, await instructions via transmission," I read aloud, glancing at her. Her eyes remained unreadable. "The mission is as discussed, and reward will be paid upon completion."

"I guess we know someone didn't want me alive," she said.

"Let's not stay here, then. We'll leave tonight...head for Southampton."

"Agreed. Whether MI6 is involved, the Bureau, or both... the Mirror is too dangerous. We have to do something."

"Well then," I said, motioning toward the door. "Shall we?"

———

I woke before dawn, when the only light came from the moonlight that filtered through the window. Alicia and I had stayed at a boarding house close to the waterfront, waiting for the morning before we made our next move. It was cheap and smelled of salt and fish, but it was better than risking my ransacked flat. We still had no idea if the man who had attacked us worked alone or if he had help. I stood and glanced at her.

She was sleeping quietly on the bed, her face gentle and soft. Lighting a cigarette, I paced back and forth in the room, discomfort settling in. Something wasn't right—something didn't add up yet. How did they get a working Mirror—if it were true? The Mirror, the Bureau, MI6, Krane... something had to have been secretly smuggled out or discovered. Krane was dead, that much I was sure of. And the Mirror itself had been destroyed when we'd fought him—at least the one he had. So what happened? I glanced at Alicia again, and as if on cue, she sat up and opened her eyes.

"Morning," I said.

"Up long?"

"Not too long."

The morning rays had just begun to shine, and we packed in silence. I had meager savings enough to contribute to tickets and hotels, and Alicia's work these past few months had apparently been lucrative—she carried a hefty sum herself, more than enough for both of us. The night before, I had called around, making sure I knew which ships would be departing and the places where we were most likely to find tickets back to England. We set out through the dim, foggy drizzle that streaked through the air like lines drawn from the blue-gray clouds hanging low over the tumultuous ocean. By the time we reached the quay at Alcântara, the bustle of Lisbon had begun. Men, mostly sailors, walked here and there, and several gave gruff but respectful nods toward Alicia as we passed.

Old men smoked near the warehouses, and the damp gangways were busy as we moved through. The place itself smelled of oil, salt, paint, and the sea. Checking my watch, I realized we didn't have long to wait; we wasted no time finding the vessel that would take us on the first leg of our journey. Stepping aboard the old ship, we quietly made our way along the deck, and I glanced back at Lisbon one last time. I felt a sudden pang of sadness and resentment. It was here that I called home. This was where I wanted to stay. And yet, here I was, boarding the Infanta Dom Maria, a godforsaken, patched-together coastal steamer heading for Cherbourg that seemed as aged as I was, ready to begin another journey. After all the years I'd spent working, risking my life, and discovering that time itself wasn't as solid as most men think, here I was again about to embark on another challenge. I figured I must be mad.

We quietly entered our cabin, and I glanced around. It was clean enough, and though it was simple, I couldn't complain. It wasn't like my apartment in Lisbon had been spectacular either. Alicia and I kept our guns close as we settled in for the day, and it was then that I finally remembered what we'd delayed the night before.

"Shall we see if the code works?"

"The one-time pad? What are the chances it's connected?"

"I'd bet rather good, actually," I said wryly, snuffing out a cigarette and pulling the small sheet from my pocket. I hadn't told Alicia, but that figure I'd seen in the mirror next to my bed... it must have been there for a reason. I just didn't know what the reason was yet.

"Well then," she responded, "where's the code you intercepted?"

I carefully slid it out from the label in the back of my coat. Alicia smiled slightly as she watched me but didn't say anything. I placed it carefully next to the pad and started. Here was everything I needed. My mind whirred as I pieced it together: the numbers, the keys, and the codes. I read it with ease, which almost frightened me. I couldn't remember my own damn life, and yet this was child's play. I didn't even need to align the pieces—this I could do in my head. As I made it out, however, I fished a pencil out of my pocket along with a crumpled piece of paper and began to write.

ISRB // KINGSWAY // STOP.
EXECUTE AS PLANNED.
AUTHORISATION // H.A.R. PHILBY.

"Alicia..." My voice trailed off as she glanced over the paper alongside me.

"What is it?"

"Well, I'm not sure what any of this means... But I recognize this name."

"H.A.R. Philby?"

"I worked with him at MI6. And I am sure I have seen him

since, but I have no recollection of where or when or why. It's a complete blank."

I stared at the paper in silence, my eyes rapidly scanning it, taking in each piece of the message. I knew the ISRB: the Inter-Services Research Bureau, based in Baker Street and a cover name for the SOE. They operated laboratories and workshops throughout England. They also had ties to MI6 and likely a connection with Philby.

What did this mean? And why did the man who tried to kill us have the code for this message in his room?

Outside our small cabin, the ship's horn wailed, an eerie sound that cut through the mist that had settled around the ship. Southampton, London, and Rosyth lay ahead, but I wasn't sure I wanted to find out what awaited us.

CHAPTER 3
ELLIOTT ENCOUNTER

There was no other way to put it—the cabin felt too small. I had shared tighter rooms before, with strangers, soldiers, and enemies, but not with a woman I was so close to yet so distant from. Alicia sat across from me on the small bed, her eyes fixed on the porthole as if something was fascinating about the waves that lapped against the hull of the ship. Everything outside was gray. It was the same, old, endless ocean that we'd passed hours ago. And it continued on.

The Infanta Dom Maria wasn't built for comfort—that much was clear. She was a ship you'd trust to get you to your destination simply because she'd done so a thousand times before.

What made this trip so awkward for me was simply how I couldn't read Alicia—and how much memory we'd lost together, and how much we'd remembered. I still felt the sting of forgetting her in Lisbon, which remained fresh in my mind—and though I didn't care to admit it, I wasn't entirely sure where we stood. We'd been lovers, roommates, agents of espionage, and even briefly enemies before—an intertwined fate that felt as if it were a gigantic puzzle, all thrown together with pieces that didn't quite fit.

It had been a day and a half since Lisbon, and the ship had

sailed through rough waters. We'd set out for Cherbourg—there were no direct ships from Lisbon we could reasonably take, and it was likely a safer port anyway. We had both known the journey would be tedious. Still, as the coastal steamer carried us northward through the cold seas, the drizzle, and the fog, I found that silence had become all too commonplace between us. I had tried to strike up a conversation with her that morning, speaking of Rosyth, but her answers had been short. Truthfully, I had been grateful for it, and we'd fallen into this silence after, neither of us willing to break it. Conversations, at least for my part, stung as they reminded me of the growing gaps in my memory.

My memory, which had always been one of my most prized talents, was filled with gaps—and I didn't know which memories were even real anymore. Everything felt real, of course, but every so often, I'd catch myself remembering something—some trip with Alicia, a kiss, or something else—that had never happened. The memories came and went, so real that each one carried the weight of reality, yet just a second later, they felt fake in comparison. And so I sat, stewing in paranoia and a lingering depression.

The storm outside began to worsen, and the ship began to rock as thunder rolled across the waves.

"At the very least," I said to her at one point, watching my reflection in the small porthole glass, "they won't suspect our route. It's not direct."

"That's true," she replied, without shifting her eyes. "You holding up?"

"As well as you, I'm sure," I responded, though I knew why she asked. I didn't want to give her a full answer, but in the same instant, I knew she understood I was purposefully being vague.

She shrugged, and we settled back into silence again, though the edge of the silence had been cut slightly and felt less than before. The monotony of the journey, as the sunset outside turned into dusk, began to wear on me. I sighed deeply, rubbing my eyes. They were tired, and my mind began to slip. I kept seeing the Mirror—every time I had encountered it before, and each temptation it had offered me.

"You're thinking loudly," she said, breaking the silence.

I jolted, glancing at her. At some point, she had lain down on the bed and was smoking a cigarette as she observed my face. Her eyes traversed mine, searching me, and I grinned almost sheepishly.

"Maybe I was," I admitted.

"Maybe? Well, either way, Max, we should really try to get some rest. It's late."

"Oh, it is... isn't it?" I glanced out the porthole, seeing nothing but the pitch black night.

I lay on the floor, clasped my hands behind my head, and closed my eyes. The wooden floor creaked, the ship groaned, and thunder rumbled outside. But when I closed my eyes, the noises faded, and I saw her.

The first time we had ever met.

I felt sleep pulling me, but the memory pressed itself against my thoughts, tearing me from sleep as I remembered her.

She had looked very much the same back then.

———

Istanbul was "one of the great espionage entrepôts of the war," according to MI6's official historian. When Alicia and I first met, this was absolutely true. The city was just forty miles from Bulgaria, the Nazi-occupied gateway to the Middle East, serving as an access point for the Allied forces into occupied Europe.

I was, without question, walking into a city that listened more closely than it let on. It was a place where coal dust, oil, and political espionage mixed in almost perfect quantities—a place where men and women were never what they said, and where one wrong move could put not only you but your entire organization into jeopardy. The authorities here were prepared to tolerate espionage by foreign powers, as long as it didn't impinge on Turkish society, and as long as the spies didn't get caught. That was the crucial deciding factor. Intelligence agencies could mix and mingle here in Istanbul, allowed to bribe, seduce, and betray, each agency with a vast network of agents, double agents, blackmailers, arms dealers, pimps, forgers, hookers, and con artists. Rumors and secrets circulated wildly, swirling around back alleys like the cigar smoke in pubs—some true, countless others built on lies.

Everyone spied on everyone else. The Turkish police, the Emniyet, spied on them all. It was a system of pure, cold efficiency—a game built on the international nature of the place, with even Turkish officials being drawn into the fold, often to share intelligence if the price were right.

Sooner or later, however, someone would go too far, prompting the Emniyet to stage an arrest. Then all the agencies would back off or claim to, only to resume their activities as if nothing had happened. The Park Hotel was the chief place where even the most lauded members of intelligence agencies would spend their time, though not without impunity. Whenever one of those recognized men walked in, everyone else played the game of pretense, acting as if they were not recognized.

But not the bands that played there.

Right on cue, they would strike up the song "Boo, Boo, Baby, I'm a Spy" and play it to their faces. The intelligence chiefs would ignore it, continue on their way, and pretend as if nobody knew who they were—and everyone else would do the same.

I'm involved in a dangerous game,
Every other day, I change my name,
The face is different, but the body's the same,
Boo, boo, baby, I'm a spy!
You have heard of Mata Hari,
We did business cash and carry,

Poppa caught us, and we had to marry,
Boo, boo, baby, I'm a spy!
Now, as a lad, I'm not so bad,
In fact, I'm a darn good lover,
But look, my sweet, let's be discreet,
And do this under cover.
I'm so cocky I could swagger,
The things I know would make you stagger,
I'm ten percent cloak and ninety percent dagger,
Boo, boo, baby, I'm a spy!

Back then, Istanbul was an enjoyable place. It was like a giant game of chess, with dozens of teams, all trying to break the rules —and lying about it.

Beneath the surface, there was an undercurrent of tension. If anything happened, it was possible to find Moscow blaming the Gestapo, the Germans blaming the Allies, and everyone suspecting British involvement, though the Soviet NKVD was usually likely to have been the real culprit behind it. All of this was always most apparent at Ellie's Bar, a favorite of British military personnel, serving a ferocious dry martini with the kick of a horse. Even though Ellie herself had a reputation for speaking English like a native and hating Germans, she was actually on their payroll. That was Istanbul. One particularly remarkable fellow I had known there worked for the Abwehr, the SD, the Italians, the Japanese, and the Brits—all at once.

As for the Bureau, our presence there had been minor when I first arrived. That was the way the Nine preferred it. If you didn't run clean, tidy tradecraft, the Emniyet would step in, and then things would get messy. And the Bureau largely operated as a decentralized network, with the exception of its core work-force that consisted largely of sliders and other agents. So by and large, operations within Istanbul were confined to only temporal anomalies—no surprise, since we operated officially as the Office of Temporal Anomalies and Strategic Intelligence—and those were rare.

But the first time I arrived in Istanbul, I didn't know all that. Though I had some inkling, I was still fresh to the game… especially to the likes of Istanbul, which was so drastically different from other, more covert cities.

The safe house itself was a small, second-story apartment just off İstiklal Avenue, with a good view over the endless buzz of crowds and the rattle of the trams. It was the kind of apartment that looked less than desirable from the outside—chipped paint, faded shutters, and a rusty railing—but was reasonably furnished on the interior. The Bureau was always efficient with their safehouses—picking locations that blended in and seemed almost too mundane.

She was already there when I arrived.

"Bureau too? Why'd they assign you?" I said in a rather condescending way, looking down at her. She was a full head shorter than I, but glared back up at me with a defiant stare.

"Maybe you hadn't noticed, but there hasn't been any progress made here as of yet," she retorted, and we went back to evaluating each other in silence.

"Well." I finally shrugged. I was annoyed, but it wasn't at her —it was at the damn mission and the fact that Hawthorne had assigned me someone to work with. "It's not your fault. I'll ask Hawthorne what the hell he was thinking when we're done with this mission. Name's Calder."

She hesitated but finally answered. "My name is Artemis."

"Using code names, are we?" I said, grinning as I lit a cigarette and offered her one before I walked over to the window of the safe house where we were stationed and glanced down at the street below. "Fine by me—in that case, you can call me Raven if you want to, even though I don't like it or like using it."

That was how it all started. That was when I first met her.

But the tension between us didn't last long. She was already on assignment when I landed, and it was my unfortunate task to inform her that the operation control had been split between the Bureau and MI6, rather than an exclusive operation. She challenged me on it, of course, but eventually, we reached an agreement; this case wasn't up to either of us. Orders came from above.

Hawthorne, specifically, had given us a target—Felix Haurowitz. He was a brilliant academic whose work was among the most cutting-edge in his field, half-protected by his work at Istanbul University. The man was working on something so far-fetched that even the Bureau wasn't sure of its legitimacy: hemoglobin mechanics tied to quantum phenomena. Yet, it had piqued the interest of the heads of the Bureau, and though I couldn't follow the science, I knew better than to dismiss it completely. Even more important, Felix had contacts under Nazi occupation who made him an indispensable asset for other intelligence agencies as well.

With Felix as an open asset with so much raw potential, both MI6 and the Bureau were keen to claim him as theirs for separate reasons. And since nobody was willing to concede him entirely until he made his loyalties clear, the Germans, the Soviets, and even the French circled like vultures in the dark. A successful alliance with the man was necessary—and so, our instructions were clear. The morning after my arrival, we were to head to the Park Hotel and speak to Nicholas Elliott, the head of the MI6 wing in Istanbul.

Before the sun had fully risen, Artemis—I didn't know her real name yet—and I departed the safe house, heading down İstiklal, past storefronts, pubs, and cafés, until we reached the square. Artemis wore her hair in a tight bun, with a velvet-red scarf wrapped around her neck. Her appearance stood out—she was foreign enough that most men would notice her, yet sharp enough that not many would dare to approach. I trailed slightly behind her, smoking a cigarette and choosing to watch the people around us as was my usual way, rather than focus entirely on the mission. Soon, the Park Hotel loomed into view, a towering building that seemed intimidating to anyone visiting for the first time.

It was there that we met Nicholas Elliott. The man was exceedingly fashionable. He wore round glasses, a perfectly polished outfit as any Englishman should, and a nice enough smile. Despite his appearance, his eyes were sharp, and every word was carefully spoken, betraying his true motives.

We introduced ourselves and took a seat across the table from him. I noticed another man with him—one whom I recognized from my previous work with MI6. His name was Finch. He was a younger man who had been a fresh recruit during the time I worked alongside the organization, and his enthusiasm was still evident. His eyes darted here and there, curiously and almost too eagerly, though he was clearly playing the role of a mediator. And it proved invaluable that he did.

The discussion itself was predictable—Elliott demanded the official channels, proper credit, and priority access. The man would have demanded more, if possible, but Finch reined him in and allowed us to actually bargain, which I took the lead on. Artemis watched me carefully as we spoke, her eyes fixed on my face as I discussed the Bureau's preferred position—we wanted the first dibs on the debrief, priority streams, and of course, the classic Bureau level of discretion. Though it was a tense situation, Finch was always the man to break it up. This attitude, of course, proved invaluable for the man later in life as well—only a few months after this, the Bureau would go on to recruit him as an agent. But for this discussion, he played the side of a friendly MI6 agent.

"In other words," Finch interrupted with a smile on his face, "Felix will work with both of us, but the Bureau will hold first priority in terms of tech. In terms of his connection to the Nazi contacts and credit later, that will go to MI6. Yes?"

"Well, I'm not entirely—" began Elliott, but I interrupted.

"That will go well with the Bureau if MI6 is open to it."

"And how, exactly, should MI6 trust you specifically,

Calder?" Elliott glanced at me with disdain. "We know you… moved organizations. We have that data."

"So what?" I stared at him, almost daring the man to challenge me. "What does that matter, Mr. Elliott?"

"Please, gentlemen," Finch said, clapping his hands gently. "There's no reason for this. I have the list of MI6 requirements right here—and this'll do just fine. Let's shake on it?"

Begrudgingly, Elliott agreed to Finch's phrasing, though it was clear the man resented it. I shot Finch a quick smile as we left the building, and this time, Artemis followed behind me.

Our plan was set in stone, and Artemis had a role to play. I watched, impressed, as she moved quickly, integrating herself among Felix's peers at Istanbul University. She posed as an academic researcher from Montevideo and played her part flawlessly. She knew the language and had the poise for it, attaching herself to seminar groups and finding her way into the professors' dens where men shared their drinks and gossip. Her goal was to get in touch with Felix without any other organization realizing we'd made contact—and through her reports, I noted that she did so flawlessly. The man was cautious, but so was she, and through her patience and cunning, she arranged our first meeting. It was a follow-up "lecture," and I was sent to run the exchange.

The MI6 agents had a role as well—they focused on counter-operations, ensuring that no foreign entities attempted to make contact before us and determining the actual meeting area. The room they had chosen was small—a cramped backroom office, overcrowded with books on physics, quantum mechanics, and even chemistry.

Felix himself sat at the desk as I entered, his wiry frame fidgety but his eyes sharp as he glanced at me. I could tell from my first interaction with the man that he wasn't experienced with foreigners or espionage—but he wasn't entirely unaware, either.

"My main goal is to continue my teaching," he said quietly as he adjusted his glasses. "But in Berlin, they do not allow… these thoughts. Here, it seems safer. Safer still if I guarantee my safety through alternative routes."

"Yes, that's what we're here for. You'll have protection and a platform," I assured him. "So long as you work with us—exchange of notes, names, analysis—and of course, your research. That's all."

At that moment, however, there was a sharp knock at the door. I spun around, my hand halfway into my coat as I reached for my pistol, but then I saw his face. It was Nicholas Elliott, smiling politely, his coat pressed and his glasses perched on his nose.

"Doctor," he said smoothly, "your value is certainly paramount to us in Britain. Allow me to introduce myself—I'm Nicholas Elliott, with SIS. I'm sure Max here has explained to you that he's currently offering you joint protection between his organization—which currently wishes to remain unnamed, of course—and SIS itself."

"Yes, he has," Felix responded.

"Good, good. I'm here because I want to offer you an individual offer—separate from the joint one. It's not that our joint offer is bad—but I'd like to extend something which may be more tempting to you. SIS is prepared to offer you protection, official grants, and even relocation to Cambridge in a chief position, if required. You'd work exclusively with SIS, however."

"I'm guessing Mr. Calder here wasn't aware of this deal."

Elliott stayed silent, but he smiled slightly. I had cursed in my mind. Negotiations weren't my strong suit—I got annoyed too easily. But I had to keep a straight face because these dealings were crucial.

"I believe," I said carefully, "that Mr. Elliott is indicating our joint deal does still stand. And the longevity that's offered by Elliott here means very little in the event of any failures. What our joint deal offers is resolute promises and the ability for you to remain relatively independent, without interference from either organization."

"Well," Elliott said with a smile, "it appears the deal is up to you, doctor."

Felix sat there, drumming his fingers on the desk. He still seemed nervous, but a faint smile played at the edge of his lips as he thought. It was clear he understood exactly what Elliott had done, and the situation amused him. Finally, he looked up at us and spoke.

"You're both correct, of course," he said, nodding. "But you ask me to choose, and I will not. This, of course, is a choice in itself—I will work with you both. I will keep at my lectures, record my notes—here, this is the current book." He slid it across the table toward us and continued, "So long as it will serve the cause of defeating Germany, I will work with both organizations."

"Very well," Elliott said, a forced smile on his lips. "I appreciate your time, doctor."

Without another word, he turned and left. I shot him a wink as he walked through the door, then redirected my attention to Felix. I finished up the discussion and dealings as I had originally intended, bringing the matter to a close.

As I left the room, I saw Artemis leaning against the wall and shot her a smile. She smirked back—we'd grown closer over the past few days. As we walked down the narrow hallway, she lit a cigarette and offered me one.

She finally spoke. "I found out about Elliott's intention to double-cross us, but I assume from your expression it didn't go well?"

"That, exactly," I responded. "I don't think the good doctor took too well to trusting an organization that would so easily try to undermine a deal it had itself agreed to."

"Well, that's good, then."

I smirked. "Good work on the gig. You didn't slow me down."

"Slow you down? You could barely keep up."

"If you say so."

"Name's Alicia, by the way."

"No more code names?"

And just like that, we had worked together for the first time. Whether it was fate or something else entirely, a strange spark had formed between Alicia and me, and we found ourselves taking job after job as we worked for the Bureau.

———

I felt my consciousness slipping as I smiled to myself. Our connection wasn't always the best, and it was riddled with memory loss, paranoia, and betrayal. But she was someone I knew I could trust.

Oddly enough, even when I forgot her, I still knew I could trust her.

As I fell asleep, my last thought was of my earliest years—before I'd even known her, before I had ever become an agent for MI6 and then the Bureau.

How far I had come. Sister Agnes would be proud.

CHAPTER 4
LINCHPIN LONDON

When I awoke, it was to the gentle sound of water colliding against the iron sides of the ship. The vessel groaned beneath me, and I mirrored its sound as I stretched. The bed wasn't the most comfortable, but I'd slept in a variety of places less enjoyable than this. The rocking had lulled me into a deep sleep, and I'd dreamed of my childhood rather than the Andes temple that continued to haunt me. I pushed it to the back of my mind as I glanced around. Dim light filtered in through the singular porthole of the small room, casting a grayish-blue tint that made it seem darker than it was. I wished, only for a second, that I was still back in Lisbon—next to my typewriter, with my collection of radios, and my whiskey on my desk. I turned around and saw Alicia sitting against the furthest wall, her hands behind her head, her eyes staring off into space. As I moved, however, she focused her gaze on me, and I knew finally that my life in Lisbon was gone… at least for a while.

"Good morning," she said.

"Did you sleep much?"

She hadn't slept much. Her hair was tied back loosely, the auburn tint reflecting the little visible sunlight. I could see from her posture that she was tired, and I knew she'd likely spent the night thinking and keeping watch instead of resting. I smiled at her, and she smiled back.

"Still tired?" I asked.

"Not that much," she responded, glancing around the small room. "But it's hard to sleep in such a cramped space like this."

"If I weren't so tired, I'd agree with you."

She chuckled. "Max Calder—never thought I'd see the day you were tired."

"I'm ready for retirement," I said jokingly, though I was serious.

She leaned forward, her expression clouding as she looked around. "I've been trying to piece things together: Lisbon, Rosyth, the photograph, and now the message. What does it all mean?"

"And you have a theory?"

"Well, it doesn't make any sense. Unless, of course, MI6 somehow knew about all this—somehow had access to our files, or data, before we even knew it."

"Assuming it really is MI6, of course. I'm not entirely convinced the message is…" My voice trailed off.

"How do you figure?"

"It sounds like MI6. It's signed off by Philby… and he works for MI6. But the play doesn't seem like something MI6 would pull."

"Your instincts have been better than mine. But that Philby name—it keeps coming up."

"Yeah, Philby. If my memory serves, he's a weird fellow. I met him once, in my early days at Broadwayc—just a quick document hand-off—but something about him seemed off-putting to me, even back then. He behaved like we had met before."

"You didn't trust him?"

"It wasn't that. Back then, I didn't think long enough about him to even consider it. But what seemed so strange was how he interacted with me. He seemed like he was equal parts scared and intrigued by our conversation, but I have no idea why."

Alicia stayed quiet for a moment, and I listened to the waves outside our cabin. The ship creaked, and I exhaled slowly.

She sighed and lit a cigarette. "So, all that. And now, he's authorizing broadcasts and an assassination attempt."

"I'm not so sure…"

"Right," she said, "you're not sure that message was from Philby. But his name is connected, at the very least."

"Yes, and that alone is a lead."

"Well…" her voice drifted off for a second, but she focused again and continued. "According to my current sources, Philby isn't a small fry anymore, like when you last met him. He'd certainly be capable of issuing something like this… and his name keeps coming up connected to the Mirror. The most recent report I've accessed has him as a section head, and he's establishing his own reach within the organization. My source says he has half the loyalty of Broadway already."

"Which means the chances of his name in that message being a coincidence… are low."

There it was—the point we'd been getting at this whole time, I knew. Alone, each piece seemed like it wouldn't fit together, but when you connected the puzzle, it made sense. The photograph, the doppelgänger, the man in Avenida Palace, the assassination attempt, and the radio intercept—all linked to Philby's name. It was all tied to something, even if we didn't know what it was yet.

"Then there's Kingsway. Do you think that ties in?"

"Kingsway…" I recognized the name. Kingsway was certainly associated with MI6. It was the network of underground tunnels beneath Holborn in London, one of the key secret sites of MI6. A place sworn to secrecy by anyone who knew about it.

"Could be anything," I said finally, though my tone betrayed me. "It's likely the street in Holborn—Kingsway. If that's the reference, it's deliberate. MI6 used to bury cables there—whole networks of telegraph, trunk lines, and the like. Hell, half the calls in England went through that place and ran under that road."

"How confident are you?"

"Fairly."

"We'll need to track it, then. If it has any connection to the Mirror, we need to know before we track down the Rosyth issue."

A silence fell between us as we sat there, staring off into space together. I felt close to her, but I didn't know what to say. She seemed foreign to me, and yet she was the only person I really knew. There was no bitterness, no anger, and our connection was no longer strained. But even so, we were two people who still weren't quite sure how to act when together.

"Max...how much of your mind do you think the Mirror took?" Her voice cut through the silence like a knife, and I glanced at the floor.

"More than I expected. More than I want. I'm not sure, but these memory issues—hell, I forgot you. That's got to mean something, right? Sometimes I remember places we've been and things we've done—and sometimes I forget them. And then, other times, I remember, only to later realize that what I remembered wasn't true."

My words hung in the air, and I could feel her watching me. The Mirror had affected her less, for whatever reason—probably because she was tied to it as Project Caliber, as Hawthorne revealed when we were in the Andes. She had always been the connection. I was the anomaly.

"So if the Mirror can take memories," she said slowly, "then what does that mean for you? What really makes you different from a doppelgänger?"

"I've thought of that before. It means that I'm no longer the most complete Calder."

"Well," she replied, "I think you're the original Calder, and that's enough for me."

"I wish it were enough for me as well. But I want to remember everything I don't. I want all the files, the memories, and the life that's been stripped out of me."

"Well, let's find the missing Mirror then." Alicia stood and walked over to sit next to me. I felt her lean up against my side and tensed for only a second before I relaxed.

"We explore Kingsway first," I said, my voice softer now. "Kingsway first—and see if we can figure out what hell-given role Philby plays in all this. If he's involved, we'll drag him into the light."

"Finally. A plan." She whispered it, but I heard a slight smile in her voice.

We sat there together, feeling the ship rock beneath us. It felt nice. It felt a bit like friendship—something I hadn't felt in months—and a little bit like something more.

I smiled.

———

Two days out of Lisbon, the sea turned choppy again, and the ship's engines groaned as we finally arrived in Cherbourg. The port was still scarred from the war—cranes half-collapsed, looking like giant insects, warehouses pockmarked by shellfire, and entire docks barren, but the liners arrived regardless. Their white hulls rose above the battered French docks like survivors of some great battle—and they were.

Towering above it all, immaculate and gleaming, was the Queen Mary, stopping at Cherbourg on her way from New York to Southampton. Her sheer black hull blotted out half the sky, while the Cunard lion crest caught the weak sunlight like a medal polished for a parade. This grand ship was to take us on the next leg to England. She was a ship after my own heart—built by John Brown on the River Clyde in Scotland, close to where I was born in the Gorbals of Glasgow. She proudly held the Blue Riband for the fastest Atlantic crossing.

The rain had finally ceased by the time we fully entered the port. Alicia and I disembarked, moving with the stream of passengers along the covered gangway. Diplomats with their attaché cases surrounded me as I clutched a case of my own. Families shepherded their children, French porters heaved large trunks stamped with distant addresses, and sailors strutted to and fro. I kept my hat low, holding an unlit cigarette between my fingers. I didn't like crowds of too many people, such as this— not anymore. I was too focused on figuring out which of my own memories were real to evaluate everyone at once. To make a gamble on each possibility, I had to filter out the false ones.

We boarded the Queen Mary, a transatlantic liner with wood-paneled corridors that smelled faintly of polish and seawater. The interior featured grand Art Deco design, with luxurious first-class areas like the Verandah Grill, showcasing rich woods, velvet, and custom artwork. The ship also had modest, cramped third-class cabins, reflecting the ship's tiered passenger experience. Uniformed stewards guided first-class passengers to broad staircases, while the rest of us were funneled toward the narrower halls. We had fake paperwork in order—Alicia had prepared it before her trip to Lisbon even began—and enough money for a small cabin deep in the ship.

I watched from the observation deck as Cherbourg shrank on the horizon until only the rubble and cranes were visible. The horn bellowed, a deep sound that made the hair on my arms stand up. Alicia stood beside me, resting her hands on the rail, and we watched as the French coast slid backward.

"Strange how quickly ruins become scenery," she muttered.

I struck my lighter, shielding the flame from the wind, and exhaled a puff of smoke from my cigarette before responding. "Been that way since the war."

"And London?"

"You'd know better than me," I responded, "but I think it's a ruin with paperwork attached."

She smirked as she watched the smoke drift slowly toward the channel, where the sky bent low and gray over the water. "Yes, I'd agree."

Behind us, a steward passed, carrying a wireless log. I eyed the scrawls across the top: Cherbourg / Southampton—6 hours. I fiddled restlessly with my cigarette, turning my attention to Alicia's face. Her emotions were masked, but I could tell she was as eager to be off this ship as I was.

"Six hours. Then we'll be in Southampton, at least."

She didn't respond, but she relaxed slightly. The Queen Mary surged forward, her wake churning white against the ocean as we stood side by side on the deck. It was relaxing, in a way, under the colorless sky that masked the sun. We didn't even bother to return to the cabin; after a brief respite at the ship's bar, we returned to the observation deck as the boat nosed its way towards Southampton Water. I watched silently, the taste of air salty on my tongue. The Queen Mary moved through the Solent like a cathedral in fog—her black-and-red funnels rising above the vapor, her hull humming with the low vibration of engines and memories. After a brief stop at Cherbourg, the ship was weary but immaculate, every railing polished, every deck washed with salt and dew.

The English Channel was a dull pewter, calm but sullen. Gulls circled and screamed in the haze. Passengers crowded the starboard rails, wrapped in coats against the cold, watching as the coastline began to take shape—the faint outlines of cranes, masts, and smokestacks, the industrial sprawl of Southampton spreading like a rumor through the fog.

This was unmistakably British. Alicia gently grabbed my arm, squeezing it suddenly.

"Welcome back," she said.

"Back home," I muttered, though the words felt heavier than

I intended. I hadn't called this place home in a long time, and it felt strange to be back—back after the Rosyth incident.

As the great liner slipped past Calshot Spit, the harbor pilot came aboard, climbing the narrow rope ladder with a cigarette clenched between his teeth. The engines slowed to a murmur. The wake stretched behind like torn silk. Dockworkers appeared on the quays, their caps pulled low, waving faintly in the fog as the ship edged toward Berth 101 at the Ocean Terminal.

Gangways were lowered, and the first-class passengers descended first, their luggage already waiting in neat pyramids, their faces pale with fatigue and relief. A woman in a fur collar paused halfway down the gangway, staring at the soot-stained skyline as if seeing it for the first time. Behind her, businessmen adjusted their hats, sailors joked quietly, and a few children leaned over the rails, pointing at the crowds below.

Southampton itself was still half-shadowed by rationing and reconstruction. The war had bitten deep here—bomb scars still pocked the warehouses, and cranes stood idle where ship-building had once thrived. The air smelled of salt, industry, and the faint sweetness of spilled fuel.

Customs officers waited at the foot of the gangway—all khaki and politeness—their clipboards held like weapons. Behind them, a line of black cars and lorries waited, engines idling, exhaust curling into the morning chill. For the disembarking traveler, the sound of England was unmistakable—the low toll of ship bells, the hiss of steam, the rhythm of footsteps on wet planks. Even the gulls sounded colder here.

Inside the terminal, a brass sign read, "Welcome to Southampton—Gateway to the Empire." It gleamed with irony. The empire was fading, and everyone knew it, but the sign remained—polished daily, as though denial were part of the decor.

We disembarked quickly, stewards directing passengers down the gangways and into the customs hall. The place smelled of damp stone, and clerks moved briskly with efficiency under the watchful eyes of uniformed inspectors. A young officer glanced at my passport, flipped through the travel papers, and stamped them without question. He took slightly longer with Alicia's, but in the end, her papers received the same treatment. There was no fuss and no raised eyebrows.

"Looks like we're still good at hiding secrets under paperwork," Alicia joked quietly as we finally left customs, the sky already dulling into a nighttime hue. A line of black taxis idled under the drizzle. I paused to light a fresh cigarette.

"I miss Lisbon," I admitted. "But London—London is where we'll have to go next if we want to figure out Kingsway and Philby's signature."

Alicia nodded toward the waiting taxis. "Then let's go."

"I think," I said, "we should stay the night here first. Let's pace things."

She hesitated for a second, then nodded. It was clear she wasn't sure if I was delaying for practical reasons or because I wanted to avoid what we might find. I wasn't sure myself. We climbed into the backseat of a cab, resting as its engine coughed to life and it pulled away from the docks. I glanced back, catching sight of the Queen Mary, her hull looming black against the gray sky. She had carried thousands across the Atlantic, and now she'd brought me back to a place I didn't want to go. The taxi rattled through the drizzle to a small hotel next to Southampton Central, the soot-streaked clock tower visible through the fog over the platforms. We didn't head to the station yet, though—that would be for the morning.

I hopped out of the cab, my boots hitting the damp stones with a thud. The night air was much colder here, far more piercing than in Lisbon, cutting through my lungs in a vile manner. The air mingled with coal smoke, dockyard soot, and the faint breath of the sea I could still smell. The rain had turned to a mere drizzle, but the streets were already soaked, and I had no doubt it would rain more in the morning.

I paused beside the taxi, waiting for Alicia to step to the curb, pulling the radio case with her. I carried our other minimal belongings, and we made our way quietly into the small hotel situated opposite the station. The overhang dripped with a constant, satisfying pattern as we passed beneath it, and the hanging sign next to the door was faded. Inside, the small, dimly lit reception was clean enough, though quiet, and the faint smell of kerosene penetrated deeply into the fabric of the place. We waited politely, and soon the clerk appeared, glancing us up and down. His eyes lingered for a second on Alicia's vibrant scarf, and he pursed his lips, but he didn't say anything, handing us the keys without a problem. It was a one-night stay, no questions asked—and none answered.

The small room had only one bed, and I set my bag down beside it before sitting down and stretching. The curtains were drawn over the window, and I made no motion to open them. Now that we were back on familiar soil, an almost nostalgic sense of paranoia had settled in. I knew that if I opened the curtains, the station would be visible from here, the trains groaning and clacking across the tracks all night and day, and I knew sooner or later a whistle would blow. But I didn't want to see it.

"Max," Alicia said as she sat down on the edge of the bed beside me, resting her head against my shoulder. "Are you sure about this? I know I came to you… But if you want to go back, there's still time. London, Kingsway, Philby, the Mirror—maybe it's best you leave it all behind."

I didn't answer right away. I sat there with my eyes almost closed, my mind flickering between all the memories I had—the good ones, the bad ones, even the memories of Alicia's death. Everything seemed to be tying me into this. All the sleepless nights, all the ciphers and broadcasts, and that photo of the other me, the doppelgänger, somewhere near Rosyth, his face just like mine.

"If the Mirror is truly connected to this," I finally said, "then I can't leave it all behind. It'll find me, like it's been doing. No matter who's behind this—if Philby's got his fingers in it, or if it's someone else, running isn't going to save us… either of us."

"You're right," she said quietly. "We're already here, aren't we?"

"Yes."

"Well, then, tomorrow," she said, lying back on the bed finally. "We take the train to London."

I lay back next to her, staring at the ceiling. I wanted to do more—to say something, or to touch her again, but I didn't. I just lay there, listening to the train whistle that permeated the silence, and stared up at the ceiling. And then, I slept. The same Andes dream haunted me once more.

———

Southampton Central lay heavy with smoke and echoes, pulsing with the weary rhythm of a country trying to remember how to breathe after six years of holding its breath. It stood wide and low against the skyline, hastily rebuilt after the bombings. The new concrete façade was still too clean, as if the city hadn't quite earned it yet. Behind it, the platforms stretched toward the docks like a promise, and you could almost hear the echo of wartime orders. Steam drifted between the tracks, rolling in from the waiting engines, thick enough to hide faces and intentions. Porters shouted names through the haze, their voices roughened by years of rationed tobacco and night shifts. The iron girders overhead glistened with condensation, dripping onto the stone like sweat from the city's brow.

The station clock, still war-surplus, ticked with mechanical impatience. Its face was cracked but reliable—a survivor, like everyone else in Southampton. It hung above the concourse where soldiers had once queued for troop trains, and where now families gathered in awkward silence, clutching suitcases that smelled of mothballs and hope.

Civilians waited for trains to London, soldiers headed north for postings that no longer mattered, and seamen—British, Norwegian, Polish—drifted between the platforms in search of the next ship, the next pay packet, the next illusion of purpose. The port was open again, but it didn't feel like peace; it felt like an aftertaste.

A faint tang of oil and seawater rode every gust of wind through the station's open doors. If you stood on Platform 3 and looked west, you could see the cranes along the docks, silhouettes against the gray morning—tall, patient, rusting. Beyond them, the masts of merchant vessels bobbed like antennae for a different world.

The lights flickered when the weather turned; they always did. Someone said the current was bad, but others swore it was the station itself—that the war had left it slightly haunted. Ghosts of men in khaki still waited for trains that never came, their breath mingling with the steam, their shadows stretching toward the exits.

In the early morning, the city's heartbeat had slowed. Passengers huddled in the glow of the lamps—pale light, sharp edges. Cigarettes burned down faster in the wind. The guard's whistle pierced the air like a lie told too quickly. Southampton Central was a crossroads of endings—ships leaving for faraway ports, trains vanishing into fog, lives quietly rearranged between arrivals and departures. It wasn't just a station; it was the sound of a nation still waiting for its next train to mean something.

We left our hotel room early, leaving the keys at the reception and departing into the fog of the morning. A queue formed at the booking office, and we stood silently, waiting our turn. Alicia quietly slid money under the grille, and when asked, responded that we wanted to travel to Waterloo.

"Waterloo, ten past eight," the clerk said curtly, stamping the tickets twice without looking up.

We waited, and moments later, the loudspeaker echoed the same words. I folded the tickets, checked the station clock, and watched the minute hand slowly tick forward. A porter in a frayed waistcoat pointed us toward Platform 3, and we walked briskly past a tea stall and a newspaper stand. Chalk on a blackboard spelled out our route: Waterloo—8:10—Winchester, Basingstoke, Woking, Clapham Jct.

We moved with the tide of the crowd, navigating quietly toward the glass and smoke. Waiting for us at the platform was a Merchant Navy Pacific, which looked more like a beast than a machine. Its malachite paint was dulled black by soot, but the engine roared with a fiery energy that inspired confidence. Next to me, Alicia tugged her scarf closer, watching the locomotive carefully. I glanced up and down the station, taking in the scenery and the crowd. Lisbon had felt restless but alive—Southampton was busier yet seemed tired, its movements mechanical and etched with exhaustion. Everywhere, there was a sense of repetitiveness and despair.

As our departure approached, we made our way onto the train and found our compartment. It was paneled in dark wood, the upholstery sagging, and the brass fittings dulled by years of wartime paint. We settled into the carriage, and as the guard's whistle shrieked, the train pulled free, rattling its way past sidings stacked with coal wagons and cranes that still etched their position into the sky.

"To London," I murmured.

"To London," she responded.

Beyond Southampton, the countryside opened into low, wet fields. Sheep grazed peacefully in hedged meadows still damp with the morning dew. Distant chalk ridges rose pale against the sky, and I leaned against the window, watching the landscape through it and staring at my reflection. Alicia read the paper, as she always liked to do, which gave me time to think and reflect. I watched as the train slowed at Winchester, the great cathedral looming pale and immense over the slate rooftops. The cobbled streets and Georgian terraces sloped away from the line, and I smiled slightly. This city was older than the Bureau—older than we were. It was ancient—and it felt like I belonged.

Between Winchester and Basingstoke, the downs rolled in long, empty swells, with hedgerows broken by the occasional farm. Smoke from the chimneys curled low, caught in the damp air. The fields bore the scars of war—bomb craters had turned to ponds, and small corrugated huts lingered in the forgotten corners. Basingstoke itself was a study in survival. Bombed-out shells of shops gaped beside new red-brick council houses, and the station still bustled with those who bore the scars of the war as well. Further north, the air seemed to grow thicker, and the train shook and rattled as it continued along the rails. I couldn't help but close my eyes for just a moment, dozing off. However, as I dozed, the compartment began to tilt sharply onto its side, nearly at a ninety-degree angle. My eyes fluttered open, and I glanced around, taking in the scene.

As I registered what had happened, I jolted, grabbing for the leather strap above the window, only to realize that everything seemed to be holding in place. I glanced toward Alicia—and saw nothing but her scarf. Though her scarf remained as if it were wrapped around her neck, she was nowhere to be seen. The sudden silence was the most shocking part; the roar of the engine had ceased, and I heard nothing.

"Hello?" I asked cautiously.

I glanced around before pulling myself out of the sliding door of the compartment, hoisting myself into the corridor of the train. I stood there and rubbed my eyes.

"Damn, am I dreaming?"

As if to answer, a sudden, leaden tolling noise came from above me. I wasted no time. I pulled myself out of the window, which was now positioned above me, dragging myself hand over hand until I had clawed myself upward to what was now the "roof." And there, standing against the white sky, was a figure. It seemed to have no face, no distinguishable features, and yet, it was unmistakably a body. It was roughly my height, almost my build, though its shadow was connected as if by seams to the train itself. It stood there, the silhouette shimmering slightly, and stared at me. The sound continued to toll, though it didn't come from the figure itself.

I opened my mouth to speak, but nothing left my lips. As I stared the figure, it seemed to lean toward me slightly, as if studying me, though I still could make out none of its facial features. Then, just like that, it was gone.

I jolted awake, sitting upright in my seat, sweat dripping from my brow. I glanced around. There sat Alicia, still holding her paper. The train hadn't tilted, and the world looked normal. The wheels clacked against the rail, and the engine roared in the background, steady as ever. Alicia glanced at me, her face etched with concern.

"You jolted awake. Are you okay?"

"Just sleep—nothing else," I said, my voice raspy. I rubbed my forehead, blinking slowly. "Just another trick of my damn mind. It's falling apart."

She didn't look entirely convinced and glanced at me once more but finally nodded and returned to her paper. I kept my eyes open, determined not to close them, and glanced out the window again.

Woking brought the first edge of London's reach—sidings crowded with coal wagons, warehouses patched with corrugated iron leaned against water towers. I watched as a shunter walked along the platform, lantern swinging rhythmically. As I watched, only for a second, I thought he appeared two yards further along the platform, his gait identical. But then I blinked, and he was back in the spot where he had always been. I shook my head. Was I going crazy?

Between Woking and Clapham, the countryside thinned, villages giving way to suburbs. Rows of commuter houses pressed closely to the line, their gardens littered with chicken coops and shelters left from the Blitz. By the time we reached Clapham Junction, the world had transformed from countryside to steel and steam. The junction was spread broad, like a forest of rails, locomotives crossing every which way, whistles shrieking, and brakes screeching. The air stank of oil and coal, and I wrinkled my nose. I hadn't missed this.

Crowds hurried across the platforms—women in factory coats, men in rough outfits, porters shouting over the din, and children tugging at their mothers' skirts. But our train continued on, shrieking beneath the vast glass-and-iron roof of London Waterloo, finally slowing down beneath the great station clock. The hands continued to tick, incessantly keeping time as we finally arrived. By the time the train had finally slowed for London, the light had faded to that particular gray that made the city look so drab. The smell of coal thickened the air, and the station bustled with unrivaled activity.

I crushed a cigarette beneath my boot, grinding it into the ground as we exited the train. "Back in the Bureau's backyard."

"The Bureau and MI6 both," Alicia said softly.

CHAPTER 5
FORGETTING PHILBY

At 54 Broadway in 1942, Calder was working quietly at his desk, surrounded by papers, codebooks, and files. It was cluttered in a way that only he could parse, but that was how he preferred it. Stacked like miniature towers around him, each book held its own purpose—years of use had left their edges frayed and their pages imbued with the scent of age, yet they were crucial to his work. Some books contained cryptic notations in various hands, their margins stained with fingerprints, words circled here and there, pages torn out, and some pieces barely legible. Others were new, representing the latest pieces of MI6 codebreaking technology that served as up-to-date guides on the newest ciphers they worked on. His young, almost boyish face was vastly different from how it would later become, and a glint in his eye still shone with the excitement and ambition of a young man. His mind, though burdened with work, remained vibrant and sharp.

Outside, London's cold, foggy night air was permeated with smoke and dust, and through the singular window of his office, Calder would glance occasionally, watching the street below. In the distance, he could hear the incessant tapping of typewriters and the occasional ring of a telephone. Here and there, a clerk padded past, occasionally stopping by his office to wave or deliver a message. Broadway was a place where many worked, and each man knew his role in full. It was like an ant colony, with workers going here and there, carrying their messages with a singular goal in mind.

Calder sighed, dipping his fountain pen into ink and slowly scribbling on a sheet of paper. His work was indecipherable to anyone outside MI6, but to him, it was a puzzle—and he enjoyed it, for the most part. The only downside was that he had become bored with the incessant desk work, and his body craved something more active, which would eventually come. But still—this was his language, one that he had been trained to speak.

Outside the door, he once more heard footsteps approaching. They disrupted his rhythm, however, because they weren't the hurried footsteps of a clerk approaching with a message. These steps were quieter, more careful, and stopped right outside his office door. Calder glanced up, watching as a man entered. The man didn't look like war, and though his eyes were sharp, his face looked almost boyish. His face was clean-shaven, his hair slicked back, and his features polished. Yet the way he carried himself was smooth, as if he was accustomed to this type of environment. Calder sat up slightly straighter, nodding to the man as he entered and closed the door behind him.

"Can I help you?" Calder asked, watching as the man's eyes searched his face, a slight smile playing at his lips.

"Calder."

The name was a statement, not a question. There was no clerical "sir," no gesture of rank or other identifier as was usual within MI6. Calder raised his eyebrows and waited. Few men in MI6 would speak in this manner, and so it piqued Max Calder's interest. The man, meanwhile, hesitated for a second, then continued politely.

"Kim Philby," he said, extending his hand in introduction. "Though I would have suspected Cambridge would have been a certain source of recognition. You look...young."

"Quite so," Calder responded, his mind whirring.

"Curious, isn't it?"

How did Philby know about his time at Cambridge? If so, why did he bring it up here? It wasn't uncommon for men within the ranks of MI6 to be recruited through Cambridge, but Calder cherished his anonymity and had pressed the higher-ups to speak little of his past to other agents within the organization. Had he crossed paths with this man before, perhaps at Cambridge? His mind worked speedily, running through scenarios and memories. Faces, names, classmates, and even debates at pubs while drunk—his memory was as close to flawless as a man could get, and yet he had no recognition of this fellow who stood before him.

He smiled politely, deciding in that instant that he wouldn't let on how little he knew. Something about the way the man spoke was off-putting to Calder, so he figured it was better, for the moment, to let Philby believe he remembered.

"Quite the time," Calder said politely.

Kim Philby stared at him, his eyes searching Calder's face. He strode forward, pulling a brown folder from under his arm and sliding it atop Calder's labyrinth of books and papers. "They asked me to deliver these to you. Instructions are enclosed, I believe. You'll forward summaries to Section IX by the end of the week."

The way Philby spoke carried no arrogance; only a matter-of-fact quality to it. The man seemed entirely polite, but something about the manner in which he spoke exuded charisma and confidence in the same manner.

"How long have you been with MI6?" Calder asked as he reached for the file, his fingers brushing over the cover.

"Not too long, now. July of 1940."

"Oh, newer then."

Calder opened the folder, pulling out some of the contents and rifling through them. Mission notes, transmissions, and data. It was more routine than it had initially looked—agents in

Spain, Soviet connections, code bursts received that required investigation, and a fresh German cipher that looked as if it would be the cause for headaches going forward for everyone in Section V. Calder slid a few pages across the desk, scanning them with his usual surgical speed, then separating them into piles and sorting them out into the given spots on his desk. He was brisk and calculated with his motions but couldn't help but feel that Philby was watching him.

And Philby was. The man leaned back against the wall, watching Calder as if studying him. Calder finally finished sorting the files out and glanced up to see Philby staring down at him.

"You're not surprised?" Philby asked.

"About what?"

"The files. The Soviet connections in them. Most in this office don't like the mention of Russia at all. Do you?"

Calder raised an eyebrow, scratching the stubble on his jaw as he thought for a moment. He wasn't sure what Philby wanted to press him on, but it was clear the man was fishing for something.

"Ciphers always make for entertaining work. We'll see if anything pans out."

"No qualms over who the enemy is?" Philby continued with a polite smile on his face.

"I think it's best to let the office decide who the enemies are. I don't care much about the moral question of it—my role is to decipher the codes."

"You seem different."

"Different how?"

"Never mind. Anyway, it does seem the Soviets tend to over-commit, doesn't it?" Philby pulled a cigarette out of his pocket and lit it as he spoke, offering one to Calder, who declined. "They've always been sloppy with their tradecraft. Their loyalty is respectable, though."

"I wouldn't know much about that," Calder responded,

beginning to scribble notes on a piece of paper as he continued to work. "I'm not very familiar with the Soviets. Are you?"

"Certainly, in one view of it. Well, I'd best be off."

Calder nodded curtly as Philby stubbed out his cigarette in the ashtray on the desk, smiled politely, and left the room, shutting the door behind him. The man exited with the same measured, careful footsteps as he had entered, vanishing down the narrow hallway from where he had entered. Calder sat there for several moments, the only motion being his scribbling, which he continued absent-mindedly as he thought.

There was something unsettling about the man he had just spoken to.

Though Max Calder was always confident in his memories—his perfect recall—something told him he had overlooked a key detail. From the Gorbals to Cambridge, from bars to tram journeys and even dark alleyways, Max Calder always remembered those he spoke to. He recalled faces with a mathematical clarity that made him an impressive asset to any intelligence organization, which was part of the reason he had been recruited in the first place.

And yet, there was Philby. The man stood before him, speaking to him as if they'd known each other, and yet Calder had no memory of him. He glanced down again at the folder which Philby had passed off to him. Other than the details stamped neatly in the center of the folder, there was a small signature in the upper-left corner, written neatly in a precise fashion: H.A.R. PHILBY.

Max Calder sighed, tapping his desk as he finally finished writing and carefully set his pen down.

Philby was someone he definitely should have remembered, he thought. And yet, he couldn't.

CHAPTER 6
TUNNEL TRAUMA

We left Waterloo Station behind, stepping out into the drizzle and coal haze. The concourse rang with echoes—guards calling out departures and the travelers bustling around us as if we didn't exist. I led the way, Alicia close behind, her eyes focused ahead while mine took in every uniform and face. It was here that we found a taxi, which carried us east along the Embankment, the Thames black and sluggish under the weakened gas lamps. London looked worn thin— bomb scars patched with fresh brick, scaffolded skeletons looming in the fog. The war was over, but the city had yet to fully recover.

I tipped the driver near Holborn, and we walked the last few streets in silence. Holborn still carried the smell of dust and ration paper. The war had ended three years earlier, but in this part of London, peace felt provisional—as if the Luftwaffe might return any night to finish the job. Kingsway ran like a scar through the district—a wide Edwardian boulevard meant to symbolize modern London before the bombs reminded everyone how fragile modernity could be. It was half shadow, half scaf- folding. Some of the old office blocks stood clean and proud;

others were still missing their top floors, their windows replaced with plywood and good intentions.

The trams clattered up and down from Aldwych to High Holborn, their bells echoing like ghosts of a better decade. Buskers played cheap saxophones under the bridge near Southampton Row, their music drowned out by the traffic and the soft hiss of postwar rain. The light at dusk was always the same—amber and gray, the color of a cigarette end.

Most of the offices along Kingsway had switched tenants since the war. Law firms, insurance brokers, and shipping agents shared walls with unmarked rooms that didn't exist in any official registry. They belonged to departments that had names like Special Operations Reserve or Foreign Communications Liaison —MI5 and MI6 shadows. Men in tweed jackets who drank too much tea and said too little.

The air carried a faint scent of coal smoke and typewriter ink. Women in dark skirts and sensible shoes hurried between buildings with folders clutched to their chests—the new clerical army running the machinery of secrets left behind by the old one.

After dark, Holborn changed its pace. The pubs filled early and emptied late. The "Duchess Arms" and "The Fox" were regular haunts for intelligence officers posing as accountants and real accountants trying to seem important. Smoke hung low, and laughter erupted in short bursts. If you stayed past closing, you might hear someone slip into the kind of conversation that never reached the morning papers—about German scientists now working for the Americans, Russian couriers passing through Lisbon, or something called the Mirror that supposedly went missing up in Scotland.

Holborn wasn't glamorous like Mayfair or dangerous like Whitechapel; it was something worse—watchful. It was the kind of place where too many people knew too much about what they shouldn't while the rest pretended not to notice. It was gray, smoke-stained, and quietly menacing.

Though I had never personally entered the Kingsway tunnels, I knew where they were—my memory of that, at least, I was confident hadn't failed. Near Chancery Lane station, I found what I was looking for: a discreet service door marked "Post Office Telephones" in flaking paint. To anyone else, it would look normal.

I paused and glanced at Alicia, then pointed toward the door. "The hinges are rusted, but the padlock is new. That's not normal."

"Someone's been tending to this?"

"Yes, for sure," I replied. "And from the looks of it, this is MI6 hardware. They've been back down here."

"Then what do you think we're getting into here?"

"Could be nothing. Could be something. Keep watch."

Alicia scanned the street, vigilant. It was empty, except for the water that trickled through the gutters. I pulled out the picks from my coat pocket and got to work on the lock. It gave after three tries, and I pulled the door open, wincing at the loud, rusty creak. A gust of stale air spilled forth, and, pulling a flashlight from my bag, I stepped into the dark.

I led the way, with Alicia close behind me. The stairwell spiraled downward, the brick walls damp with condensation. The beam from my torch flickered across old posters plastered to the walls—"Dig for Victory" "Careless Talk Costs Lives." Their colors had faded, but the letters remained legible against the dark. The sounds of the city above faded into obscurity, replaced by the dull thud of our boots as we descended further. And finally, we reached the bottom. The tunnel opened into a long corridor, lined with heavy iron doors. Dust lay thick against the floor, but in places, the marks of boot prints had disturbed it, even before our arrival. I crouched, running a finger against one of the prints.

"Thoughts?"

"Not long ago," Alicia said as she bent down next to me. "Two, three days maybe."

"Well," I said, rising again, "that means we're not the first ones down here recently. Question, though, is who? And why?"

Alicia glanced up and down the corridor, taking in the empty darkness that stretched in both directions. "Whoever it was, they didn't care to erase their tracks. That's either careless, or they were confident that nobody else would show up down here."

"It's also possible," I said, "that it's a trap set for us."

She nodded, her fingers moving closer to her coat, where I knew she kept her pistol. I motioned along, and we continued down the corridor. The only sounds were from our boots and the occasional drip of water from some old pipe. The walls ahead were covered in peeling paint, the damp bricks covered in mildew, and any directional boards stained with age. I saw the occasional letter visible from the flaked paint, covered up by new stenciling. Walking closer to one of the signs, I examined it carefully.

"This is MI6, alright. Let's keep on."

Alicia nodded and pressed onward. There were doors and dusty switchboards connected to abandoned telex machines that sat covered in a fine gray layer of particles. The area had broadened, and there was less damp and more dust. Still, the tunnels were narrow, and claustrophobia would have threatened to envelop anyone. I, in particular, was forced to keep my head bent as I navigated the tunnels, which had clearly not been built for a man of my height. We pressed on, occasionally looking toward the doors that were now positioned frequently, passing the reels of derelict cables, more switchboards, and signs that indicated this had once been a primary hub of MI6.

We continued until the cables became sparser and the corridor began to narrow even more. It was clear that even MI6 agents had rarely ventured here. But ahead of us, in the dust, was that fresh set of boot prints.

"What exactly are we looking for, again?" Alicia asked as she followed me. I kept swinging the beam of my light to and fro, scanning the doors and cables.

"Well, whatever the guy who walked here before us was trying to find, for one. But for two—" I glanced closely at one of the signs that was against the wall, "—that. See there?"

Alicia stepped closer, examining the old chipped paint. "That's old Bureau signage."

"Covered up by MI6 layers, yes. Scraped over, stamped over, but still visible there enough." I tapped the torch against it, and the weak light steadied for a moment. "See? They've crossed out the Bureau identifiers, not just painting over them but actually trying to carve them out. The fact that they did it this way means whoever did it was trying to be very careful."

Her eyes scanned the sign closely, her red scarf drawn tightly around her neck. "So what? You think this area used to be Bureau?"

"Not officially, I'd wager," I said. "But there are signs that something changed hands down here. Whoever was responsible for covering up this signage likely had a hand in both the Bureau and MI6 and made attempts to erase this fact."

"We're close, then."

I nodded in agreement.

We continued on, our footsteps echoing heavily throughout the tunnels. Alicia silently reached into her coat, and I knew she held her pistol tightly, ready if we were to run into any trouble. We continued for what felt like minutes. By now, it was unclear how far we'd ventured into the tunnels, but we pressed onward. And then, just as I had begun to wonder if it was a dead end, we came across a door unlike the others. And toward this door, the boot prints turned. The door itself was old, wooden, and sturdy, though it had begun to twist a little with age. Crooked brass numbers still clung to it, green with rust, and faint words were painted in stencil above the numbers, black and visible in the dim light.

SECTION IX

Alicia stopped next to me, and I could feel her draw her coat tighter around her shoulders. It was cold down here, as if the air had begun to grow stale the further we walked. I tossed her the torch and pulled out my lock picks, bending over near the handle of the door. The iron lock that clasped it shut was rusted, and it caught for a bit, but as my stiff fingers grew accustomed to the arid cold, I finally heard a click, and the lock slid open. I tossed it to the ground, wincing at the clanking sound it made as it fell, and leaned my shoulder against the old door, pushing my weight against it. The door barely shifted, groaning as I shoved against it, slowly opening as if it didn't want to reveal the secrets that lay inside. But finally, it opened, and Alicia carefully shone the light into the old room.

Stacked to the ceiling were crates upon crates, clearly scrawled with Bureau markings and sealed with Bureau seals. Many of these box markings had been stamped out, their Bureau markings replaced with MI6 ones, but it was clear that whoever had stashed these here didn't think they would be found. Glints of copper peeked through bundled panels and hollow frames, but what caught my eye were the newer boxes, which appeared to be MI6, without any clear Bureau influence. Walking toward one of these newer wooden chests, I ran my fingers lightly over it, then lifted the lid. Dust puffed outward like a cloud and fell free from the lid. My fingertips traced the inside of the chest, feeling into the very corners of it. The chest was filled to the brim with papers. I picked up several and read them for a moment before tossing them aside.

"Most are redacted," I said.

"Other than this," Alicia replied, stooping to point at one of the papers I had tossed aside.

I picked it up again, peering carefully at the corner she had indicated. On the edge of the paper, in faint lettering, were the initials C.F.S., along with a faint imprint of a date stamp.

"C.F.S.," Alicia muttered, her voice low. "Any idea of who that is?"

"Not entirely," I replied, "but it's possible… yes, it might be. Actually, I don't see who else it could be: Charles Fraser-Smith."

"Fraser-Smith? Didn't the Bureau try to recruit him?"

"Yes. Failed, though. Fraser-Smith was MI6's technical magician. But if he's involved, this runs deeper than we thought."

Fraser-Smith was a name that anyone who had worked for MI6 at a high enough level recognized. He was the man responsible for the Q gadgets, named after the Q-Ships of World War I, but often much deadlier. Working primarily for Section XV of the SOE as well as MI6, he was a brilliant inventor who had turned the tide of the war, creating everything from hairbrushes that held concealed storage to pens containing a compass with a secret compartment for a paper-thin map, and a magnetized clip that could be balanced on a pin to provide an emergency compass. He also developed tunic buttons containing an explosive charge and was involved in the infamous Operation Mincemeat in 1943, a successful British deception operation during the Second World War to disguise the Allied invasion of Sicily. He aided secret agents, saboteurs, escaping prisoners, commandos, and the SAS.

If he were involved in this, then there was no telling what else we were about to uncover. I glanced around, shining my torch deeper into the cavernous room.

"I'd wager most of these boxes are either empty or the files are redacted. Look at the dust."

Alicia nodded. She had noticed it as well—the dust that should have lain thick atop most of the crates and boxes was displaced, as if whoever had been here before us had rearranged the place... or emptied it of anything that mattered.

I suddenly stopped, thinking I had heard something, and walked slowly forward, shining my light around piles of crates, motioning for Alicia to be silent. In a second, she had her pistol in hand and crept behind me as we made our way deeper into the room. It wasn't just intuition that made me suddenly go silent—it was a faint, steady humming that emanated from the darkest corner of the room that lay hidden by stacks of crates and boxes a head taller than me. I squeezed shoulder-first between the tall stacks, the wood groaning and creaking as I passed, edging my way toward the furthest reaches of the chamber, where the light from the torch faltered.

And then I saw it.

It wasn't hidden exactly, but surrounded by files, boxes, and crates, I saw it. It sat there, in skeleton form, with heavy copper plating built upward. They had turned brown and green from age but were still unmistakable. The cabling that was apparent in the frame rattled faintly with a staticky hum for no apparent reason, and the entire frame seemed to vibrate at a slow, steady pace.

It wasn't large; it appeared as though it had been engineered as some sort of test—a creation that only existed to test the theory of the project before building something greater—but I recognized everything about it.

My blood ran cold as I stared at it, and Alicia paused beside me, her breath catching as she too saw it. There, in the very furthest corner of this old, locked room at the bottom of the Kingsway tunnels.

Another Mirror.

It wasn't new—that much was obvious—but it was evidence enough. The beam of the torch reflected off the surface, where plates were bolted together, revealing several unfinished areas. It was clear that this Mirror had been built roughly, like a prototype discarded halfway, an echo of the machine Krane had crafted with detail and fervor before we'd destroyed it. But it was alive, humming faintly as if it were in some sort of stasis.

"Hell, Max," Alicia's voice echoed softly in the chamber as she stared at it.

"They—someone—had the pieces," I muttered, walking slowly toward it. "It shouldn't be down here."

"But it is."

"How long do you think?" I asked. My voice didn't feel as if it belonged to me. All the crowded boxes, the redacted files, the crates, and even the cables seemed insignificant compared to the weight of what we'd discovered.

"Hard to tell."

Almost in a trance, we moved closer, carefully stepping around scattered bits and pieces of metal that lay around it. My throat felt dry when I spoke next, and I could feel the words forcing their way out of my mouth. "If Fraser-Smith got his hands on this… or helped, somehow—"

"Hell, then MI6 likely had a deeper role in it than we thought. And God only knows what they were doing with this."

"And Philby. Philby—his name is connected to this somehow, too. His name on the message, along with Kingsway—that can't be a coincidence."

"Max… do you think it works?"

"I'm not sure," I said, stepping forward and placing my hand gently against the frame. "But it doesn't look like it is right now, at least. And if it did, I don't see why they would have left it here."

"But if they left this here…" Her voice trailed off, but I knew what she meant.

If they left this here, what had they taken? What was worse than this?

As if suddenly making up her mind, Alicia bent down, placing her hands on some of the boxes and flipping the lids open. One by one, she tore lid after lid off the boxes, and after several moments of staring at the Mirror, I joined her. Most boxes were empty, but not all. Some yielded nothing—just dust, stale wood shavings, and paper long since blotted black with deliberate redactions. But, after digging through some of the smaller boxes, I pulled out a bundle of reports partially covered in the thick strokes of black ink that were used to hide information. Several words, however, remained visible and escaped complete obliteration.

"Alicia, look." I motioned for her to read the line I'd spotted.

There, on the paper in front of us, was a clear line of text at the bottom of one of the documents: H.A.R. PHILBY—CLEARED.

Beneath that, though faint and barely legible, was a typed line of text that read "SECTION IX."

I glanced at Alicia. Though the light of the torch had dimmed, I saw her face—grim, worried, and drawn. She looked at the paper, then back at me.

"Max, if Philby knew about this… then what are the chances he's behind it?"

"Could be," I said, forcing a grin. "But hey, at least your intel on MI6 seems to check out."

"Well, at least we know where to head next."

"Rosyth. Let's grab any of the files that have information in them and get the hell out of here before the torch dies."

Alicia nodded, and silence enveloped us as we continued to work in the dim light. We didn't stay for long after. Anything that survived redaction and anything that still remained, we filed away into a small briefcase or tucked into our pockets where it would fit. Glancing one last time at the Mirror—which continued to hum faintly but did nothing else—I finally led the way back through the tunnels, navigating the dust and damp-ness until we reached the spiral stairs once more. Every step upward felt like a struggle, and we walked in silence, both contemplating what we had just seen.

Though Alicia's intel had indicated another Mirror was oper-ational, seeing proof of it was completely different. It was some-thing I hadn't wanted to really admit was possible, yet now I had to come to terms with it. Down there, beneath London, inside the Kingsway tunnels, sat another Mirror—clearly a prototype.

Even though neither of us said it, our minds were focused on the same conclusion. If the prototype was here… then what was at Rosyth?

At last, as the light from my torch began to flicker and give out, we reached the top of the stairs and found ourselves back out at Chancery Lane. It was gray, and fog hung sourly over the streets, the lamps still aglow as if we'd never left. The rumble and noise of the city were loud, and the light was abrasive to my eyes. I winced as I shut the door carefully behind us. London never felt friendly, but it felt even colder than usual—as if all the ghosts that haunted the city were watching us. The stairwell door that clicked shut behind us was relocked, and as we walked away from the place, I forced myself not to glance backward. It was as though we hadn't discovered anything, really—as if it were just another piece of dust, swallowed up under Kingsway's dark cover, a memory left buried where we'd never find it again. But the briefcase I held with the files was a steady weight on my arm, and this reassured me. At least we had something.

Alicia pulled her scarf tighter around her neck, shivering in the cold. Her breath formed clouds in the chilly air, and her eyes darted here and there, as if she were expecting an ambush.

"Where do we go now?"

"King's Cross. Nothing left here; we need to get to Rosyth."

"Max...when do you think we should reach out to the Bureau?"

I hesitated before responding. "Not yet. I don't trust they're not part of this. And if they find out the equipment still exists..."

"...They'll try and reboot the project," Alicia admitted slowly. "But I still think we need to make contact."

I didn't respond. There wasn't much else to say anyway—we each knew that the prototype existed and that whoever had been there before us knew that as well. If Philby's name was stamped clearly beside the project I despised, I wanted to get to the bottom of it.

We walked in silence along Holborn, shoulder to shoulder, ignoring the traffic that bustled past and the motor horns that pierced the fog. People walked past us, but I didn't pay attention to them as I usually would have. The fog shifted, clearing slightly, and I finally waved down a cab as it drove past. I held open the door for Alicia before entering myself, relaxing quietly into the back seat.

"Where to?" came the voice of the cabby.

"King's Cross," I responded, and we were off.

It was only a mile and a half as the crow flies, but in London, crows didn't fly straight. Holborn was all tired suits and half-lit windows as the rain began again—that thin, persistent English rain that never quite fell but soaked everything anyway. The driver grunted, lit a cigarette, and pulled away.

The cab turned north, tires hissing over wet cobblestones. Outside, shopfronts blurred—tobacconists, stationers, a ration shop still displaying its faded "For Victory" posters. The driver's hands gripped the wheel in the way only men who had survived the Blitz did—cautious, suspicious, ready for the sky to fall again.

We kept the windows up. Alicia finally glanced at me and broke the silence.

"There's only one thing I'm worried about."

"What is it?" I asked as I lit a cigarette.

"Those boxes… and that prototype… looked old. Older than last year."

"I agree."

"If that's the case," she continued, "doesn't that mean that whoever did this didn't just recover the old files Krane had left lying around?"

I nodded. "And if that's the case, who knows what the hell we'll find at Rosyth?"

"Other than you."

"Yes, that," I chuckled. "Not that my experience with the last doppelgängers was that good."

"What will you do if you have to face yourself again?"

"Then I shoot," I said, smiling, though it didn't reach my voice. As much as I refused to admit it, I didn't know what I would do.

As we passed Russell Square, the rain grew heavier. The

taxi's wipers squeaked across the glass like an anxious metronome. A couple under a shared umbrella darted across the street—the woman's laughter cut short by a passing lorry. From the corner of Woburn Place, you could see the glow of King's Cross ahead—not light, exactly, but a different kind of illumination: sodium-yellow, industrial, weary.

The cab slowed past Gray's Inn Road, where the bomb damage hadn't yet been concealed. Gaps in the terraces looked like missing teeth, their edges blackened and raw. Finally, the cab turned left toward King's Cross Station—the large brick façade looming ahead like a tired sentinel. The clock tower's face was dim under soot, its hands stuck a few minutes fast, as if London itself were impatient to be somewhere else. The city never stopped moving, even when it seemed to stand still.

The taxi came to a halt, and we stepped out, making our way into the station. It looked brutal—giant black ribwork, porters moving here and there with practiced ease, the coal and iron gray color palette the only thing visible. The whole place moved like one living monolith, and I sighed deeply.

"Eyes forward, Max. Focus on the mission," Alicia said gently beside me.

I nodded resolutely, and we walked through the station, past families with yelling children, stray dogs and cats darting about begging for scraps, and the servicemen still slick with soot and dirt. Everywhere, people bustled about, but I stayed close to Alicia as she purchased tickets for the journey. Then we sat together, side by side on a bench, waiting.

A little while later, the loudspeaker crackled to life, announcing our journey to Edinburgh, and we boarded the train.

The whistle cut sharply across the glass vault of King's Cross, and the A4 Pacific we had boarded surged forward, steam rolling alongside the iron girders above. I leaned back in the leather seat of the first-class compartment—a choice Alicia had made that I didn't protest—and tipped the brim of my hat over my face. I wanted to rest and stared mutely at the polished wooden paneling of the car. Alicia sat opposite me, her hands folded neatly on her lap, her eyes watching the scenery outside.

London slid past quickly—terraces of red-brick houses, allotments, smoke-stained factories, and streets full of taxis. Soon, the rhythm of the wheels steadied into a hard, metallic chant, and the countryside opened into hedgerows and fields dotted with sheep. We were off again, heading to a hell I wasn't sure I wanted to face.

I cracked the window open a fraction. Coal smoke and cold air rushed in, carrying the scent of the damp earth outside. I closed my eyes for a moment, listening. The clatter was steady, but ever so often it faltered—as if a beat was there that seemed to repeat itself or the train was running over the same joint twice.

I opened my eyes. The same cart was passing by the window again, a horse-drawn dray piled high with hay, the driver's cap pulled low, his arms flicking the reins. I blinked, and suddenly only hedgerows remained; the cart was nowhere to be seen. Alicia met my gaze—she'd seen it too. We were already dealing with the effects of the Mirror.

York brought a flurry of activity, with porters shouting, locomotives hissing under the cathedral-like roof, and new passengers boarding the train. From the platform, I saw many men running to and fro, as if busy, but one man in particular caught my eye. He wore a dark suit, his newspaper raised in front of his face. Though he never glanced in my direction, I saw him fold his paper neatly as the train left the station, and as he remained on the platform, I couldn't shake the feeling of paranoia watching him. We were being tailed.

North of Newcastle, the landscape grew wilder as the effects of man faded, and we caught sight of the sea. The occasional castle would break through the horizon—Bamburgh, Alnwick— their ancient stones crafting a foreboding presence as the train continued on. We'd bought drinks, and I sipped my whiskey, its warmth calming my nerves. As the train moved along, Alicia pointed out the landscape.

"Scotland," she said.

And she was right. As the train crossed into Scotland, evening shadows stretched longer, and the sky became dark. Smoke trailed past the windows, curling back into the carriage, though I had long since shut the window. I tapped the arm of my seat, discomfort coursing through my veins.

"I feel like we're two steps behind, Alicia."

Her reply was calm, almost clinical. "We always are."

The train hurtled toward Edinburgh, with Arthur's Seat a black silhouette against the quickly fading sky and the castle a shadowed crown above the city. Steam roared as the Pacific braked hard beneath Waverly's cavernous roof, and I flicked the last of my cigarette to the floor, grinding it beneath my heel.

"Well… I'm finally back," I said. "Now the real work begins."

She smiled, but only said one word in response. "Rosyth."

CHAPTER 7
CHRONICLING CALDER

cotland was home. Max Calder was a man born to a life in Glasgow, already cursed to fail. He was a man whose world began in crowded, agonizing silence, born in a one-room flat with a damp, mildewed ceiling and cracked plaster walls. The Gorbals didn't notice when he was born, nor did anyone care much. The tenements were gray and unyielding —back to back, as if they had been stitched together by a shoddy surgeon or some second-rate cobbler attempting to fix a problem already too far gone.

When he was born, he was a thin baby. His mother tried to take care of him. Her layered, draped shawls were tattered already, and as she shuffled here and there among the streets, she was looked upon with pity by even the most unfortunate. She was his mother—but the father remained a mystery. The shipyards and factories provided a somewhat healthy respite for the mother and child, as the forgiving sailors would often spare her food or bread to help her get by.

But before he had scarcely turned three, she had passed away. Calder never even remembered her, really—as gifted as his memory sometimes was, he could never put a face to the name. Rumors of fever, influenza, and even a more dastardly sickness surrounded her death, but it didn't matter to him. He was alone in the world, and her absence was forgotten as he was whisked off from flat to flat, passed from relative to relative. But everyone—even the relatives—had to fend for themselves, especially during the First World War. And in the Gorbals, food was barely enough even for those who worked. By the time he was six and a half, his existence had slipped into those forgotten crevices of the city, where even those who knew he existed didn't often remember. His survival depended on a mix of charity, parish, and the street. Food was meager and late, and though Calder scraped by, he more often than not went to bed hungry.

It was in 1920 when Calder's life truly began to take a turn for the better, if you could call it that. He had grown fond of seeking aid from the Daughters of Charity, who had set up their haunts near the Gorbals, seeking to assist those they could. It was here that Max Calder met Sister Agnes—though he would often simply call her Sister—one of the Daughters who frequented the place. She smiled rarely, but her gentle tone struck a chord in the young boy, making him listen attentively even when he ignored others.

One gray, overcast afternoon, Calder had lifted several cigarette cards from the jacket of a dockworker who had passed out against some stone steps. The man's head rested against his chest, his nose dripping, and a half-finished bottle of whisky hung from his fingertips.

Calder slipped his fingers into the man's coat like a shadow, silently reaching into the pocket and pulling out those cherished cards that boys like him wanted more than anything but rarely found. To a grown man, Calder thought, these were worth nothing—but to him, they were something. To him, they were shiny treasures, tempting visuals of far-off places and things that he'd never seen before. He scampered off, excitement flooding his veins at the prospect of showing the cards off to the few other boys he played with in the streets. Before he had made it barely three streets away, however, a firm hand caught his wrist. He flinched, recoiling until he recognized the voice that spoke to him.

"What are you carrying there, Max?"

Sister Agnes was standing over him, her eyes firm as she searched his face. Calder froze, lowering his gaze. She'd given him stern lessons before—to never steal, even if it were the smallest, most inconsequential thing. He expected a lecture at the very least, but it wasn't what he got. She crouched down at eye level with him, her knees popping as she did. The old woman waited until he finally spoke.

"I'm sorry, Sister. I…"

"You've quick fingers, Max. And a quick mind—something I don't see often in these parts. It's quick enough that you can survive, but quick enough that you can throw yourself right off a ledge if you go too far. Understand?"

"No, Sister."

She sighed, her voice measured and weary. "The reason, Max, that I don't want you to steal is because you do have smarts. Being smart makes everything easier… and that goes for the bad things, too. It starts small at first, but you'll quickly realize you've a knack for stealing things. That's not good. You'll realize, sooner or later, that you never really fit in. But the way you decide to deal with that is what'll help you survive… or leave you to starve."

"Yes, Sister. I understand," Calder said, though he didn't entirely.

She gently took the cards from his palm, examining them briefly with a glint in her eye. Then, suddenly, she handed the cards back to him. "Keep the cards if you want. But remember, Max—you'll have a knack for anything you set your mind to. So set your mind to something good. That'll keep you alive."

Half an hour later, the cards were back in the drunkard's pocket.

It was just one of many lessons that she taught him. Sister Agnes, though aging, continued to devote as much attention to Calder as her position allowed. He was never sure why she focused on him—perhaps it was because, as she had told him on many occasions, she thought he was simply too different for the Gorbals—but he was glad for her help. As the year continued, the Sister began to give him errands. They were small at first, such as carrying notes up and down the alleyways, or keeping a basic track of the donation sheets as she began to teach him math. It seemed as if no one else but her noticed the boy picking up things so quickly, or repeating the information he learned with the precision of a scholar beyond his years.

As Max Calder continued to grow, his housing became more stable, with the assistance of Sister Agnes. Using her own meager funds, she helped the boy to find a flat in one of the better tenements in the Gorbals. Though it was by no means a palace, the small area that he now called home was far sturdier than what he'd known before, simply by the nature of it being a place he could call home. The local area, though crowded, was somewhere he could return each night—and for the first time in his life, he wasn't fighting for survival.

Sister Agnes didn't stop there, either; she continued to nurture and teach him whenever she could, helping Calder to find small jobs so he could begin to contribute to his own welfare. "Don't steal things you've not a need for. Don't fight unless it's for survival. An' don't beg unless you've no other way."

And so, he worked. At first, it was largely with her help—but as time went on, he began to do small tasks for others who resided within the Gorbals—a note delivered to a doctor, an errand to the coal yard, and other small tasks that allowed him to have his own independence. It was during this time that Calder began to notice that he picked things up more easily than the rest of the kids. It wasn't simple, by any means, but he realized he had a knack for memorizing the routes of the town, each street and back alley, and the men and women he spoke to. By the time he turned ten, Calder had changed from a starved, barely recognizable, impoverished boy who roamed the streets into a more wiry, keen survivor.

Around his thirteenth birthday, Sister Agnes began to fall ill. Although she never spoke of it to Calder—the two spoke less these days—he noticed her cough growing heavier in the winter, and her movements became slower. One morning, while Calder was delivering a message to the mission, one of the Sisters beckoned him to approach.

"What's wrong, sister?" Calder asked, noticing the worried look on her face.

The woman stared at him in sorrow for a second before she spoke. "It's Agnes, lad. She's taken to bed, an' she's not lookin' good."

Calder nodded silently, then thanked the sister for telling him. He wanted to visit Sister Agnes, but he suspected that she didn't want him to know or see her in such a state. And so he left, keeping his thoughts to himself and his feelings suppressed, only stopping once or twice to stare up at the dark sky as snow began to fall. By nightfall, she had passed, and Calder was once again left alone. He attended the service, staying near the back and not speaking to anyone there, simply watching and observing as he'd always done.

Though in his later years he never spoke of Agnes much, he always followed the rules she had taught him to the best of his ability. It was his way of repaying her for saving him from the Gorbals. As he grew older, he began to spend more time around the public houses and bars, working the door and breaking up scraps between the clientele. At these bars, he quickly realized that his brain was the true selling point of his services. Rather than working the doors, he began to drift toward the interiors of the taverns, taking down names, faces, and voices, all within his mind, while listening to idle boasts the men made after one pint too many.

"Ah, boy, when I tell ye o' the size of the haddock I've

caught, you'd scarcely believe it!" one man yelled, his face flushed and red, his beard wet with ale.

"Wasn't it only last week you said you caught not a thing in months, Tam?" Calder had been leaning up against the bar, a rag in his hand as if he were cleaning, but his mind was firmly focused on the conversation.

The sound of laughter caused Tam to turn even redder than he'd been, but only for a second, as he began to laugh. "Well—aye, that's right, boy, but you've never seen the likes of fish I'd caught before that!"

"Aye," another man chimed in, "I can attest to that."

And so the conversation and laughter continued, but Calder took note. He listened with a grin, watching their faces closely. He'd never poke them too harshly—never starting a fight—and only kept at it enough to rile them up. Men who felt flustered, who felt challenged yet reassured, were men who spent more in the bar.

Calder motioned to the bartender, and a second later, the man had slid a drink across to him. It wasn't anything fancy, but the owner of the establishment, O'Dwyer, had promised Calder over conversation that he'd provide free drinks for the boy at no cost, so long as Calder "did his thing." And so he did.

Later that night, two of the regulars were arguing over their pints, voices growing louder as their disagreement escalated. Calder drifted nearer, listening carefully, a slight grin on his face.

"You say I didn' pay, now? You know damn well I had my pocket turned inside out for all'us last night!" said one man, whom Calder recognized as Ewan.

"You're chattin' rubbish," the other man replied, his voice slurred but the anger clear from his tone. "You left bloody early, an' I bought five bloody rounds, 'member?"

"Now, fellas, I think you're both misremembering," Calder said as he leaned in, tapping his fingers on the table. It wasn't close enough to startle the men, but close enough so they could hear. "John, you did buy five rounds that night. Bought 'em for everyone, and said a good man would never let a glass go empty."

"Aye. Aye, I did say that," John replied slowly.

"Yes, and you—" Calder pointed to Ewan, a smile on his face. "You covered the last two, after John disappeared with that bar whore… I was there; he only reappeared later, after you'd left."

Ewan's mouth opened, then shut again as his face twisted in thought. "That's right, that's right…" he muttered, squinting. "So 'en, who pays tonight?"

"Well, John bought five—and Ewan, you came in with the last two… but arguably just as important, after John left, that is. A tie, nearly," Calder said, grasping both of them by the shoulder in a friendly manner as he did. "The matter of tonight's pay shows different, eh? Tabs are all different sizes now, an' you can hardly blame each other for payin' any less the other night."

And just like that, the potential barfight was averted. The two men muttered under their breath, but the anger had dissipated. And Calder struck.

"Lads, lads," he said, jovially. "Another round? Only one way to settle this now—and that's one apiece."

"Aye, one apiece," John muttered, a sheepish grin on his face.

"Aye, that'll settle it," Ewan grumbled, though his tone was no longer angry.

Calder faded away, leaving the two men as they raised their hands for the barkeep. For O'Dwyer and the other pub owners, he was as good as an extra set of hands. He could fight if he needed to—and often did—but his true value was in soothing tempers and helping every man see the use of an extra round of drinks.

As his reputation continued to grow, Calder became known by many of the owners as a reliable bouncer and assistant, respected for both his fists and his memory. His early years had forged him into a valuable asset, and his work at the bars gradually became rougher. Whereas before, the men had only relied on him for his smooth talk, they now relied on him to handle the drunks, sailors, and the odd unruly razor gang member, all at a higher price than he'd initially charged. Word soon began to travel that Calder wasn't to be messed with—he fought rough, observing how men moved and thought, using the environment to his advantage. And though violence shadowed his work, he used it more as a learning tool than a means to hurt. He learned each time he fought, and by his late teens, he'd gained a serious reputation in the Gorbals.

Yet the more he worked to survive, the more it bored him. His mind began to itch for something other than the constant pattern of bar fights, drunks, sailors, and the type of men who frequented these places. A restlessness overtook him that he could no longer ignore, and he began to explore places other than the bars. With meager savings, he began to dip into that as he spent more time at reading rooms, printers' shops, and even the stray book he could find in second-hand shops. He had long since taught himself to read, with help from Sister Agnes, and he began to vigorously consume history, argument, and detective fiction—consuming non-fiction textbooks alongside works by Conan Doyle and Christie in equal measure. His eyes grew accustomed to the finer things that he consumed, and human nature began to fascinate him.

When reading was no longer enough, he began to experiment with himself. He began to learn to draw buildings and architecture, and when he found that enjoyable, he began to experiment with forgery, copying forms and letterheads. At first, he simply did it as a hobby, but soon he discovered a practical application —a simple fabricated note would land him day work at the coal yard, no questions asked. While he rarely used such methods, it began to confirm what he already knew—intelligence was how you truly survived in the world.

When even his hobbies began to bore him, Calder switched his attention to conversation. He began to slip into the more upper-end regions of Glasgow, conversing with educated men and learning about the schools they had attended. During his conversations, Cambridge emerged as the pinnacle—it was a place that the men spoke highly of and where the brightest minds seemed to gather. It wasn't admiration that made him focus on it, but the challenge—and he became obsessed.

Despite his growing obsession with books and the allure of the finer world he saw from afar, he continued to work in the bars. He had to support himself, after all; to pay the rent, he dealt with scuffles, bar fights, and rowdy customers. Night after night, he'd lounge at the bars, sipping on alcohol provided to him and watch, waiting for the crash of broken glass or the heavy thud of fists. Though it had once forged him, it now felt repetitive and boring.

Eventually, however, Calder's breaking point arrived. He was at O'Dwyer's, where he usually worked, when two men began shouting at each other from across the room—one a sailor, the other a tattooed man Calder could only assume was part of a razor gang. He stepped in just as one of the men lunged for the other, shoving the sailor against the wall and twisting the wrist of the tattooed man until he dropped his glass and the shards skittered across the floor. The tattooed man cursed, and Calder noticed a commotion from the table where he'd been sitting.

"Now ya done it, lad," said a third man, rising from his seat. He rushed from the table, pulling a small knife from his pocket.

Calder backed up, shoving the tattooed man to the floor as the other man approached him. Though he'd dealt with his share of razor gangs, they usually never pressed the issue—even these men knew when being a drunkard had gotten the better of them, and they typically held no grudges against him for doing his job. Still, it was dangerous to fight them while they were drunk and violent. The tattooed man rose, and the two circled him until the one with the knife lunged. Calder dodged backward, swinging a chair upward and knocking the man's head with a solid thump. The guy collapsed, but the tattooed man was already on top of Calder, and the two struggled, fighting for a second until Calder broke one of his arms free and landed a solid punch.

O'Dwyer himself must have heard the commotion because he came rushing from his upstairs loft, his arms raised. "Enough! Enough, lads—that's enough!" he screeched, trying to wrestle the tattooed man to the ground. The man resisted, cursing and striking Calder in the face. Calder returned the blow, driving a sharp elbow forward toward the man's face, but at that moment, the man thrashed and broke free.

With a dull thud, Max Calder's elbow landed solidly on O'Dwyer's temple.

The man staggered, his eyes wide but blank, before collapsing to the floor like an empty burlap sack, blood seeping from a cut across his brow.

"Christ, you've killed him…" a voice from the silent tavern echoed.

Calder bent quickly, his hands fumbling with O'Dwyer's shirt, his finger pressed against the man's neck. "He's breathing," he muttered, but the words were heard by nobody but himself. Without a backward glance, Calder stood, wiped the blood from his hands, and barked at a man who stood nearby to fetch a doctor. Then he walked into the night.

O'Dwyer survived, though he caught a fever and was bedridden for a week. Calder kept tabs on the man but never returned to visit or showed his face. It wasn't his fault—he heard talk of that through the crowd—but he blamed himself. His words failed him when they mattered the most. From that night, Calder knew he was done with Glasgow and with the Gorbals. He no longer wanted to live the kind of life he had so far, and as he sat, watching the dark sky and the smoke drift through the air, he knew that he wanted to leave it behind.

Just like that, Max Calder began to disappear. It was in plain sight at first—a new second-hand suit that made him look somewhat respectable, a different way of standing, and a new cadence to his speech. He left his haunts and began to migrate to the wealthier side of Glasgow, where he wasn't known as Max Calder. Here, he began to use a new name—Jack Fontaine, a man more familiar with this type of life. He spent his evenings in hotel lobbies and tea houses, testing accents until he became unrecognizable and practicing his signatures and letters by candlelight until his forgeries were so neat they were practically perfect.

The months passed, and by the end of 1932, Calder was ready. With his briefcase full of fake papers and a threadbare suit, Jack Fontaine boarded a southbound train. As he stepped off the train and glanced up at the towering and prestigious Cambridge University, Jack Fontaine smiled to himself, an excitement in his chest that he hadn't experienced since learning to read.

Here was a smile that wasn't his, a second-hand suit, and false papers—but here also was a new challenge that would require more wit than he'd ever used before.

He was ready to play his part.

CHAPTER 8
EDINBURGH ELUCIDATION

The brakes screamed one last time as the Pacific engine dragged the train into the cavern of Waverley Station. It was a place that breathed steam and secrets. Nested in the hollow between the Old Town and the New, it resembled a bowl of iron and glass, capturing the noise of the city above it. The great arched roof, blackened by years of soot and war smoke, trembled with the sound of trains arriving from Glasgow, London, Aberdeen—and sometimes from places that didn't appear on the official timetables.

From Princes Street Bridge, the station spread out like a mechanical lung, exhaling clouds of vapor and coal dust. The city's spires and monuments loomed above, cold and impassive, while below, the platforms sweated with movement.

Electric lights buzzed weakly under the soot-dark girders, reflecting off wet stone and the gleam of uniform buttons. The war had ended, but rationing hadn't; everything still seemed rationed—the light, the laughter, the hope. Even the advertisements peeling from the walls appeared tired: "Take the LNER to the Seaside," the posters promised, but the paper was yellowed and the edges curled with damp.

At the southern end, near the old booking hall, stood a news kiosk and a tea stall that smelled of boiled milk and burnt toast. The tea was strong enough to stand a spoon in, and the milk was powdered. Travelers queued silently—soldiers on leave, widows in worn coats, businessmen pretending to be busy. The station's loudspeakers crackled with clipped, unintelligible announcements, the kind that seemed designed to hide meaning rather than convey it.

The station police moved in pairs, their boots echoing off the platform tiles. There were always more of them than anyone could explain. They claimed it was to prevent pickpockets, but those who knew better said it was to watch the couriers—the quiet men and women who arrived without luggage, stepped off the London train, and vanished into the city before anyone could ask a question. Porters darted through the mist like shadows, their caps glinting as they shouldered bags and shouted for tips, though I ignored them. They weren't why we were here.

I stepped down onto the wet platform, a cigarette already between my fingers, its glow haloed in the steam. I'd taken to smoking even more in Lisbon, and with the recent stress of the news I'd received, my smoking habits had increased. Alicia followed behind me, her heels striking against the stones, muted slightly by the damp. The air was thick with the scents of smoke, coal, damp wool, and rain drifting in from the Firth of Forth.

Above us, Edinburgh Castle loomed in the distance, half-hidden in the fog, its black outline rising sheer from the crags against the sky, as if tearing the world asunder. Arthur's Seat crouched on the other side, a darker mass against the fading sky. Between the two, the city stretched out, every window glowing dimly, and every alley cast in shadows.

Alicia drew her coat around herself, shivering. "It feels older than London."

"Older. Colder, too," I replied. I flicked ash into the puddle beneath my feet, my eyes scanning the crowd. Something seemed off, but I wasn't sure what it was yet. Soldiers on leave, businessmen clutching briefcases, women shepherding children

—but among them, there were several people who caught my eye. A man sat there, folding his newspaper slowly and carefully, but his eyes darted up to me when he thought I wasn't looking. I didn't say anything yet, though.

Instead, my mind was whirring. We were being tailed—but tails were something I hadn't considered previously. Everything happened in tails—and everything could be traced. Just as we were being followed by these men, so could anything be followed if you knew where to look for the footsteps. I sighed, cursing myself for not thinking of it sooner and brushed my hand against Alicia's waist, ever so slightly. I didn't say a word, but I knew she'd follow my lead.

I guided Alicia toward the exit, and we pushed through the concourse and into Princes Street, the rain already beading on the brim of my hat. Trams clattered past, sparks flashing from their overhead wires as they rumbled by. The Gothic spire of the Scott Monument cut sharply into the skyline, black against the wet. Shops glowed dimly under ration-era glass, their windows beaded with rain.

I felt the Mirror's tug here too, as if the city itself were bending, folding around its own ancient stones. Alicia must have noticed it as well—her eyes followed the tramlines, but I could see her entire body was tense.

"You feel it?" I asked.

"Not sure if it's just the city... or what we saw back at Kingsway."

I exhaled, watching the smoke vanish into the night. "Maybe it's both."

The rain thickened, swallowing our footsteps as we moved deeper into Edinburgh's streets—toward whatever awaited us. As we walked, the city pressed close, rows of terraces looming above us, darker than the sky itself. The gas lamps that lined the streets flickered, each light distorted slightly by the incessant drizzle. My hat brim caught the rain, funneling it down my collar, and I knew Alicia felt the same permeating cold that I was experiencing. As we walked, I glanced quickly behind us, nonchalantly as if I were simply looking around, and then squeezed her hand slightly.

She nodded ever so lightly, and though neither of us said it out loud, we were both keenly aware: we were being followed.

"How many?" she asked, her voice barely a whisper.

"Two," I muttered back as a tram squealed past, sparks lighting up the dark sky.

She shifted her gaze slightly into the reflection of a shopfront as we paused, glancing at the dull shoes and ration coats which sat on display. As we stared at the storefront, she spoke in a low voice.

"From the station, I think. I noticed them there—the man with the newspaper and another short fellow."

I nodded. She had seen the same men I had, but their patience spoke volumes about their skill. This wasn't a hurried assassination attempt; these men hung back, tailing us like they were professionals.

"Let them follow," I said as we resumed walking. "Whoever they are, they clearly already know we're here. If they're Bureau men, they want to see where we go. If they're MI6, they'll either be expecting us to spook... or probably doing the same thing that one tried in Lisbon. Either way, we can't do anything right now."

"So what's the plan, Max?"

"I thought of something when we were at the station—when I saw them following us."

"What was that?"

"Everything has a trail. Everything leaves footsteps you can follow if you know where to look—and I think I might know where to look. Whoever had the Kingsway files, or put them there, had to have taken them from official Bureau sources at some point. There's no other explanation, right?"

"I'm following."

"In '46, the Bureau moved most of its files out of London to vaults up here in Edinburgh. Every damn thing that could burn them if another Blitz ever came. Archives were swept, moved in the dead of night. All the files too sensitive or too damning to keep in London, they moved to the archives here. I don't know where most of the vaults here are, but I do know that if there's a paper trail for Section IX, or for Philby's damn connection to all this and the Mirror…"

"…It'd be here," she finished quietly.

"Only issue," I said, "is that I don't know where they stored the archives."

She paused for a moment before speaking. "Max… I think we need to reach out to the Bureau itself."

"No, no, not yet—" I shook my head stubbornly. "Alicia, we still don't know how connected the Bureau is to all this. If they are involved… that could be deadly. And if not, we might not like the stance they take."

"You're right. I guess so," she sighed. "But eventually, you'll have to make the decision. Or I'll have to go to them myself."

I nodded as we walked. I knew Alicia was more loyal to the Bureau than I was—even now, after all we'd been through. I wasn't sure if she would actually contact them, but she would certainly consider it. So I needed another solution, one that wouldn't involve the Bureau explicitly.

"I have an idea," I said, pointing ahead through the darkness and rain as a tram rattled by, its sparks briefly illuminating a blur of rain-streaked glass. "But it might not work."

She almost smirked for a second before composing herself. "Well, aren't all our plans like that? What is it?"

"Back during the war, on a solo mission, the Bureau had me run a file exchange here in Edinburgh. Picked me because I'm familiar with the locals—though I thought of it as punishment from Hawthorne more than anything else… it was mundane. Anyway, they stuck me in a terraced house—off Abercromby Place, I believe."

"You remember the address?"

The address… but not just that. It might be tied to the Bureau's file vaults, especially because of who was running it last, I heard."

"Who?"

"Guy named Cameron McLeod. He's Bureau. Born in Edinburgh, too. And what's more, I think I remember he was overseeing the file shifts back then."

"I won't even ask how you know that…" she muttered.

"Our strengths are different, Alicia. You should feel lucky I have a contact that might not hate me—or want to kill us—for once."

"Lead the way, then."

We wound through the old streets, the beautiful architecture barely visible in the dark. It was a well-polished city, and the trams splashed along the cobblestones, their headlights shimmering. I hesitated a few times—even here, my memory wasn't as sharp as it used to be—but eventually, I found a landmark I remembered, and we set off again, Alicia following me. Behind us, I knew the two men continued to trail us, but each time I glanced back, they hadn't grown any closer. Eventually, we saw it.

The terraced house sat near the corner, unremarkable compared to some of the other places we'd passed. Its windows were dark, completely curtained, and covered in dust, while its roof was slick with moss. I bent down, brushed my hand along the underside of the cast-iron boot scraper that was set into the cement step, and felt around. Just as I was about to give up, I felt it—an old-fashioned, rusty key that an Edinburgh agent would have found here all those years ago. It wasn't that I was opposed to breaking into the building, but I knew it would attract unnecessary attention, and back when the Bureau had run this safe house, they only used a set number of hiding places for their keys. I glanced up at the street, and in the distance, I could see two shadowy figures that had paused along the path, in the darkest spot between two street lamps. Then I slid the key into the lock.

It gave way, only reluctantly, and the house admitted us with a creak and a sigh, as if it hadn't been opened in ages. The air was thick with the kind of smell you find in a cupboard that has remained sealed too long, or a home that's grown old without its owners. The scent of coal dust, damp mold, and old paper filled my nostrils, and I coughed slightly as I lit a cigarette. I glanced around.

Even the wallpaper had turned yellow in places, the roses faded, and the coloring was almost all gone from the background patterns. It was an abandoned place—a safe house from a golden age long gone. The Bureau had reached its peak during the early days of the war, and after the Dockyard incident, it had slowly begun to decommission many of its safe houses, agents, and protocols.

Alicia slipped past me, her figure gliding smoothly against the weary facade of the home, the sound of her shoes quieted by the fitted rug. "What a charming home," she muttered.

"Quite the sight, isn't it? It's more dilapidated than I remember. If McLeod was using this, he hasn't for a while."

I didn't even bother turning on the light. The glow from street lamps outside illuminated the place well enough when I threw back the curtains, and my torch cast a steady enough yellow beam to do the rest. I walked ahead, looking around. In the hall, a mirror covered with dust and a staircase that curled upward met my eyes. It was very much how I remembered it, but older.

As I walked past, I caught my reflection in the dusty mirror for an instant, but it wasn't mine. I turned toward it, staring again, but the figure was gone, replaced by my regular face— older than I remembered, with dreary, lifeless eyes. I rubbed a hand across my face, staring at myself. How did I become so tired? What had happened to the agent who was first recruited into the Bureau?

"See anything?" Alicia's voice echoed from behind me.

"Only things I don't want to," I responded. "Let's check the basement. The interesting pieces are always below ground."

Cigarette in one hand and torch in the other, I kicked the shoddy makeshift door open and began to descend the steps. They were even more makeshift than the door—the type of thing meant for coal boys—but down I went, with Alicia tailing me. The air grew colder, more stale, and more silent as we went, until only the creaking of the stairs could be heard. At the bottom, I circled my light along the walls until I saw it—along one wall, there was a bench lined with coils, condensers, and even a receiver. Above it, a board nailed to the wall with a small grid of notes thumbtacked to it, and next to it all was an open ledger.

"Well, damn." I stepped closer. "Wonder what the hell they were broadcasting here."

I glanced down at the ledger. It was a log—dates, times, call groups, all written in a sort of neatness that almost made it seem printed, yet I could tell it was all handwritten. Some lines were more hurried and shorter; others were erased and overwritten with a careful tact that made it almost indistinguishable. Tacked above it all was a thin, yellow card.

Post Office Telephones—Engineering Access Permit
Holder: C. MCLEOD
Authority: [REDACTED]
Pass No. U-1794 Valid to 31/XII/46

"That's him," Alicia said, tapping the permit with her finger. "Found your man."

"Looks like it." My eyes were already on the penciled note to the right of the board, though it was nothing more than a hastily scrawled line that was already half faded. I squinted, trying to make it out, and bent closer until the writing became legible: Kingsway switchrooms—C.F.S. // H.A.R.P.

"Both of them. He was listening to London, it seems," I said.

"I'll search the rest of the room, then. And check the logs—there might be something there."

I flipped through the documents carefully, taking it all in. This is what I was good at—what I was trained to do. Seeing patterns in information that shouldn't be seen. But the more I flipped through it, the more mundane it seemed. Sure, there were occasional scribbled entries, but most of them seemed to belong to a hobbyist—except for the ones that had been carefully erased from the pages of the book.

"Not much here," I called over my shoulder. "If this is McLeod's bench, he took his work seriously."

Meanwhile, Alicia had searched the small room. When we reconvened a few moments later, she tossed a box of QSL cards and various postcards onto the table next to the ledger. They were small, paper-thin, and moldy from age—postmarks from Leith, Copenhagen, and even Lisbon. One of the cards in particular had a smudged address written across the back: 18 Inverleith Row.

"Think he lives there?" she asked.

"One way to find out. But first, let's check upstairs."

We walked back up the old wooden stairwell, balancing carefully until we reached the main floor. Here, we made a quick detour into the kitchen, checking the shelves for anything that could help us.

The shelves were mostly bare—the stove was rusty and empty, and the only food remaining was a tin of treacle that looked almost embalmed from age. The rest of the rooms at ground level were very much the same—stripped of anything that could have been of use to us, other than an old armchair, the fireplace pokers, and the hall mirror. Finally, it was time for us to explore the attic. Alicia led the way this time, pushing at the attic door and heaving it open as I finished my cigarette.

"With our luck, it'll be empty," she said dryly.

It wasn't. At the back of the attic, we spotted an old trunk, half-buried behind a tangle of broken chairs and moldy rugs, barely visible in the dim light seeping through several of the broken boards. It looked old, made of dark wood, with brass corners and intricate carvings. I grabbed the lock and fumbled in my pockets to find my pick.

"Wait, here's an easier way."

"Oh, that'll do the trick," I said, grabbing the small chimney brick that Alicia had pulled from one of the floorboards.

I slammed it against the hasp with a dull thud, tossed the broken metal to the side, and lifted the lid. The smell that emanated from it was that of paper—old, stale, worn paper, but paper all the same. The folders inside were the Bureau's standard issue, folders I'd held a thousand times before, with areas completely redacted in black ink. There were no signatures or discernible factors on the front of the folders; of course, organization policy prevented much of that. But the dates on the tabs were fascinating—dates that made a dull sense of dread settle in the pit of my stomach.

1943 and 1944 were the main two. The war years—years that should have been largely filed away by now.

"Whoever kept this trunk here went against Bureau policy," Alicia said, her voice low.

I nodded as I thumbed through the files. As was expected, most were redacted—but here and there, a line or two slipped through, and they made sense. Routing diagrams, memos labeled 'KINGSWAY—S IX SUPPLY Installations at Kingsway Tunnels,' and a neatly signed note at the bottom: "Liaise with F.S." I cursed as I finished thumbing through the last of the folders and tossed them back into the trunk.

"What's wrong?" she asked, concern etched in her tone.

"It's not enough. We already know the damn rooms exist under Kingsway. We already know they weren't sanctioned, and that Philby—and Fraser-Smith—have something to do with it. But it's not enough... it doesn't tie together. Hell, nothing ties together."

"Explain, Max." Alicia watched as I began to pace the room, kicking at some of the rolled-up rugs in frustration.

"I don't have the smoking gun," I muttered. "We've got the gun itself—Kingsway, Section IX, Philby's clearance, Fraser-Smith—and we can feel the damn thing is still hot, but we don't know what it shot at. We don't see the smoke, and we don't see the target. Or maybe all we see is the smoke. I just need one line that ties it all together. Anything, at this point. A work order that points to Rosyth, or some indication of how closely Philby and MI6 are involved, or how he even managed to pull all this damn magic off. Without knowing what the target hit, we're left with a gun that's going cold, in the attic of this damn house."

I could hear myself pacing the floor. The boards creaked and protested beneath my boots, dust rising from the beams and hanging in the air as if disturbed. The smell became even more nauseating, but I couldn't help it. I wanted to smash the trunk to splinters and tear the ink off those damn redacted pages.

"What about the message?" Alicia asked, her voice quiet. I could tell she sympathized. "About Kingsway… it said as planned, didn't it? That might be your bullet."

"It's just a tease. It doesn't have the substance we need," I muttered. "And it was probably about us—getting rid of you, at least, rather than anything else of substance. And I still… something still doesn't sit right with me about that message."

"So then what next?"

I didn't respond. My head throbbed, a headache that felt as if I'd been suppressing it for days, bursting at the seams of my forehead. It was an ache I knew well—one I only felt whenever I dealt in Mirror business. I could feel the missing shape of my memories whirring around, like scrambled eggs that could never be made whole again.

"We've got enough to know that something exists," I finally said. "Enough to know who set it up—I think—and definitely enough to get killed over. But not enough to stop the whole project, and not enough to head directly to Rosyth. I should have left that man breathing in Lisbon. One minute—one minute might've been all it took for his handler's name, or a meeting time, or something of substance. Instead, we've got a prototype beneath Kingsway, and dead ends everywhere else.

"So then what are we missing?" Alicia was still calm, even when I wasn't, but it helped me gather my thoughts.

I stopped pacing as I made a decision. "We're missing paper. And the life of the whole thing. For paper, we need a trail—the logs, ledgers, dock passes, or anything with a signature. We need to know how Fraser-Smith and Philby got all that material, and who betrayed the Bureau to do it. They didn't just materialize there—hell, they were boxed, loaded, and signed for. And then we're missing someone—someone who can testify. Someone who was there when it happened."

"And you're thinking that might be McLeod?"

"McLeod is our best bet," I replied, a sliver of hope in my voice but none in my mind. "His permit's on the wall. He wrote that note about Kingsway in his own hand. He kept this trunk… which we know he shouldn't have kept… goes against all protocol. If anyone can point a finger at who's really behind this, it'd be him. Or he's dead."

"And we know his address."

"Well, his last address, I suppose. Could have been years ago, but it's our best bet."

"What makes you think he'll talk to us?"

"He owes me one," I said, motioning to Alicia as I headed toward the faint, glowing exit of the attic. "Lisbon. He's not the type that'd forget."

We took only the few papers that still had something of substance on them and then left. Down the stairs, back through the old, yellow hall, and out into the wet darkness that surrounded the city, we made sure to close the door behind us until it latched just the way we'd found it.

The two men who had been trailing us hadn't gone anywhere. They were quiet, not looking directly at us, but I spotted them quickly across the street. They were patient—but I knew they weren't stupid. They likely knew by now that we'd spotted them out, and that concerned me even more. Most men would panic—once they were found out, they'd stop trailing and attempt to call off the mission. A pro, though—a pro would keep at it.

Alicia glanced up and down the street. "Inverleith Row," she said. "Guess we hope he's still there?"

"If he isn't, it's likely someone knows where he went." I raised a hand, waiting for a cab to pull out of the rain, its lamps shining and glimmering through the fog. "And if he is there, he's going to talk to us. I'll make sure of it."

We slid into the cab, the seats already slick with damp water beneath us, and I motioned to the driver. "18 Inverleith Row." Just like that, we were off, the cab rattling along the dark streets until the buildings began to thin and the rain let up slightly.

"So, what is your history with McLeod, anyway? What does he owe you?" Alicia murmured as the cab drove onward.

"It's a long story, but it's one I haven't forgotten. It was in Lisbon, actually—in 1943. McLeod was MI6 back then, just barely. He was still green, not really experienced in the field yet. He was running a courier chain for the Embassy and was doing a solid job on paper, but one of his couriers was an Abwehr double. I was in Lisbon on one of the missions we didn't run together at that point—working on something entirely different. The Bureau had me tracking down a rumor. But the Abwehr man crossed my path, and so I followed him after I watched him tail a Brit courier into a café near the river. Didn't even think twice about it; didn't know the Brit he was tailing was McLeod. Didn't know that the Germans planned to get rid of him for good and dump him in the river—but you know how I am. I usually follow my instincts.

"I still remember how it was back then. The night was so damp you could taste the salt on your tongue, could smell it eating through the brickwork—and the lamps were barely visible. The café was mostly empty, of course, other than a few drunks. I saw two tables away, McLeod waiting for the courier to make his drop. Then, three men walked in—I knew they were Germans instantly. The courier signaled to them, but I knew McLeod hadn't noticed. The man was just too new to the job at the time.

"But I waited and kept biding my time until they followed him. They weren't even going to wait till he was outside—meant to grab him before he even walked out the door, but I shot first. I took two of them down, the other two fellows ducked for cover, and I grabbed McLeod, dragging him by his collar through the kitchen and out into the alley. He kept asking what was happening and who I was, but I didn't answer—just told him to keep his mouth shut and to keep moving. I'd left my car about two blocks down, so I pulled him there—shoved him in and took off before he could even protest. The whole thing probably took three minutes, but all he knew was that I saved his life… that much was clear.

"I didn't want MI6 to know the scope of my mission, though, and wanted to make sure he wouldn't inform on me, so I made sure he knew that he owed me one before I dropped him on the road near the British compound and left. That was it—but since then, every time he's seen me, he's been thankful about it. And he's never repaid me, either—so if he's still alive here in Edinburgh, he's going to pay the debt."

I leaned back against the damp seat, closing my eyes as I lit another cigarette. It was quickly becoming a dangerous habit. Alicia had listened in silence the whole way, her face blank except for her eyes, which examined me closely. She probably knew that I didn't usually speak this much, but she didn't ask why today was different. Instead, she shifted, and as the cab finally slowed to a halt, she spoke.

"We're here."

The cab let us out at the corner, only a few feet from our destination. I scanned the street and saw a dark vehicle idling slowly in the darkness. I smiled slightly and tapped Alicia, who nodded. She knew as well. The place was an old stone building and had clearly been there for quite some time, with black iron railings slick with rain in front of it and a white-tinted door in the very center. The windows were dark, and the entire place exuded an air of mystery. It was well into the night, and the street was quiet enough to hear the tram two blocks away and the soft patter of rain on the ground below. I sighed as we approached the place. I swung open the gate, not bothering much with subtlety. The men who trailed us already knew we were here, and we didn't have the resources or the time to shake them. Instead, I marched right up the steps and knocked at the door—three quick raps—then stepped back. At first, there was silence, but only a moment later, I heard footsteps inside. I waited patiently, watching as the door opened barely an inch, and a tired face peeked out.

Though I could scarcely make out his features, I heard the shocked inhale and the half-muttered curse as he tried to close the door, but I had my foot in the crack before he could pull it shut.

"Can't speak," he muttered, his voice hoarse and quick, though unmistakably Scottish. "Not here, not now—an' not to you. Don't come back."

"Lisbon, McLeod. You owe me one."

His grip on the door loosened. He opened it wider, then stared at me, and I could see his full face now, his eyes calculating and grim. He looked past my shoulder, down the street, and then back quickly to me, as if calculating how long he had before everything went to hell.

"Two hours," he said. "On the dot—I won't stay. Meet me at The Northern Bar and come clean. Don't let them track you."

And with that, he shut the door. I moved my foot this time, letting him slam it in my face. I glanced around at the vehicle behind us, then at Alicia.

"Two hours," she murmured.

"Let's use that time well."

And we did. We didn't go straight there; instead, we looped our way through the back alleys, pretending that we were interested in window shopping on the next street down. We cut through another alley before taking a tram two stops northward, stepping out, crossing the track, and then taking the southbound tram back. Our goal wasn't to lose our trackers, but as we finally crossed town, I caught Alicia's sleeve and jerked my head toward a narrow lane wedged between two small, shuttered shops. It was scarcely visible in the darkness, and I knew it would provide the perfect cover. We slipped into the small alley, our boots splashing in the puddles, then cut through a service yard and emerged onto another back alley that spilled onto a main street again.

We kept moving, darting into another alley before the men caught up, swiftly jogging now—and then another alley, and yet another, until I finally paused, listening. There were no sounds but the rain.

"Gone, you think?" I asked.

"Gone," she replied.

Though Edinburgh wasn't my home turf, it was close enough that I felt comfortable navigating the area—and confident I'd still be able to find my way to The Northern Bar. Sure enough, we found our way there just as the two-hour mark approached and slipped inside with two minutes to spare. He arrived exactly on time, his coat wet with the rain, his eyes scanning the room before they landed on us. We'd already taken our seats at a table in the corner, and he approached, sliding onto the bench opposite, his back to the wall.

The Northern Bar was a flurry of noise, smoke, and hustle, but McLeod still looked nervous. His eyes were shifty, and he glanced around several more times before speaking.

"Debt's not forgotten," he said, quickly glancing at Alicia before refocusing his gaze on me. "What do you need?"

"Section IX," I said, my voice quiet as I leaned in.

He flinched slightly, his face twitching as if uncomfortable, before he collected himself. "Figured you might be after that. Here in Edinburgh, after all... it was unsanctioned. Off the books —nothing about it in the Bureau nor MI6—rooms under Kingsway that weren't on any plan."

"Built when?"

"Back before the incident. You know which I'm talking 'bout. And then expanded when we shifted the files north; some crates were diverted to it."

"Fraser-Smith?" Alicia asked.

"If you've got him, you know near as much as I do. There were others, too. H.A.R." He stared cautiously at my face, as if trying to read me, then continued. "And even others I still can't mention."

"So what's left?" I asked.

"Enough for a trail if you're lookin' for it. Barely, but it's there." He reached into his coat, producing a brown-wrapped parcel, thin and damp in spots, but still hanging together. Rather than slide it across the table, he dropped it beneath the table, into his lap, and slid it over. I felt the package hit my knees beneath the table and grabbed it. "Key's in there. Bank of Caledonian Merchants. Three-seventeen. Be wary of what you find there."

"One last thing," I said. "You kept a radio bench on Abercromby. Had Philby and Fraser-Smith scribbled on the wall. Why?"

He shook his head. I could tell he was getting uncomfortable. "I regret some of the things I've done. But Calder—steer clear of those men."

"Rosyth," Alicia interrupted as he began to stand. "Does it connect?"

"I won't answer that. I'm payin' a debt, not digging my own grave. We've all made sacrifices to win the war. Hell—" he said, and for the first time, his voice grew louder and more emotional, "I've sacrificed more than most. But damn it if sometimes the choices we make aren't the right ones."

Before I could speak, I felt Alicia tap my shoulder and glanced toward the door of the pub. It had swung open, and two men walked through it—the same two who'd trailed us before. They hadn't caught sight of us yet, their faces blank and masked, their eyes roaming the room. McLeod glanced around to see what we saw, and when his face caught sight of the two men, he stood.

"Debt's repaid," he said. "Those two men—they've been trailing me since halfway through the past hour. Thought I gave 'em the slip. Guess not. Back door for you, Calder. I'll take the front. Don't look back till you've got to the Bank and found what's in the deposit box."

I nodded. "Watch yourself, McLeod."

He didn't respond, moving through the crowd and disappearing into it as the two men still scanned the room from the doorway. Alicia and I stood as the two men glanced in opposite directions, sliding along the wall toward the back end of the pub until we'd found the service corridor. Alicia went first, and I followed behind her, glancing around to make sure we hadn't been spotted. The back door gave way easily, and we slipped out into the darkness, which was beginning to grow lighter.

I felt beneath my coat—the package was secure, safe from the rain.

Now it was our time to find what McLeod had hidden at the Bank.

CHAPTER 9
EVIDENCE EXTENDED

We walked along the slick street, our coats turned up, and the parcel McLeod had given me safely tucked under my arm. The rain had given up now, at last, as the morning light began to break through. The gray, downtrodden city slowly became more visible as we walked, and I glanced up and down the street, a sense of urgency overtaking me. I wasn't sure where the men who tracked us were, but I knew they would be close by now.

"St. Andrew Square," I said to Alicia as the street opened up, the flow of early morning traffic carrying us slowly in the direction we needed to go. The Bank of Caledonian Merchants sat on the eastern side of the square, standing tall in the early morning fog—royal and old. It was an incredible building, ancient—undoubtedly crafted by architectural hands far more skilled than mine could ever be. I smiled slightly—something like this would have been nice to learn as a talent instead of espionage.

As we entered, I slipped the hat off my head, tucking it beneath my arm as I almost reached for a cigarette before thinking better of it and glancing at Alicia. She stood next to me, her red scarf fastened tightly around her neck, her face unreadable, as was typical for her.

The manager found us before we could find him. He emerged from one of the side doors, a ledger tucked under his arm, his eyes darting between our faces. It was clear we'd attracted a certain level of attention—we were likely not the usual clientele. He was a Scotsman, well-groomed with an impressive mustache. His chin was clean-shaven, highlighting a slight double chin, though he held himself up straight, and his jagged nose slanted at us, as if defying any sense of indecency we might have brought with us.

"May I help you?" His question was polite, but there was no smile on his face.

"We're here for a safe deposit," I replied. "Box three-seventeen."

He glanced nervously at the parcel I had produced from my coat for a second, nervously twirling his mustache. "I would like to see the note then, sir, and of course, the key—provided you have it."

I set the parcel on the counter, unwrapping it carefully. The brown paper fell away, revealing a stiff card, a box number in ink, a stamp, and below it, an old-fashioned key worn thin. The man glanced down at it, then his face flicked back to mine.

"Sir—I'm afraid, with my deepest apologies, we maintain the strictest protocol with our security… and our depositors. You'll understand that simply producing a card and a key is—"

"—It's why you're the manager," Alicia interrupted, and I suppressed a smile. What seemed to be a genuine, respectful smile played on her lips. Her face was innocent, a slight tilt to her head that told men they need not be careful around her. She wasn't dangerous. "Of course, you'd be respectful toward your bank—and your well-paying clients. The gentleman who left us this key left his instructions as well. He asked us to retrieve the items from the bank, and he chose your bank because of the excellent reviews from your customers. I'm sure, Mr.—what was your name again?"

"Campbell. Mr. Campbell," the man replied.

"Well, Mr. Campbell, surely you wish to keep a promise to your well-paying customers?"

He glanced at her—for the first time, it seemed, properly. Her face did the work, and her charm did the rest—she kept her eyes on his, watching in that unreadable way that a man could interpret in any way, and often did. It was an old trick, but it worked every time. It wasn't that he trusted us, but it was a sense of duty—a sense of honor that would compel him to agree. And sure enough, as if on cue, he gulped once, then spoke.

"May I see the card, please?" he asked.

I slid it over to him, hoping everything was in order—I wasn't entirely sure I trusted McLeod's package. It had been years, after all, and what he had originally stored away might be of little use now. Seconds later, however, the man looked up, a newfound respect and fear kindled in his eyes.

"P—please, follow me," Campbell said with a slight stutter, his voice too loud, then corrected himself. "Discreetly, if you will."

He led us silently down a narrow staircase into the bank's underground, where iron doors protected it, their old paint cracking with age. He opened the door with a key he produced, each scrape of the metal echoing as the outer gate swung open. He then pointed toward the rows of safety deposit boxes along the wall, all requiring both a bank key and a customer key to open them.

"Three-seventeen," he muttered, sliding his master key into the bank lock and inviting me to use the key I had brought with us in the second lock.

I walked forward while Campbell stood back. I noticed he gave me a wide berth, his eyes nervously darting anywhere but toward the box. I opened the lock, the key sliding in effortlessly as if it had been used many times before. Inside was a small chest, which I carefully slid out, lifting the lid as I did so. Alicia sidled up next to me, her eyes taking in the contents. The smell of paper emanated from the chest—old paper, but paper nevertheless.

Inside, there were ledgers tied with cloth tape, rolls of manifests stamped "King's Cross Goods," and even authorization slips with clipped corners. Alicia let out a quiet breath and leaned in as I watched. She turned the pages, each delicately, careful not to harm the evidence we'd just been presented with. She opened the ledger carefully, and we read it in silence. The handwriting matched what we had seen at Abercromby Place. In particular, two notes stood out:

SECTION IX / KINGSWAY—Cleared, H.A.R. Philby.

SECTION IX / KINGSWAY—Cleared, V.A. Haldane.

"Hell," I said, letting the word simmer on my tongue. "What's this, then?"

"Let's take the numbers," she responded, her voice low.

Setting the chest down on a table, I copied the information fast—each piece, ledger entries, dates, shipments that had been diverted to the Kingsway Tunnels—everything that gave us connections, I wrote down. Alicia worked swiftly as well, copying margin notes and other information that I had skipped.

Behind us, Campbell stood silently, never interrupting or telling us to hurry. Instead, with hands clasped, he stared firmly at the wall, as if we were invisible. I wanted to take everything, but I knew it wasn't worth the risk—though McLeod hadn't confirmed it, I suspected that others might be aware of the contents he'd hidden. And so I pocketed only what might go unnoticed—a torn stub, a brass tag etched with the box number, and several smaller receipts—until we'd finally gone through the entire chest.

I slid everything back in the box, carefully closing the lid, replacing it, and locking it again with a click.

"Are we finished?" Campbell asked quietly as we finally turned toward him.

"Yes, I do believe so," Alicia replied, a warm smile playing on her lips. "Thank you for your discretion."

"We are an old institution," he murmured, his voice still distant and his eyes blank. "The things we keep are none of our business, and, dare I venture to say, none of our knowledge."

"Indeed," I said.

With that, we went back up. The lobby was louder than before, busier, with more clientele making their way into the bank. Outside, a curtain of rain splattered against the street, which crawled with people and bustled with trams. The entire place was wet, downtrodden, and gray.

"Four of 'em," I said in a low tone as Alicia and I took in the scene.

"Trailing us?"

"One by the kiosk, one by the door—two more by the taxis across the street."

"Twice as many."

"They must be having a busy day," I said, shrugging my shoulders.

She smirked, and we stepped into the traffic and crowds of the street beyond the bank, ducking between two vehicles that bustled along. As we did, like clockwork, Alicia whipped off her scarf, stuffing it into her coat, then quickly pulled a folded beret from her inner pocket and tugged it low over her auburn hair, tucking the glowing strands rapidly beneath the woolen brim to hide the color. I slid my hat onto my head, pulling the brim low and sagging my posture until I was nearly a head shorter than I stood normally. We merged seamlessly into the crowd—now parted slightly—and let it carry us along as we disappeared.

Only a few streets down, we reconvened, both emerging into a small, dark, coal-smelling alleyway. It was an old trick—turn partners into separation, with one following and trailing behind the other. In this case, Alicia followed me nearly a field away, keeping track of my hat as she followed slowly through the crowd. When I ducked off the main street, she followed minutes later, like clockwork.

"Well, what do we have now?" Alicia asked as she joined me.

"Let's see," I replied, producing the case we carried with us from beneath my coat and pulling out the papers I'd taken from the bank. I sat down carefully on a nearby bench, and Alicia sat next to me. I carefully slid open the briefcase, making sure to lean over it to prevent any drizzle from falling on the papers, while Alicia sidled closer.

Here was everything we'd collected so far: all the evidence we'd taken from Kingsway, the papers we'd found, the notes from the ledger, the tag, and all of McLeod's files I'd managed to snag.

Near the bottom of the case, we carried our money and personal effects as well, so as not to take up more room than necessary. I carried the case, and Alicia carried the radio with her —other than this, we traveled light. But for now, my attention wasn't on the other contents; it was on how full the case had become with evidence.

"Putting aside the fact that none of these authorizations are even connected to the Bureau," Alicia said, "there's one thing that doesn't fit. How did any of this information survive Rosyth and the Dockyard?"

I sat in silence for a second. It was a memory I didn't want to recall. "You're right. It should have all been lost. Or so everyone said."

"If Philby's signature cleared a route to Kingsway, and the paper trail is here in Edinburgh, then someone built that bridge."

"So then how did Philby gain access?"

"...to the blueprints?"

"To everything needed to build a damn Mirror," I muttered, and I could feel a sense of paranoia creeping into my mind. I wasn't sure what to think.

"It had to have been Philby… or do you have another idea?"

"Yes," I said. "So either Philby gained access to the archives… the files… before Rosyth, or someone in the Nine used his signature as a cover-up."

"The Nine? Max, you don't think they're behind this, surely."

"I'm not sure what I think. Damn, I can't even trust my own memories—are you absolutely sure the Bureau is to be trusted, and that this is all on MI6?"

She hesitated for a second before responding. "Well, he obviously had inside help. McLeod alone might have been enough."

"McLeod helped reroute supplies," I shot back, "but that isn't enough alone."

"You're right, of course. I guess we're done with paper?"

"Rosyth," I said, though I hated the word by now. It wasn't just a place; it was a memory that I hated. But the ledgers pointed straight to it.

"We'll need a new travel method," I said. "Something that isn't as traceable and doesn't draw attention. No more trains, no more ships. Ministry surplus, maybe… a jeep or something."

"You're more familiar with Edinburgh. Know of any disposal depots?"

"One out near Sighthill," I responded.

"Perfect. Cheap, I hope. Our funds are running low."

I stood, packing up the case once more, and we left the alley, winding through the side streets, past the factories by tram, making our way out through the outskirts of Edinburgh as the fields began and wire fences became more prominent than buildings.

We finally stopped at a gatehouse—its Ministry green paint peeling and cracked. Beyond it stretched a yard full of decommissioned wartime equipment: Bedfords, Humber staff cars, and even Norton bikes. I quickly spotted what I was looking for— two jeeps with mismatched panels that looked the worse for wear.

The man at the gate took us in with one dismissive look—he seemed to be the shoddy, downtrodden type who sold to people like us, who didn't want receipts.

"What you after?"

"Something that can take us places," I said, "and for cheap."

"You'll be wanting ugly, then. Plenty of that here."

"Would we be here otherwise?"

"True, sir," he chuckled, leading us into the depot yard as he swung the gate open.

Less than half an hour later, we drove out of the yard in one of the two jeeps I had spotted. It wasn't fancy, but it was a vehicle I knew could be trusted—and it was a way to avoid prying eyes.

Somewhere beyond the Forth, I knew that Rosyth was waiting for us.

<h1 style="text-align:center">CHAPTER 10
ROSYTH REVISITED</h1>

We drove along, the rain finally clearing up at last. We had only stopped briefly at a store for supplies before embarking on our journey—a Geiger counter from an Army Surplus store, bolt cutters, some food, and several other useful adornments for our journey now that we had a place to store them. The road stretched out before us, long, wet strips that twisted and turned around the foothills, the water still fresh on the grass and trees. The jeep handled better than it looked—which was to say, barely—and with each bump or crack in the road, it jolted, the tired suspension barely keeping us stable.

Alicia sat in the seat next to me, her coat buttoned up to the top and her red scarf wrapped tightly around her neck. Although the rain had cleared, fog began to settle in, swallowing our surroundings until we could only see a dozen yards ahead. I didn't mind it—and I didn't mind the silence—the drive was enough for now.

Rosyth wasn't far—about half an hour away, though slightly slower due to the weather—but the closer we got, the more the air seemed to change. The road down to South Queensferry twisted and turned like some thought I shouldn't have followed. The wind off the Firth carried along the sour smells of oil, salt, and something older—iron, maybe, from the great boats that passed. The war had already ended, but the air here still tasted metallic and carried ghosts along on each draft of wind. Finally, we arrived at the ferry.

The queue for the ferry stretched along the cobbles, engines idling, men smoking against the chill with open windows to let it rise into the sky above. The great red ribs of the railway bridge loomed overhead, each beam lit in the hazy dusk light, the kind of monument only Britain could build to remind itself it was still an empire that had conquered all. It was something that made me yearn for the old days—the days when I was still young and ambitious enough to share the feeling. Below it, the ferry waited —a squat, workmanlike vessel with a flat deck and chain-hung ramps, its paint worn and scratched down to steel, salt, and rust.

A deckhand in an old, sod-ridden navy coat waved us forward. "Easy now, easy. Keep 'er straight."

The ramp clattered as the tires met it, the incline slick from spray. The jeep jolted once, then settled steadily onto the deck beside a lorry stacked with crates. I glanced at them with some amusement, noting that they had been stamped "ROSYTH." A boy chocked the wheels with old timber wedges and nodded at me, signaling I could kill the engine. The whole thing smelled of diesel, smoke, and rust. I stepped out into the harsh wind, leaning on the rail.

The Forth was restless, dark as pitch. Seagulls rode the updrafts around the bridge pylons, cawing like they'd been wounded. Across the water, North Queensferry crouched under the hill, a scatter of stone houses and lamplight. The chilling air cut through my coat, straight to my bones.

It rested heavily around us now—the type of cold, suppressive feeling that never left once it stuck to you. I felt a weary, grim series of thoughts threatening to overwhelm my mind—

memories of the incident, memories of the Andes, and memories of my time growing up in the Gorbals. Everything seemed so far away now.

Alicia broke the silence first, as if noticing my thoughts.

"It feels like driving backwards in time," she said, quietly joining me on the deck.

"How do you figure?" I asked as I smoked, not taking my eyes from the water.

"You know what I mean. Back to where everything happened… and where everything started."

"Back to where we were cursed."

"Exactly."

"Yeah," I muttered. "Too much like before."

We fell silent again as the boat seemed to shudder. Neither of us needed to voice what we really felt or what we really thought of when we thought of the Dockyard—the Mirror. The ferry groaned, engines turning over like tired lungs. A horn sounded, low and bellowing, and the deck trembled as we surged forward. The crossing took about fifteen minutes, long enough for the cold to find its way to the center of my bones. The water slapped the hull in a rhythm that could've been a heartbeat if you wanted to believe in some kind of life beyond yourself. I didn't.

Halfway across, the deckhand wandered by. "Three shillings, sir. Sixpence for the lady." Soon after, Alicia and I slipped back into the jeep, waiting in the cold for the trip to be over.

The north slipway came up fast—the ramp waiting like an outstretched tongue. Chains rattled, brakes hissed, and the ramp dropped with a bang. One by one, the cars growled forward, bumping up onto the cobbles. My turn came, and the tires screeched as they caught the wet steel. I glanced back once. Fifteen minutes across the Firth of Forth felt like hours—a border crossing not just between shores, but between lives. Then and now. The ferry was shrouded in smoke, the bridge above it vanishing into mist. It was a crossing I didn't want to make again, but at the same time, a part of me didn't want to leave.

I pressed the pedal down, feeling the jeep surge forward with an energy I was sure it hadn't felt in years. I wanted to make good time.

Rosyth soon appeared exactly as I remembered. It was a ghost of empire wearing a navy coat. The war had ended, but no one had told the Firth of Forth. The cranes still moved against the horizon like slow mechanical giants, their rusted arms creaking over half-empty dry docks. The air smelled of oil, salt, and the kind of smoke that never quite left your clothes. The dockyard sprawled as it always did—a confusion of slipways, storage sheds, and barracks built to outlast the men inside them. The Forth Bridge itself, red and skeletal, loomed to the east like some great iron cathedral to precision. Beneath it, the tide moved sluggishly—silver at noon, black by dusk—carrying the silt of centuries and the whispers of whatever the Admiralty had dumped there during the war.

The dockyard was supposed to be in a peacetime transition —"post-war reorganization" was the phrase they used. But the reality was a kind of suspended animation. The Royal Navy had scaled down, but the secrets had not. Behind the chain-link fences, work continued—unlogged, unmentioned, and unseen.

The surrounding area was tightly controlled. Armed sentries patrolled the perimeter, their boots echoing off the dock walls. Even the local fishermen had been relocated downriver. The nearest pub, The Admiral's Rest, was still open—a lonely outpost where engineers drank cheap Scotch and spoke too loudly.

As evening approached, the dockyard became visible from a distance. It was still active, though parts and pieces had been dismantled, abandoned, and left for dead. Our goal was those areas where nothingness embedded itself like a warning.

Alicia shifted the Geiger counter in her lap, fine-tuning the dial until the red needle swept back and forth across its face.

"Think there will be something worth measuring?" she asked.

"I think we'll find out."

"Optimistic."

"Unfortunately not," I replied as the jeep rolled to a stop beneath a cluster of trees, a short distance away from an old supply shed I'd spotted. The engine sputtered once or twice before dying as I turned it off, leaving us in silence. These were the thrilling moments before a mission began—the moment when you felt the excitement course through your body, making you forget all the pain it took to get there.

"You still want to do this?" Alicia asked. "Up until now… well, we've just been tracking. Following leads. But this might change things."

"I don't think I have a choice," I said, pushing the door open. "Let's go."

I had almost closed the door before I suddenly had a second thought that made me pause. "Along with the tools, let's bring the radio."

"The radio? Why?"

"On the off chance someone does find this jeep, I don't want them tying it to me."

"Smart," Alicia said, reaching into the seat to grab the attaché case where it sat.

We crept along in silence. The darkness had settled in, and we kept to the shadows, ducking behind stacks of corrugated sheets and crates that were set here and there, towering above us. These provided shelter from the floodlights that illuminated the dockyard, though not from the rain. It had begun again, this time pouring in a torrential downfall that made me glad I wore a hat.

Somewhere close by, a guard coughed, and Alicia and I froze, waiting for him to pass. His torch beam cut through the fog, only inches from my boot. I pressed tightly against a stack of crates, not daring to breathe until he'd passed and his footsteps had faded away in the rain.

Though it felt like hours, we arrived at the Bureau's annex about ten minutes later. It was an underground facility that lay beneath the old yard, beyond a stretch of tall fencing where the old Bureau door gave way to the facility below. It was dark, and I could barely make out the place, but as we cut the fence and rolled beneath it, I felt an uncertain chill as I realized the doors and entryways had been hidden—covered by what looked like a large storage warehouse.

"This is different than when I was last here," I whispered. "Where do we enter?"

"I think the main door is inside the warehouse," Alicia whispered back. "But do we risk breaking in?"

"If we have to. But let's check out the perimeter first."

Suddenly, she pointed. "Look there, near the foundation of the warehouse—see the paint?"

"Ah, clever," I muttered. The paint was a signature type of Bureau gray—a color that to most untrained eyes, meant nothing. But to me, I knew well that it was the same dark, dull color that had been chosen for most doors and storage casings during the period I'd worked for the Bureau.

"Looks like someone unearthed it before us," Alicia said quietly.

Just visible behind a set of barrels and rusting chains, the outline was faded and rusty, but unmistakable. Alicia brushed her hair back behind her scarf, crouching low beside me as I crouched down to examine the hatch more closely. She tapped the Geiger counter she held in one hand with a gloved finger, then sighed.

"No spikes yet, but I'll keep it on."

"After what we saw at Kingsway," I said, lifting the bolt cutters from beneath my coat, "let's not get ahead of ourselves."

"Looks like we have found the entrance," Alicia said.

"Well, one of them, at least. Not the main, but..." My voice trailed off as I pressed the cutters together. With a snap, the bolt yielded, and I heaved at the latch, which groaned in protest. Just like that, the door opened and fell inward with a soft pop of suction that felt almost too easy. As it swung open, however, I nearly recoiled in shock—the air inside wasn't stale, wasn't old or silent. Faint, glowing lights emanated from within, and a strange, low humming noise echoed out of the hatch.

"What the…" I hadn't been sure what we would find, but this was the last thing I'd expected.

"Still powered."

"That's impossible."

"Doesn't mean it's untrue."

I stepped through first. My boots echoed against the metal, the smell of the interior heavy with ozone. The narrow corridor ahead was lined with pipework, cables, and the occasional dim red light that still gleamed with current. The power should have been gutted years ago, but instead, a gauge on the nearest wall ticked, a small green needle vibrating around the midpoint. Alicia followed closely behind me, closing the hatch carefully behind us. The sound was like the lid of a tomb closing, and I felt a chill against my skin. We'd been busy on our trip, but now, finally, we were here—and I wasn't sure this was where I wanted to be.

Sub-level one of the Bureau underground at Rosyth was all offices—each meticulously partitioned, with typewriter desks left unattended, and old, dusty echoes of the remnants of employees still lingering. Though a fan spun lazily on the ceiling, the entire place felt abandoned—covered in dust and fully empty. The lighting here was luminescent and yellow, and I remembered with a shudder the times when this level had been filled with agents, Bureau officials, and sliders.

"Christ," Alicia whispered as she ran her fingers along a file cabinet, tracing the dust. "It brings back memories. But do you hear that?"

"It does… and I do." A faint mechanical hum whispered

through the air, pervading the whole place as if it came from everywhere at once.

"What do you think it is?"

"I think we both have a guess," I said. "It sounds somewhere deeper—past sub-level three, maybe."

"Then we'll keep going."

We passed through each corridor and level with a sense of unease. The glowing lights meant I didn't even have to use my torch—the whole place was visible, illuminated with an eerie glow, so familiar yet unsettling. This was where I—and Alicia— had worked before it happened.

At sub-level three, the temperature began to drop. It was cold enough for me to see my own breath, and when my boots hit the concrete flooring, a faint layer of frost shimmered with each step. It was the type of cold that you didn't feel right away but that cut through your skin and embedded itself in your very bones. The Geiger counter in Alicia's hand ticked once, then slowed, steadying again into its regular rhythm.

"Residual?" she asked.

"Residual shouldn't pulse," I replied.

But we pressed on. The chamber where the incident had happened all those years ago—where the Mirror itself used to sit —lay beyond a set of double doors and an observation room. Reports indicated that after the explosion, the doors had been sealed with welds and concrete to prevent any potential residual, uncontrollable slides or time dilation.

But they were not.

As we approached, I could see the doors hung slightly ajar, as if they had been forced open a long time ago. Light leaked through. I braced myself against the frame, pushing the door open. There, in front of us, was a Mirror—or what had been built of it.

Suddenly, as if I were seeing a vision, I saw a flash of light shimmering across the exposed metal, and for an instant, I saw her. The woman I had known in my MI6 days as Locket—Lucy

Howard—stood on the platform where the Mirror had once been. Not as I'd last seen her in Cairo, where she almost got me killed, but younger still, with an expression of amusement. Her mouth moved, but no words came out—and in the next instant, she was gone. I blinked—I had forgotten all about her. Forgotten about our past… what we had shared, and what we'd lost. Everything came flooding back. It was overwhelming.

Alicia's hand caught my sleeve. "Max, what is it?"

"Nothing," I muttered, my eyes still on the platform where the Mirror's frame stood. I blinked, pushing back all those visions I had of that woman flooding back—the good and the bad. "Just the light playing tricks, I think."

Alicia glanced at me, suspicious, but I focused on the task at hand. I wasn't going to tell her. It was too painful. I took in the scene before me—the partially built Mirror.

The central amphitheater was covered with a network of copper tubing, wires, and control consoles—these were mangled and covered in dust, yet still alive. In the very center, where the original Mirror used to be, was a sprawl of new coils, wiring, and pieces. Rising from the very spot the original Mirror had been constructed was a newer frame. It was sleek, simplistic, and almost Machiavellian in nature compared to Krane's subtle and intricate handiwork. Almost as if on cue, Alicia's Geiger counter began clicking, steadying into a low, continuous chatter.

"Someone's been working here," Alicia muttered.

"Recently," I said. "Weeks, maybe days. But were they building this?"

"What do you mean? It looks like they were starting over."

"It looks that way," I said, approaching the Mirror's frame and kneeling down. "It's no doubt a newer model than the one we found at Kingsway, but look at this. See?"

"What?" Alicia asked, bending down until her gloved hand brushed the edge of the frame.

"The bolts—look. They've been sheared," I said. "Not loosened—cut clean out. Someone took pieces off this… maybe still is. See the impressions? The outer skeleton of this was used to hold something, probably the panels themselves. But they're gone."

"So this frame's been… deconstructed?"

"Exactly. Look—drag marks." I pointed toward the frost-blackened floor, where curving marks from the center ran toward the hatch near the back of the room. "Whatever they pried free, they hauled away. It was big—heavy too."

"So it's a salvage…" Her voice trailed off as another noise suddenly interrupted her.

I froze, listening—then glanced down in shock.

The MI6 radio in the leather attaché we had brought along suddenly hissed, then filled with static before flaring to life. It was a mangled, distant voice, but unmistakably a man's, half-obscured by the interference.

"…warning…evacuate now… Section is compromised…you have company."

A burst of static blared, and the voice cut out. I stared at the case in shock. There should have been no way for it to receive a transmission, but as I watched, the voice ebbed through the static again. "The Nine. Watch… contact the Nine—repeat, the Nine—"

And with that, it went silent.

Alicia's eyes were fixedon me, her face betraying her emotions for the first time in ages. Her eyes were wide, her face whiter than usual.

"Did he say what I think he said?" she asked in a quiet voice.

"Yeah. The Nine. But the Nine aren't MI6; they're Bureau."

"We need to make contact with the Bureau, Max," she said. "We're out of our depth."

"We can discuss that," I said, resignation heavy in my voice. "…but that's not what worries me."

"Someone else is here."

"If we believe—well, whatever that was, then yes," I said, my pistol already drawn. "We need to get out of here soon."

We stood there quietly for a moment, listening. There was no noise other than my own breathing, and even though all my instincts told me to leave, my mind was whirring with suspicion that I couldn't ignore. I motioned quietly to Alicia, and she followed me.

As we left the amphitheater, I stole one backward glance at where the unfinished Mirror sat. I half expected to see her again —to see Lucy standing atop the platform, her blonde hair dancing in a breeze that wasn't there. She was on my mind now, and I couldn't help but wonder if she was still alive. I had never double-checked those rumors of her death... so maybe....

I pushed the thought from my mind. My focus was on the mission—here and now—and on Alicia.

We moved in sync, passing the unfinished Mirror frame, through the doors, and down a passage that curved downward into another auxiliary tunnel.

"Shouldn't we leave, Max?" Her voice was barely a whisper.

"First," I whispered back, "I want to know where the power comes from."

She nodded, and I knew she understood. Powering the whole facility would have been a monumental task, something that wouldn't be as simple as flipping a breaker switch. As we were familiar with the facility, however, I was confident we could find our way to the power room to see what equipment had been set up and what had been installed to power the facility. I opened a side door in one of the passageways, descending a stairwell that spat us out into a large, cavernous bay. Dim flood lamps buzzed here, their lights flickering with a greenish hue.

I walked along, pistol still drawn, with Alicia just several steps behind me. It wasn't that I was afraid—I wasn't even sure if the voice that had echoed through the radio was telling the truth—but I knew something was off. That much had been clear since we entered the facility. I spotted a coil of cables that descended through the ceiling of the bay and further downward.

Several new cables had been added, routed along with the dusty ones, which confirmed my suspicion.

"You see that?" I asked.

Before she could respond, though, I saw movement. It looked like a reflection or some kind of silhouette that dashed past the furthest end of the bay, nearly ninety feet ahead, vanishing as quickly as I had seen it. Same shoulders, same trench coat, same gait.

"Max." Alicia caught my arm.

"I saw it."

I aimed my torch down the cavernous bay, flashing it here and there. Nothing. Only the icy-cold shimmer of the air, the fog from our breath, and the vast bay bathed in an eerie green light in front of us.

"It looked like…" Her voice trailed off.

"Me."

Without another word, I broke into a run, chasing the spot where the figure had vanished. As I approached, I noticed a long corridor to one side and shone my torch down it, illuminating the dark passageway.

I could see a figure still running down it, far into the distance, and as I watched, he turned the corner and vanished yet again. He was too far—and if it were me, we'd never catch him. Not with how I'd been moving lately. I silently cursed myself. When had I become so old?

"Damn it," I muttered.

"Max," Alicia said quietly. "Just leave it."

Silence settled between us, even heavier in the dim air. I felt an aching, dull pressure between my eyes—a headache that seemed to have implanted itself the moment I saw the figure. As we stood there, the entire place began to flare white, glowing brighter and brighter. A strange sensation overtook me, as if I was everywhere at once and as if my entire body had turned to liquid, like ocean waves crashing against the side of a tossing ship.

I glanced at Alicia.

"Slide—" I forced out, but it was all I could say as the world turned blank, as if we were everywhere at once, and time itself was unraveling. I glanced around, looking for somewhere to steady myself, but it was too late.

I reached out for her hand—the only thing I could still see— but missed. The world cracked open sideways.

CHAPTER 11
DOCKYARD DELUSIONS

blinked, slowly at first, then faster, trying to clear the confusion from my eyes. I glanced up, then down—the world around me was no longer the frost-choked bay we'd been in moments before. There was no Alicia, no Geiger counter, and no shadowy figure that looked a bit too much like me. Instead, I felt as if I'd been dropped into a photograph, the colors too vivid and the sounds a bit too muffled.

Where the hell was I?

I tried to move, but found I couldn't. It was like my body was no longer connected to my mind, trapped in a dream that wouldn't end. I felt a sense of panic, but it subsided quickly as I remembered—back in Hell's Kitchen when I'd first met Alicia again. Back then, I had felt something similar—the partial slide where reality bent without fully breaking. It was a visual slide, cognitive maybe, pulling me into some echo of time. And just like last time, I was pulled back to Rosyth. The same sub-levels, the same corridors, the same haunted feeling, but bustling with activity.

And there, right in front of my face, was me—not me exactly, at least not anymore. Now, I was gray, old, and weary. Now, I had weathered skin, a tiredness in my eyes I couldn't shake, and a hatred of the world for being more dishonest than I could have ever imagined. But the man in front of me had none of this—this was the version of me from before.

He was younger, sharper around the edges, moving with that cocky stride I used to have before the Mirror broke my mind, chipping away at my greatest gift. He—or I—stood there, wearing the standard Bureau garb, moving seamlessly as he had done a thousand times before. This younger Max held a clipboard, and I recognized the day almost instantly. I had normally been out on missions or on slides to "change the world," as we had been told. This day, however, Krane had made a specific request for most personnel to put in extra effort for another Mirror test he had planned for the day after.

This day was September 19, 1945.

The younger me was talking to several junior agents who were hauling crates through the hallways.

"Double-check those," the younger me snapped, his voice impatient and leagues different from what I remembered. "Last thing we need is Hawthorne to get on our ass again."

The men nodded, carefully maneuvering the loads they carried. The sub-levels looked just as I remembered: concrete walls reinforced with steel, lights buzzing overhead, and the faint hum of the Mirror when it was active. Bureau agents hurried past—sliders, spies, and scientists—all moving in motion for what was touted by the Bureau as the largest scientific advancement of the last decade. But why was I seeing this now? What had caused the slide?

I drifted along, not in control of my movements any more than waves control the shore they crash upon, following my younger self as he walked through the corridors. He stopped at one checkpoint, flashing his ID to a guard who waved him through without a second glance. Of course, he wasn't questioned. Max Calder was one of the top agents of the Bureau and well-respected among the men who worked there.

But something felt off.

As I watched, I noticed things—small, subtle things, but they stood out the more I took in. The guard who waved me through wasn't the regular man. The regular guard I had known by name —a certain McNay who was friendly to me—and I was certain I did not recognize the guard who had just waved me through. I tried to turn around to see his face again, but we had already moved past.

The younger me turned a corner into one of the supply bays, where stacks of crates towered above the workers bustling around like bees. I watched only haphazardly, distracted by what I had seen on the crates as we passed. Though it was only for a glimpse, I was sure of it—the labels had mentioned "Radar Trials" and had been routed to Edinburgh. That alone stirred suspicion within me, but something nagged at me even further. Sure, the Bureau dabbled in covert ops that involved advanced radar systems, but these crates were being routed to London. And because the Rosyth base was almost entirely dedicated to Mirror infrastructure, I doubted that these crates actually contained what they said. And the volume—dozens of crates, far more than any simple test would need.

I thought back to Kingsway, and the connections began to flicker in my mind. Those "radar" boxes could have been smuggling parts right under our noses: copper plating, energy conduits, wires, and even Mirror pieces. Diverted from official channels via Edinburgh, these items were sent along to be filed at Kingsway instead of any official Bureau operation.

Philby's clearance stamp on those old ledgers... Fraser-Smith's gadgets... the Mirror under Kingsway... was this all happening, even on the day of the disaster?

Had someone been building a shadow project even then, right under the noses of the Bureau, siphoning off resources while we were too busy to notice? But how had Krane let this happen? I simply couldn't believe it.

Younger me, however, didn't seem to care a bit. He signed off on a manifest without a second glance, chatting idly with a friendly tech. "Get those to Krane," he said. "He's been riding everyone lately, just like Hawthorne, I'd say."

The tech nodded, but I saw it—so quick it was barely visible, but unforgettably vivid—a flicker in his eyes, a moment's hesitation. It was all wrong. It was all a puzzle I hadn't even seen back then because I was in the middle of it, too focused on the Mirror and my next slides to ever consider the larger game that was being played around me.

I wanted to shout, to warn my younger self, but none of it mattered. The scene blurred at the edges, and I felt myself drifting away. I tried to resist at first, but I watched as the entire place turned to light.

———

The next thing I saw, the younger version of Max Calder had vanished, and I was nowhere to be seen. Instead, I saw a dark, small room that looked dimly lit—some kind of office or briefing chamber. At the head of the table sat none other than Emil Krane.

He looked just as I remembered him—his glasses, his face stricken with equal parts of madness and intelligence, his Bureau suit polished and impeccable. Around him were several agents, many of whom had vanished after the incident. They leaned over the table, discussing blueprints as I watched.

"...the Mirror is stable," Krane protested, his accent unmistakable. "But we need more power—more test runs. Maybe one tonight?"

One agent—a man by the name of Vickers—nodded. "We have enough power for tonight. But no tests, not tonight, Krane. Hawthorne is already on our asses for your tests. You've already scheduled one for the 20th, and that was barely allowed. One tonight without a vote would be career suicide for you."

Krane's lips pursed, and anger spread across his face. "You restrict perfection," he said. "You know this, right? We could be the premier organization by now, not some infested, side-ridden second-rate…"

But his voice grew faint, like a radio signal fading away. Time distorted, faces smeared, and I could feel myself being pulled forward in time. Wearily, I wondered where I would go next.

———

Suddenly, I was back in the main chamber. The clock on the wall read 21:00, its hands ticking without pause or effort. The place was quiet, silent, and empty, just as it had been when Krane ran the unsanctioned test that started it all. I saw him staring ahead into the pulsing Mirror, his face alight with eager envy, his eyes gleaming. He was speaking, though I couldn't hear the words he said, and when I looked at the Mirror, I saw my own face in it, just as I had in the slide in Hell's Kitchen.

Then, my vision began to fade again—and suddenly, the clock on the wall read 23:00. It was darker than ever, and the hum from the Mirror was almost deafening. But the clock… I watched it. I knew what would happen when ten minutes passed because the official reports said the explosion struck at 23:10. That was when Krane finally pulsed the Mirror too hard. That was when everything went sideways.

But 23:10 came and went. There was no pulse, no failure—nothing except Krane continuing to work. I watched, confused.

Then, at 23:11, it happened. Krane smiled slightly, a madness glinting in his eyes, and his fingers ran over the controls. A white-hot flash erupted from the Mirror, pulsing through the air like an unleashed energy bomb.

The pulse blasted outward, so powerful it shattered consoles. I knew that outside the room, agents were dying by the dozens. Men were aging, their bodies shattering in a temporal effect that couldn't be undone. Blurry, torn faces turning to three hundred years and then dust in an instant. All their features would be eroded, and Rosyth would be shut down.

My body shot backward in the slide, and I felt myself traveling at the speed of the explosion outward. I passed through walls in my visitor state, overlooking the place. Through the smoke and chaos, figures moved—not just agents, though, not just terror. Instead, I saw men bending over, deliberate, and working quietly. Then, right before it all ended, I saw my own face.

The world fractured, and a sharp pain pierced my head. My memories split, and my mind felt like it was on fire. Why was everything so different? Why was this slide different?

Suddenly, I was back. Reeling and disoriented, I glanced around, grimacing. Where the hell was I? The world before me, which had seemed so real, was gone. Now I was back in the real world—if you could call it that. I was no longer standing in the facility. Where was I? Why was it so dark?

"Max!" Alicia's voice cut through the burning pain in my head as she grabbed my arm. "Where are you? What happened?"

"Where… what? Where am I?"

"That's what I'm asking you, Max."

"I…" I paused. "Did you not slide?"

"We both slid," she said, confusion etched in her voice. "We are now somewhere near the exterior fence line of the Dockyard, from the looks of it. But where are you?"

"Did you not see it all? Krane, the explosion…everything?"

She looked at me as if I were crazy—as if I'd seen a ghost. Rain beaded on her lashes, and the glow from the distant floodlights shimmered through the darkness, signaling just how far we were from the Bureau segment of Rosyth.

"Max…last second we were underground, and then we were here."

"You didn't see it?" I asked, steadying my voice as I watched her carefully. "You didn't see Krane, the chamber, the pulse, the time…none of it?"

"I blinked, and we were here, at the fence. One second we were at the sublevel, the next outside. But—"

"—I didn't, and it's later now," I finished. "Look at the lights; they're changing the watch."

CHAPTER 12
OBSERVER OVERRIDE

The roar of machinery from the dockyard interrupted us, and we waited in silence. The lights along the perimeter were as they always had been, but moved as the shift rotation began. We had timed our entry to coincide precisely with the first shift change, which meant some time had passed. Maybe an hour, maybe more, or maybe less—but there was something that had changed. Alicia pulled her watch from her coat pocket, checked it, and then nodded slowly. It confirmed what we both realized—the hands were exactly where they would have been had nearly an hour passed.

"Forward," I muttered. "We slid forward."

"That's a thing now?"

"Not before. Not like this. But I suppose it makes sense," I muttered. "A slide forward in time is infinitely easier than a slide backward—the only changes you have to make to the timeline are the removal of whatever you want to send forward and to place it in some sort of stasis."

"...And for you, that stasis wasn't full."

"Precisely," I said, rubbing the base of my skull to try and make the dull headache behave itself. "But it also means that someone's got a live Mirror—one that's actually working. Not a dead prototype in hibernation like in Kingsway, or a half-built model like here. A real one. Working."

"The only question," she responded, nodding, "is whether or not the slide was intentional or not. Remember Krane?"

"He had no idea," I said. "No idea at all that we were linked to the Mirror. I wonder if it's the same thing as here?"

Her eyes drifted past me, watching the fence line. "Not sure," she said. "But if we're on someone's radar, I'd prefer not to be."

"North line," I said, following her gaze. "Let's hug the fence and find our way back toward the trees. The jeep should still be where we left it. If time only slipped an hour or so, it's likely the jeep still hasn't been discovered."

We sprang into action, crouching near the fence, the wire brushing against our shoulders. The wet, slippery peat caused us to trip occasionally in the dark. We didn't dare turn on our torches—this close to the Dockyard, we'd be caught instantly. Instead, we moved in silence, the faint blue of the Forth appearing and disappearing behind sheds, crates, and the towering machinery of the dockyard.

The world felt haunted—silence interrupted only by the screams and groans of machinery, darkness interrupted only by the lights that illuminated the dockyard. Somewhere behind us, a guard's boot struck metal, and we froze. His torch cut through the fog, and I threw myself down against the wet ground. Alicia did the same, and we waited with bated breath until he moved on.

I sighed, straightening up again—my body felt tired. My prime was past; I could tell that much. When I'd worked at the Bureau during the height of the war, a mission like this would have been child's play, but now, I felt a pervasive sense of weariness that wouldn't leave.

The northern fence gradually bent toward the trees, and the ground softened underfoot. The wire here sagged, and signs of wear showed. It was clear that generations of yard men had neglected the fenceline here, caring little about how it was taken care of. After all, we were farthest from the core dockyard by now.

"Max."

I noticed it at the same moment she did. At the edge of the wood, a dark figure suddenly appeared—neither here nor there, but everywhere at once, like a splice in a film. He sprang out of the darkness, like vivid, crisp pieces of glass suspended in the air, each piece reflecting light as if the air didn't know where to keep him. We moved in sync, breaking out in a run toward him.

He heard us coming and tried to run as well, but it seemed he could barely move. He tripped, lurching sideways into the brush. He threw out a hand on one of the trunks to steady himself. But instead of his hand meeting wood, he fell forward, his arm halfway through the tree before it became stuck. The man whimpered in pain, yanking his arm, then grimacing.

As I approached, I didn't even need to see his face. I somehow knew everything about him before I'd ever fully seen his scar. He was me.

"Hey!" I called out, my voice cutting through the air. "Take it easy."

The man turned to face me, and my face looked back at me. He looked thinner, more gaunt, his eyes almost a pale white near the edges with a film covering them, as if they had been the first thing to go. He opened his mouth as if trying to speak, but no word came. Instead, a rattle escaped his throat—half breath, half sound. He shook his head as if he were trying to clear it, and I watched the edges of him shimmer and twist as if he were only partially here. A searing pain suddenly ached in the back of my head, and I grimaced but remained focused.

"Don't," I said, holding my hands out. "If you can't talk, just wait. We'll try to help."

It was the first time I hadn't fought another version of me, but the man didn't acknowledge my offer. Instead, he reached into his coat—a slow, deliberate movement that seemed inten-tionally disarming. Alicia's pistol still snapped up, steady, aimed at him just in case. But the man continued to move, his hand rising from his pocket slowly into the damp air, holding a badge. It was dark, but I instantly recognized it as a Bureau-style pass. I stared at the words that were embedded on it.

SLIDER—VAR 6F

He jammed it into my outstretched hand, hard enough to hurt. Then, he opened his mouth, struggling, and this time, he managed to speak. "An...gus," he rasped, the words tearing against his throat. "Or...acle...Loch."

Then, it happened. He didn't so much fall as simply dissolve. His body began to shudder, or vibrate, and his shoulders turned to air and light all at once. The rest of his body seemed to echo, resonating with the environment around it as if he were suddenly allergic to existing, and the hand that had held the badge only seconds ago dropped and hit the earth, falling against the mossy ground. In a few seconds, even the hand shone with light, and then everything was gone. Nothing was left but an echo of a hum.

I stood there, the badge stinging my skin, listening to the noises of the dockyard in the background. Alicia slowly lowered her gun, shock evident on her face. She glanced at the badge I held in my hand. "Variant 6F... variable, maybe?"

"Not sure," I muttered back. "Variant seems most likely."

"You ever seen one degrade like that?"

"Have you?" I shot back, my voice harsher than I intended. "We've fought doppelgängers before... but this felt different." I shoved the badge into my coat.

"Yes," she said. "He said Angus, Oracle, Loch. Any of that ring a bell with you?"

"ANGUS," I said, tapping my forehead. My headache had all but vanished. "Old cover site I heard about while working at Broadway for MI6. It stands for Advanced Navigation and Geospatial Utility Station. People think it's about radar, but it isn't. It's what they stamped on papers when they needed an official name for a black site beneath the water at Invershiel."

"Under a loch."

"Yes," I replied. "Loch Duich. Invershiel. A tidy place on the surface. They didn't let any details leak about it, but it's always been a place that MI6 stored things they didn't want to admit existed officially."

"And what about Oracle? Did you ever hear of that at MI6?"

"That one," I said, "I'm drawing a blank on. It's not Bureau nomenclature I know of, and it's not any MI6 project I was aware of. It does sound like a project codename, though. When I worked at MI6, they loved their classical references."

She nodded resolutely, determination flashing in her eyes. "Then we go north."

We followed the wood line more cautiously now until we arrived at the jeep. I arrived slightly before she did, sliding behind the wheel while the rain pattered steadily against the hood, cranking the engine so it sputtered to life. I sighed, relaxing at last. Though the motor coughed slightly when starting, I had faith in this old vehicle.

Alicia slid into the seat beside me, and I revved the engine, slowly pulling out of our hidden spot beneath the trees. As I did, however, the radio in the attaché case sputtered to life again—this time, the static was minimal, and the voice came through clearer than ever. It still sounded muffled, but it was unmistakably English.

"Max, the badge is important. Echoes will collapse when their anchor amplitude goes thin."

Alicia's hand was already on the volume before the voice finished speaking. "Who is this? How do you know his name?"

"I am an observer," the voice echoed, crackling slightly as the man spoke. "Your window is short. Time is limited."

"Which window?" I asked. "What do you mean?"

"That was a forward-chain event. The system is trying to equalize entropy across its anchors and uses the highest observer amplitude available. You… are the connection. The control."

"Explain," I responded.

"Difficult," the voice rasped. The static seemed to be increasing. "The Mirror doesn't just tune time and space; it tunes to people. Everything is fundamentally the same. Every run you make lays down an anchor—a memory for the machine itself. You are the weight, the tie. We call this observer amplitude. It is the quantum strength your entanglement holds within the overarching system—the platitudes are repetitive—but observers are the key to the quantum. It is the strength of attention you project—other versions, weaker versions, will unsuccessfully occupy the same coordinates. You… Max… are the observer—your amplitude overrides variants and weaker echoes. When you focus on a weaker copy, it forces a resolution within the system—one will be annihilated in order to rectify the imbalance."

My mind was whirring. I was familiar with some quantum explanations—I'd been taught those while at the Bureau—but this was new to me. Before I could speak, however, the voice pressed on. This time, it was barely intelligible through the static.

"If a site is coupled to another—like Kingsway to Rosyth—or if a Mirror-to-Mirror connection is present via quantum entanglement, then sometimes it will cause… other connected entities to be affected as well. It's called the Atlas Effect: when something moves imperceptibly at its core, reality tears itself apart at the periphery.

"And doppelgängers," I said, "do those appear where we're remembered by the system?" The jeep jolted here and there as I drove, bouncing over rocks and cracks in the ground.

"Echoes," the voice responded. "Almost unidentifiable from doppelgängers scientifically, but unique enough to deserve a separate classification. Echoes of you will try to resolve at the strongest points within the quantum web. But the variants unravel."

"Why 6F?" Alicia asked suddenly.

"6F? I do not have access… to this information," the voice responded after a delay. But clearly, the echo you faced was weak. A very thin Max."

"And Oracle?"

The voice fell silent. I shook my head quietly as we drove, then glanced at Alicia. She was staring off into the darkness beyond the car's windshield, her eyes focused on something she couldn't see. For the first time in a while, I wasn't sure what she was thinking. Suddenly, the voice sputtered back to life.

"Not… much longer. The Nine… contact. Philby… caution. Be careful of both. Find the secret."

Before I could respond, the voice went silent again, and the case went dead. The little light that had no business being on in the first place blinked off again, and we were left alone together in the jeep. Alicia finally startled from her stupor and glanced over at me. I knew by her look what she was going to ask before she spoke, so I cut to the chase.

"Fine," I said. "We'll call the Bureau."

She nodded, a smile playing on her lips. I knew she loved being right. "We call the Bureau." We bumped along silently in the jeep, jolting here and there, down the Military Road until the dockyard was far behind us and no longer watching. A few minutes later, we made it to Inverkeithing, quickly finding one of the few hotels located in the small town. I parked and turned off the jeep. Several minutes later, we found ourselves in a room over a shoddy bar that smelled of damp wool. The clerk was barely awake, only looking at our money as he handed us the keys. That alone made the place worth it. I sighed, lighting a cigarette as I kept watch at the window.

It had been a long night, but it was far from over. As I watched the street below, Alicia turned her attention to the single telephone accessible in the room, dialing the operator chain and then the number she knew so well. It was time for us to finally contact the Bureau. I despised the idea, but then again, I figured I had become more cynical lately, and so I let it slide.

"Operator," the voice on the other end of the line echoed.

"This is Artemis," Alicia said, then gave her callsign and codes that only she knew. I saw her face change ever so slightly as she spoke, as if somehow she had slipped into the character she played for the Bureau. "Priority contact for the Nine. Two things to pass—compromise at Rosyth, operational power live on the sub-levels. Kingsway, Section IX rooms active, Bureau equipment filed under clearance stamps, including H.A.R. Philby and V.A. Haldane. Requesting advice and permission to make a drop."

The voice on the phone remained silent for a minute. Then it spoke. "Is Raven operational?"

Alicia hesitated. I could tell she was unsure whether to speak, but I nodded my consent, and she replied, "Affirmative."

"Message received. Stay off-grid. Clearance review is under discussion. Until then, you are not to return to primary sites. How long can you hold?"

"The night, at least."

"Then hold. Updates will follow," the operator said, and the line went dead.

For a few minutes, Alicia and I sat in silence, alone in the cheap room, our collars and hands still cold and wet from our venture to Rosyth. I ate meagerly from the food we had, though I suspected a warm meal would have been nice compared to what I was eating now. Maybe a plate of haddock or something even more hearty. I lit another cigarette, opening the window to let the smoke drift out into the rain.

"You buy any of that?" Her voice broke through the silence.

"From the Bureau?"

"No," she laughed. "Always the cynic, Max. The observer amplitude, the anchors, and the variants."

"We both saw it at the treeline," I said. "The other me. We always knew the Mirror had a sort of... connection... to us. I mean, hell, you're intricately tied to the whole thing anyway. You were the key, remember? Maybe we just pretended we'd finished the job, but it was never really done."

She sighed, her face suddenly tired. "I don't like to remember that," she said, "but you're right. Whoever—or whatever—that voice is, it makes a lot of sense."

"Rosyth's the oldest place that has any juice left," I said. "Kingsway's the London site of the Mirror… but I suspect there's another—what they might call Atlas core, the biggest one, at Invershiel. We are feeling the peripheral effects of it. Maybe ANGUS, maybe Oracle, whatever that means. Either way, that place is probably the trigger for everything we're seeing."

"Which does explain why the echoes are showing up now," she said. "They're not just showing up randomly; they're showing up in places where the machine knows you exist."

"What bothers me the most, though, is the badge. Someone had to assign that badge… that number. And what does 6F mean? Does that mean there are six others, at least?"

"I don't think we'll have answers. Not yet."

"Which is why," I responded, "we're going to the loch. Find out what MI6 decided to build under there and see how deeply involved Philby really is."

"What about the Nine?" It wasn't resistance in her question but an open resignation that signaled she was willing to do as I thought best.

"The Nine… they can decide whose side they're really on," I muttered. "I'm tired of trusting the Bureau and everyone else in my damn life with things, only to realize that my own damn mind is faulty. I still don't know what I saw today. What I saw when I slid—did the Bureau itself betray me?"

"Max…"

"At the very least," I continued, "the Nine will know what our plan is. They can make their decision, but you already gave them a heads-up. By the time we get to Invershiel, someone will have decided exactly how important we are… and whether or not we're friends or enemies."

"Max…" she said again, and for a second, I thought she was going to protest what I'd said about the Nine, but she didn't. "Have I ever betrayed you?"

For the first time in a while, I wasn't sure what to say. Despite our history, Alicia rarely ever exposed her real feelings to me. But here she was, staring into my eyes, searching for something that even I hadn't seen. I felt a pang of guilt, as if I'd betrayed her in some way.

"No," I said at last. "No, you haven't."

She reached out, caressing both sides of my face with her hands—no gloves. She'd taken those off when we entered the room—and I felt her soft fingers against my rough, weathered skin. "Then use me as your anchor."

I nodded. I wasn't sure of what to say. Finally, I gave her a weary smile. I knew that she was one of the few I'd felt such a close connection to—and unlike others, she was the only one who hadn't betrayed my trust yet. Unlike Locket, Alicia had never left me for dead. She had never sacrificed me for the mission.

"I trust you," I said.

Her mouth curved slightly, a hint of a smile near the corners, but she still watched me carefully. "I'm not tired yet. I'll sleep after breakfast."

"You and me both," I said.

We didn't sleep, of course. We lay on our backs and watched the ceiling turn from pitch-black to smoke-stained gray as the silence began to be replaced by the occasional vehicle or dog bark. The road outside stayed misted with rain and plumes of smoke from chimneys. Near 0400, when the hour had waned and the silence had deepened into something I didn't even dare break, I turned my head to see if she had fallen asleep. She was already watching me, her hair loose around her face, her eyes slightly lidded with the sort of exhaustion that has more to do with life and less to do with sleep.

The world outside was cold, damp, depressing, and sometimes felt as if it was draining the life away from me to power the cars, rain, and engines that surrounded us—but not here. The space between us lessened, though I wasn't sure if it was her or me who initiated it. Then, she crossed the gap. The kiss was gentle at first, then rougher—something to bring us back from the edge we found ourselves teetering near. Something to remind us we were alive.

She drew closer, her legs against mine, the coldness of her buttons touching against my skin. My fingers moved as if they had a mind of their own, without thought, and no words were spoken. The air was thick—the tenderness and urgency all at once, a desperate anchor for both of us to each other and reality. The wall creaked, the window fogged up as the street outside grew gradually lighter, and for a while, we forgot our troubles.

An hour or so later, I lay back on the bed, sweat riding my body and dripping from my brow. She stayed close, her hand resting gently on my chest, her breathing more rapid at first, slowly returning to the same pace we had before. Neither of us spoke. The light coming from the window had begun to brighten, and I knew too well that sleep wasn't going to come for us, not really—in only a few hours, we'd be back to the real world. The world outside the room.

I thought about the other me. The one who had died. He'd said three words to us before he had vanished—Angus, Oracle, and Loch. The first was a lie, a cover used by MI6 to hide their true intentions. The second was a fiction—something I wasn't sure of but could only guess. And the third was the place we needed to go next, the place we were about to travel to.

The light outside the window was fuller and brighter. Alicia's steady breathing indicated to me she had fallen asleep, and I felt my eyes closing as well. The Nine would talk amongst themselves. Invershiel would remain buried beneath peat and rain, waiting for someone to discover it again. And soon, Alicia and I would travel to that dark loch in the north, where we might just find the truth at last.

I closed my eyes and drifted off to sleep. This time, the Andes dream did not revisit me.

CHAPTER 13
NAMELESS NINE

Pristine sunlight filtered nowhere this deep—five floors below the foundation, beneath Holborn's soot-stained heart, buried under brick, steel, and layers of earth that remembered fire and empire. It was a place built not to be found but to be forgotten.

The corridors here wound like veins through a sleeping giant—a hundred passages, with more beyond them, none mapped, none aligned with the world above. The air was dry, filtered, old. The walls emitted a faint hum—electric, underground, almost biological.

This was the Bureau's core, the nexus where all invisible lines converged. Officially, it didn't exist. Unofficially, it decided everything that did. Those who entered came without titles and left without names. Only a handful of people in the living world knew it existed—and most of them had been absorbed by its gravity long ago. The rest were controlled entirely by its reach. And then there were two others.

The Bureau Conference Hall sat in the innermost chamber—a perfect circle of authority, carved from precision and paranoia. The air carried the scent of ozone and metal warmed by current. White lamps hung from delicate brass stems, steady but soft, their light rippling faintly across the long marble table like water under ice. The surface was polished so flawlessly that reflections appeared almost too sharp to be human.

Steam pipes and electrical conduits traced the high ceiling like thick metallic arteries. They groaned, pulsed, and whispered as if the building itself were alive—and in some unrecorded sense, it might have been. When the wind shifted in the tunnels, you could swear the pipes were speaking—syllables caught in vibration, replaying the past in static fragments. The doors were hydraulic, triple-locked, opening only to those whose names appeared on a list no one had ever seen.

At the center of the marble table sat nine identical leather chairs. They faced each other in perfect symmetry, forming a pattern of mutual suspicion. No plaques, no nameplates. The Nine had no fixed seating—a tradition meant to keep identity always secondary to voice.

When the meetings began, the lights dimmed slightly, and the soft hum of the circuits deepened. Above the ceiling, the entire building seemed to listen. No one raised their voice here; they didn't have to. Power this concentrated didn't shout; it breathed.

The Nameless Nine were never photographed, recorded, or officially identified—not even in the Bureau archives. Each belonged to a different branch of service, and each owed allegiance to something they claimed to despise. Together, they balanced the world like surgeons holding a dying patient steady —not to save it, but to keep it from waking up. The chamber lights flickered once, briefly, when decisions were made—as if the circuits themselves recoiled at what they carried.

Eight figures sat around the table, their faces cast in shadow from the lights above. They were only eight—one was missing— the Nine needed their leader. Their coats hung from the rack near the door, mostly navy, charcoal, or gray, each exhaling rain and soot from the city above. The eight spoke softly among themselves, waiting patiently, their chatter almost too relaxed.

They'd become weak since the war, and the power of the Bureau was waning because of their lackluster decision-making—even the most mundane agents within the organization gossiped about this.

Then, one of them mentioned the man.

"...he's been a real nuisance, even before Lisbon," one said, shaking his weary head side to side like a pendulum.

The room froze, and silence spread uncomfortably among the eight who sat there. Their gazes shifted toward the heavyset fellow at the far end, a colonel by name officially, but unofficially the second in command behind the Director.

"Don't," Vickers muttered, his voice disinterested. "We wait for her."

The clock continued to tick, mounted over the door ornately as it counted the minutes—two passed, then five.

"She was due at 0900," sighed Dr. Nkosi, the chief and most esteemed scientist among the Nine. He was a nervous, sunken, gaunt man who constantly smelled of tobacco and other smokes, but his insight was continually brilliant, matching even the likes of Hawthorne, Turing, and Krane. "We can't simply begin the meeting without knowing whether she—"

But at that moment, the latch of the door handle clicked, and the room went silent, all eyes fixed on the door.

Elspeth Moreau stepped through the doorway at last, a file tucked under one arm and rain on her dress. She was a small woman, not physically commanding, yet her posture was precise and her demeanor was almost cold. Her hair was set in a bobby-pinned twisted bun that served yet again to craft the delicately created narrative she'd set about herself, an elegant warning to those around her at every turn. On instinct, Vickers rose from his chair, but she waved him down, dismissing him with a gracious nod.

"Apologies," she said as she seated herself at the head of the table. Her voice was quiet but firm. "I was detained on sub-level three. New information presented itself—this morning, in fact—but before we move on to that, I want updates."

She placed the folder in front of herself, visible to the entire table, neatly unbuttoned her coat, and glanced around expectantly. The entire room was silent at first, except for the ticking of the clock.

Finally, Vickers spoke. "Director, since our last meeting, MI6 has pressed a formal request through liaison channels. They want access to the Mirror documents recovered from Rosyth… the excuse given is shoddy; they claim there were incorrect filings among documents traced down by their agents and are demanding an agency-wide evaluation for transparency… with this baked in."

There was a shifting among the chairs, and a curse followed.

Moreau's eyes shifted from the unopened file in front of her. "That's a poor excuse, even for Broadway."

"Yes," Vickers replied, his voice downtrodden. "But they're threatening to request a joint audit committee from Whitehall if we stall further."

A ripple passed through the room, accompanied by murmurs and dissatisfied sighs as several board members leaned closer to each other, speaking in dull monotones. Moreau, however, didn't move.

Vickers continued. "And I'm sure I don't need to say—"

"We no longer have the organizational strength to outright refuse. If we do, we risk political exposure," Moreau interrupted. "MI6 has friends among the government who have been overly critical of our continued use—as of late."

"Yes," he continued evenly. "They claim that declassification would be partial—they would be given technical schematics and other well-detailed files we have access to, and they have even proposed a so-called joint analytical board to evaluate it. Section IX, in particular, seems to be involved."

"Names?"

"Victor Haldane, the Assistant Director of Section IX, appears to be chiefly involved. Along with him, we have evidence that Fraser-Smith and Philby are additionally leading this attempt."

"If my memory serves," Moreau said, "it's been three months since we first intercepted some evidence of this subterfuge. Are we aware yet of when it began?"

"It runs deep. Our intel is still unclear, but we assume this is a plan put in motion from years ago… even perhaps during or pre-war."

Moreau glanced around the table, her eyes hardened. "So we're compromised."

The room was silent. At last, Dr. Nkosi interjected. "Regardless, if MI6 plans to copy us, it cannot be successful. If we assume they wish to replicate our technology—the Mirror we had built—their technology will likely be insufficient. They'll need a key, or a functioning prototype at the very least. Both—thankfully—are far beyond their capabilities."

"I wouldn't be so sure of that," a younger woman interrupted, her accent indistinguishable. "The keys may not be lost."

"Meaning?" Moreau asked.

"A field report from this morning," the woman answered. "We've been keeping tabs on the two agents responsible for most of the Mirror recovery and dealing with the Krane post-Dockyard incident. Agent Artemis has re-established contact. Just this morning, actually—transmission confirms she's in Raven's company, apparently en route northbound."

"Re-established? Artemis?" Vickers' face grew uncomfortable.

"Yes, I had become aware of this as well," Moreau said, "We wondered if Raven had survived, and so I've done some liaison of my own."

"And what have you found?"

"What I just received my report on this morning," Moreau replied, her face growing even more stern as she tapped the folder in front of her. "Whose idea was it to try to remove her? To execute the Caliber protocol?"

The faces flickered with confusion as the eight around the table glanced at each other and back to Moreau. For several long seconds, no one spoke. The tension cut the air like a knife, and the room remained so still that if a feather were to drop, it would sound like a thunderclap rolling over the hills.

Finally, Vickers' chair creaked. He straightened slightly, his fingers laced together as he composed himself. "Director," he said slowly, "this is the first I'm hearing of this. What intel do you have?"

"That was why I was delayed when I arrived this morning. Aside from Artemis and Raven reaching out… aside from their investigations into this matter so far, we've just received… I have other intel. . From separate investigations and from agents whom I will not disclose, I have received information that there was an attempted execution of the Caliber protocol when she first sought out Raven in Lisbon."

"What? From one of our own?" Vickers' face was red now. "But why did you run this investigation without informing the rest of the board?"

"Because, clearly, we are compromised. Or, at the very least, someone's hand was played without my knowledge."

"So then…"

"—Yes. And I'd best not be misheard," she spoke, her voice commanding. "Do not pretend to mishear me when I ask again. Whose idea was it?"

Her eyes glided around the table, like a cat waiting to pounce. It passed Dr. Nkosi's cigarette-stained fingers, the young woman fidgeting in her seat, the colonel's nervous eyes, and landed on a pale fellow three seats down from Vickers. Hargrave sat there, his jaw working nervously, his bulging eyes blinking at a faster rate than usual.

He swallowed. "Director," he began, striving for steadiness that waned as he spoke. "It was my mistake. I assumed—well, we assumed—that such an action with agents no longer affiliated officially with the Bureau would be sufficient to erase our tracks. Anomalies that must be cut out. I had standing authorization for external suppression when such a leak fit the criteria, and of course, the man was deniable. No evidence leads back to us, none whatsoever. If it went well, Artemis would no longer be a prob—"

"Oh, yes. I was aware of this, as well. You staged it to read as Broadway," Moreau interrupted, her voice glib. "You stamped Philby's initials into a one-time pad and used an Able-Baker cadence on a civilian set. You attempted to kill a former agent in cold blood, two streets from a public café. And when it failed, you dropped it off at MI6's door as a countermeasure."

Hargrave's face was as white as a sheet. "Director—"

"What I'm most curious about, Hargrave," Moreau spoke, her voice icy now, "is how you knew of Philby's involvement so closely? How were you, of all people, aware that Philby's stamp would be believable and set off an organizational bout with Artemis and Raven caught in the middle when the rest of us at the board had only learned of Philby's involvement this morning or several days ago at the earliest?"

Hargrave didn't speak. He sat there, his eyes blinking at an unprecedented rate.

"You've made a grave mistake. It only confirms what I believe to be true: some of us at this very table are compromised —whether by the Soviets, the Americans, or in some cases our very own MI6. Some of you are working to take down our organization from the inside. And," she held up a finger, silencing any protest from the board, "I will find out who. There will be an internal inquiry. Comprehensive. Every paper, every cable, every back-channel that led to this. If any of you were involved, you will be purged from this organization. Hargrave, you are stood down from authority effective this second. You will surrender your files to Vickers' office immediately and will remain under surveillance until our investigation is conducted and concluded."

Hargrave's lips moved soundlessly. Finally, he nodded,

stood, and left the room without another word. Moreau motioned toward the young woman, who nodded, stood, and followed the man silently. The six others sat around in uncomfortable silence, not daring to speak to Moreau, until Dr. Nkosi cleared his throat, a rasping cough that left the room colder than before.

"Director... if I may. Even with this misstep—an obviously vicarious one—the reality is this: if MI6 is really reconstructing from Rosyth, they cannot possibly have a fully functional Mirror. They will need a key."

"The Caliber," said another voice from the furthest corner. "Whether we use that name or Artemis, the physics hold. They will likely need one as well, or an anchor."

"Indeed," Dr. Nkosi added. "If they have employed the same technology as we—stolen technology from us—then inherently these two are important to the system."

Moreau nodded in agreement. "But we cannot butcher them. Not yet—they have chosen to move, and for now, we must decide whether to move with them or against them. But I will not have our organization shoot our own former officers in back alleys like some mongrel dogs, or work with MI6 to destabilize us."

Vickers nodded. "Then we must bring them in, Director. If MI6 is pulling this power play, they have much to gain. We should claim our agents first."

"Agreed," Moreau said. "Artemis asked for advice and permission to be granted. I say we give her more than that."

She drew the folder toward herself, opened it, and read through several pages that only she could see. "Motion," she said without lifting her gaze, "that we extend provisional clearance Beta to Artemis and Raven for purposes of this current... crisis. Funds, equipment are at the usual places. We will monitor them with internal agents, obviously, and they will remain unofficial until we are certain who caused this instability within the

Bureau in the first place, but other than that, we will offer full clearance."

"Seconded," said Vickers.

"Any opposed?"

But there were none. One man shifted slightly in his seat but thought better of speaking when he saw Moreau's face. Instead, a chorus of "Aye" resonated around the table, and the motion was done.

"Good," Moreau said, standing. "If there is no other business, I have somewhere to be." She was gone before anyone could speak, heading to her office—the place where she spent most of her days.

———

The office was narrow—far narrower than most men expected when they heard the title. It had a high window that overlooked London's gray skyline, a black telephone that had survived more wars than the Bureau itself, and a desk situated in the very center. The desk itself was special—hardwood, sourced from Montevideo's finest carpenters. On its surface lay the morning's traffic: a stack of intercept summaries, a sheet of MI6 liaison notes, and the thin folder that she had not yet let out of her hand. Moreau sat there and sighed, resting her head in her hands. For the first time, her frame seemed frailer, no longer imposing, and she appeared weary.

She read it again: Kingsway, disturbances, rumors of echoes and doppelgängers running amok, and Rosyth—lights where there should have been none, and a Mirror frame. She knew more than she let on, more than the other members of the Nine knew. She suspected, at least, how deep the corruption ran—but she had no confirmation of it, and thus could not act. But the names. The names of those two—H.A.R. Philby and V.A. Haldane—stamped neatly on the paper request, shepherding

Section IX, yet always five steps ahead, as if they had Mikhail Botvinnik himself in their back pocket.

"Damn you," she said softly, as though the curse itself might save her the trouble of dealing with those two. "Damn you to hell."

She wasn't stupid. Moreau knew full well that the Bureau—the organization formally known as the Office of Temporal Anomalies and Strategic Intelligence—was on its last legs. It was a behemoth crashing down in slow motion, and she could not stop it. All she could do was temper the fall and prepare those she cared about for success. After the disaster that had been the Dockyard incident, the Nine and their organization had suffered immense outside criticism, investigations, and even cases levied against them.

The organization that had once seemed invincible was now at the mercy of other, more powerful organizations that had begun to overtake it. She hoped—more than she liked admitting—that Raven and Artemis would save it. Not the Bureau itself, but something more precious: time.

A pair of agents and a trunk filled with old ledgers, against whatever MI6 had persuaded itself it could do. The hope was meager, but she knew nothing else would stand a chance. She gingerly picked up the old phone on her desk and dialed a number. An operator answered—a voice she'd never heard before, yet one she knew would direct her truly. Sir Stewart Menzies' secretary informed her stoutly that Sir Stewart was not presently at his desk and would be unable to speak.

"Tell Sir Stewart that Director Moreau wishes to speak to him," she said, and the voice on the other end of the line went silent.

A minute later, Sir Stewart himself was on the line.

"Director Moreau," he said, his voice warm. "It has indeed been too long."

"Longer than either of us would have wished. You've developed something of an appetite for our old projects."

"Projects? I am sure I don't know what you mean."

However, Moreau was in no mood for pleasantries. "You want Rosyth's other files," she stated directly. "You want the schematics and a joint board. Your Section IX is planning to overtake our project—our biggest accomplishment—don't pretend you aren't aware of what Philby and Haldane requested."

"Ah, that." She heard him pause, as if considering what to say next. "We have… interests. The war has left a great many interesting objects and projects unattended. We are simply trying to mitigate what losses we can, for King and country."

"You are messing with something you don't understand. You'll find that if you stick your fingers too far into a bear trap, they're likely to be broken off."

"Is that a threat, Director?"

"Simply a warning, Sir Menzies."

"A warning of what?"

"A fair one," she replied. "Between us, I am fully aware you've taken what is not yours. I will make MI6 pay for this, and I will air your deeds to the public if I must, even if it destroys the Bureau in the process. But beyond that, I am fully warning you. You have no idea what the project you are undertaking is capable of."

"Once again, Director, you have nothing for me. Only platitudes and dancing around the truth."

"If you, Haldane, or Philby wish to have access to the Bureau's files," she responded, "you'll have to find them the way you found whatever it is you have access to now."

"You'll fold," he said, his voice now icy. "You have no leverage whatsoever."

"Not yet," she replied. "But I know more than you might think."

"You were always stubborn, Director," Menzies said, his tone friendly again. "Oh well, we will be in touch."

"Good day," she said and set the phone down before he could.

The office quieted into an eerie silence once again. The rain had deepened, and the sky had gone from a light gray to a duller one. Moreau sat, her hands still for the first time since she'd entered her office, and her eyes drifted slowly toward the corner of the desk, where a small frame lay face down. She reached for it tenderly and turned it over, running her fingers along the chipped edge of the photograph.

A little girl smiled up at her—hair pinned the way Elspeth wore it now, chin raised, and a small, innocent smirk that lit up her cheeks. The little girl seemed so small, so distant, that Elspeth felt tears threatening to overwhelm her. But she hadn't gotten as far as she had by being unable to control her own emotions.

"I miss you," she whispered, caressing the well-worn photograph one last time and setting the picture down again.

CHAPTER 14
ELSPETH MOREAU

Her hands returned to the telephone, action overtaking her once again. There were strings yet to pull and a battle to be fought for the sake of Raven and Alicia. The memo on her desk from MI5 lay there, tempting her with what she knew must be done. Her MI5 contact, a chief advisor to one of the greatest men in the organization, was frequently complaining to her as of late that MI6 was encroaching on home soil. They "acted like an embassy on home soil," the man had written in a furious hand, and she had half a mind to enlist MI5 to assist Raven and Alicia. But she sighed. She knew she could only help so much. Ultimately, the pair would have to either succeed—or be killed—all on their own.

Suddenly, she paused. The thought of that girl just wouldn't go away. It grew stronger and threatened to overwhelm her until she couldn't ignore it. She took a deep breath and thought. Just for today—just for half an hour—she would indulge herself. She would allow herself to think and remember what she had lost.

She turned the photograph back over and let it breathe as she did. The edges had gone soft and yellow with years of handling; a neat, small tear was in one corner where it had been crushed and met the edge of her purse one too many times. The girl in the frame was on a beach, a taut kite line burning into her palm, her auburn hair blown full of sand, grit, and light by that haunting Mediterranean wind. She was fifteen, perhaps, her eyes closed as she laughed. The sky behind her was the shimmering essence of late afternoon, and the sea lay like a tranquil sheet of mirrored grace. Elspeth traced the outline of the photo with one finger, the way you'd desperately touch a dying friend, yearning only for them to return to you.

She turned it facedown again, gently, but didn't put it away. Not yet. Not now. Just for another half hour, she wanted to remember and be human.

———

Montevideo in March 1930 was a beautiful city, standing at the crossroads of two worlds—the fading elegance of the old century and the mechanical hum of the new. It faced the Atlantic like a gambler across a table: poised, graceful, and quietly desperate to stay lucky.

The heat lingered in the streets that month—not the fierce, sunburning kind, but the heavy warmth that clung to linen collars and made cigarette smoke curl slowly upward. The air smelled of salt, diesel, and the faint sweetness of wilting jacaranda blossoms in the parks. Out in the harbor, ships from Europe and Buenos Aires lay at anchor, their funnels streaking the sky with soot as longshoremen shouted amid the fog of industry.

Along the Rambla Sur, the grand seaside boulevard, families in white hats and wide skirts strolled beside the seawall, while boys dove into the shimmering shallows for lost coins and luck. The sea beyond looked like a tarnished steel mirror, reflecting the endless blue above. Couples walked arm in arm, the women's parasols bright against the distant hum of cars. The modern world was arriving, but slowly—the city resisted rushing, like an old song resisting translation.

Cafés and confiterías lined the avenue, filled with cigarette smoke, tango melodies, and the aroma of coffee roasted too long. At Café Brasilero, men in Panama hats debated football and politics in the same breath. The upcoming World Cup was on everyone's minds—Uruguay would host it that July, and the discussion was feverish with pride. Waiters carried cups of espresso and glasses of vermouth on silver trays, amid bursts of laughter and the scrape of chairs.

Down at the docks, sailors and dockworkers mingled with artists and exiles, drinking cheap grappa and debating revolutions. Montevideo was neutral by nature, but it was never naive. The city served as a crossroads of trade, gossip, hidden funds, and disappeared men. Couriers from Europe arrived with briefcases that never opened publicly. Letters passed through cafés in envelopes stamped with false consulates. Dozens of languages floated in the smoke: Spanish, Italian, English, Portuguese, German—the sound of an empire unraveling and being rebuilt in whispers.

Above all, the wind from the Río de la Plata carried the scent of rain and distant lands. Montevideo was a port city, yes, but it was also a state of mind—caught between Europe's last breath and South America's first cry. The city was vibrant with contradictions—cosmopolitan yet provincial, glamorous yet weathered, modern yet haunted by nostalgia. A city of mirrors and whispers, built on the edge of the known world, already waiting for the next ship to bring news, money, or trouble.

Standing at the seawall just before dawn, the world smelled of salt and coal, with the first ship lights flickering on the horizon. The city behind still glowed faintly, caught somewhere between the promise of day and the memory of night—exactly where Montevideo had always belonged.

Back when her name wasn't Elspeth, the name she had chosen after the accident, she was Maria. Back when the river smelled of fresh air, the cut fruit, and the gardens smelled of fresh flowers, and the sky was always blue. Her girl—Alicia—

was thirteen then, kneeling in the sand with a stick in her hand, tapping at the beach. Dots and dashes formed in the sand—a private language Elspeth had taught her.

"When will Daddy come home, Mama?"

"He will soon," she had responded. "He will be here soon." But it was a lie she only wished were true. Her husband had gone where men go when they choose the world over those who love them. Where exactly he was, she knew not. He had always been a man of great deeds, but his actions often outweighed his abilities—and he would end up caught in something far worse than he imagined. It had happened that way, and he had vanished, leaving only the whisper of a rumor behind him. Alicia would always ask her why her father had left.

But each time, Elspeth would answer that she did not know. Then, Alicia would ask the other, more pressing question.

"Will you ever leave me, Mama?"

"Not so long as I live, my darling," she would respond.

But promises are not always kept.

Elspeth carried the kites and the biscuit tin and the blanket—Alicia ran beside her, carrying the rays of sunlight that bounced and reflected from her hair. Near evening, they walked through the market where men called out prices for things they could not afford. Alicia skipped ahead, a red cord looped carefully around her wrist so her kite wouldn't fly away.

And with a crack, the world shifted.

With a thunderous boom and a pulse, it turned on its head. It seemed to bend inwards, folding on itself. For a brief moment, Elspeth saw an older girl flash through the corridor of air that created a rift in front of her—auburn hair bright as blood, a pale face, a red scarf, and a coat she'd never owned—and then her own little girl was gone. The cord drifted away with the kite, and Elspeth ran after it, crying, screaming, and grabbing onto the only thing left of her daughter. The kite, which was all that remained, hovered where a child should have been.

She cried out, screaming Alicia's name, begging for her little girl to return. She tore the city apart searching for her daughter but found nothing. That night, she sat at the kitchen table, her chest heaving until breath took her no longer, and she fell asleep. But as the days turned to months, the physics papers she'd translated for money began to make sense. The math played in her mind, and things began to make sense. When she'd exhausted every other possibility, the only thing left was probability. And probability, mechanics, and science were her last hope of finding her daughter.

She dedicated years to it—bookstalls, letters to scientists in Paris, and notes in every margin of the pages. Her grief became her driving force, and she forced herself to focus only on this. She began to make friends. Her theories and science spread like wildfire, and by November of '32, the French Deuxième Bureau contacted her on a cold night, asking her to show them her model. She did, and for the first time, nobody scoffed at her theories.

"Parallel, you say?" The man nosed his glasses slightly higher on his face. "That is intriguing. How much funding do you believe you'd need to create a functioning device? We are prepared…"

But Elspeth was barely listening. She knew this was her only chance to find her daughter again.

By '43, Elspeth had constructed the original prototype. It was a strange, brutal thing—copper ribs, glass, and bolts that looked like knobs, and a power draw that would alone sap an entire city. She called it her project—unnamed, something only dedicated to her daughter. Though she had been supported for so long by the organization she claimed to have built it for, she didn't care.

She turned it on without authorization, and she alone knew how to use it. Though she had no real way of controlling it, she journeyed through it into a foreign world. The prototype she had built tore her away from her timeline, setting her down in a parallel branch: London, 1932. She wasn't going back.

It would be months before anyone even knew her name, and not the same world she had experienced, so she made certain this time would be different.

She worked her way through the timeline—slightly differently, slightly more cautious—she had realized that, try as she might, she simply couldn't solve the final equation that would give her a more complete control over a device that allowed her to breach timelines. And yet, as she maneuvered her way into the seams of a new century's bureaucracy, she began to realize this timeline would not be the same. Thus, she became Elspeth Moreau—a quiet woman who learned that the true equation she had to solve wasn't one of mathematics, but of people.

She began to navigate toward politics rather than science and slipped into London's climate when it became clear this was where the future lay. She understood, earlier than all others, that the machine did not simply tune space-time, but minds. It needed a constant. Though she herself had become a doppel-gänger within the world that was foreign to her very DNA, she knew that somewhere, Alicia would resurface. Somewhere along this branch, the system would try to use her again.

Eventually, she found Alicia from this timeline as well. In Montevideo, she hid herself away, watching the young woman from afar at a train platform and noted how beautiful she had become. Even though this wasn't her own daughter, she couldn't bear to harm her, leaving the young woman to grow up with her mother in this timeline, in the desperate hope that Alicia would never become involved in such an entangled web.

But even Moreau couldn't predict what happened next. The very organization she had a hand in forming—the Bureau—where she gathered the most brilliant minds on the planet, and, when she got wind of Krane's theories and plans, recruited him instantly, would become this timeline's undoing.

Time has a way of connecting—and reconnecting—the constants throughout parallels, and Elspeth experienced this firsthand. Though she found herself rebelling against her own flawed morality, she realized that she had no other choice but to use the Alicia of her new world to find her real daughter—and thus, Caliber was born.

But despite her best attempts, the Mirror never came to fruition. Even at the height of its success, right before she made her move, other forces plotted against her. Three weeks before she had decided to venture forth into another parallel to find her daughter, the Dockyard exploded, and the Mirror was lost.

One unsanctioned test was all it took.

One brutal moment that cast the world into chaos, dismantling everything she had worked for and destroying the network. She had grieved for weeks, knowing that it would be nearly impossible to recreate the Mirror to achieve her true goal.

But as she mourned, a new goal began to form in her mind. Though she would never stop seeking her real daughter, she knew the Alicia of this timeline needed her, too, and she set out with the purpose of helping the auburn-haired woman of whom she had grown so proud.

———

Elspeth caressed the photo that was face down on her desk. That girl… it wasn't hers. She had nothing left of her daughter. Nothing to remember her by. Tears fell from her eyes onto the desk, and she let it happen. She knew, somewhere deep in her heart, that she would never see her little girl again.

The photo she had snapped—of this world's Alicia at fifteen —wasn't even her real little girl. This Alicia wasn't hers. And yet, Elspeth couldn't let this one go. This version of Alicia had lost her father, too. Elspeth wouldn't let her lose her mother—or the man she knew this Alicia loved.

She turned her attention again to the MI5 memo on her desk. She had given Artemis and Raven enough rope to climb with, or hang by, no matter what their final decision was. She had done everything she could without burning the place down.

Work. Back to work. She had felt enough.

She slid the MI5 memo aside, scrawling her own note for Vickers in the margin—stall the audit. She knew that if they requested Whitehall oversight, MI6 would suffer. Whitehall wouldn't suffer MI6 scrutiny, and it was a plan as much as it was a bluff that would buy them time.

Elspeth picked up the phone, dialing a number she knew all too well.

"Vickers," she said when he answered the phone. Her voice was calm again, and no hint of her mourning betrayed her. "Send a message to our contact near Rosyth. Let's have her monitor those two. As for MI6, let's look at any of their agents involved in this. If they want to steal our project, I want eyes on every agent responsible." There was a pause on the other end, then a response of weary acceptance. Moreau softened her tone slightly. "We're nearly out of time, old friend. You know as well as I that the Bureau is standing on its last leg—but we are still standing."

She set the phone down with a click. Outside, London bustled, cars driving over the cobblestone, their tires hissing and splashing through puddles. However, Moreau did not allow herself time to enjoy the outside air, nor did she glance at the street below for more than a moment.

"Alicia," she murmured more to herself than anything else. "I will bring you home. In one world or another."

She rose, smoothing her dress as she made her way to the door of her office. With only one last backward glance at the photograph lying face down on her desk, she left the office, her heels clicking with a rhythm against the corridor. Somewhere far beyond London, the two agents—her last remaining hopes— were making their way to Invershiel.

And if Invershiel contained what she believed it to—if the rumors she'd heard of Project Oracle were correct—there might be one last chance for her to find her own daughter.

CHAPTER 15
ANGUS ASSAULT

woke, stretching, yawning, and ravenous. Alicia still slept beside me, her breathing gentle and barely a whisper above the steady patter of rain against the small window. For a while, I stared at her—hair frazzled across the pillow, one arm stretching toward where I had just been, the glow of early afternoon casting streaks of light against her skin. It was something that made me long for a life other than the one we knew, a life that would never be mine. I knew it as well as she did. I sighed, and my stomach grumbled as if it were a waking bear.

I slid out of bed, careful not to wake her. The floorboards creaked beneath me, and I sighed, feeling impatient. This small hotel room in Inverkeithing was a far cry from what I would have desired. A constant chill permeated the air, crawling into my bones no matter what I did to avoid it. Outside the window, the street below was quiet. One lone car passed, the engine whirring, and then silence fell again.

I lit a cigarette and made my way to the bathroom, shaving as I smoked. Smoking had become a habit I relied upon to think, and I needed to think. I stared into the mirror above the sink, looking at my own face. I barely recognized it. The threads we had right now were frayed, and I was barely able to put them together. Kingsway, Rosyth, the radio voice that seemed to know everything we did and more: ANGUS, Oracle, and Loch Duich. Everything just seemed disjointed.

Except for that. My slide at Rosyth was still fresh in my mind, and as much as it filled me with dread, I was beginning to understand exactly what had happened… or at least, I suspected it. If the explosion had happened a minute after the official records, then the official records must have been a lie.

And if the records were a lie, then my memories were as well.

Alicia stirred from the bed.

"You worried?" she murmured, her voice still slurred from sleep.

"When am I not?" I chuckled back.

She sat up, pulling the sheet halfway over her chest, staring at me as if she still couldn't believe what we'd done the night before. "Breakfast, Max?"

"To be damned with Rosyth, Invershiel, and all of it," I chuckled. "Breakfast comes first."

She smiled, and for a second, my worries faded. We enjoyed a Full English, and a little after noon, we were back on the road. The jeep had survived the night, just as we had. Though it looked a bit worse for wear from all the rain, it still ran and idled perfectly fine. A Bureau package had arrived for us as we ate—delivered by a young courier with a hat drawn far over his eyes. The package was scarcely more than an embellished envelope, but it contained everything we needed: a sheet of clearance orders, a map, twenty 5-pound notes, and a small letter containing a handwritten scrawl. I had opened the package and read the note. It was the first time I had seen her handwriting. Though I knew Director Moreau by name, she was an elusive operative whom only the highest agents within the Bureau had met.

You are cleared to proceed with full Bureau authority. Included is official clearance, funds, and, to follow, instructions and further intel.

Assume MI6 presence. Philby's supervision confirmed. ANGUS and Invershiel confirmed.

　—Elspeth Moreau

That was all. Nothing more, but that alone eased my mind a little bit. Knowing that the Bureau itself had decided not to interfere with our progress was a relief, and so we embarked on our trip with fresh minds, full stomachs, and less worry. Alicia unfolded a map we had bought as I drove, scanning the little lines that traced their way through the Highlands. "Invershiel's another two hours, maybe more. There are service stations— 'petrol stations,' to you, Max, at Pitlochry and by Glen Moriston."

"Provided the rain doesn't prove to be too much," I muttered, glancing up at the overcast sky.

"Same as Lisbon," she said. "Do you miss it?"

"I miss when this was easier," I said, pressing the pedal down more.

She smiled and went back to studying the map laid out in front of her. The jeep bounced, rattled, and shook as we drove over the rough roads through the foothills and mountains. They were shrouded in mist now, behemoths that rolled along like some giant stone waves of the sea. The further we drove north, the more foreign the place became, and the less of society remained. Sheep fields, moorland, and wet boulders scattered here and there created a haunting backdrop to our journey, and the long, twisting road ahead.

I lit a cigarette as we drove, the ember's faint glow flickering in my peripheral vision while I guided the jeep. Alicia read aloud occasionally, pointing out coordinates and speaking loudly so her voice would carry over the wind and rain.

"Bureau clearance should provide us with some much-needed resources," she said, "but it won't help us with MI6 or any other organizations we'll need to deal with. And I have a feeling the Bureau is prepared to claim ignorance if we're caught. They are very good at plausible deniability."

"I assumed as much," I said. "Other than the provided confirmation on Invershiel and Philby—and the funds, of course—I doubt we'll find much assistance from the Bureau. Just as always, we're on our own."

"It isn't that bad," she said. "It might be difficult, but I think we can sneak our way to the loch via this forestry road—the one you mentioned."

"Yes. Don't mind me—I've been more cynical as of late."

"Max, you always were," she chuckled.

"Maybe. But lately," I said, "I feel as if the world is against us."

She didn't respond, but pungently placed her hand on my arm. I smiled slightly, then reached into my pocket, pulling out the small badge I'd taken from 6F. Just a second later, however, I nearly dropped it. Cursing, I tossed it to Alicia.

"Shit!" I exclaimed, rubbing my fingers together.

"What happened?"

"Damn thing burnt me. What the hell?"

"It feels cool to the touch to me."

"I guess," I said, "that it has something to do with that observer amplitude thing. Though I'm still not sure about all the details there. What I already know is complicated enough."

"Speaking of that," she said, reaching for the attaché case in the footwell. She flipped it open, adjusting the dial on the radio as we drove. The static swelled and grew sharper.

"Trying to see if the voice returns?" I asked.

"Yes," she replied, still fiddling with the dial. "Wonder if there's a specific frequency..."

But despite her efforts, no voice returned. No matter which frequency she set, or how she fiddled with the dials, the radio remained silent.

We drove onward. By the time we reached Glen Moriston, the sun was low in the sky, almost entirely covered by thick clouds. It had stopped raining, and as I pulled into the petrol station, I noticed that the air seemed thick with silence. The petrol station attendant barely glanced at us as he filled the tank. He was a thin man, his face blackened with grease, his eyes bulging out of their sockets.

"How's the road to Invershiel?" I asked.

He shook his head slowly, though his eyes darted up to me nervously and then back down again. "Road's narrow. Weather's not the best… folks don't go much past Shiel Bridge these days. Construction… other things… you know, we get to talkin' 'bout…." His voice trailed off, and he went silent. His eyes flickered toward Alicia, then he lowered his gaze and turned his attention back to the fuel pump. I thanked him, paid, and we left without asking what he meant.

Back on the road, it began raining again—only a sprinkle this time, but steady. The tires splashed through the puddles, and dusk set over the hills. The jeep's headlights cut through the fog, but as we drove, suddenly, Alicia squeezed my arm.

"Max. Look ahead."

I shook myself from my stupor and leaned forward, peering through the misted glass. Far in the distance, maybe a hundred yards or so, a convoy of military trucks rolled toward us—four unmarked 4x4s, their bodies sleek with the wetness. They moved at a steady pace, fast enough that they seemed to glide toward us as I watched.

"Army?" I asked.

"Maybe," Alicia replied, "but there are no markings. Definitely not Bureau, either."

I whipped my hat out and pulled the brim low over my eyes as the first truck passed. I saw Alicia do the same, and I snuck a glance out the side of the window at the men driving. They wore field caps, but there were no emblems or insignias I recognized. Their faces were hardened and expressionless, as if they had been set to a task they understood all too well.

"Keep your head down," I said in a low voice, though I knew she was already doing so. "Just in case."

The convoy thundered past us, southbound along the same

road we'd just driven on. I watched their taillights in the mirror until they vanished into the haze, slowing the jeep to a halt so I could eye them.

Alicia finally spoke. "If they're MI6, they're not hiding it well."

"Maybe," I said. "They seem to be in too much of a rush to care."

"Why would that be?"

"Rosyth," I said. "They must know we were there by now. If they want to keep from being compromised, they'll clean the place out."

"Or," she said, "they could want us to see them. Be making a show of it—to let us know they know what our game is."

"Possible," I replied. "Either way, from the direction they are headed, it seems they're going toward Rosyth."

"Best make good time, then," Alicia said.

We traveled in silence a while longer, both listening to the rhythmic drumming of the engine. A brittle fog rolled over the hills as the rain ceased, and to our left, the outline of a loch—though not the one we drove toward—flickered, dancing now and then through gaps in the hills. It was a restless mirror of black water that caught reflections as easily as a flytrap catches flies.

Alicia unfolded the map again, her fingertip tracing the thin line that indicated the road we had traveled. She pondered over it for several minutes, then finally spoke. "If I'm correct, we'll reach Shiel Bridge in less than half an hour. After that, we'll have to deal with Invershiel."

"And ANGUS," I said.

"And ANGUS. Maybe we'll enlighten ourselves as to what Oracle means as well."

"Yes—" I began, but at that moment, the radio flared to life.

The shortwave attaché crackled, static flaring over the frequencies, followed by the sound of a distant roaring and breathing noise. I slammed on the brakes—I wasn't going to risk losing the signal, if that was even how this radio worked. We listened with bated breath as we waited.

"Max…" Alicia whispered.

"Turn it up."

She did. For a moment, the static continued, and I had the fleeting thought that maybe it was nothing more than a sporadic spark of interference, but then suddenly, a voice spoke across the waves.

"Do not approach Invershiel directly. Repeat: hold for a day. Repeat: Invershiel on alert. Forces already at work."

The speaker clicked, and just like that, it fell silent again. The tone died, and empty air was left between us. We exchanged looks, and I could see the worry etched on Alicia's face.

"That's the same voice," Alicia said. "Same phrasing, same cadence. Do we trust it?"

I hesitated. "We listen," I replied at last. "This man—or whatever he is—hasn't steered us wrong yet, as far as we know. We'll stop before the bridge and see what's moving up there."

I cautiously guided the jeep off the road onto a gravel turn-around where the mist gathered thick, the rain soaking the gravel and grassy hills and the dark water of the loch beyond. The engine sputtered down to silence, and for a long while, neither of us spoke. Rain tapped gently against the hood like the rhythmic ticking of a clock. It was a haunting, eerie moment that left both of us slightly more worried than we had been just minutes before.

"He said forces," Alicia finally said, her voice low. "Plural. I doubt it's the Bureau… but could it be?"

"Probably MI6… and maybe something worse," I said. "A lot is going on; we still don't know."

I recalled the slide at Rosyth and the strange suspicion that had been growing in the back of my mind ever since. I sighed deeply and leaned back in the seat. In the distance, a faint yellow light glimmered and danced through the fog—perhaps a flame or maybe headlights bending along the road. I couldn't tell, and in the next instant, it was gone. The air carried a slight scent of gasoline, and the rain didn't help with the odor.

"So, what's next?" It was a question we both knew the answer to, but she asked anyway.

"We wait till dawn," I replied. "Like the voice said. Find a pub, blend in. We'll approach Invershiel from the forestry road when there's light, unless something changes."

"According to the map," she said, sighing, "there's a small stop around two kilometers back. I saw the sign on the road a while back as well."

"Name?"

"I…ah, it's right here on the map—Glenshiel," she said, squinting. "Or whatever's left of it. Just a dot off the main road; it might have a hotel and maybe a restaurant if we're lucky."

"Perfect. The smaller, the better. We don't want to be tracked…or followed."

I swung the jeep around, and the tires hissed and popped over the gravel as I doubled back along the road. The rain darkened the sky, and the entire horizon began to take on a somber, amber glow. The jeep rattled as we hit bump after bump, and every few moments, the headlights would catch on the mist particles that ran thick now and reflect back toward us before cutting further into the darkness again, illuminating our path.

"It feels like we're running," she muttered.

"We are," I responded and revved the engine.

Glenshiel wasn't much, though it had never really pretended to be. Dominated by the dramatic mountain landscape of the Five Sisters of Kintail, the glen consisted of a single street lined with several stone cottages that seemed half-collapsed, a small church, and an inn. It was clearly near closing hour, but as it was typical of places such as this, closing was defined less by the hour and more by the arrival of the rare visitor who requested room and board. And today, that was us.

I parked outside and killed the engine. Alicia and I sheltered our heads and luggage, making a short run for the doorway that swung open. A blast of warm air hit our faces—dry from a coal fire and infused with the smell of smoke and a faint tinge of whiskey. A few locals sat huddled in the room, which served both as a dining pub and the entrance to the inn, their low voices cutting off entirely as we stepped inside.

We were strangers here, I knew—and out of place. I just hoped none of these men were more than they appeared to be. The woman behind the counter glanced at our papers without reading them, then nodded toward the far stairs. "Room back there. Two beds. Or you'll be wantin' one?"

"Two works," I muttered, paying her without haggling. The woman nodded curtly, and we ascended the narrow staircase, the boards groaning in protest with each step. It was clear this place had seen better days.

When we finally arrived at our room, it was nearly pitch black outside. I glanced down—we overlooked the main street of the village, or what passed for it. There was one lamp opposite our room, which provided a gloomy, flickering light. Underneath it, several rats scattered as a noise spooked them. The window panes were covered in condensation even with the latch open, and the room smelled slightly musty with a hint of peat. It was an old place, but it was as good as we could have expected. Alicia settled first, dropping the radio case onto the small table and rubbing her hands together to fight off the chill.

"It feels like the war all over again," she said.

"It does," I replied, glancing out the window once more. I knew we were closer to Loch Duich and Invershiel than we had ever been, but I still didn't feel complete. I hadn't felt complete since Rosyth.

"Think the voice will find us… even here?" she asked.

"Don't know where it's coming from… but it's found us everywhere else."

She nodded, and we didn't speak again. Outside our window, the Highlands were covered in a frosty mist, but I slept well without the dream of the Andes and Krane haunting me.

———

Morning arrived with the rising sun, battling the mist and the cold, which fought back mercilessly. A dull, gray sky pressed low against the hills. Alicia and I ate in silence, enjoying a small but hearty breakfast of eggs and what appeared to be a sort of bacon—thin rashers crisped over the pub's stove, served with a generous helping of black pudding. The tea tasted of smoke and was almost stale, but I was grateful for some warm food. The landlady didn't look at us as she served us, but I knew she was grateful for some money—and the potential for new gossip.

Around these parts, gossip was all they had. I remembered it all too well from my childhood in the Gorbals. By noon, the clouds had begun to finally clear, and I set out to check on the jeep. The fuel gauge said half-full, and the tires seemed to be holding up—though they were paper-thin. We packed, and Alicia poured over the map we had used to navigate so far. We'd received another small package from the Bureau overnight, delivered anonymously and without any trace of the courier who dropped it off. It contained several more detailed maps of the area and the latest Bureau intel.

It was a Bureau classic—how they knew our location, the agency would never disclose. But though the Bureau was far past its prime, the Nine still had eyes and ears everywhere, so I was only half-surprised.

"You said Invershiel's northwest from here, right?"

"Yes," I replied. "Why?"

"It lines up with Bureau data."

"Not surprised," I said. "The Bureau likely got most of their data from people like me—agents they turned from MI6 and recruited during the war."

"Well, let's take the forestry track then. Yes? It looks like it branches just past Dornie, so we can approach from the ridge above Loch Duich."

"Dornie...I've been there before."

She raised an eyebrow. "Seriously?"

"Believe it or not, yes. It's near the meeting point of Duich, Alsh, and Long, and the A87 to Skye passes right by it. Beautiful place—old fishing village—I had to stay there a night when I was still with MI6, I think." I was struggling to recall the memory. It was a struggle I hadn't had before, but I pushed the worry to the back of my mind. "It was some small mission up north of Fort Augustus. Just paperwork and waiting for a courier, nothing major. I remember passing Eilean Donan Castle on the way there—a haunting place on a small island. Wish I'd stopped and enjoyed the mission more; looking back now, I should have."

She gently punched my shoulder, laughing slightly. "You've gotten soft, Max. Spending more time reminiscing and remembering than you ever did before."

"Maybe because that's what I fear losing the most."

She smiled, her eyes understanding. She knew me better than anyone else. I knew that much—even more than Sister Agnes had all those years ago. But she knew it would do no good to speak of it, and so she changed the topic… and I was grateful for it.

"So, the forestry track? Only issue I see is it's unmarked."

"So is Rosyth," I replied.

"Well then," she said. "Let's go see what MI6 has built under a loch."

"All's packed," I responded, and we were off.

For the next few minutes, we spoke little.

As we drove, the road lifted us into the mist as if it were pushing us along through the clouds and toward something darker. The dusk around us settled in oppressively, like a blanket against the folds of the hills. As the light thinned, the rare trees turned into papery dark cutouts, and I took a few minutes to hood the jeep's headlights before we continued. I let the jeep idle low as we inched past Dornie, finally reaching the forestry track that split off the main road.

It was only two tire tracks that cut through the peat. No sign, no outpost—just a small road that signaled our path toward Invershiel. Loch Duich lay to our left, mute as glass, its dark, shiny surface reflecting any light that touched it, yet none at all. Not even a single ripple could be seen on its surface. Not a sound, either. There were no birds chirping, nor any foxes calling. Even the wind itself seemed to have calmed.

"Here," I said suddenly, though I wasn't quite sure how I knew. I turned the wheel, driving down one of the smaller tracks that branched off the forest road. The track we followed curled through small pines and cut stones, eventually making its way to a stand of trees. The fog thickened even further here, pressing right up against the windscreen until we could barely see through it. It was like a wall of soft, billowy white clouds keeping us hidden. It felt comforting in a way. Somewhere on the other side of that wall, something moved and then fell still again—maybe a rabbit or a spectre of someone I wanted to see. I didn't mention it to Alicia. I wasn't even sure if it was real.

False memories began to invade my mind. I recalled being on these ridges before—another war, a different woman next to me —and yet I knew I had never been here before… at least, not to Invershiel. Though Alicia held out the map and pointed out directions, I didn't need it to drive anymore. The jeep bumped and crawled along the road until we reached the end. I slowed it to a halt as the tires nosed up against a slab of poured concrete set into the earth like some gigantic, flat rock.

I killed the engine. The silence was absolute; nothing left but the fog.

"That looks like a culvert," Alicia said, eyeing the stone.

"I doubt it is," I replied, stepping out into the dark, gloomy fog.

As I inspected the slab, I noticed it seemed almost too perfect, as if it were multifaceted—crafted to appear obscure and old, yet each surface served a purpose. It had been poured into specific, tight angles, as if constructed to run much deeper than it looked, with the moss and peat forming around it in a way that seemed to indicate it had been there for many, many years. Still, if this was it, there was no handle and no obvious door to enter.

As I thought, I slipped the badge from my pocket that 6F had jammed into my hand back at the fence line, holding it carefully with one of Alicia's handkerchiefs. In the cold air, the little rectangle already felt warmer than it should, but the handkerchief was enough to do the trick.

"You ready?" I asked her.

"Always," she replied, following me into the fog.

We made our way carefully along the gigantic concrete slab, feeling here and there, looking for any suggestion of an entrance.

"Maybe further down," she said, motioning toward the area where the flat land turned into a rocky slope that I knew led to the dark water of the loch. "If we go further down, maybe there will be an exit tunnel or some entry shaft we can find."

"Sure," I replied, and we traced the concrete downward, tripping over stones, loose rocks, and boulders, and making our way around the trees.

As we walked, I noticed something unusual. It was almost as if the badge in my hand was growing warmer and warmer the farther we went. I tried to think of what it could mean and of any explanation when suddenly it hit me.

"Alicia," I whispered.

She froze behind me. "What is it?" she whispered back.

"I think," I said slowly, "I think we're near the source."

"The source?"

"Yes—of the doppelgangers or echoes, or whatever you want to call them." I lifted the badge. "This badge... it deals in observer amplitude, correct?"

She nodded silently.

"If that's the case, then wouldn't that mean if there were another strong observer—similar to me—nearby, the badge's effect would be amplified?"

"Yes, and what of it?" she asked.

"Well, the badge has been growing warmer as we've walked. That means we're getting close… to something. Another echo, or maybe another Mirror."

She nodded resolutely, and we continued.

Soon, we came across several large grated openings—round concrete culverts jutting out of the edge of the hill, each covered with thick iron bars. I peered inside one of them, glancing into the tunnel. The gaping tube was at least twice my height, and there were four of these culverts lined up in a row.

"Where do you think these lead?" I asked.

"If I'm guessing," she said, "probably into whatever has been built here."

I nodded and smiled grimly. "Well then, do you think you can fit through?"

She examined the bars carefully. "I think I can," she replied. "But what about you?"

I sighed, stretched, and rolled my shoulders. "I'll have to try my best."

About ten minutes later, we had both managed to slip between the bars. Alicia did so easily; the spaces between them were more than enough for her slender body to slip through. As for me, it was a slightly more embarrassing task. It ended with me almost buck-naked as I slid through the cold iron. The bars pressed against my skin, and I had to struggle—for a moment, I thought I was caught. But with one final heave, I managed to pull myself through.

"Damn," I muttered as I sat down against the curved, circular surface inside the culvert. "That was something."

She nodded, smiled, and handed me my clothes back.

We followed the tunnel. It sloped downward, which was unusual for something like this. I still wasn't sure what this culvert was—whether it was a vent or something else—but we followed it until we came across a small access door, seemingly set into the rounded concrete like a scar, edges smooth and barely visible. I barely noticed it in the dark, except for when the beam from my torch swept over it. Off to the left side of the door was a square that looked bizarrely beveled and glossy in the darkness.

"Locked," I said, but I wasn't too worried. I had an idea. A moment later, I pressed 6F's badge up against the glass, and with a click, air and mist shot from a seal I couldn't see. "And now it's unlocked."

The cement door slowly slid upward, and I squinted as the bright, artificial light stung my face. It revealed a hallway the color of white plaster—almost too clean, too empty—lit without shadows, and I could hear the distant hum of power and noise of energy somewhere far deeper into the core. There were no guards, no dust, and not even a hint of shadow in the place—it felt almost too surgical.

"Let's go," Alicia said, and I followed without further prompting.

We moved in sync, our feet padding against the impossibly smooth cement floor. "ANGUS—ACCESS E. SERVICE—LOW PRESSURE LINE" read a small, white sign along the corridor. Whatever this place was, I figured we were inside something that had likely been abandoned years ago, simply because the entrance itself was so heavily disguised. If we didn't have the badge from 6F—which I only suspected worked because he had mentioned Invershiel and ANGUS in the first place—we would have never managed to invade their base so successfully. A stairwell opened up to one side as the corridor grew larger—the entrance darker than the well-lit passage we had followed so far. We descended one flight, then two, then three more.

I lost count.

The deeper we went, the hum deepened until it seemed to make the very metal stairs beneath my feet vibrate. At the bottom, there was a door, securely latched, with a similar black, beveled glass scanner as before. I tapped the badge to it, and without protest, the door slid open.

Ten minutes passed, maybe thirty, and I began to lose count

of all the passages we had turned down. Though Alicia hadn't spoken a word, I could hear the frustration in her footsteps. I had almost given up when suddenly I saw it.

As we left the smaller corridor and merged with a much broader one, I noticed something: a large metal door lodged securely in the wall. It was riveted, ribbed, and looked as if it had been reinforced hundreds of times. As I glanced up at it, the sign on the door caught my eye—the letters stenciled there as if daring me to read them:

RECURSION CORE—VERSION THREE

Alicia inhaled sharply, her breath catching in her throat. I didn't say a word—only held up 6F's badge to the small eye of black glass that was implanted by the door. For a second, nothing happened. I tensed, half-expecting it to be a trap. Then a voice crackled over a loudspeaker somewhere near the door.

"Credential class: SL-series key, 6F confirmed. Authentication complete. Proceed."

I heard the bolts within the door creaking under the weight of the metal, and it parted, swinging inward.

The chamber was a vault that seemed to have been converted into some sort of laboratory. Whatever this place was, it appeared to be as tall as the stairs we had descended. The walls reached upward into the darkness, the lighting only at eye level and slightly above. The whole place was dim, but the air inside seemed to pulse with a faint electricity as if it were alive. I knew what that meant. Sure enough, in the center, where cables spiraled away from the walls and toward it, was a tall, crude frame, at least twice my height. There was no interface, no controls that I could see, and nothing to hold it down. It simply stood there, a tall and unmoving behemoth, as if it were daring me to approach it.

It was MI6's Version Three.

It wasn't in stasis like Kingsway, nor was it dismantled like Rosyth.

This Mirror was alive—a thin skin of black light was etched over its impossibly smooth surface, quivering gently as if it were the ripples of a pond that stretched endlessly in every direction. From deep within it, a hum emanated.

My heart sank as I saw it. "So much for destroying the Mirror."

"Can it ever really be destroyed?"

I didn't respond, but I wished I could. I edged toward the gigantic thing, my hands itching to break it. Itching to destroy it. I wished more than anything that I could take a sledgehammer to it, beat the thing down until it was nothing but dust—but here it was, and I was virtually helpless to stop it.

Alicia had slipped away to the side, her hands quickly and precisely sorting through a collection of folders arranged on a long bench next to a terminal mounted on the Mirror, the word "Oracle" etched neatly into the panel.

Out of the corner of my eye, I saw her wake the screen with a touch. I wasn't sure what she had found, but only a few seconds later, her voice sounded urgent and unnerving.

"Max, come look at these files."

There was a fear in her voice she didn't bother to hide, and it made me turn away from the mirror. On the Oracle terminal, I saw three lines—three lines of text floating in a field of black:

CALDER SERIES—VARIANTS SL-001 THROUGH SL-042
OBSERVER LEAKAGE
SECTION IX—K. PHILBY

A signature block sat below it, crisp and vivid. Beside the terminal, pinned as if it were something they had examined countless times, was my photograph. It was unmistakably me— a Bureau ID crop. Someone had stamped beneath it in neat handwriting: CALDER SL-000.

Almost as if on cue, the light from the mirror began to brighten, and the hum increased. I could feel the pulse now, beating through the air as it always did right before something happened, right before an activation. It was as if it sensed me… as if it somehow connected to me as I stared at my face pinned next to the terminal. I turned just in time to see the surface shatter inward, and time felt as if it were stopping. Then a face broke through it, like some desperate, drowning woman surfacing from a lake for the final time. It was unmistakably Alicia, but older. Her hair was white with frost, her eyes covered in a filmy gray that made it seem as if she were almost blind. I could see her screaming, but I couldn't hear it—no words, no sound, just the hum of the machine. Then, in the next moment, the crack in the mirror healed, and she was gone again.

"We need to shut it down," Alicia said quietly, her voice not betraying what she felt.

"With what?" I glanced around, looking for breakers, buttons, anything—any control other than the dead panel in front of us. There was nothing, just cables and conduit—nothing that seemed as if it would help us. But as I scanned the room, something caught my eye. It was nearly buried under a coil of spare wires—a small, satchel-sized box, the sort of thing a wireless field operator would use. It was wrapped in carefully oiled canvas.

On top of the thing, three bare copper coils lay like ribs, each carefully laid and meticulously hand-wound across the box. It didn't look like any Mirror tech I'd seen before, which was why it caught my attention. I walked over to the workbench and looked at the box closely.

Along the front edge ran another thin strip of brass, etched with a small inscription that I read with squinted eyes in the dim light: MODEL INDUCTOR ARRAY—FRASER-SMITH—KX-7.

"Fraser-Smith," I muttered, pulling the box from where it was buried.

"There's something from him here?" Alicia asked, glancing over.

"If anyone would try to put a leash on the Mirror," I said, "It would be Fraser-Smith. But what does this thing do?"

"Could it be a kill switch?"

"Maybe," I said. "Or maybe it's a control board."

On the very front of the box was a small rotary dial and a toggle lever with three positions stamped next to it: NULL, COUPLE, BREAK. Next to this was a small pressure switch

My fingers hovered above the small switch, itching to pull it, but I hesitated. Alicia, as if she had read my mind, shook her head.

"Don't," she said. "Whatever it does, I don't think we should find out. We'd be going in blind."

She was right. I set the box down, carefully again, then turned my attention back to the task at hand—The Mirror.

In that instant, the facility erupted with noise. Sirens blared around us, emanating from every speaker mounted in the walls. "Unauthorized access. Recursion Core Three. Units respond," the intercom barked. I could hear boots on the floor outside and radios chattering.

"Quick," I motioned to her, "take what you can grab."

But Alicia was already moving, stuffing the smallest items into her coat—ledger cards, a brass file tag, and a small memo that lay on the desk. I grabbed a handful of folders and shoved them into my own coat, jamming them under my belt where they would be secure.

Glancing around wildly, I spotted a low service hatch, half-hidden behind a bank of cable conduits. I dropped to one knee, spun the latches, and the panel popped free with a sigh of cold air.

"Down!" I said.

We slid into the cable trench, the air warm and stale, the smell of hot dust and insulation overwhelming. I wrinkled my nose in disgust as I pulled the hatch shut above us and flicked off my torch. Seconds later, I heard the thunder of boots and voices in the laboratory we'd just left. Someone's torch flickered over the vent for only a second, illuminating my face. I silently hoped they hadn't seen me.

"Someone or something, activated it—the core's hot," a voice snapped overhead, angry and commanding. "No intruders found yet—but there is one. 6F's badge was used for entry. Sweep the floor. Every inch if you have to."

There were several voices, but Alicia and I didn't wait. We crawled along silently in the cramped space, barely able to move because of the size of the trench, inching along as silently as we could.

I could still hear the echo of the speaker above our heads. "Unauthorized access," it blared again and again.

We passed hatch after hatch, but each time I shook my head when Alicia glanced back at me. It felt as if it took hours, and my knees began to ache. My muscles stung. After a while, another trench split off from the main one, and we crawled along it until we reached another hatch—this one opening up to a blast of fresh lake air and the night sky. I tried to unscrew it—once, twice, and again—but each time I couldn't quite grab the small bolts that fastened it shut.

"Damn it," I cursed.

"Let me try," Alicia called back gently.

"No, not yet—" I could hear the boots thundering above us. I didn't know if we had time. I pulled the 6F badge out of my coat pocket. "Let me try something."

I carefully unwrapped it from the handkerchief and held it in my hand. I could feel it burning my skin, and it began to glow red hot, hissing wildly. Then, I pressed it firmly against one of the bolts on the grate—and sure enough, a second later, the bolt sheared loose and fell into the dark.

I burned the next, then the next, and the gate sagged on the last bolt. With a shove, it popped off, and I slid out carefully into the slick, dark, damp world we had left behind. My hand hurt, but I could feel the pain going away as soon as I wrapped the badge again. I pressed flat against the cement as floodlights combed up and down the foggy slope. I could hear voices shouting in the distance, and radios crackled.

"Not back yet... left instead," I whispered, and she followed behind me. Instead of heading back toward the jeep directly, we dropped down the slope toward the shore, crawling between trees and behind rocks. The ground turned from wet, moist peat to spongy shoreline, and our feet made no sound as we silently vanished into the night.

I found a hiding place wedged between two large boulders and several trees that sheltered us from view. We waited with bated breath, watching from a distance as a search team moved here and there, shining lights in the culverts for several minutes before they vanished back into ANGUS.

When the lights finally dimmed and silence reigned again, we made our way back uphill, pulling ourselves up the steep incline until it began to stabilize and become flat once more.

Stumbling through the darkness, for we dared not light our torches, we finally made our way back to the forestry track, which surfaced from the fog like a long-forgotten friend. I still kept low, motioning any directions to Alicia as she followed behind. When the jeep came into view, I froze for a second, listening. There was no sound of engines, no barking dogs, and no footsteps against the moss—simply silence.

"Go," Alicia said, her voice cutting through the silence, and we hurried back to the jeep.

I leapt into my seat, turning the key. It stuttered to life, and we rolled it idly down the road until it became gravel, and we finally made our way back to the main path.

Only then did I pause to remove the light covers and guide us away from Loch Duich.

CHAPTER 16
ARCHIVE ASTONISHMENT

Silence hung heavily in the air around the inn. It felt like a warning. One wrong move, and we were done for. It was the kind of silence that sits in your very bones—the kind you feel before the rain comes. Every time, it's inevitable… and every time, you can feel it, inching ever closer.

We took the upstairs room again; it was the only thing that wasn't already damp. The same inn we'd used the night before now sheltered us once more. Heat from the fires below seeped into the walls, making our room slightly warmer than it would have been otherwise. But it wasn't much, and I still felt the chill in the air.

I spread out what we had looted from the vault across the small bedside table. The folders were still warm as I pulled them from beneath my coat, and Alicia did the same. It wasn't much, but it was better than nothing.

Alicia stripped off her coat and her clothes and hung them over the chair back to dry. She glanced out the small window, looking down at the street. I knew she was thinking what I was and hoping we hadn't been tracked. If they had found our tire tracks, they could find us here.

She lit a cigarette, sat on the edge of the bed, and stared up at the ceiling. For a minute, we listened to the rain—the solid patter against the roof and the wind sweeping across the hills.

As we sat there, the radio in the attaché case crackled to life, and a voice spoke. "ANGUS was always a trap. Oracle needs an anchor."

The voice echoed through the room, steadier than ever, and more human than we had ever heard it before. Then it went silent.

Alicia glanced at me, her skin pale in the lamplight. "An anchor," she said.

Her eyes rested on my face for a second too long before she looked away. The word didn't need a question mark; I knew what she was thinking. It was me.

I opened one of the folders we'd stolen from the vault and laid it across my legs, joining her where she sat on the bed. The file contained information about an early Entanglement Unit, complete with a Bureau stamp and dated only four days before the Rosyth Dockyard incident. The information was mostly a blueprint, but it was enough that they would have been able to build almost anything we had. From my limited knowledge, Entanglement Units were one of the core quantum technologies used in building any Mirror. Even though it was an early version, having access to this blueprint would have given MI6 almost everything they needed.

"We saw Philby's name on Oracle," Alicia said suddenly. "What do you think that means?"

I was silent for a second. She had reminded me of my own photograph pinned right next to the terminal itself, but I pushed those thoughts out of my mind. "I'm not sure what it means," I said. "But I don't think they're just copying us. I don't think they just copied the Mirror. I think that is our Mirror."

"What do you mean?"

"I think somehow they stole Bureau technology," I sighed. "Not just blueprints—actual pieces."

Silence fell between us, and we fumbled through the rest of

the files, fatigue addling our minds. The files were relatively bland and felt incomplete. However, I did notice the covers. Almost every cover was marked in a nondescript municipal hand that wrote "EDINBURGH ORDINANCES, NAVAL RESEARCH," complete with the stamps of the main Bureau office located in Edinburgh. I had been there many times, so much so that I had no trouble remembering the address. There was no mistaking it. I flipped one of the files over, examining it closer. Sure enough, the Bureau's old cataloging system was stamped on the back. Whatever MI6 was hiding had likely been misfiled into some anonymous storage in Edinburgh—buried in the Bureau's sub-basement archives.

"Classic," Alicia said, exhaling smoke. "The Bureau was always one for burying things, not burning them. And if MI6 learned from the Bureau, then they would have misfiled it sideways in a place no one bothered to pull."

"They learned from the best of us," I said. "And we learned from them. Remember, many of our agents used to work for MI6. Whoever did this was an insider—not just MI6, but the Bureau as well."

It reminded me of Finch. Finch—the man who had worked with me after the Istanbul mission, where I had first met Alicia. Finch. Always eager—almost too eager—to join the Bureau. But he had left the Bureau soon after joining and returned to MI6 after disagreements. I didn't say anything to Alicia yet, but I had my suspicions.

"Get some sleep," I finally told Alicia as I caught her blinking a little too slowly.

She nodded without arguing and lay down on the bed. No clothes and no blanket. Her face was serene, and her body peaceful.

I dimmed the lamp and cracked open a bottle of Scotch I'd requested at the counter earlier when we booked the room. I pored over the folders and files we had found, but there was little of use within them. My memories were blurring, too, and I could barely remember where we were now. I closed my eyes, mentally repeating everything in my head. The last word I said was "Edinburgh." Edinburgh. That was where we needed to go.

I sighed, finished skimming the last file, and turned off the light. I glanced out the window one last time to check on our jeep. It was still there, still untouched. A few doors down, however, my eyes caught sight of a car. The windows were black, reflecting the sky. Whatever car this was, it wasn't local. It was far too clean and far too still.

I carefully took my gun from my coat pocket, and as I lay in bed next to Alicia, I made sure it was within reach. I slept only halfway, my mind always awake even if my body slept.

———

We were off before the first light. The road southward was a slow drive through wet moorland. Alicia navigated, one finger tracing the map as she held on to the radio. It had been sputtering all morning, speaking gibberish for the most part.

The car from the night before kept its distance in the mirror—sometimes a dark smudge on the horizon, other times almost close enough to see who was driving it. But all the while, it followed us as the radio mumbled on, speaking incomprehensible words.

"...sub-basement… Edinburgh… anchor… sub… basement… Edin…"

It wasn't much, but it was something. The car that had been following us trailed us all the way, including across the Queen's Ferry to the city's outskirts, before finally peeling off toward Leith as if it hadn't ever been following us, but I knew better.

"Shall we tell the Bureau we're here?"

"Well, I'd be very surprised if they didn't already know," I answered.

Telling a desk officer we were Bureau seemed inevitable. We were no longer sifting through old, forgotten files in an abandoned safe house. We were heading for the main thing: the Bureau's Edinburgh Station, the official repository for everything filed away during and after the war.

The Station occupied a Georgian townhouse just off Charlotte Square, the kind of address that promised respectability at first glance and secrecy once you stepped inside. The stone façade had been scrubbed clean, the paint fresh enough to smell faintly of turpentine. The brass knocker shone too brightly for the soot-dark street surrounding it. Curtains remained drawn no matter the hour, with light leaking only as a narrow seam across the sills.

Inside, the air carried a mix of polish and old paper—the kind of polished quiet that said upper echelon. The front hall was narrow, floored with chequered tile worn smooth by boots that never stayed long. A single electric lamp hung above the stairs, humming quietly, its filament caged in frosted glass. Somewhere deeper in the house, typewriter keys clacked and then stopped.

A small bell over the door chimed as we entered—soft and precise, as if it was timed to remind visitors they were being noticed. Behind a mahogany counter sat a clerk in a dark waist-coat, ledger open to a blank page. He looked up slowly, as if I'd broken the rhythm of a day devoted to silence. Everything about the place suggested civility—polished banister, framed naval prints, a faint smell of lemon oil—but the stillness underneath told a different story.

Past the hall, narrow doors led to rooms lined with steel filing cabinets disguised as bookshelves. Each drawer bore small stenciled codes instead of titles. The farther back you went, the colder it got, the hum of machinery rising under the floorboards. Somewhere below, beneath the varnish and bureaucracy, the real archive waited—the Bureau's heart beating slowly under layers of respectability.

I nodded, and the counter clerk nodded back. "What do you need?"

I handed him our clearance without a word. He studied it for a moment. "Temporary status noted," he said. "Follow me."

"I suppose that's how it works these days," I said. "Where are the archives?"

"Archives?" he asked.

"Yes, archives. I'm aware that this Bureau location is used to store away secrets."

"Mundane ones," he said.

I nodded, confirming those were exactly what I wanted.

He sighed as if it were a major inconvenience and showed us the stairs. We descended three flights until we reached the archive level, a labyrinth of metal shelves and filing cabinets blanketed with dust.

I motioned to Alicia. "Let's split up. You hunt for any misfiles. I'll look for absences."

And so we did. I searched carefully, looking for anything out of place—drawers that felt like they should have had weight but didn't, labels too inconspicuous for their own good. Whoever had been through here had filed things away tidily. There wasn't much to find.

Half an hour into the cold, boring monotony, I heard her voice from the next aisle. It wasn't loud, but it was urgent.

"Max."

She was kneeling, a folder balanced on her knees. The cover title was bold: "Naval Ordinances, Rosyth Dockyard, 1945." She flipped it open.

Inside were Bureau technical specifications—component lists I knew by heart—the same ones I'd once seen Hawthorne poring over late at night on the missions we used to run together. Shipping manifests stamped with a date I knew too well—the date of the incident.

She spread a page on the floor and tapped it. "Move... secure storage, 1715. Items—Entanglement units, 4. Resonator coils, 12. Coupled frame assemblies, 2. Prototype paneling, misc. Signed ... S.FINCH."

I was astonished. That name sealed it. I shook my head in disbelief. "But I was there," I said. "Wouldn't I have noticed a train of boxes rolling past me?"

She didn't answer. Her eyes were already on the next page, scanning all the clearance stamps, the Section IV ink where it didn't belong, and the storage records with no addresses. Everything we needed.

We kept digging deeper into the drawers near where Alicia had found the "Naval Ordinances" file. At the bottom of one, I found something else: metal cans labeled "DOCUMENTATION. PERSONNEL RECORDS—CLASSIFIED." The exact date of the dockyard incident was scrawled in fine handwriting along the bottom.

"What do you think is in these?" I asked, tossing them lightly in my hands.

"Let's find out," she replied. "There should be a projector room or a viewing room down here, right?"

I nodded and led her toward the far end of the archives. I'd seen the door earlier as we had passed it. The viewing room was the size of a crate, barely large enough for both of us. I threaded the reel—my hands moved through as if I'd done it a thousand times before. The screen flickered to life. The date code in the corner confirmed everything I suspected.

Rosyth, whole and alive, just as it had been before the incident. Men moving about. Crates wheeled through the far door. And in the foreground, there I was—the younger me, at my station—standing there, oblivious. The timestamp said it was thirty minutes before the blast.

"What is this?" I asked, my voice hoarse. "What are we watching?"

Alicia touched the screen's edge. "The Germans ran a closed-circuit system in 1942 for weapons. We stole it. Officially live only, but unofficially, we had a recording capability, even during the dockyard incident." She watched my face carefully. "This could have been recorded. It's not out of the question. Or maybe it's a fake, designed to make you doubt your memories, Max. Careful."

"Either way," I said, "I need to watch."

The first reel ended, and I put on the second. I saw Krane now, the light reflecting off his glasses. He was talking to someone just out of frame. He pointed toward the Mirror chamber, that familiar glimmer in his eyes when he spoke about his one true love—what he considered his creation. Then the image jumped. A cut. Something had been removed.

"Right there," Alicia said, squinting. "Something was inserted on the leader. Someone scrubbed something out and left just enough."

I sat back. "What does that mean?"

"I'm not sure," she said. "But whatever they removed, you don't remember either."

I nodded, my face cold. "They changed my memories," I said. "Changed what I saw." Because there I was again, in the room, oblivious—as if Krane didn't exist. I stood in the background this time, but I knew this was never a memory I had.

"There are two more," Alicia finally said after the silence stretched and the reel finished. She reached into her coat and pulled out two small wire spools, each labeled "TIDAL RESEARCH." Not video, but audio. The wire recorder in the corner whirred to life. Static, and then voices, clear.

"...the schedule," Krane's voice was clipped and irritated. "You want it done, you don't cut my time down."

Then another voice, smooth as polished marble. I recognized it, even though I'd only heard it once all those years ago. H. A. R. Philby.

"The components must be clear before you overload," he said. "Overpulsing will ruin everything. Give me five more minutes—five minutes prior to overpulsing—and my men will take possession of what we need."

"Your men," Krane said. "You will not do this on my floor without—"

"We'll do it where it's least visible," Philby interrupted, amused, as if Krane were a subject animal he was entertaining. "Hawthorne's clock isn't my clock, Krane. You know damn well that's why we're doing it at night when the Bureau won't be supervising your experiment."

"I suppose…" Krane's voice trailed off in dissatisfaction.

"And what of Calder?" Philby asked.

"Calder is the anchor point," Krane said. "The machine needs him awake and nearby to hold the phase. We'll initiate when he's in the station."

"What of his memories?" Philby said.

"He won't remember a thing. Before I overload the thing, I'll make sure to fry his memories."

The recording broke up—other voices bled in, voices that shouldn't have been on the line. In the tangle of words and sounds, someone said my name. One voice in particular—raspy, dark—curled around the edges of my own. Familiar and wrong. And then the wire cut to silence.

I stared into the darkness, unwilling to hear what I had just heard. But the noise was already in my ears. I didn't want to believe it. I didn't want to admit it. And yet I had heard everything.

Alicia spoke at last, as if afraid I might lash out. I was too numb.

"So it wasn't an accident," she said softly. "They stole working pieces of the Mirror, turned you into an alibi, and killed everyone else—everyone else in the facility."

I didn't respond. Minutes ticked by. She waited for me to say something. I didn't. I didn't want to.

Footsteps pounded down the stairs in the distance—purposeful, not the slow shuffle of a bored clerk. The clerk's protesting voice echoed beyond the door of the room, and then another voice, sharp and deep, cut through.

"We have signed warrants under Whitehall authority. Step clear."

Alicia's eyes met mine, and I nodded, mute. She killed the machine. I flicked the projector bulb off. We gathered what we'd brought into the viewing room, tucked it into our coats, and slipped out.

The voices were at the corner now, down the hall, out of sight in the stacks. "Are there any visitors here? One would be male, tall. A scar on his left cheek or jaw, possibly traveling with a woman."

The clerk stuttered, but the man pressed on. "Our warrant says seizure of Rosyth material under joint audit…" The words trailed off.

"Let's move," I said.

Two doors down from the viewing room, there were no other exits, so we crouched in the dark behind a shelf and peered underneath until heavy boots strode past. At least five men followed the clerk, who nervously showed them the way. As they disappeared from view, we dashed for the stairs.

At the top, I glanced down the long hallway. Several more men stood at the entrance where the clerk had sat. I shook my head, slipped into a side door, and motioned for Alicia to follow. We navigated a web of corridors until I found a service exit and shouldered it open, grimacing as the hinges squealed.

A minute later, we were on the street. Edinburgh—busy, cold smoke in the air, a thin smear of sunlight through clouds. We didn't run; running gets you caught. We walked slowly, and I held the documents tight beneath my coat.

As we moved with the crowd, the radio crackled to life. Heads turned as the voice spilled through it: "They know you found proof. ANGUS was always a trap... Oracle needs an anchor. You've always been the anchor."

I sighed. I didn't want to hear the voice anymore. I knew all I needed to know now. The slide I'd experienced at the dockyard had all but confirmed it. I had sensed something was wrong, but I'd made up stories, lies, and alternate explanations. I'd tried to hide the truth from my memories, but I couldn't anymore. Now I had the evidence.

"What's next?" Alicia asked, her voice as numb as I felt.

"For now," I muttered, "we keep the papers. We keep the evidence. And we figure out the next step."

She adjusted her scarf, tucking the red fabric around her neck. "Max."

"What?" I asked. I couldn't muster anything else.

"If they changed what you saw," she said, "it wasn't your fault. They didn't change who you are."

I nodded.

Together, we vanished into the crowd. I didn't know our next step. But whatever it was, I wanted to end whatever had twisted my life into this.

I wanted to stop whoever caused the dockyard incident.

CHAPTER 17
FINDING FINCH

Only an hour later, we sat together in the jeep, the cold air lashing against the windscreen, and a small city map we'd picked up spread wide on the dashboard. The jeep was idling, but it did little to keep out that pervasive cold that seemed impossible to escape. I sighed, staring carefully at the map, squinting to see better in the dimming light. I squinted so I could see and focused so I could forget.

There was nothing more that I wanted to do right now than to forget. But how could I? I felt as if I were on the verge of breaking down—all I needed was one more push, and I'd go hurtling over the edge. I wanted to stop. To stop all this madness and return to Lisbon, defeated, losing my memories, but happier at that prospect. Memory had always been such a weird phenomenon to me. I valued my mind—valued my intellect and my recollection. And yet, now that I was presented with memories that had been hidden, I wanted nothing more than to forget.

Memories. Of Krane. Of Philby and their betrayal. It was cemented as fact now—Alicia knew full well, as did I, that Philby had somehow come to an agreement with Krane, and the two of them, and perhaps more, had plotted to remove Mirror materials and designs right from under my very nose.

They'd used me as a scapegoat to do it, and as the anchor to activate the damn device in the first place. I figured the plan had been simple: "If Calder can't remember when he resurfaces, then how will there be any foul play to track?"

I could hear Krane's voice echoing in my head now, though I wasn't sure if it was a memory that had returned to me or a false idea planted in my head by my newfound hatred of myself that was kindling itself like a fire.

"What now?" I was startled as Alicia spoke, interrupting my thoughts. Her voice was hoarse and tired. I knew she was feeling shocked, as was I.

Inside, I felt broken, shattered, as if there were nothing left to live for. But I focused. I focused because I knew she was counting on me.

"Now we must find Finch," I said. "Finch's name was on those ledgers. If anyone saw the sleight of hand—or was responsible for it—it was him. He was always friendly to me. But the fact that his name was there, to me, indicates he was also a traitor."

Alicia cocked her head, skimming my face with her unreadable gaze. "How friendly? Is it possible he's still a traitor?"

"I don't think so," I replied. "At most, he was an unwilling participant. Remember in Istanbul, he kept Elliott honest. Later, the Bureau brought him in. On paper, he died after the Dockyard —same as I did. But paperwork also says there was no theft."

"Then let's ask someone who might have the answer," Alicia suggested, reaching for the glove box.

"Any ideas?"

"I was hoping you might have a lead, Max. You used to work for MI6, after all."

I nodded slowly. "He'll be old by now," I said, "but my old MI6 handler might be willing to do me one favor."

She pulled a small purse of coins from where we'd stored them, and we made our way to the nearest phone booth. This one was my job. Though Alicia usually kept in contact with Bureau news and investigations, I was the one who dialed the phone and waited for the old man to pick up.

A voice answered after the third ring—old, likely in his seventies or eighties by now, gravelly but clear. I knew he hadn't expected to hear from me—the slight shock before he gathered himself gave his surprise away.

"What do you want?" he asked.

"I want to know about Finch," I said. "And before you say he's dead, don't. We both know that's not the case."

The voice sighed, then paused, as if he were contemplating how much to tell me. "Glasgow. An' don't call back."

With a click, the call ended. But it was enough. He wouldn't lie to me.

We hurried back to the jeep, taking the back roads west while the city slumbered. We passed lanes that slept, with only the occasional dog barking, and houses that were shuttered to keep out the cold. I kept our headlamps low as we coasted by a police cruiser that sat idling along the road. No one followed us yet. If MI6 were watching, or if they'd tailed us, they would have expected us to leave by the main road.

Soon, Glasgow's silhouette rose in the distance, darkened by smoke, coal, and grime. It was late, so we rented a cheap place off the river—the kind of hotel you only consider after inspecting the room first. It was a sleazy place, but here in Glasgow, it felt like home to me. I parked the jeep carefully behind a building near the hotel, in an alleyway, hoping it wouldn't be robbed or vandalized in the night. And we slept.

The next few days were a blur. Although the man had told us Glasgow, I feared that was all he had to offer—and all we had to go on. We sifted through the underworld, and I found my way back into places I'd sworn to leave behind. Finding Finch would be harder than we'd thought. Ancient bars where a man's name was worth less than his tab, small shops where smoke was thicker than smog, and whispers preceded any arrival. Alicia and I split up most days, talking and listening to men we didn't trust and thought even less of.

Eventually, caught a break. In a bar I'd frequented when I was young, a man nodded me over and motioned for me to sit. I took the seat. He kept his cap low, his face in shadow, and spoke in a low, gravelly voice. I knew his type—the kind who would trade secrets for whiskey and who would sell out his own mother for twopence.

Who he was specifically, I didn't know. Maybe he was a disgraced high-ranking government agent trying to buy his next drink, or a genius who had grown up on the streets, addicted to the bottle and the information he sold in equal measure. He was someone we called a "nose," and the streets called him a "tout."

"You looking for Finch?" he asked.

How the man knew his name was none of my business… just as it was likely none of his. I nodded. "You know his whereabouts?"

"It'll be a price." He grinned.

I slid over half a purse of money.

"A price more than that."

I sighed, sliding over the rest. He finally smiled again, more at ease.

"He's got a limp. Works as a porter now, from what I hear," the man said. "Talks to nobody, but everyone knows him. Goes by the name James Kerr. But be careful, Calder. You asking around like this has got people talking about you as well."

"Which station?" I asked.

"Central."

That was it. I met up with Alicia that night. "Central Station," I said without pause. "We'll have to leave the jeep here at the hotel. From what my source said, people have taken note of us."

"So we have to go ghost again?" she asked.

I chuckled. "Exactly. This reminds me of our jobs before… all that happened with Krane and the Mirror."

She nodded wordlessly. That was all that was needed. She'd been there for everything. We left the jeep where it was parked and made our way to Glasgow Central Station. It was a vast echo chamber of postwar Britain—part cathedral, part factory, part confessional for a city that hadn't yet caught its breath. The war had ended, but the station still operated on a wartime rhythm: efficient, weary, and slightly suspicious of good news.

Glasgow Central dominated the city's heart like a piece of Edwardian armor—seven acres of glass and iron spanning Argyle Street. From the outside, the main sandstone façade on Gordon Street was stained by a decade of coal smoke and rain. Pigeons roosted in the crevices of the clock tower; the clock itself ran five minutes fast, as if to remind travelers that Glasgow was a city that couldn't afford to be late.

Inside, the great train shed roof—a lattice of wrought iron and glass—filtered the light into a greenish haze. Some panes had been replaced after the Blitz, but others still bore the faint frosting from blackout paint. When the clouds broke, shafts of sunlight cut through the steam like spotlights searching for something that didn't want to be found.

The concourse was a geography lesson in motion. Soldiers still in service khaki shared benches with shipyard workers carrying tin lunch pails, while women in headscarves queued for the ticket windows under the British Railways (Scottish Region) signs that had been newly hung after nationalization. The old LMS initials were still ghosted on the stonework underneath. Vendors hawked tea from aluminum urns and meat pies that tasted of memory. The station tea rooms had returned to civilian use, though half their crockery was chipped RAF surplus. A sign at the buffet read "No Coupons Required," and that was reason enough for a crowd.

When the wind swept down from the Clyde, it carried the smell of shipyards and iron. The station's glass roof amplified it, trapping the scent until it became part of the architecture. I inhaled deeply. This was home. And if Finch was really here, I would find him.

Alicia tapped my shoulder twice, and I stopped. She'd seen him first. He was leaning against a pillar near the second-class side. He wore a gray wool newsboy cap pulled low over his eyes, his face gaunt and shallow, his flask lifted high as he drained it. I could tell from his stance that the limp was real. His face was haunted now—nothing like the jovial, slightly round face I'd known. But his eyes—I recognized those instantly. As intelligent as ever, though sunken deep, almost to the bone.

"Max," Alicia said softly. "He knows we're coming."

I nodded. "But he won't run. He never did like making a scene."

I walked up slowly, greeting him as if I were a passerby asking for directions. Alicia drifted to the right, her hand inside her coat, and I knew it was on her pistol.

"James Kerr, huh?" I said. "You haven't been keeping in contact."

His mouth twitched. "You were dead, Raven. They said so."

"That makes three of us," I said. "But who wrote the death certificates?"

He chuckled—a sad laugh, more hollow and empty than his face. "I've been hearing about you. Heard you've been nosing through basements, finding old files."

"I need the truth," I insisted. "I don't care if you were involved, Finch—at this point, it's a given. But I need something more."

He studied me, eyes raking me from head to toe. Finally, he spoke. "MI6 took it. Pieces. But you already know that. Before the Dockyard." He flinched, as if recalling a bad memory. "You think they built a Mirror from nothing but blueprints? They don't have the minds or the capability. Krane was one of a kind. They called it salvage, ran it right under your noses, and I stamped the right forms."

"Section IX," I said.

"And friends among them. We used your schemes and our trucks." He chuckled suddenly. "Well, back then, it was the opposite for me. Back then, when I worked with the Bureau—" His voice trailed off.

"Who else was involved?" I asked.

"Don't ask. You wouldn't want to know."

"So, Version Three? What do you know about Version Three?"

He laughed, and regret flickered in his eyes. "They didn't just stop at three, Max. There's a fourth. Far more dangerous and far more potent, if they can get it working. Can't say more than that."

I sighed, but before I could press him, Alicia cut in. "And Philby?"

Finch fixed his hollow eyes on her and smiled wryly. "He and I were close for a bit. Why do you think I worked with him? He didn't tell me what he'd planned at the yard, though. Didn't tell me what he was willing to do just to get pieces. He's a clever boy, I'll give him that. Didn't tell me he was gonna kill to get what he wanted."

"I know you, Finch," I said. "I know you're a good man... and I know you regret what you did. But if you're holding anything back..."

He didn't answer right away. His hands fumbled in his coat, and he drew out a small black envelope, placing it in my hand. "I'll atone for what I've done wrong. Only you open that," he said, his voice low. "Don't trust no one with it. Not a clerk, not a director, not the Nine. Don't trust no one, you hear?"

"What is it?" I pressed. "Come on, Finch. You've gotta know this is the end of the line for us. We need something more."

"I've been looking," he said, his eyes darting as if he were being watched. "Philby isn't just MI6, he's—"

A crack split the air, violent and loud. Finch's head snapped forward, a bloody hole where his eye should have been. His body hung in midair for a second, arms falling limp to his sides, the flask slipping from his fingers. Alicia caught his shoulders before he collapsed and gently slid him down onto the platform, her hands already moving.

My gun was in my palm before I knew it. I scanned the girders and spotted the shooter where the roof trusses met at an angle—a dark shape in a service uniform, too still and out of place to be a worker, though his face was obscured. He ran sideways along the roof, then suddenly he vanished like a whisper in the wind, either dropping through a hatch before I could mark it or fading into smoke, gone without a trace.

A whistle blew, then another. I crouched, my gun low along my leg, watching for other angles from which a man could shoot. I still wasn't sure who the intended target was, but it didn't seem to be us. The man had only taken one shot—clean, precise—and then gone.

Alicia searched Finch's body quickly. He was already dead. There was nothing we could do for him now.

"Nothing but coins," she cursed. "A ticket stub. Half a map. Nothing else. Do you have the envelope?"

"It's on me," I replied.

Uniformed officers began to converge on the commotion. I slid the pistol back into my coat and nodded to her. She was on her feet in a heartbeat. Before we could be questioned by the police, we melted into the luggage and the crowd and made it out to the southern end of Hope Street, near the junction with Argyle Street.

Rain lashed my hat as I stepped into the street once more. We didn't talk, and we didn't run. Instead, we quietly and calmly traced our way back to the hotel, my hand resting on my gun the whole time.

———

As we neared the hotel—two blocks away—I stopped dead. A second later, I pulled Alicia into the shadows.

A black vehicle idled at the alley mouth where our jeep was parked. Another sat across from the hotel lobby, lights off. At the hotel itself, two men stood near the door, pretending to read newspapers and smoke, but by their posture and the way their eyes swept the street, they were as far from ordinary guests as you could get.

"They've already searched our rooms," I said. "I'd bet money on it. And our jeep will light us up the second we go near it."

"Think it's the same ones from Lisbon?" Alicia asked.

"Could be," I replied. "Could be the same people who hired the assassin to take us out. Whoever dropped Finch timed us to the minute."

"We can't go back," she said.

I nodded. "Let's get to a safe house. There's one still on the ledger. I remember where. It's likely decommissioned by now. Dead, just like Finch was supposed to be... and I suppose is, now."

On the way, we stopped at a phone booth. Alicia fished in her pocket for coins.

"You or me?" she asked.

I knew what she meant. "You're better," I said. "They'll answer your call, and they actually like you."

She lifted the receiver. A few seconds later, a voice came through the phone. "Operator." The voice had the polite, flat English accent I knew too well.

"Artemis," Alicia said, and gave the key phrases.

A pause, then another voice came on the line—whoever this was, it wasn't the operator anymore. A woman's tone, masked by an accent I couldn't quite place.

"What's the report?" the voice asked. For a second, I thought I heard a flicker of sorrow in it, but then it was gone.

"A shooting at Central Station," Alicia said. "Subject Finch. Alias James Kerr. He's dead. Source admitted MI6 took pieces from the Dockyard. Confirmed Section IX and confirmed Version Three, with potential advancements beyond it. Sniper took him out, disappeared after." She hesitated. "We'd like an official assessment and investigation. Is this tied to the Lisbon attempt? Did MI6 or the Bureau have anything to do with it?"

Silence. For a moment, I thought the line had dropped. Then the woman spoke again.

"The Lisbon attempt was not this," she said. "It was a rogue sub-cell within the Bureau. We have identified them and are in the process of weeding them out. The incident will not recur. Whoever the shooter was today, it wasn't Bureau-sanctioned. And we have no intelligence linking it to MI6 either. Be cautious. Go off-grid if you can."

"Acknowledged," Alicia said.

"One more thing," the voice added, as if it were an afterthought. "Don't open anything you were given in public. Keep it safe until you can read it without prying eyes."

The line went dead.

We kept moving. By the time we reached the decommissioned safe house on the outskirts, night had settled. It was a two-story building covered in bad plaster, almost at the edge of the Gorbals. I shivered; my distaste was plain for anyone to see, but I didn't care—I had never wanted to return so close to where I'd grown up.

Inside, the air was stale. The Bureau had stripped the place years ago. Only a kettle, a chair, and some dust remained.

I rolled my shoulders, feeling the stiffness in my bones. "Well, I guess we sleep on the floor tonight."

She nodded.

We spoke in low voices about our next steps. "Philby," I said. "If he's been playing the Bureau, he might be playing MI6 as well. Finch seemed to confirm that, too."

"Then we find him," Alicia replied.

She glanced at my coat. "Shall we open the package?"

Without another word, I opened the envelope.

Inside were only a strip of negatives and a key, with no

signage to indicate what they were. I carefully slid them both into an inner coat pocket and buttoned it closed.

"Any idea what those are?" Alicia asked.

"Not sure."

"Well, that's not as helpful as I had hoped."

"Wish he'd gotten more time to finish his sentence before he died."

"We're running out of friends," Alicia mused suddenly.

"We never had many to begin with," I responded. "But you're right. Luckily, we've got enough for now."

She lit a cigarette. In here, in this abandoned safe house, cold to the bone, cigarettes were the only warmth we had.

"Who do you think's behind the shot?" she asked. "Philby?"

"No. It feels too loud for Philby or MI6. Besides, the voice on the phone—she'd have let it slip if MI6 had a hand. From what I gather, that was one of the higher-ups."

"Who do you think it was?" Alicia asked.

"I'm not sure," I replied. "But she spoke with confidence. She's someone important."

We fell silent. I unrolled the half map we'd taken from Finch's pocket and, taking the negatives back out, laid them beside it. The map showed a coastline, jagged and weathered. The tear in the map was almost too neat to be an accident. Still, there wasn't much here. I didn't know what to do next.

"What are you thinking?" Alicia asked, her voice cutting through the silence.

"I'm thinking that Philby might not be just MI6. Finch tried to warn us, and the moment he did, he died. If Philby's been playing the Bureau, he's been playing MI6 too. The man can't be trusted. Maybe the Soviets, maybe someone else. But wherever his loyalties lie, I know it's not with us—and I don't think it's with MI6."

"So what's our plan?" she asked.

"We have enough information for the Bureau to go after MI6," I said. "That's not the problem anymore. However,"—I tapped the side of my head—"we need to find Philby himself, press him, see exactly what makes him tick."

"Are you up for it?" Alicia asked.

I sighed. All the memories of these past few days came rushing back, uninvited. "I don't think I have a choice," I said.

She nodded. "Well then, let's get some sleep."

"Tomorrow," I said. "Tomorrow, we'll find Philby."

CHAPTER 18
GLASGOW GAMBIT

We never got the chance to find Philby. The next morning, bright and early, a paper had been slid beneath our door. I woke to the city stirring—the trams humming, the smell of coal, and the bustle of commuters outside. As we descended the creaking stairs from the bedroom, I saw the note wedged under the front door. The safehouse door didn't offer much protection against the elements, as the crack beneath it was more than an inch high. Sliding a note underneath it had been child's play.

I picked it up. It was hotel stock, folded carefully. On it was scrawled a time and a signature.

Meet 1300. H.A.R.P.

I wrinkled my nose. "Philby," I said.

"He's taking the initiative," Alicia said, dropping to the floor and crossing her legs. There was nowhere to sit except for the chair that looked nearly unusable. "He's known we've been onto him for quite some time—or wants us to think we're on the right path."

"Either way," I said, holding the paper up to the window's

light, "we go." The hotel crest was embossed in the corner, reading "Grand Central Hotel," though there was no watermark beyond that—no sign of anything hidden. "No Bureau. Not yet."

"We'll tell them after?" she asked.

I nodded reluctantly. "After."

We dressed in silence. As I pulled on my coat and combed my hair, my hand brushed the lump of Finch's envelope. The negatives and the key rested comfortably in my pocket. Whoever had shot him, I wanted revenge.

"Well, at least now we have Finch's word that everything ties together," Alicia said. "We have the signage—and we saw that Rosyth wasn't a ruin. And that Oracle was built… and working."

"And now," I said, "we get to talk to Philby. There are only two missing links."

"Which are they?" she asked.

"Number one: wherever the variants or echoes are coming from. And number two: whatever Finch was trying to tell us. I don't think Philby is just MI6."

She watched my face. "You think he's working more than two sides?"

"I think he's working more sides than there are on a die," I replied. "I don't know where his true loyalty lies, but we're going to find out."

We left the safehouse, walking through the dim Glasgow morning. Before heading to Glasgow Central Station on Gordon Street, we backtracked to our original hotel from the night before and found our jeep. No one lingered near it anymore. We pulled our briefcase, the attaché radio, and the rest of our belongings from the vehicle, then set off for the address on the note. I opted to leave the jeep behind for now—by now, it was clear that whoever was tracking us knew about our vehicle.

The Grand Central Hotel was a Queen Anne-style monument to endurance—still beautiful, still standing, but carrying every year of the century on its shoulders. Its glamour had hardened into something else: discretion. The war had left marks on its walls and in its service, but it remained a crossroads for anyone moving between past and future. Built into the eastern façade of Glasgow Central Station, it was only walking distance from where, only the night before, Finch had met his demise.

This hotel was much nicer than where we'd previously stayed. Inside, the reception hall opened like the nave of a church—high ceilings, marble pillars, and a checkerboard floor worn smooth by half a century of boots and heels. The light came from chandeliers that had survived the Blitz but not the blackout paint still clinging to their crystal drops. Everything smelled faintly of coal dust, furniture polish, and the scent of alcohol—the standard postwar perfume of Britain in recovery.

For me, it was exactly the kind of place that felt safe because it was too tired to care who you were—a place where secrets blended with the smoke and left through the same revolving door as the guests.

Alicia and I found our way to the hotel bar, once a temple to whisky and cigars, now surviving on blended scotch and black-market cigarettes. The barman, a veteran with one good eye, mixed drinks with military precision. American servicemen occasionally drifted in, talking too loudly about dollars and jazz. Everyone needed someone to blame or envy. We took a corner booth near the back exit. I put my back to the wall, and she took the seat just off the aisle, angling her legs to clear the way if it came to that. I watched the door like a hawk; though I didn't expect Philby to set a trap, we couldn't be too sure.

"For diplomatic relations," Alicia murmured. "I doubt they'll paint this place red in broad daylight or try anything else too funny."

"I agree, especially with our official Bureau backing by now. But who knows how far they'll go otherwise?"

She nodded.

Philby arrived exactly on time. Neat, fashionable, well-dressed—tailored coat, polished shoes, and expensive cloth. His boyish smile could have charmed the harshest schoolmaster, but there was a strain behind it, and his eyes were sleek and cunning. H. A. R. Philby was a man who had rehearsed every inch of his appearance. He scanned the room at a glance, then his eyes fixed on me. He slid into the booth across from us. No hat, no gloves.

"Kim," I said, looking at him with distaste.

"Hello, Max," he replied, a curious smile playing on his face.

"Funny, isn't it? How we're all supposed to be on the same side of things, and yet… Well, here we are?"

"Well, I'd like to think it's just a part of the job," he responded. "These things are never easy, but still…"

"You know," I said, "you seem to know a lot more than you let on, Kim. Tell me something: MI6, the Bureau… everything you've been working for here. What's your goal?"

"What about yours, Max?"

"What do you mean?"

"You're not asking the right question." He sighed, glancing at his watch as if he had somewhere to be. "We're all pawns; everyone is. But that's the point, isn't it? Either you're a pawn or you're not—but the game always moves forward. It never ends, even if you're in control."

"Well then, Philby—tell us what exactly you control. You're good at your job, I'll give you that—but you wanted to meet for a reason."

"Oh, that," Philby laughed. "Ah, Max. We're not on the same side, but that's the nature of the game. However—" He paused for effect. "—you've become quite the thorn in my side lately. You and Artemis here."

"I'm flattered," Alicia said.

"So am I," I nodded at him. "But I fail to see the reason for our conversation."

"I'm giving you a chance, Max. Consider it a warning—this game you're playing is nothing compared to mine. Drop it now, or you'll realize only too soon that you're the pawn… of everyone."

"Speaking of being everyone's pawn," I said, "how's that going for you, Philby?"

"Right, right," he chuckled. "You mean MI6? Well, Max, that's really none of your concern—you no longer work for us."

"MI6, among others."

His face twitched slightly, as if I'd struck a sore spot. "What is it you're claiming, exactly?"

"Nothing more or less than MI6 stealing the Mirror… or at least, pieces of it. Are you going to deny that?"

"Not at all," he replied, "since I suppose the cat's out of the bag now."

I watched his face carefully. Something didn't sit right with me—it was as if he was giving up this information too easily, as if he didn't care what we knew, so long as it was only about MI6.

We continued to speak, Alicia watching the door carefully. I was grateful for her—she always had my back, even now. Philby never mentioned Oracle, not once, but when he called it "technical consolidation," I could see his smile falter. He didn't deny Rosyth either, and he smiled when Alicia mentioned the radar trials.

"Most of it was Krane's idea anyway," he said, laughing. "Krane hated Hawthorne, you know—he really did."

"But I doubt Krane made the plans," I shot back.

"Oh, you're right," he responded, "and I'd deny every single thing on record. You see, nothing you have—none of the evidence—will ever make it to court. Because—" He paused, gesturing between Alicia and me—"you trespassed to get it."

"All the evidence? How sure are you of that?" I asked him. I didn't let him see in my eyes that I knew he was largely correct. The only evidence we had collected legitimately was bits and pieces, circumstantial ones, that wouldn't hold up in court, and I doubted it would get us anywhere. We'd be tied down with years of litigation if the Bureau tried to pursue it officially.

"I know you've been to Invershiel," he said, laughing again.

"Max, there are more players than you realize. The only reason I even asked for this meeting was to warn you."

"Warn me? Philby, you've always been the type to play both sides. Take what you can from the board and keep the game to yourself."

"I'm flattered, Max. But if this is a game of influence, I've already won."

"Have you? There are liabilities everywhere, Philby. The truth has a way of catching up to everyone—I've found that out firsthand."

"Not to me."

"How so? What do you think will stop it?"

He paused, almost as if debating what to say next. Finally, he spoke. "The target is on you now, Max."

"What do you mean by that?" I asked.

"I mean," he said, lighting a cigarette, "you should drop it. Now."

"What do you mean? Who's after me?"

"You'll know soon enough," he smiled. "But I'm done here. Either come to your own conclusion or find out the hard way. I'm off to London—have to be there by morning. Your last chance to let me know your final decision will be tonight."

He set his lighter on the table, stood, smoothed his jacket, and turned without a backward glance.

Alicia and I sat there for several minutes, motionless.

"Well," she said at last, "on the plus side, you always did look good with a target on your back."

"I've had more than I can count," I said. "And he admitted to more than he had to. That's the tell."

"What do you mean, Max?" she asked, her eyes still on the door.

"He admitted to MI6 and its theft so quickly you'd think that was all there was," I replied. "But Finch had already started to say it, remember? Philby isn't just MI6. Finch died before he could tell us, but I have my suspicions. Whoever Philby's performing for, it's someone who's not MI6—someone who benefits from us thinking it is. Even more fascinating, I think Philby requesting this meeting and trying to scare us away was a bluff on his part. If we really couldn't harm him by researching MI6's schemes, why would he try to stop us? He doesn't care about us personally, so there's no reason to warn us of anything. He's afraid—afraid we'll find out who he really works for."

"And how do we prove that?" she asked. It wasn't impatience; she just didn't see where we could go next.

I rubbed my forehead, feeling tired. "I'm not sure. We'll have to use what we have: the negatives, the keys, the files—even the radio, if we can get the voice to talk again."

"And the Bureau?"

"We'll give the Nine what they need without giving them any more," I said. "Let's tell them he conceded 'consolidation' and that we have corroboration across three sites. They can pursue Broadway while we try to find more."

She nodded.

As we stood to leave, the room began to spin. I knew what was coming—a partial slide. There it was: a foggy but unmistakable memory of Cambridge. I saw Philby as if through my own eyes—not my younger self's eyes, not the version who had been at Cambridge, but an older me. Philby was leaning against a stained-glass window, telling me something, and I felt anger as he spoke. Then the scene split, and I was back in the bar. I cursed in my mind as I tried to grab onto the memories—the memories I was sure I hadn't known before. How did I know Philby back at Cambridge? How... and for a second, I remembered that one fleeting meeting I'd had with Philby all those years ago at MI6.

Was this what he had been referencing? But no—the memories were fading again, slipping out of my grasp as if they had never been there to begin with.

"Max?" Alicia's voice was tight with concern. "What happened?"

"Nothing," I replied. "Later."

"Do you want to sit down?"

"No. Later."

We walked out. I lit a cigarette. In my coat pocket, I kept the note from Philby. Even if Alicia wasn't entirely sure, I was already convinced.

He was working for someone, and I was going to find out who.

CHAPTER 19
KIM AND KRANE

Kim Philby had never been one to be surprised by his own lies. He followed the gray path of falsehood as easily as he wore his suits, keenly aware of which of his own flaws were known to others. He had a knack for it. Broadway had taught him well that the real truth was what others believed—not what actually existed.

He had been working for Broadway when he first heard mention of it. It wasn't a name—not at first, at least. It was encrypted Bureau traffic that bled across a narrow band retained by Section IX, consisting of small five-letter groups in an unfamiliar cadence. Yet, everything seemed to spiral around one word—one noun—that he didn't have access to. He had dedicated his time to it, whatever that thing was.

As time went on, Philby brought his discovery to the men in charge of MI6—powerful figures like Victor Haldane, who had endorsed his discovery and championed it as something they should pursue.

"Yes," Haldane said as he rifled through the papers Philby had presented. "I believe we should make... tactical advancements toward this technology. What say you, Kim?"

"I'd readily agree," Philby replied, "so long as I'm one of the players in charge of the repossession of it… and the infiltration."

He spoke so bluntly, and Victor, always the man who respected power, agreed. Of course, it hadn't really been Victor's decision… nothing had. Philby planted the idea so expertly, so tactfully, that Victor thought it was. The theft was to be executed under the belief that MI6 could use the Mirror to secure British supremacy in the power clash between the two competing agencies, as well as global espionage struggles, particularly against the Soviet Union. And so, by September 18th, 1945, Philby had made contact with a man inside the Bureau ranks—a man by the name of Emil Krane, who had promised him the world—and more—due to his dissatisfaction with his current status.

He snuck into Rosyth Naval Dockyard late one night under the cover of darkness. It was easy to get in. Krane himself had paved the way for him. And so, only hours later, he stood next to crates with "RADAR TRIALS" stenciled across their flanks—crates that had fake manifests and everything else fake, except for their signatures. The signatures were the trick. With the help of Finch, another MI6 loyalist, several scientists and guards MI6 had paid off or blackmailed, and Krane, it would be easy to reroute any crates they needed far away from The Bureau and toward Kingsway and Invershiel.

Krane met him in a thin corridor near a bend where their conversation would not be caught by prying eyes or ears. Krane was always the sort of man who seemed fanatical, and Philby resented him for it, but he never said as much.

"So," Krane began, without introduction, "what do you need from me?"

Philby smiled politely. "Well," he replied, "you're the scientist. I don't understand this thing, so you need to tell us how to move it… you said you'll pulse it?"

At once, Krane responded, "An anchor. Not the device—the system. It's alive, you see. And the brain—the brain gives weight to the waveforms. Your people don't understand this."

Philby nodded—politely, though he didn't understand it either. "My people," he said, "we will ensure that you have your time and that you have your escape. We have a plan."

Krane's mouth twitched at the edges. "Plans are good," he said.

The facility beneath the dockyard was now mostly empty, with only a few scientists and guards remaining, and none near the Mirror itself. Krane guided Philby carefully along, past the observation gallery, toward the central amphitheater. In the center stood the Mirror itself, and next to it a tall man with a scar on his jawline, who stood with a clipboard, half-turned away.

"Is that—" Philby hesitated, trying to remember his name. "Is that Max Calder?"

"Calder," Krane confirmed. "He's ignorant, but he's essential. The machine and he have a certain connection. He's the anchor for it. He'll be here tomorrow as well."

Krane continued walking, and Philby followed him. The first two crates had already been stamped properly.

"ISRB/KINGSWAY," Philby said, glancing at the crates. "That'll do for now. Invershiel later."

"Finch, sign the crates," Krane said, motioning to the jovial man who stood behind them, his broad face etched with stress, and Finch nodded, stepping forward.

Philby left a tag as well, one only their people at Kingsway Station would read. "ANGUS spares to ISRB/KINGSWAY; crates to INVER—." Then the crates were rolled out.

"The 23:10 pulse," Krane said a while later. "Will you have it all clear by then?"

"We should," Philby said. "Might need one extra minute, just to make sure everything's out."

The two men then shook hands—the kind of handshake you only give when you don't fully trust the other. And then Philby left.

A day later, near dusk, he returned but didn't sneak into the facility this time. Instead, he stayed nearby, waiting at a distance from the Dockyard, where Krane had assured him it would be safe. He stood outside the dockyard, waiting for that inevitable scene to unfold.

At 23:11, a pulse tore through the amphitheater and the entire Bureau facility, like a gigantic wave of energy. Philby was thrown backward and blinked in shock. He waited a while, then made his way back to the meeting point they had agreed upon. There stood Krane.

Philby smiled at him. "Welcome," he said, then motioned to a car he had left idling a little way off. "Follow me."

"Where to?" Krane asked.

"The Bureau will think you're dead. MI6 will think you're dead as well," Philby responded. "I'll arrange your papers and make sure that all the reports are filed saying that you never even lived."

Krane nodded. They agreed to part ways and never speak of each other again. That night, Philby filed what MI6 expected to see—destruction. In truth, he gave them damaged fragments of the Mirror: pieces, incomplete, but pieces all the same. It wasn't a betrayal, he told himself. The Soviets were the ones in the right. MI6 was just another pawn in his game—just as it always had been, ever since the Soviets had recruited him at Cambridge all those years ago. Ever since that man, who seemed to appear from nowhere, had tried to stop him. Later, under pressure from Moscow Center, he would break the pact and expose Krane's trail—but not that night.

October arrived, fast and cold like a freight train dragging winter's chill behind it, rattling through London's fog-choked streets. Broadway had become a sort of prison for Philby, though it had always been a large stone fortress that held more secrets than employees. Now it kept him from his one goal.

The schematics he carried under his coat were partial at best

—merely fragments of Mirror blueprints padded with jargon to keep Moscow Center hungry but not starving. The theft had gone smoother than expected, and the crates were rerouted to Kingsway under ANGUS cover, disguised as navigation and geospatial kits that no one would question. But soon after, security tightened, and access to the complete blueprints was restricted to Haldane and a handful of loyalists who believed they were rebuilding Britain's edge in the world—an edge of conquest.

Philby cursed internally as he walked toward his office. The sheets he unrolled under the desk lamp's glow were plans for the Mirror's design, but they weren't enough. Krane had promised more, but the man was a ghost now, and he couldn't be found. And Moscow Center was getting frustrated. They had demanded full deliverables, but he was forced to string them along with nothing but scraps. Philby sighed once again, examining the components.

With MI6 clamping down, Oracle had become the new wrapper around ANGUS, a front hidden at Invershiel. As the weeks passed, Philby grew more frustrated, as did Moscow. It didn't seem like there was any other option for him—until luck struck once more.

In early 1946, Krane resurfaced in Paris. Philby first heard whispers of his name—of a mad scientist claiming he could open a doorway, metals that sang, and demands for funding to complete his research. The man was begging any sponsor he could—Nazi remnants, Soviets, or even Americans—asking for funds and equipment. Krane was a liability, but Philby still couldn't deliver full schematics. The ANGUS security was ironclad, and so he broke the pact and broke the promise.

Sending a wire to his Moscow handler, Philby said, "Asset available. The defector. The brain behind the Mirror."

Moscow Center accepted. Soon after, he brokered Krane to Marshal Grigory Kulik, painting him as their golden goose. And Kulik, always the optimist, took the bait. Krane vanished into

Soviet hands soon afterward, and Philby was left with some relief as Moscow pressed him less than it once had. He had sold Krane as a trophy defector who could build what paper and partials could not. As the brain behind the operation, naturally, Krane would be able to reconstruct the Mirror from the simplest details.

And so for a while, Philby thought his position was secure. But time has a way of dashing securities against the wall and breaking them in two.

————

Trouble began to arise when Kulik's messages of praise turned sour, and the disgraced general began to complain of sabotage and unwillingness to cooperate from the asset. By June 1947, Philby was nursing a glass of brandy as he read through the latest developments—news of how Krane, now holed up in a remote laboratory, had initially promised wonders, yet his work was continually delayed again and again. His promises fell short, and by extension, so did Philby's promises.

Then, one night, following the failure in Prague and the disruption caused by those two agents, Krane disappeared without a trace. Rumors circulated that he had fled to old Nazi allies in Argentina, but attempts to locate him were to no avail.

For Philby, this spelled disaster. His handler, Yuri Modin, fired off letter after letter, chastising him for his shortcomings and the failure to produce a working asset. "You promised a machine," Modin wrote in one encrypted dispatch. "A machine that could have changed the tides of war, and yet we received a madman who ruined our future."

Philby would pace the floor in a rage, his mask slipping only when he was alone. How could they blame him for this? He hadn't known Krane was such an unstable lunatic—hadn't known that MI6 would clamp down on security so tightly until he could barely get a memo out to Modin, let alone find any useful information pertaining to the Mirror blueprints.

Suspicion among the Soviets, blossomed, and other players in the game began to surround Philby. It was as if he were being pulled in every direction at once. Modin was growing suspicious of his slowed results, Haldane had grown angry at the failure of the MI6 scientists to provide a fully working Mirror; and Angleton—James Angleton, that damn American, the very man he'd mentored, was everywhere he wasn't supposed to be.

Somehow, that crafty CIA operative had managed to obtain backchannel details involving the Mirror, though they were highly classified, and had reached out to Philby himself, requesting a collaboration between agencies to investigate further. The two men had been friends for a long while, but this latest contact had begun to interfere with Philby's plans. It wasn't anything too out of the ordinary, but Angleton's mentions of "peculiar experiments at naval sites" and "the undefined Project A" worried Philby. After all, if Angleton probed too far into the details, he risked discovering all the dirty secrets Philby had worked so hard to keep hidden.

"Kim, old chap, do you think we could trade a few intelligence secrets these days? Just like the good old times, you think?"

"Right so," Philby had responded as he kicked his legs up on his desk, the phone pressed against his ear. "What are you interested in?"

"Well, fella," Angleton continued, "some strange stuff is going down in Vienna. See, one of our men heard rumors of a British military courier dead there recently, and we've been tracking down leads since. But whoever orchestrated the event, well—they're a clever man."

Philby had stayed silent for a second. "Ah, right," he said at last. "I've heard of that." He knew all too well what Angleton was pressing at—the courier had been carrying a heavily protected transcript detailing Project Oracle.

"So…" Angleton continued when Philby didn't respond for several seconds, "any details you can give me on what the man was carrying?"

"Well," Philby responded, "I wish I could, old friend, but I'm severely lacking in that department. They've got me on desk duties these days."

By late 1948, the atmosphere was cold and tense, and the pressure mounted from all sides. Haldane, back at Broadway, began to lean harder on Philby, assigning him to the project closely, and yet never letting up on the security. "These frames we've built just don't… damn work," Haldane barked at one meeting. "We need results, and Project Oracle is turning up dust. Results, Philby!"

Philby nodded his head respectfully, though he seethed inside.

Modin's memos began to tighten as well, and the man reached out, requesting a meeting in person. Philby, of course, had no choice but to entertain the fellow, for though the trials at Invershiel had proceeded, the actual information he could provide Moscow was still relatively useless.

He continued to promise more—more drawings, more blueprints, and more results—but only so much could be trafficked to the Soviets. Though he continued to plead for time, the noose began to tighten.

Yet, in the quiet hours, as Philby sat in front of his fireplace, the logs crackling and the smoke rising into the air, he reminded himself that though he walked the razor's edge, it was all worth it… in the end.

It was all worth it for the Soviets. They were right—justified, even—and the game would continue on. He just needed to lie a little bit more.

Lie to a few more men, and then everything would fall into place.

CHAPTER 20
MODIN MOTIVATION

hilby's hands shook as he sat alone in the back seat of his car, watching the street through his tinted windows. Just earlier, he'd heard—through credible sources he had carefully vetted—that someone among the Nine, the Bureau's infamous group, had staged an assassination attempt on Max Calder and had used his name. It hadn't resulted in anything; he knew that much. But he also knew that it was a message—a message from his Soviet handlers that meant one thing: "Keep failing to deliver results, and we'll use you as an alibi," were the words that he could hear in his own mind.

Now, of course, was the night of his meeting with Modin himself. Philby felt as if he could hear the river if he listened just the right way—the dark, deep thrum that pervaded the landscape, the swirling black waters. He wondered if, by continuing to let down Moscow, he would eventually end up in a river like that. He breathed slowly, trying to calm himself down. He straightened his tie and ran his fingers through his hair. Finally, he stood, stepping out and crossing the road to the door of the safe house.

It was less of a safe house and more of a warehouse, of course. An old warehouse that smelled of damp plaster. But it had been fashioned into a homey enough place—a place where he and Modin had their meetings. The curtains were still drawn over the windows, blacking out any of the remaining light that would filter through. Philby flicked the switch of a lamp, the yellow light shining beneath the shades, and sat waiting in the room.

Modin entered several minutes later, without so much as a knock. His hat brim was dripping, his overcoat beaded. He was a small man, but his presence was imposing to everyone who met him, especially Philby. He took the chair opposite Philby, as if he'd expected it to be empty when he arrived.

"You are late," Modin said in Russian, his voice mild but dangerous.

"I am here," Philby replied in English. "I came from Glasgow. The roads were—"

Modin dismissed him with a wave of his hand. "What is happening, Kim?"

Philby exhaled. "It's all going according to plan. I did what you asked. Section IX has fallen into my lap. Kingsway is under my control. If you want access to the variant in Scotland at Invershiel, we are already inside the rooms."

"You didn't promise us access," Modin replied. "You promised Moscow a machine."

"The damn machine refuses to work," Philby said, his voice sharper than intended. "We've copied everything we could. We have Krane's notes—whatever was findable, at least—and coils and frames that match the Bureau's. The Mirror has power. It has a hum. It has a pulse. Then nothing. It's almost as if it rejects us. I think," he added, holding up a finger so Modin would let him finish, "it wants some sort of anchor, or so the scientists say. It tunes to observers."

"And who is it tuned to?" Modin asked.

"I don't think it's ever untuned," Philby responded. "It wants that bloody Slider, if the legend is to be believed."

"And who is this?" Modin asked.

"Max Calder," responded Philby, and Modin turned his head slightly.

"You mean the same Calder who caused Krane to go missing in the first place?"

Philby nodded.

Modin sat back, his face composed but his eyes filled with anger. "You infiltrated your service. You have access to their secret rooms beneath the loch, and yet you have delivered us nothing. One scientist who disappeared as soon as Calder interfered. Diagrams none of our men can decipher. And other than that, simply hearsay."

Philby clenched his jaw. "You know what I've put at risk to get even that. I signed the releases at Rosyth Dockyard and took it apart piece by piece. I've fed you intel, and I've fed you blueprints. I've killed men —"

"I've killed men too," Modin interrupted. "What have you delivered? Your sacrifice is irrelevant. We need results."

Philby laughed. "I am loyal."

"You are ambitious," Modin responded. "Ambition makes a good spy, but it also makes a man who is incapable of controlling such a device as the one you have access to. You keep three loyalties in your pocket at once and take out each whenever it has the best light. Machines like this one will resent such a man as yourself with split loyalty."

"This machine isn't theology," Philby shot back. "It's physics."

"And yet your physics calls its missing piece an anchor and needs human weight to steady it." Modin leaned forward. "We need something more."

"Then we take it," Philby said at last. "The core. Version Three at Invershiel. I've seen it. I've worked on it. If we can get it out—even parts of it—your engineers in Prague, or wherever you like, can use it, can build on it, and we can make it work."

"Steal it from your own service?" Modin asked, as if contemplating the option. "Simply walk into a secret, secure

British military installation and walk out with a machine such as that?"

"We can create the window," Philby responded. "It's simple mechanics."

"No," Modin said at last. "I will not send my men on a suicide mission for you, Philby. This is your mess. You bring us the machine or a large enough piece of it that we can make it work. Otherwise, your calls will begin to go unanswered."

"What is my timeline?" Philby finally asked.

"By the end of the year," was the response. "By January 1st, I expect to be able to tell Moscow Center why I still accept your calls."

"Are you questioning my loyalty?" Philby asked.

"Simply observing your nature," Modin replied. "If the device is truly as fantastic as we have heard, then you will do anything in your power to steal the thing. But do something while you can still choose your path forward."

Philby laughed, a mix of a genuine laugh and something almost panicked. "Understood," he said.

"Deadlines," Modin responded. "I have faith in you, Kim. But be careful of your Bureau man, Max Calder. He knows something is off with you already. Be careful, because for some reason he has not yet told your service of your betrayal."

And just like that, Modin was gone.

Philby sat for a little while longer, the coursing through his veins. He breathed deeply, his eyes closed, and let it flow out into the floor, waiting until he was composed and calm again. Then he stood, checked his pockets, as he always did, and left the building, making his way back to London.

The air tasted metallic and damp. He drove the path he always took, a habit he had long maintained. Though he glanced in every mirror for a second, making sure that no one from MI6 was following him, he was soon distracted. He cracked a window, letting the cold air hit his face and letting it numb him as he drove. He thought of the loch—Loch Duich—and the

Mirror beneath it. And he thought of Max Calder's face. Something about Max Calder didn't sit right with him. Either way, it wasn't his problem to deal with. His problem was to deliver the Mirror, or at least a piece of it, that would be enough to rebuild it again. He would not be dismissed by Moscow Center like a minor pawn in their puzzle. He drove through the fog, finally smiling to himself as he thought. Calder was an interesting puzzle piece, that was for sure. Why hadn't he told MI6?

He continued to wonder and drove onward.

CHAPTER 21
TRAITOR'S TIES

As we walked away from the bar, I made up my mind. Alicia trailed behind me, her hands jammed into her coat and her chin tucked into her autumn-red scarf, bracing for the blast of cold air as we stepped outside.

"We're not done," I said.

"I figured," she replied. "Do you want to shadow him?"

"I want to know where his loyalty really belongs," I said. "MI6, Moscow, or someone else? And we're not going to call the Bureau—not this time."

"Why not?"

"Because," I said, "I trust them about as much as I trust MI6 right now. Who knows who he works for or where his loyalties lie?"

She hesitated. I could tell she disagreed, but she simply nodded. "All right, then."

We traced our way back to where we had left the jeep in the alley. As we turned the corner, the spot was empty. No jeep—just a pair of fresh tire tracks and half a boot print near where it had been.

"It's gone," I said.

"I suppose they were watching."

"Must have been one final trick from Philby. Fine, then." I rolled my shoulders and thought for a second. "How about we go shopping?"

"I like the way you think," she replied.

We found our pick on a side street around three blocks away. An old Austin 10 sat under a lamp whose yellow bulb flickered. The engine block was still warm. Someone had driven it only a minute ago.

I nodded to Alicia, and she took the other end of the street, watching for passersby. A few minutes later, I was in.

"You never lost the knack," she murmured.

"Only thing left is to swap the plates," I said.

I found a nearby Morris Eight whose owner would never notice, as long as he kept up with his parking fees, unscrewed the plate, and carefully affixed it to ours.

Then it was time to find Philby. He went by his initials, as he always did. We used a pay phone and called around at the most popular hotels in town until we found him, where his initials were booked.

We headed straight for the hotel, parking near the entrance, where the valet would guide his car when he was ready to leave. It was time for a stakeout.

The stakeout lasted through the day and into the afternoon. Many hours later, in the mid-afternoon, a black Humber nosed up right under the canopy, and out of the hotel walked Philby. His boyish smile was gone, his mouth twisted into an unpleasant expression, as if he had taken a mouthful of something he greatly disliked.

We let him get four cars ahead before we joined the flow of traffic. Alicia watched carefully ahead as I navigated.

"Wonder where he's going?" she asked. "He mentioned London, didn't he?"

"He did," I replied. "And I doubt he was lying. London is the hub, and the last thing he'd expect is for us to trail him after that. He doesn't know what Finch said, or that we suspect him of something more. Whether he's going to report to MI6 or someone else entirely, he'll likely take A74 down and avoid trains to keep from being counted."

"Then let's make it a convoy," she said.

We followed from a distance, down the soaking-wet A74, hedgerows trimmed and pristine. We kept our lights dim and our distance elastic, growing closer and then falling behind when we needed. In the fading daylight, the Humber was a smudge that moved quickly along the road. Sometimes we lost sight of it. He stopped at a small town for petrol, and we did the same—at a station slightly farther along the road.

Alicia picked up two small bottles of pop.

"You sure you're up for the drive?" she asked.

"I've driven worse roads," I replied. "Besides, what else would we do? Sleep?"

And so the rest of the afternoon and evening was spent driving down past Carlisle and then south, even further along what some called the artery of England. We followed Philby closely, leapfrogging him through transport cafés and dirty lay-bys. Neither of us rested.

London welcomed us with the falling night—dark, smoky, and gray—as the last rays of sun dipped below the horizon. The buildings appeared tired yet impressive as always. As Philby's Humber turned and vanished into the lot beside the warehouse, we let the distance open up. But we hadn't lost him. His car slowed in front of the old building—damp plaster walls, curtains blacking out the windows, the faint hum of a lamp inside.

Before we settled in for the long wait, we made a detour. Along the drive, I'd discussed with Alicia what we needed—and now, we navigated toward a damp, shabby part of Camden, where black markets still frequently thrived in the post-war atmosphere.

Here, Alicia slipped into a dimly lit electronics shop run by a contact of hers—a man who dealt in surplus gadgets under the table. Only a minute later, she emerged with a Webster-Chicago

Model 80 wire recorder, a coil of insulated wire, a contact micro-phone, and a basic preamp kit.

"How much?" I asked.

"Free," she replied. "He owed me one."

I chuckled, and we drove back to where Philby's car was located.

We parked three streets away in a space between two delivery vans and made our way back on foot.

"Two men in raincoats watching out front," Alicia said. "They're covering it in case there's something obvious."

We had made it just in time, too. Another car slid to the curb. Several men stepped out and took up positions near the door. One man went inside.

"Covering the front," Alicia said.

"Let's hope they are not covering the back," I replied.

The lane behind the warehouse was narrow. A loose vent grate sat near the back wall. We scaled a low stack of crates to reach it quietly. I slid the spike of the contact mic into a mortar seam just below the vent and felt the wall under my palm. Alicia crouched beside me, balancing the Webster on a crate. The wire recorder looked like a metal lunchbox with electronics.

"I've wired the preamp," she said. "Keep an ear out."

I listened carefully. The spike picked up everything at first—the sounds of London, pipes, useless gossip. But then I heard voices. The first was Philby's, smooth and clipped.

"Can't move it any earlier," he said.

A second voice answered in Russian. It was the kind of accent that didn't bother to hide itself—Moscow. I couldn't hear the full sentences through the buffered line and static, but I made out several words: "deadline," "Invershiel," "Soviets," "Calder." Alicia's eyes flicked to me, but I was too focused. I adjusted again and watched the thin wire vibrate slightly.

"Yuri Modin," Philby said, as if he were speaking to an old friend.

That name cut through me like ice. Meanwhile, the little steel wire on the Webster kept taking everything down. Out front, the car continued to idle, but the men never scouted the back. They weren't worried; Philby clearly hadn't told them about me.

Seconds later, chairs scraped. I heard one of the men excuse himself. I motioned to Alicia; we killed the gain, plucked the spike free, and wound the Webster's wire back onto its spool.

"Time for a dead drop?" she asked.

I nodded. "Under that bollard."

Two streets away, at the base of an iron post, there was a small box that nobody ever tightened. I worked it loose, tilted the base just enough, and slipped the spool inside like a letter into a slot. Seconds later, I had the screw back in. The drop was finished. If we weren't caught, we'd pick it up. If we were—well, hopefully, someone would find it.

We watched from the corner. A man left, his hat pulled low over his eyes. A while later, Philby himself left, his hair slicked by the drizzle, anger visible on his face. I figured that this was all the information we needed. Alicia and I hopped back into our car and made for the nearest phone booth we could find.

"Switchboard," a woman's voice said.

"This is Max Calder," I replied. "Put me through to Section V —Nicholas Elliott."

There was silence, then a click.

"Section V desk," said a young man's voice.

"Don't need the desk," I replied. "Elliott."

"Name, please," came the reply.

"Calder. Max. Formerly MI6, Section V. Clearance code 7VK9." I gave him the rest of the information.

"I see the record," the voice said. "I also see a transfer. You're Bureau now."

"Maybe," I said. "But I'm telling you, one of your men is coordinating with Moscow. Let me speak to Nicholas Elliott."

"Please hold," he said.

Several minutes later, he returned. "Do you have any proof of this?"

"I have it all on recording," I said. "If you want this to be yours, you have less than two days before it becomes a very public piece of evidence."

"Bring it to Broadway, then," the desk officer responded.

"I'm not stepping foot in your building with evidence you want to burn," I snapped. "You want it? Let's meet on neutral ground."

"Where, then?"

"Invershiel," I finally said. "Send Elliott or someone he trusts. Section V, not Section IX. My terms."

There was another long pause. I heard someone else murmur a sentence in the background.

"That seems hardly neutral… but agreed," he said. "A representative from Section V will meet you there. Give the time."

"Two days."

"Mr. Calder, please remember, we still consider your loyalties compromised. You left us."

"Noted," I replied.

"Very well." The line went dead.

Alicia was watching my face carefully.

"Broadway?" she asked.

"No," I replied. "They'll come north. To Invershiel."

"Why did you pick Invershiel?" she asked.

"Because that's where Philby would least like to meet."

"Fine," she finally said. "But this time, we contact the Bureau."

I was reluctant, but the defiance in her eyes made it clear she wouldn't take no for an answer. Alicia sent a quick note to the Bureau with updates. We swapped the Austin for a battered Vauxhall two neighborhoods over, then set off on the road northward, checking what resources we had left. We were headed for the small place on Loch Duich, where we were going to meet our fate.

"Do you think Broadway will show, and that it's not a trap?" Alicia asked.

"They'll show," I replied. "They'll want to know what we found out."

She laughed. "You really can't let Philby go, can you?"

"Philby's the reason my mind is broken," I said. "I'll drag him down into the ground with me if I have to."

We drove onward into Scotland, where the lochs were still black and the sky was still gray. London's skyline retreated behind us.

Up above, the moon shone bright in the sky.

CHAPTER 22
BELIEVING BETRAYAL

didn't want to go. Not really. But for once, I actually believed I might be able to put an end to something.

To put an end to all the missing memories and all the betrayals I had faced over the years. To put an end to the one man I knew now had instigated it all: Kim Philby.

So, Alicia and I were off yet again. Off to try and stop the inevitable.

We cut south off the embankment before dawn, doubling back through Holborn as if we'd taken the wrong turns and simply gotten lost. I backtraced our steps naturally, finding our drop point and working the screw loose with my fingers. The screw was wet and slippery from last night's rain, but it mattered little to me. I slid the spool from the hollow base and felt its weight in my hand. It felt sturdy, as if it were the security I needed to finally put my ghosts to rest.

"Does it look good?" she asked.

I cocked my head and put the wire to my ear, as if I could hear the very noises and the evidence inside it.

"I think so," I replied, slipping it back into its tin.

We drove north up the A74, a road that felt endless—just as it had felt before. We didn't talk much because there wasn't much to talk about. The air was thin and cold, and the Highlands shouldered up out of the earth, dark, hulking shapes under the morning sky. The air was cold, but the car we drove now was better than the old jeep we had abandoned—or rather, the jeep that had been taken from us. And so we continued on, driving toward our fate.

Ten miles shy of Shiel Bridge, however, the Bureau found us. Two Hillmans swung out of a layby, their dark shapes against the horizon. They had no lights and no siren. For a second, I thought it was MI6. But then I saw one of the drivers inside, and I saw the familiar Bureau outfit he wore, and I knew what was happening.

"Damn it!" I cursed, anger flooding my veins. "What are they doing?"

But I had no choice, and so I pulled over. A tall man stepped out of one of the Hillmans and walked up to our window. He nodded at me, then addressed Alicia.

"Director Moreau insists that there be official attendance at this meeting."

"We've got it," I replied. "We are the official attendance."

He smiled wryly. "You would think that. But not quite. You're attached, at the very least. Now, hand over your toys."

They followed behind us, one Hillman ahead and one behind. It was like a convoy now, and as I drove, I gritted my teeth in anger. I could feel Alicia watching me, and I knew she didn't disapprove of this situation as much as I did. But we kept going. I had no choice.

We arrived at the forestry road, where several men were waiting. Several wore MI6 windbreakers, while others wore Bureau suits, along with a Ministry sergeant who held a clipboard in his hand and sported an elaborately twirled mustache. A small decontamination tent had been pitched at the verge of the entrance, and we were ushered inside.

"Standard precautions," said a man with sergeant's stripes as he reached for my attaché case.

"For what?"

"Simply electromagnetics, sir," he responded. "We've had interference… the nature of the projects within—"

His voice trailed off; he realized he'd said too much.

"I'd like to see you damn well try to take it from me," I said, but I stopped as Alicia's gloved fingers pressed against my sleeve. She shook her head silently. I sighed, giving up the attaché case and watching it disappear through the flap.

"Lose it," I called after the man, "and I'll make you a missing memory."

"Duly noted," he said as he walked away.

All of our items proceeded as such—every case and everything we had. As we waited, I glanced down at the loch. It was dark against the gray sky, tidily framed by the trees and the horizon above it. And then there was the site at Invershiel—ANGUS, as it was better known.

We were ushered inside, and there stood none other than Nicholas Elliott. He was slightly more gray than he'd been in Istanbul, but he was there nonetheless. A Bureau man stood there as well, introducing himself as Vickers. Apart from those two, there was Haldane—a man I only recognized from after my tenure at MI6—and Dr. Nkosi, whom I knew from personal experience was rumored to be one of the Nine.

"Where's Philby?" I asked.

"He'll be here soon," Haldane responded curtly. "Let us wait."

Philby arrived late, his mouth arranged in an apologetic manner.

"Now, Mr. Calder," Elliott said, "and Miss Rayes—shall we begin?"

I nodded. An uncomfortable silence fell over the room. Vickers began.

"For the record," he said, "this is a joint convening of the Bureau and MI6 concerning Invershiel and Oracle—"

"ANGUS," Haldane interrupted, correcting him.

"—and its immediate status," Vickers continued, glaring at

the man. His fingers tapped a folder he held, and he skimmed it briefly. "Our position is straightforward enough. We request it be shut down immediately."

Haldane smiled, as if challenging any Bureau agent to force him to do it. "We've repeatedly informed the Bureau," he said, "the equipment is not functional. This is simply a testbed. There's no weapon contained, and at present, our results are embarrassing."

"Embarrassing?" I said. I could feel my blood pressure rising. I rarely got angry, but this was getting on my nerves. "Your lies are embarrassing. I can hear the hum of the mirror at this moment."

Haldane ignored me. "Come now, come. We're far less proficient than the Bureau gives us credit for—unfortunately so. In fact, every activation attempt at Version Three has culminated in noise and false positives. The only thing we've created are aftereffects."

"Variants," one of the MI6 scientists said from the back.

Vickers cocked his head. "Define artifacts—and variants, for that matter."

Haldane glanced at Philby quickly, then refocused on the Bureau agents in front of him. "Transient apparitions," he responded. "Something of a superimposed phenotype. Unstable residue. We've begun a sort of misnomer internally—calling them variants for clarity—but they're nothing so advanced. All we're doing currently is cataloging these anomalous recurrences we believe are tied to an observer's prior exposure."

Elliott shot him a glance. "English, please," he said wryly.

Dr. Nkosi's cigarette burned down as he listened. "You're describing an anchor," he finally said. "An anchor for the machine. Have you seen his face? Who is the anchor?"

Haldane shrugged. "We've seen many faces. Non-consequential. All brief. Non-stable. They degrade."

Elliott's eyes drifted to me. "And you, Max. We're aware of

your ventures into our facilities. Have you been aware of such noise?"

"I suspect," I replied. "If there was any evidence of such ventures, it would already have been brought against me. As for any such noise, you've got your taxonomy wrong. These aren't artifacts. They're men. Echoes. And you've been logging them." I stared at Philby. "SL-001 through SL-042. Does that ring any bells?"

Philby remained impassive. Haldane's eyelid, however, twitched slightly, and I could see Vickers staring at me intently.

"Regardless," Vickers said suddenly, snapping out of his thoughts. "Variants or not, aftereffects or not, echoes or not—we're not here for this. We're here because we have credible evidence that there is a live Mirror frame within ANGUS, and we want you to close the site."

"Agreed," Elliott responded before anyone else could speak. His face didn't betray a single emotion. "We agree to shut it down temporarily until we can conduct a sane audit."

Haldane shook his head angrily. "You're trying to audit something that can't be understood," he spat. "But if it calms your nerves, very well. I'll defer to Elliott."

Vickers looked at me and then nodded. It was time to present the evidence. I set the tin on the table.

"We're also here for this," I said, staring at Philby. "And you."

His face lit with genuine confusion. "Max, whatever are you talking about?"

"Don't even. Two days ago, you met with Yuri Modin. You promised him a machine. He gave you a deadline, and you asked him for time. It was really pathetic, actually. And it's all here. Names, dates—even you speaking my name like it was some sort of prize—all recorded through your wall and your own coal chute."

I smiled as his eyes narrowed and his face drained of color. I carefully placed the spool in my palm. "Mr. Elliott, you do prefer proof, don't you?"

"Always," Elliott said, not glancing at Philby.

I cranked the Webster on the table and slid the spool onto its prongs. With a click, the wire ran. The little gauge trembled, and it was as if the entire room had gone silent, waiting for the evidence. And yet, as I stood there, waiting, there was nothing. Simply static. I increased the volume again and again. The static thickened, but no voices played from the tape. Confusion trembled through me and surged to my head. A splitting headache bloomed; I winced. Why was there nothing?

"Well?" Haldane said. "We're waiting."

Alicia's eyes were on me now, and I could feel her waiting just as the rest of the room, with bated breath—could feel her wishing that Modin's voice would play through the wire. She hadn't even heard it yet. I'd been the one listening to the wire as it was recorded, and now it was playing nothing.

The spool ground to a stop and ended with a polite click. I stood there in silence.

"Whatever that was," Haldane laughed boisterously, "it's clear you didn't present proof."

"You did something to it," I stuttered, glancing wildly between the MI6 agents. "Before the gate—the tent—what did you do with it?"

"Sir," one of the MI6 technicians said politely, "we degauss metallics crossing the threshold. It's standard, of course."

"Oh dear," Haldane responded. "A magnetising field would erase magnetised recordings, Mr. Calder. You should have told our men you were smuggling a wire into such a sensitive site. Then again, I doubt you had evidence on it in the first place."

Elliott sighed. "Max," he said, "maybe—"

"Maybe what?" I spat. My head felt like it was splitting open, and I could feel the hum throbbing beneath the floor, traveling into my very chest. I could see everything—the amphitheater through the wall, the coil chain, and that old woman I had seen in the mirror as it split open. Then I snapped back to reality and glanced around at the men—and Alicia—

watching me, as if I had emptied my pockets and dumped a handful of sand at their feet, as if I were the boy who cried wolf.

"Mr. Calder has suffered episodes," Philby said, regaining his composure and with it faking compassion. "The dockyard incident that the Bureau is so well known for left a mark on him. Everyone there has seen strange things, but from what I hear—and from the reports—Mr. Calder is particularly affected. In fact, it makes certain good men monsters."

Neither Elliott nor Vickers nor the doctor moved. Finally, Vickers spoke.

"The site will be shut," he said, "as agreed upon. Today. Division of custody as agreed. No activation, no tests. MI6—you'll sign, yes?"

"Of course, of course," Haldane responded. "It is our pleasure to cooperate with a fellow government agency."

"And the variants?" Nkosi asked.

"Simply noise," Haldane replied. "It will be taken care of."

Philby spread his hands in a gesture of fake surrender, almost too politely. "Come now. I'm sure all of us here want the best for our country. Not a single man in this room conspires with Moscow."

Alicia said nothing. She simply watched me, waiting to see what would happen. She knew I was crumbling inside.

I followed the rest of the agents out of the room and above ground. I felt numb. All our items were returned to us. But I didn't care. I could feel the spool still resting in my palm. The spool was now empty. The spool that had contained the only memories and the only proof I had of Philby's betrayal.

The convoy returned down the road in silence, stopping at a petrol station near Dumbarton to refill. Alicia stayed by the pump, but I wandered off as soon as I could exit the vehicle. As the drivers ducked into the café for tea and Elliott walked to the phone booth to call Broadway, I slipped away, silently pulling the attaché case and the 6F badge out of the vehicle, as well as the small purse of coins Alicia and I had left. All I wanted was to be alone.

Around the back of the petrol station, I hopped over the small stone wall and down to where a creek ran with cold, fresh water to the other side and continued walking. I didn't want to be here any longer. I glanced back as I walked over a hill, all alone, and saw the loch lying below, like some damn mirror reflecting its surroundings so perfectly. I continued to walk.

"Damn it!" I yelled, punching a nearby tree that was unfortunate enough to be on the receiving end of my rage. "Damn it! Damn it! Damn it!" I punched it again and again and again until my knuckles bled and I felt as if I had broken my hands, until the rage subsided, replaced only with sorrow and fear.

Had I imagined it all?

I picked up the case and walked onward, the blood dripping and falling on the ground like some crimson puddle.

I arrived in Glasgow by dusk. My hunger pangs ignored, the wire still in my pocket, I stumbled along, ignoring anyone who shot me a strange glance, until I reached the one place I wanted. I knocked, and the door opened.

There stood a man in front of me—Italian by heritage—with a peculiar moustache and a bald head, and a belly that looked at least three times as large as the rest of his body. He stared at me for a second, squinting, and then recognition dawned on his face.

"Max Calder," he said, laughing. "What brings you here?"

But then he saw my expression and my hands, and his face became etched with concern. "What's wrong?"

"Everything, Mario," I replied, stumbling inside. "I need you to fix something that's broken."

"What's broken?"

I set the spool onto his workbench. "Tell me how to fix it."

He wired it into his own player and ran the wire under a pickup coil, his ear to the monitor. As he did, his face fell. He played with it for several more minutes, flipping it through the machine to test, but the needle returned nothing.

"It's been wiped," he said.

"By what?" I asked.

"Some sort of field," he replied. "Alternating. Strong. It's a nice uniform randomisation. There's no residual bias. No wear, no age, not even heat. You either walked it through a huge coil, or the field off some big machine—whatever was humming out there—did the job, or someone took a handheld magnet to it, like they were giving it its last rites."

"Could it be done by accident?" I asked. "Some sort of machine?"

He grunted. "I doubt it—unless it's a machine I've never heard of."

I thought of everything: the tent, the polite man with the clipboard, Haldane's cheerfulness, and Philby's surprise. Philby hadn't known. He hadn't even known I had brought it. No one there should have known. The only people who knew were Alicia and me. But I didn't want to think of it. I pushed it out of my mind.

"Can you retrieve anything from it?" I asked.

"It's gone, Max," he said. "The best you'll get is a clean conscience."

"But it was there," I said numbly. "I heard it."

"And I believe you," he said. "Whatever was there. But whatever it was, it's gone now."

I nodded, thanked him for his time, and left. Outside, Glasgow's rain sharpened and pelted down on my face. I followed the smell of beer to a place that used to be mine back before I had left. O'Dwyer wasn't there anymore. Nothing I knew was. And hell, even if I remembered something, how could be sure it was true?

I sat down and placed a few coins on the table for a drink. I let the first go down without tasting it. And then another. And then another.

I glanced up, and in the reflection of a mirror that hung next to one of the doors, I saw a shadowy figure standing there watching me. Its red eyes looked at me, almost tauntingly, almost alluring. And it smiled. It was a perfect mix of a Wild West outlaw and a shadow—a silhouette of a man that wore a low hat. I closed my eyes. I didn't want to see it anymore. I didn't want to see El Cuadro, or anything else for that matter. The room thinned around the edges. Thinner and thinner and thinner.

I knew now that Philby was working for the Soviets. But if he were, the Mirror wasn't going to be destroyed—not by men like Haldane, and not while men like Philby had deadlines baked into their plans. Philby was going to steal it. I knew that much.

As for Alicia, she deserved a note. She deserved to hear from me, but I couldn't bear to tell her. I knew she hadn't betrayed me. She was the one person I trusted. But if I wanted to fix anything, I couldn't tell her now—not when she had just reestablished her relationship with the Bureau and had begun to build trust with them again.

As for me, it was time to go back. I sighed deeply. There was only one way now, and it was forward. I left before the fourth drink could convince me otherwise—convince me to rot away in Glasgow, as I had throughout my childhood.

So, I made my way back to Invershiel. I hotwired a small, old car near the outskirts of Glasgow and drove back. I still had the V6F access card, but not much else—just that card, the reel, and the attaché case with the radio. Those were all my belongings now, and I didn't want anything else.

By midnight, the forestry track was dense with fog. It felt empty; the only sign of other people was damp footprints ghosting the verges. I could still hear the hum in the ground. I stumbled down to the culverts, which glistened wet. I had taped the V6F card inside my cuff. It wasn't skin to skin, but I could still feel the burn.

A plan began to form in my head, as if it were a storm that

was brewing. It was stupid, simple, and wrong. But it was my only option. I knew that at this point, if I didn't take action, I would die. I couldn't keep living like this.

So I formulated the plan: get inside, stand in front of the frame, and go back—back to Cambridge. That was what Philby had mentioned to me all those years ago—telling me we'd met at Cambridge. Well, I figured if that was what he believed, maybe I should give him a taste of his own medicine. Perhaps I could convince him what loyalty truly costs. All I had to do was sabotage a single conversation or convince him that Moscow was evil, and that might be enough to break everything going forward. And if not, I'd die in the place that had been trying to kill me for years.

I breathed slowly, then slid through the bars and into the culvert, as I had done with Alicia before. It was time.

Time to turn back time.

CHAPTER 23
SHATTERING SLIDE

The cold iron bars seemed to squeeze the life out of me as I slid through, and my ribs ached. I had the V6F card taped inside my cuff, and I held the attaché case in my hand. Even though the tape bit into my skin through the heat of my sleeve, I knew it would be worth it. This card was the most important thing I carried. The radio—well, it had been quiet since the dockyard. But I still carried it because so far, the voice had been right.

Soon, I reached the access plate. I slid the V6F card across the reader; it blinked once, and then the door opened. The corridor beyond was white and sterile, just as it had been the first time I was here with Alicia. Down the stairs, along the corridors, I snuck along. No one should be here now, I thought. Not a single soul, now that the place had effectively been decommissioned.

I reached the big door with the words: Recursion Core Version Three. I sighed and placed the card against the beveled glass. The door parted as it had the first time, and I walked through. Cable arrays curled off the walls like braided ropes. The Oracle terminal sat next to the mirror frame in the center of the room. The frame was so large that, as I stared up at it, I almost felt intimidated. But I was too numb to care. My only goal was to stop this all from happening.

The Oracle terminal was already awake. Someone had left fragments of their day scattered across the desk; I assumed they were documenting everything before fully decommissioning it. There were stubs of pencils, scrawls in messy handwriting, and several spools of wire sitting next to the terminal.

The terminal itself was unfamiliar to me. I had never operated one of these before, and the screen was crammed with utilities and other technical jargon I wasn't quite sure how to use: Anchor waiting, Observer amplitude, Target location. All of it was far beyond my training.

But my goal was to reach Cambridge. I wanted to stop Philby once and for all—not expose him to the world, because he'd wriggle through that net like a slippery eel, grinning in that stupid, irritating way—but to stop him before he even truly got started.

I set the attaché case on the desk and began tapping the terminal, testing various settings. From what I could tell, this mirror operated slightly differently than the previous ones. The coordinates input here were mostly unsuccessful—many of them even disabled—as if this Mirror itself didn't have that capability. However, I noticed I could pulse the mirror, using its energy signature to turn it on. That seemed simple enough.

As I worked, I thought of Kim Philby, of his boyish smile and the betrayal that hid behind it. Anger flooded my veins.

Suddenly, the radio in the attaché case flickered to life, and I could hear static bristling from the case, as if someone were speaking.

"Almost there," it said.

"What?" I asked.

Then the voice came through, clearer than I had ever heard it. "You're almost there, Max. That is how you program the Mirror."

"Say it plainly."

"Cambridge, 1933," the radio responded. "You are the anchor for the system. Your mind controls the success of the slide."

I increased the pulse, feeling the throb from the mirror behind me as it glowed with a dark light that cast an eerie sheen around the room.

"Make sense," I said to the radio, almost chiding it. "What do you mean?"

The radio sputtered, and then I heard the voice laughing. "You're already sliding."

I lifted my fingers off the keys and glanced around. Sure enough, the room was turning white, almost as if it were spinning, and the Mirror's surface was cracking open—that classic Mirror look, like black glass shattering in on itself. Through it, I could see Cambridge.

I grabbed the attaché case from the table and, without a second thought, leaped through the surface.

———

Cambridge hit me all at once. It wasn't one of those remote slides I had experienced before. This was a classic slide—the type that only happened for us sliders. I could hear the bells: loud, lively bicycle bells cut through the morning fog, followed by the low grumble of a delivery lorry over the cobbles.

It wasn't cold here. Not as it had been. It was summertime. Cold smoke lay sweet in the air. I could smell the faint tang of beer from taps being wiped down in the kitchens.

I still wore the same clothes as I always had. That was how slides really worked: anything sent through was sent through all at once. And yet, confused, I looked down at my hand and realized that the attaché case with my radio had vanished. That had never happened before. Still, I figured it was simply an unexplained phenomenon, due to the Version Three Mirror Recursion Core being different from any Mirror I had gone through before.

So I walked through the town, glancing around, trying to get a feel for where I was. By the look of the shops, I was on Trinity Street. I glanced at my reflection in a cracked café window and saw my face. I grimaced. I wasn't the best-looking man, at least not now, with three days of stubble and the gray streaks in my hair. It was something even an impostor wouldn't trust.

Luckily, I still had some money in my pocket. The first step was to find lodging. I made my way along the street until I found a boarding house near Jesus Lane, with narrow stairs and a quiet, smoky air. I was greeted by a landlady—an older woman with blonde hair—who smiled at me sweetly as I entered.

"I'm here to read," I explained, and she nodded quietly, choosing to keep her thoughts to herself as she booked my room.

Because I was in Cambridge, I took on my old alias: that of a studious man who learned as he walked and enjoyed the finer things in life. After a quick trip to a secondhand shop, I had a fresh suit. I was clean-shaven, nicely groomed, and ready to begin my conquest. Along with this, I picked up some rudimentary supplies, forging a letter to keep in my pocket, just in case anyone asked about my whereabouts or why I was here.

It brought back memories of my first time in Cambridge—the time after I had fled from the Gorbals and found my way here in search of something more, something more challenging. The time when Hugh Sinclair recruited me into MI6.

After a few days, I found him. He wasn't hard to spot; he was a popular man here, just as he was everywhere else. At the Union that afternoon, I followed along, watching with the eyes of a hunter as Kim Philby drifted through the debate, here and there, laughing with his friends. His hair was neatly parted, his eyes amused without ever really sparkling. He looked like the sort of man who had been born into privilege, but who was restless in a way.

When I first saw him, he stood there with Guy Burgess by a hearth, and I knew then that this was already when Philby had begun to turn. Still, there was no use in trying to change him too fast. First, I needed to know what actually made Kim Philby tick, and so I didn't say anything that day. Instead, I let it breathe and continued to watch him.

That first night, I sat alone at The Eagle, eating dinner and watching the conversations around the room. The second night, I began to get closer. I began to mold myself back into that old version of me—the man who was so familiar with Cambridge that his vowels and his sentences sounded as if he had lived there all his life—though I kept my name: Max Calder. I had almost gone under the name Jack Fontaine, but I didn't want anyone to make the connection.

By now, Philby knew of me. That much was clear. I was well-read enough to keep up with the conversations here, and from the way he glanced at me once, I knew he was intrigued by my story. That was what I was counting on.

On the third day, I introduced myself to Philby. He was alone outside the hall after a Union speech, smiling up into the air as if it owed him money. The evening had been good for him; that much was clear.

"Mr. Philby," I said.

He looked up, his smile ready. Then it faltered a bit when he saw who I was. "What can I do for you?"

"Name's Max Calder," I said. "I'm trying to catch up. Came to your talk, enjoyed the fireworks, felt I should introduce myself."

My name and face meant nothing to him.

"Kim," he replied, "you don't look like you've just done your Part I, that's for sure."

"No," I said. "Life was busy. I've come back to do it again if I can."

He laughed, genuinely. It was the laugh of a man who still hadn't quite been fully corrupted.

For a minute, we talked about trivialities—football scores, the price of books, and the news from the Continent. He was charming, but I could tell he was slightly bored with the conversation.

He was an intelligent man, no doubt, but he knew how to perform and feign interest.

Still, I didn't want to push. I excused myself and left.

After that, I became his orbiter. Three days turned into five, and I slowly began to fall into the edges of his circle. I learned his patterns, where he ate, and where he talked. I would drink weak beers in rooms overcrowded with bookcases, where Burgess and Blunt spoke, and even Maclean—whose name I learned—occasionally offered his thoughts. I watched carefully and learned, slowly, that Philby wasn't the only one being turned. There were five of them—five men being groomed into Soviet assets.

Then, finally, I found my moment. It was now or never. Philby stood alone one evening, smoking as he stared off into the distance, his eyes focused on nothing at all. I nodded to him, and he nodded back. Then I approached.

"Hello," he said.

"Walk with me?" I asked.

He looked at me suspiciously for a second, then nodded. We walked along, the wet grass beneath our feet, and finally stopped in the shadow of a chapel, where I turned to face him.

"So… Kim Philby, not Harold, right?"

"That's right, Mr. Calder. Yes?"

"Glad you remember," I laughed. "Can I ask—what's with your name? Kim? It's not common, is it?"

"My father's fault. He called me Kim when I was young… comes from a novel by Rudyard Kipling. But what do you want, Mr. Calder?"

"Call me Max. Anyhow, Kim, I've noticed you seem to prefer the company of ideologues."

"You're not wrong, but it's hard to think without some sort of ideological fuel, you know? The world is changing, and the future of Europe is in the hands of people who can't simply keep their eyes closed any longer."

"You mean Marxism?"

"There's something beautiful about it, isn't there?"

"Maybe… but ideology can be a dangerous thing if it's not tempered by experience. Sometimes, people get lost in their beliefs and they find it's too far to turn back when they try. You can't change the world with ideals alone, Kim."

"You sound like an old man, Max," he laughed. "What do you know about it, Jack? I'd guess you've lived as sheltered a life as I have."

"You guess wrong," I responded. "Risking everything might sound exciting when you're young, but take it from someone who's risked everything and lost much over his life… sometimes, burning everything leaves you standing in the ashes."

"Yet sometimes, you have to burn down old structures to make space for something better. If the world you're living in is so deeply flawed, what else can you do? If the system is so corrupt and broken, and we have the power to tear it down… shouldn't we? Why do you think we have all these brilliant minds here at Cambridge? We're the future, Max. People like us, with the right beliefs, can change everything."

"I think you're wrong, Kim. Beliefs can be dangerous—especially when they blind you to reality itself. If you are caught up in ideologies, you'll lose sight of realities. Because once you take down the system, something else will step in and take its place."

"You make it sound like it's a choice between two bad options. But there's always a better side to choose, Max. History is written by those who dare to act. Look at all the great leaders, the revolutionaries. You know what they have in common? They act—they don't just sit by the river and reflect."

"Kim, you're brilliant. But your naivety is dangerous. You talk about change, but have you ever wondered what kind of change you're actually creating? Power corrupts, Kim. No one ever sees it coming, not until it's too late. Just… take it as a warning. I don't want to see you become a pawn in someone else's game, whether you like it or not."

He looked at me with visible disgust. "You can't scare me

with those old warnings, Max. This isn't about fear; it's about action—about changing the world for the better. History will look back on us and remember the ones who dared to take control. I won't sit idly by while the world rots from within."

"Then you're already lost, Kim. The greater good is a dangerous illusion. You'll learn that soon enough. I just hope, for your sake, that when you wake up, you won't be standing alone in the ashes," I turned, walking away as I spoke. "If you ever change your mind… you'll be able to find me."

When the conversation ended and I walked away, I knew I had failed. But I hadn't exactly lost the war. I hadn't turned him, not outright. But I had left a thought in his head that would, hopefully, begin to blossom into something more. Later, as he lay in bed and closed his eyes, perhaps he'd think about the words I'd said and remember what I told him.

Still, I didn't want to go back through the Mirror yet—not back to the Recursion Core, and not back to Alicia yet. I'd realized now why Philby had brought up Cambridge when I'd first met him at MI6 in Broadway. It must have been the conversation we just had that had caused that memory for him all those years later. Our timelines were clearly out of sync, and I had no memory at that time of something that hadn't happened yet—at least for me. It was prior to the slide. A Mirror paradox.

For now, my plan was to move. If I couldn't pry Philby off the cause alone, I could ruin the cause itself. That meant I needed to infiltrate the circle that had formed around him.

Guy Burgess was the easiest to get near, and so I began to follow him as well. I let him talk to me naturally at first, drifting into his presence, learning his ideals. Sure, you can't out-argue an idealist, but the plan began to crystallize as I learned more about him and listened to them speak. It was a simple plan, really: if I could learn more about Philby, I could exploit his weaknesses. If I couldn't turn his head, I'd have to cut his legs out from under him.

After nearly two weeks had passed, something happened

that pushed Kim Philby out of my mind. I noticed it. As I walked at dusk, I felt eyes on me and glanced around—quietly, just for a second. There was a man tailing me. He wore a long coat and had his hat pulled low over his eyes. It was an ordinary hat, but I could tell instantly from his movement that he was a professional. He kept pace with me, even in the darkness, and his footsteps made no sound.

I pretended not to notice, but drifted across a lawn, down to the Backs, and over a footbridge, all the while watching and waiting. Fog rose from the river. The nights were cold here, even though it was summer. When I caught his shape again in the river's reflection, I cut down a brick alley—a dark, thin corridor where the lamps flickered and the light ran yellow.

The street was empty. I glanced around. Had he stopped following me?

Then, all of a sudden, the first shot cracked the night open. The brick above my ear spat powder and dust. The sound tore down the alley like thunder. I ducked, cursing. Whoever this was, he was a professional. But how had he found me? He shouldn't have known about me. No, this had to be something else. Had MI6 discovered my slide and sent someone after me? But that should never have worked. For all intents and purposes, for them, my slide should have been instantaneous, or at the very least, only a few hours.

"Why stop me?" I shouted down the alley.

"You should have stayed gone," the voice called back.

I could tell his voice was disguised, as if he held a pebble in his mouth to make it deeper and more gravelly. The next shot was close—so close that I could feel the bullet graze my ear, and the brick less than an inch from my head exploded into white sand. The blast from the impact sent me reeling, and I fell to the side, clutching my ear.

Hot, metallic-smelling blood dripped from somewhere beneath my fingers, and I stumbled for cover.

The dark streets of Cambridge shimmered around me, a city

of brick turned into a battlefield. I could scarcely see straight as I stumbled along, hand against the wall, looking wildly back.

Was he following me?

It hadn't gone as planned. Not at all. The mission hadn't been this—a damn death trap—when I'd started it. Everything was supposed to be simple: bring Philby over to our side before he betrayed us, and it would have been a success.

I glanced backward again and flung myself behind a brick pillar in the nick of time. A flash of metal. A gunshot. The bullet tore a hole through the railing beside me before I could speak, dust from a shattered brick rising into the air.

Another shot rang out and nicked my coat—the small piece that still remained visible—tearing through it as I shuddered.

"What the hell do you want? Why stop this?" I shouted.

"You should've stayed gone."

The next volley ripped through the night air, bullet after bullet ricocheting around me, down cobblestones slick with rain. I could hear shouting from guards, teachers, and sleepy students now—confusion and fear in their voices.

I had to do something. I could hear boots clacking against the cobblestones. I could hear the man getting closer. My fingers scraped against the ground, raw and painful, as I grabbed a handful of small stones.

Standing, I hurled the stones toward him and raised my own gun, firing back. A single shot caught him in the arm, and he twisted but didn't flinch. Then he broke into a run.

In an instant, he was on top of me, and we fell to the cobblestones, the water trickling down the cracks as we struggled. I saw my gun skittering away in the rain, and I flung my arms up in front of my face as he unleashed a flurry of blows down on my head, his fists raining down like hell.

The weight of his blows was mechanical, each one like a steam engine—clean, perfect, and precise. I could feel my arms stinging, but countered with an elbow and felt something crack. We rolled over the wet ground, trading punches.

"End of the line for all of us," he hissed.

But at that moment, I felt a pulse of energy—a pure, white wave blasting through us with such a powerful force that we were torn apart, and I was flung two yards away, landing with a thump that knocked the air out of me.

Everything went still.

CHAPTER 24
MERGING MEMORIES

I t was as if I were surrounded by darkness, an empty void stretching in every direction I looked. No walls, no ground, no sky. I couldn't tell if I was floating, falling, or doing everything all at once. And then the dark began to form a world, almost as if it were being painted around me, details emerging from the void.

I tried to move and realized I was falling—but not quite—as if I were falling without any weight. Suddenly, the floor appeared beneath my boots, black like the surface of a loch in Scotland. The air smelled singed, as if fireworks had just exploded around me.

At the same moment, he landed opposite me, with the same grunt that I made. He wore the same hat, though it was lopsided now, revealing his face. He had the same scar along his jaw and the same frame. But he looked younger than me, taller, and stood more confidently. I stared at my own face across from me and knew this was one of the echoes.

He grinned, lopsided. "Calder," he said. It was my voice, but cleaner, more defined. "You must be the original. I'm SL-042."

"Damn, did you run out of numbers or something?" I asked, taking a slow step back. I wasn't sure what he wanted, but he'd tried to kill me minutes ago, so I wasn't confident he wouldn't try again. "What's your purpose here?"

He cocked his head, looking at me. "My purpose? What's yours, old man?"

"I don't need a purpose," I responded, bitterness seeping through my voice. "I'm the original, aren't I?"

He smiled, his white teeth glinting in the darkness, reflecting a light that came from I knew not where. "You won't be for long."

Slowly, the world around us flexed, shifting, and we found ourselves in a dark amphitheater with no walls, cables like roots, and a Mirror standing in the center. The Mirror itself, however, was empty. There was no crack, no surface—just the frame.

SL-042 began approaching me slowly, his fingers twitching slightly, as if he were itching to strangle me on the spot.

Suddenly, I had an idea. I picked a point on his face. Anything. Then settled on the scar on his cheekbone, and I stared, tight, focused. If he was an echo, then I should be able to destroy him using observer amplitude as I had learned earlier— force the resolution and make the copy disappear like it was an overexposed print.

But he kept walking forward. He didn't blink or falter at all. Instead, he threw back his head and laughed. "Oh, that's fascinating," he said. "But, Calder—observer amplitude doesn't work on me. I'm not an echo. I'm the perfect variant."

He lunged at me—I countered. It was like fighting a Mirror, except I was no longer the optimal Calder. He smiled as I stumbled backward, caught off guard.

"You're too neat," I hissed and slammed my forehead into his. We both fell backward, stumbling.

He recovered first. "And you're too sloppy," he said, lunging forward.

But at that moment, the floor disappeared, and we both fell through. Reality shifted, and the weight seemed to change, as if we were no longer falling but floating upward. And then suddenly, I was standing in a corridor below ground, the yellow lights flickering and humming slightly.

Suddenly, I heard a voice from the wall. "Max."

It was the voice from the radio, but it was clear now—not obscured and not staticky. And I recognized it instantly.

"Hawthorne?" I asked.

"Hello, Max," he replied. "You've always been quick with it."

"But you're dead," I responded.

"A lot of things are dead," he said. "I am not one of them."

I still couldn't see him, and I glanced around, wondering where the voice was from. There was no static now, and it sounded as if he was right over my shoulder. But I couldn't see his face.

"Explain," I said. "I doubt I have a lot of time."

"Oracle—Version Three of the Mirror—was trained… on the old system," he said, smiling. "It rebuilt you from traces, echoes of your vibration, files, recordings, and even other observers' perceptions. It needed an anchor, so it built a perfect one. They named him SL-042 at ANGUS, but he fooled them—pretended to be like the others and faked his death."

"So how do we kill him?" I asked.

"You can't. You simply outlast him."

"That doesn't sound like a plan."

"Plans rarely survive," he replied wearily. "You're the anchor, Max—the system tunes to you. If there are two anchors, it'll force a resolution. You'll merge, and only the stronger will survive. Unless you break the pattern."

I shut my eyes, focusing. I tried to remember everything in London. Everything in Lisbon. And everything in Edinburgh. I tried to remember everything that had happened, and yet I couldn't.

"So what happens if I lose?"

"You'll be replaced," Hawthorne replied. "There's only room for one anchor, and one of you will fade."

"How are you talking to me?" I asked suddenly. "After we destroyed Krane's Mirror, wouldn't you have died?"

"Well, you would think that," he said. "But it was an entanglement leak—something simple enough. You see, a functioning version of the Mirror—or an intermediary version, at least—was built before you and Alicia ever destroyed Krane's new version. And so, a sort of network was created. A sort of web. I'm not flesh anymore, but my mind—" he paused before he continued, "—my mind is still here. And I have just enough strength to speak to you through the frequencies that permeate the universe."

"So why help me?"

"The reason I've always helped you," Hawthorne replied. "Because I am partially responsible for this." He sounded almost ashamed. "There were things I didn't tell you and secrets I withheld. Because she trusted me. Trusted me to save you and Alicia. And if you don't make it out—well, the world is as good as gone."

I could sense the world melting around me now, and I could sense that he was close—SL-042.

"Calder," Hawthorne said, his voice urgent. "He's going to break you down into parts until he overpowers you. You have to find your own anchor. Any memory. One thing that you can remember above all else."

"Alicia," I said.

And then the world fell apart.

———

The floor buckled, and I was back in the Mirror chamber, standing around twenty feet away from SL-042. He stepped through the Mirror frame as if he had been looking for me, then smiled when he saw my face.

"Where did you go, Calder?" he asked. "Surely you're not

fading already. I thought you might've just gone 'Poof!' like Finch did when I shot him."

"You were the one who shot Finch?" I asked, incredulous.

"Of course," he replied. "Who else? When I realized you were after this Mirror—to disable it—I quickly came to the conclusion that I couldn't let that happen. Anyhow, where were you?"

"Just getting some advice," I responded, circling away from him as he dashed toward me, springing into action. But this time, I changed my rhythm—sloppier, my stance shifted, my weight all different. He faltered.

"What are you playing at?" he snapped, circling me. "Don't try to fool me, Calder; I am you. I know what you know."

"Then you know I don't have a plan. My memories are broken."

"Exactly," he retorted, smiling. "You're breaking. No, already broken."

Then the world around us flickered.

I was in a room with a window overlooking a river. I knew where we were before I even realized it—Montevideo. It was a place I was so familiar with by now—so familiar because of her —that I half expected to see her there as I turned around. And then my heart leapt into my chest because she was there.

Alicia sat in one corner of the room, in a rocking chair, a shawl draped over her shoulders. Her hair was the color of steel, her eyes cold and white, covered in a gray film. I recognized her instantly. This was the one who had screamed through the Mirror all those days ago.

She leaned forward, peering at me. "Hello, Calder," she said. "I tried to warn you, you know."

"What do you mean?" I asked.

"Oh, never mind the details," she replied. "You always seem to pick fights with yourself, don't you?"

"This time I didn't pick the fight," I said—then paused. "Why am I even talking to you? You're not here."

"Neither are you," she replied. "Are you going to die tonight, Calder?"

The door splintered open as he kicked it down, rage filling his eyes. He was so fast. He leapt toward me before I could move.

My memories began to falter. Memories of Sister Agnes vanished as if they were broken pieces of glass. Streets I had walked a thousand times began to curve, and I barely remembered which direction I had walked. Names were twisted. I couldn't remember if Hawthorne was Elliott or if Elliott was Finch. Pieces of his life began to insert themselves into mine, and I tasted the smoke of cigarettes in a small, rickety café in Vienna. I saw myself killing an older version of Hawthorne, stabbing him in the heart and holding him in my arms as he bled out.

I tried desperately to focus. Then, suddenly, I remembered—I needed an anchor. I let my mind open up just to that and tried to find her again. A red scarf. I held onto it, clutching it desperately in my mind until I saw her beneath it.

"Do you still think you can save him?" the older version of Alicia asked. But I wasn't sure who she was asking or why she was asking. "Do you still think you can save the boy whose memories were never missing?"

I could barely speak, but I forced out six words. "I think I'm tired of dying," I said.

Suddenly, the room broke open, and we fell again. As we fell, he continued to break my mind. I could feel him gaining the upper hand, and I knew that SL-042 was replacing me.

As we fell, we were suddenly separated. The room was blank and void again. I glanced around, confused. My entire body felt bruised and broken, and I could barely remember who I was.

The third space we fell into was nothing but reflections—reflections stacked to the ceiling. An endless hall of glass and Mirrors. This was the visual manifestation of the Mirror's core. It was somewhere I had never been before but had always been part of, in a way.

There, stumbling to his feet just as I was, was SL-042. He and I faced each other in a room filled with a thousand reflections of us. Though none of them seemed to care, the reflections moved on their own, flickering and indifferent, as if threatening to replace both of us at once.

In one mirror pane, I saw a version of me, still in his apartment in Lisbon, typing away on his typewriter as his memory slowly faded. In another, I saw a variant of me lighting a cigarette, coughing as if the smoke were killing him.

Then SL-042 moved, slowly walking forward, and the room seemed to buckle under his footsteps. He was always ahead of me because he was the metronome.

Suddenly, I realized something: I didn't want to lose myself. I didn't. I didn't want to die, and I didn't want to lose my memories. I wanted to remain.

I swung forward desperately, in a way that caught SL-042 off guard. He tried to dodge, but my fist caught him cleanly on the jaw, and he stumbled backward.

I glanced around frantically, looking from mirror to mirror at all my variants. Then my eyes landed on one. This one was staring at me. He was older than I was. His hair was all gray, and his face was wrinkled. But he smiled as I looked at him, and then he stepped through his own reflection. I saw his scar was on the wrong side, and his face was older than mine.

"Who are you?" I asked.

"Hello, Calder," he said. "I'm SL-001."

"You mean..." My voice trailed off.

"Yes," he nodded, laughing painfully. "I'm the first variant generated by the Mirror—and please don't look at me too closely. I already feel as if I'm starting to burn."

I glanced away. He raised his eyes, staring at SL-042. "You're not so perfect, are you?"

It was a simple question, but SL-042 seemed confused. "What do you mean, scum?"

"You're out of sync," SL-001 said. "If you were truly in phase with the system, your observer amplitude would collapse me. Go on. Try."

He held his arms out, as if daring SL-042 to try.

And he did. The composite—the so-called perfect variant—focused on SL-001, eyes narrowing, as if he expected the old man to burst into flame under his stare. Nothing happened.

"See?" said SL-001. "You're still just a copy. You're not the true anchor, even if you're more 'perfect.'"

Then he turned to me. "He's built out of you, Calder. He knows you. So it's time for you to stop being yourself."

"How do you stop being yourself?" I asked.

"Simple," said SL-001. "You outmatch yourself."

SL-001 leapt across the room and attacked SL-042.

"It's not about hitting harder," he called over his shoulder. "Break the pattern, Max."

"That's the trick?" SL-042 asked, wiping blood from his mouth. "Overwhelm me?"

"No, the trick is to be wrong on purpose," SL-001 responded. "Which makes it right."

This time, we fought differently. I could see the old man panting, his face covered in sweat, his eyes tired, but he kept fighting alongside me. Suddenly, SL-042 began to change tempo. He grabbed a shard of glass, swinging down toward my body.

I couldn't dodge. I watched, almost as if in slow motion, as the glinting, sharp piece of glass fell toward my face, grasped in his hand.

Just like that, SL-001 threw his body in front of me, and with a thud, he fell to the ground. He rolled and came up bleeding, clutching at where he'd been stabbed.

His body looked like it was burning, glitching, and becoming more unstable. But I didn't have time to think. I spun around, kicking toward SL-042 before he could regain his balance, and I felt my boot connect with his ribcage. It was only for a heartbeat, but it was just enough—001 ran toward him, grabbing his arms and struggling to hold them.

"Now," the old Calder said through gritted teeth.

I dashed forward once more, slipping beneath his guard, low and fast. Grabbing a shattered piece of Mirror from the ground, just as he had done, I drove it into SL-042's chest and watched as he gasped for air that wasn't there.

He stared at me once more, hatred burning in his eyes, then his face fell forward, and his body went limp.

SL-001 was now alight, his whole body turning into flickering bright lights, as if he were phasing out of reality, but he smiled at me. He tried to say something, but I couldn't hear his words. Then he fell backward, still holding onto 042's body, through one of the dark Mirror frames—an empty one, where only void stretched in every direction.

The frame hummed—and all at once, every reflection began to flare, brighter than ever. And then, I saw the void again and felt my consciousness fading.

I wasn't quite sure if I'd won or lost.

CHAPTER 25
MIRROR MACHINATIONS

The next thing I saw was a light—humming, bright light that flickered in and out of existence for a while. As it came into focus, I saw Alicia's face etched with concern, leaning over me.

"Max," she began—but the floor buckled. The Mirror's Recursion Core chamber wasn't a room anymore. Whatever had happened inside the Mirror, the effects in the outside world were evident. The iron ribs screamed and protested as bolts sheared and the roof above us warped. The Mirror's surface shifted from black glass to boiling tar and back, shattering a thousand times in a second.

"On your feet," Alicia urged, pulling me up as best she could. "You left without a note, idiot."

I tried to stand, but my knees buckled. The world around me felt dizzying, and I couldn't quite remember who I was or who anyone else was. We staggered for the door together. The terminal was still awake, but as we walked, it blinked. Static spread across the screen, and it turned off. Alicia pulled the 6F badge off my wrist, where it was burning my skin, and tapped it to the reader. The door gave way, protesting as it did.

We broke into a run along the corridor, with me stumbling

behind her as the wailing sirens grew louder. Halfway up, the radio in the attaché case sputtered to life.

"Max," the voice said—clear again this time—and I recognized Hawthorne. "Good job, but all mirrors are connected on a fundamental, quantum level. All it takes is one." The radio went silent again.

We made our way through the last hatch, emerging into the air above—cool, damp, thick with the scent of rain and moss. She guided me along through the fog as the hillside itself shuddered, almost as if it were going to collapse in on itself. Somewhere under the earth, a deep rumble sounded.

Back at the forestry track, Alicia sighed, looking me up and down before bursting into laughter. "You're crazy, you know that, right?"

"Only partially," I responded weakly.

"Explain," she said, her laughter dying, her face becoming stern, as if she were scolding me for what I had done.

I leaned against a tree and raised a finger. When the world stopped spinning around me, I finally spoke. "There was a perfect variant," I said. "I tried to go back in time. Tried to stop Philby from betraying us. But the variant ruined my plans. SL-042. He was too perfect. Oracle was trained on us—files, recordings, all the data the first Mirror had. All the quantum connections. And the Mirror itself built an anchor, and it was called SL-042. He was like a metronome. Perfect. Never losing the beat. He attacked me in the Mirror, tried to overwhelm me. Then there was an older variant, too—SL-001. He helped me, and we managed to beat 042 inside the machine. When he finally lost sync, I finished it."

"That's the short version?" she asked incredulously.

"The only version," I replied.

"Fine," she said. "Let's get out of here."

———

Two weeks is a long time when there's finally nothing left to worry about. Well, nothing life-threatening, at least. We sat in rooms that smelled of suits and coffee and wrote down everything we could remember. We logged all our travel between London, Edinburgh, and Glasgow—even that initial assassination attempt in Lisbon. We documented everything and cataloged it all. We recorded what had happened at Kingsway and Invershiel, the prototypes we found, and even Rosyth Dockyard sublevels still operating in places they shouldn't be.

I handed over everything I had found: all the evidence, and the badge that had left a scar on my wrist that would never go away. Alicia handed over the rest. For the first time, we were introduced to the Nine themselves. Vickers and Dr. Nkosi were among them. Director Moreau was there as well, looking through the evidence with a stern face.

"We understand the core at Invershiel is unrecoverable," Vickers said.

I nodded. "I believe it's broken beyond repair. The one at Invershiel, at least."

"Our recommendation," Alicia continued, "is that we destroy any other versions—the one at Kingsway and any recovered Rosyth Dockyard assemblies—before someone else takes them."

"Agreed," Moreau said. Vickers nodded. "We'll pick up these pieces as quietly as we can. Perhaps," she added, a bit reluctantly, "they should be destroyed."

"Let's hope so," I responded.

As for MI6, Broadway did everything they could to interfere. Even though it had made them unpopular with government officials, Haldane still sent a letter—polished and professional—demanding more time. Elliott moved as well, working closely with Section IX and the Ministry. But Alicia and I filed our report all the same. Mirror V3 was broken, and the other two versions needed to be destroyed. That was our professional recommendation as two of the only remaining Sliders.

Hawthorne didn't come back online. I kept the attaché case

near my bedroom and turned it on occasionally, hoping that his voice would sound through the waves. But I never heard it. Cuadro stopped showing up in mirrors. Whether it had finally been killed when the Mirror destroyed itself or was just severely weakened, I wasn't sure.

But I still struggled. My memories were fragmented. Alicia tried to help. She would remind me of what we'd done that day. "We ate at three," she said. "You argued with Vickers at five, and then—remember?—we caught the night tram." I would nod, smiling, but I only remembered half of it. She tried to help with the memories of 042, too, but this slide was mine; she wasn't sure how to anchor it for me.

Sometimes, I would wake with memories that weren't mine. Memories of Vienna. Of Hawthorne's shirt pooling with blood beneath my hands. Sentences in Russian. And even Modin's name ghosting me. I'd hear myself say my own name, but in a voice that wasn't mine.

"You okay?" Alicia asked quietly one day as we sat together on a bench eating lunch.

"What do you mean?" I replied.

"Are you… you? What happened to the parts you lost?"

I laughed, my voice hoarse and painful. "I beat him, you know," I said. "But some days, I can still feel his mind in mine."

"This slide," she said. "This one was different. I wasn't there, so I can't anchor it for you. I can only help remind you who you are."

"But who am I?" I echoed.

She stayed quiet. She didn't know how to respond, and neither did I.

Some days, I would remember that damn tape—the one that held Modin's voice, Philby's voice, and all the proof of treason. Other days, that memory was blank. Sometimes, I'd see the tin, the clipboard, and the degausser winking at me as it cleared my proof, and on other days, it was gone, as if it had never happened.

I was still convinced, however. I took meetings with the highest-ranking men in MI6 and the Bureau. I told them Kim Philby wasn't just MI6's best asset; he was working for Moscow. A traitor. I told them Section IX had been his cover—his cover to filter Mirror data and information to the Soviets. I told them everything, but neither Elliott nor Haldane believed me. Whether or not they were in on it with him, I wasn't sure. But the one thing I was sure of was that no one believed Max Calder, the man with the broken memories and the paranoia, over the smooth, boyish, professional Philby.

The Nine listened. That was a benefit, at least. But they also watched my hands, and I could see their eyes shift uncomfortably as they saw the scar on my wrist. No one would say it to my face, but everyone was thinking the same thing—Max Calder could not be trusted.

Director Moreau was the only one who truly seemed to listen, her eyes softening whenever I mentioned Hawthorne's name among my ramblings.

"Listen, Calder," she said at last. "We will pursue the Kingsway lead, and we'll press on Rosyth Dockyard. We'll talk to Whitehall and bring it to their attention. Until then, leave. You're of no use to me if you have two memories—and both of them are broken."

"What about Philby?" I asked.

She fixed her eyes sternly on mine. "I believe you," she said. "But you brought us a man made of smoke and a recording you can't even play, let alone remember. If you bring me something I can put on a table, then we'll pursue him. Until then, there's nothing I can do."

I stormed from her office, anger overtaking me as it often did those days. Nobody believed me, not really. Even Alicia had her doubts. I knew it. I didn't blame her, of course. But she hadn't heard the wire. And some days even I doubted what I'd heard—the way Modin's voice sounded and the way Philby had so readily admitted that he worked for the Soviets.

But doubt isn't the same as amnesia. Patterns don't need a perfect memory for them to reveal themselves. Everything I had seen, everything I did remember, still pointed to Philby being a rat... a mole. And I was determined to catch that rat. They erased the spool and hid their tracks so well. But I knew that eventually, if I kept on long enough, I would find something.

I walked along the street, alone, until Alicia joined me, touching my sleeve gently.

"We'll find something, Max," she said. "Something solid."

"We will," I lied, but I knew even she didn't believe it.

I could live with ghosts, bad nights, and new scars. I could live with Hawthorne finally being gone. I could live with everything in my mind breaking. But what I couldn't live with was Philby getting away clean—getting away without losing something of his own.

I As I lit a cigarette, I wondered what Philby was up to now.

CHAPTER 26

RUSSIAN RECONSTRUCTION

Philby smiled contentedly, his boyish face contorted with pleasure. He glanced at his reflection in the dark window and, past that, London's damp horizon. The river was a black seam beneath the high arches, its surface shimmering with golden reflections from the yellow lamps. In the background, he saw London's skyline; beneath it, he saw victory.

Everything had gone according to plan—well, for the most part. Max Calder had ruined so much for him, but still, he had managed to salvage it, as he always did. It was officially a junk run. Section IX had signed the papers themselves, decommissioning everything. It was all backed up by the Ministry, and Haldane had signed off on it. But of course, the junk run was just what Philby wanted it to be. He made sure everything was sent off to the Russians, just as he intended.

He cut the engine and stepped out, his hat brim beaded with rain and his overcoat buttoned against the cold. He stepped into the warehouse.

"Ah, Philby, you've brought me something," Modin said.

Philby nodded, lifting the canvas. His hands unwrapped the first layer to reveal a copper hoop, and beneath it, a set of coils. Though it was in pieces, a panel of black glass was there as well.

It didn't quite reflect correctly, but it was good enough. Along with this came boxes upon boxes of drawings, blueprints, and notes from Section IX's leading scientists.

"Mirror cores," Philby said mildly, as if this were just another day. "Two were cracked, one clean. Field plates, a calibrator ring, prints and blueprints from Oracle and the other decommissioned assemblies, even microfilm of frame geometries—all verified by our top scientists."

He sighed, then added as an afterthought, "There was a witness."

Modin cursed under his breath, then crouched, studying the shape of the Mirror fragments in front of him. When he looked up, his face was only half satisfied.

"You promised us a machine," he said. "These are pieces."

"Ah, but pieces can be fit together like a puzzle," Philby said, his voice cheerful. "You were never going to walk out with a full working Mirror—not out of a secure British facility, not whole. But these, they've written off completely. Haldane himself has buried the Oracle project in forms to avoid embarrassment. And your people," he said, tapping Modin's shoulder, "will put this back together the way Russians always do."

He smiled. "And I've left enough doubt to convince Broadway that this failure should never be pursued again."

"And the failure?" Modin asked.

"Well," Philby said, "the core broke itself. The audit is closed, and Section IX has been reassigned. It was an international embarrassment—or would have been if information had reached the public. They've declared the physics impossible and gone home."

Modin's mouth twitched, almost forming a smile. Then he gestured toward one of the crates. "Those schematics?"

Philby nodded, sliding the lid off the box. "All the schematics you need. Schematics, blueprints—everything that was supposed to be destroyed, now in your hands."

"Our engineers will decide how long it will take," Modin said. "We will let you know."

Philby inclined his head slightly. Every bit of his body was taut, and yet he didn't want Modin to notice. He didn't want Modin to see how badly he wanted a drink or how tense this situation had been. Instead, he simply spoke.

"There is one more thing," he said lightly.

Modin's gaze shot up. "Yes?"

"Max Calder," Philby said. "He failed to produce a recording, which saved my life. He looked like a fool. But he's still alive, and he's still nosing around these things, still trying to investigate us."

Modin laughed then. "So? His Bureau is busy inventing reasons to be ashamed. Let the English suffer, and let them fight among themselves. Besides, our own Mirror will soon be operational. Then Max Calder will work for us, not against us."

Philby hid his distaste. "As you wish."

For a moment, Modin studied Philby's face. "London believes you have failed. Good. Do not hurry to rectify that. I've also heard from inside sources that new opportunities are opening in Washington. The Americans are building an empire. Make sure you are there to hear it."

Philby smiled, and it was genuine. If his next assignment was with Angleton, it would be easier. "They have no reason not to trust me," he added.

"Keep it that way," Modin responded. "We will move this tonight. Good job, Kim. You have done well."

"Thank you, Modin."

"Do not make me regret it," Modin said, and vanished into the night.

Philby sat there for a moment, a smile playing on his lips, then left, got back into his car, and drove slowly along the road. He parked three streets away from his flat, walking the rest of the way so no one could follow him or trace his movements.

Once inside, he adjusted his tie, took off his coat, and poured himself a glass of whisky. Oracle was gone now, buried under rubble. Kingsway would meet the same fate, with everyone thinking that the files had been destroyed. And the dockyard—well, for MI6's own benefit, they would never admit that they were responsible. His name was nowhere to be found in that story. And yet he definitely had one.

He lifted his glass slowly. "To the Mirror," he said softly, "...and Max Calder."

Then he drank.

CHAPTER 27
VARIABLES AND VERDICTS

As the weeks dragged on, London slowly became a hellhole for me. It was like a prison I couldn't escape. Hours and hours of paperwork, statements, and constant badgering by Bureau employees until my handwriting looked as if it were someone else's. Each time we told the same story, and each time we told it to a different man behind a different desk, until the paragraphs were burned into my memory. On paper, we had a victory. But victory wasn't ours. They took our report, yet nothing substantial seemed to happen.

Some afternoons, however, my schedule began to shift. Rather than telling them about Philby, Kingsway, or the dockyard, they would send me down the hall to a man I knew all too well was the Bureau's psychologist. He claimed he knew a great deal about memory. With hordes of degrees plastered on his wall, he seemed legitimate enough. He would ask me about my dreams and about how my memory seemed to break. Yet, he couldn't seem to fix it.

"Temporal dissociation," he once said, his voice confident but his face confused.

"That seems like a plausible enough explanation," I replied. "You been reading up on quantum science?"

He nodded uncertainly. "And we'll do our best to help you, Max. But it's going to take some time."

It was what they referred to as a process. It was a process I was familiar with. But I was confident the process wouldn't be successful.

———

And somewhere else, a different process was taking place. Five floors down, where no windows let light into the room, the Nine sat around their table, debating what was to be done. There were eight of them now, for one chair stayed empty. It was the chair of the one no one dared to name, the one who had betrayed them.

"Well," Vickers said at last, flipping through the pages of the day's ledger. "At least we have a result."

Dr. Nkosi inhaled from his pipe. "A result," he agreed. "The prototype under Kingsway is dormant, and Rosyth Dockyard— well, there are only residuals. But MI6 needs to suffer more."

"They staged it, we found it, and we shut it down," said the woman who sat next to him. "It's as clean as these things are going to get."

"It's as clean as they have made it look," Moreau said, and the table fell silent.

"Do you want a war with Broadway?" another man asked, his voice amused. "If we push on MI6 today, they'll have Whitehall banging at our doors tomorrow. We'll be audited again and again until we forget why we exist."

Vickers held up one finger. "Not so fast. MI5 has already shared their views. 'Overreach on home soil,' they called it. They've made it clear they disfavor MI6's actions, and Broadway's been told this failure is not to be repeated."

"Well, the Home Office does love the word 'overreach,'" someone else muttered.

"It actually matters a great deal," Vickers continued. "Our government is offended by MI6 doing science and, if anything, far more offended than by our own existence. For once, we're not the ones on the back foot."

"We have a chance," Moreau said. "We have the truth as well, and I believe that gives us a hand of cards to play against them."

"But our machine," Dr. Nkosi said, "it's nothing but a corpse. We don't have that—and that machine is what kept the Bureau alive."

They continued to argue for a while about what was to be done, and in the end, they put it to a vote. It was close.

"Enough," Moreau said at last, her hands set on the table, her face resolute. "We'll accept the shuttering of their site, take our win, and hold the cards we continue to hold. From there, we'll let MI5's bruised ego do the rest and plan for the day MI6 tries something like this again. At that point, we strike back."

"Aye," said Vickers, and the motion carried, five to three.

Afterward, alone with Vickers in a small room where no ears could eavesdrop, Moreau paced back and forth. She hadn't shown it in the meeting, but she was worried.

"He still has it," she said.

"The Mirror?" Vickers asked.

"Pieces, at least," she replied. "Enough to try again. I do think Max Calder is right. Philby is far too ambitious to stop with a failure, especially when he can blame it on us. They'll try to take something that isn't nailed down. They may already have."

"Shall I put a leash on Broadway, then?" Vickers asked. "But I don't know how much of a leash we have left."

"Just watch them," she said quietly. "I want our people monitoring the situation." She sighed. "And I want Max and Alicia out of the blast radius before something comes crashing down."

"Shall we put them on leave?" he asked.

She nodded. "Let's give them some time."

"They won't take it," he said.

"They'll take it," she insisted. "Because I will ask them nicely. Or force them to. Either way, they'll take it."

———

"Administrative leave," the officer said, staring at my face. He looked straight into my eyes, as if daring me to say no.

But I did. "I'm fine," I replied.

"You are many things, Mr. Calder," he replied. "But this is not optional. It's a doctor's recommendation, and approval comes from the very head of the Bureau. Two months. Rest. Allow yourself to heal." And he slid the paper over.

There was an order clipped on the clipboard, with the Director's authorization for extended leave, full pay, and private accommodation.

"'Refreshment of mind,'" I read aloud. "That's an interesting way to phrase it."

"Well, that's what you need," he replied.

Alicia joined me in the hall half an hour later. She had a paper, too, but it was thinner than mine.

"Clean," she said, smiling slightly. "Though I'm a little overqualified for my job—they should really give me a raise." She paused, and her face fell as she took in my expression. "I asked for the time off, anyway… to visit my mother."

"How is your mother?" I inquired.

"Alive," she said. "Though for how long, I'm not sure. But I'd like her to stay that way while I'm still someone she recognizes. I think I'll go to Montevideo. Visit her while I still can."

I nodded, and we walked out of the Bureau headquarters, out into the gray, cold daylight, and sat down on the steps, watching London bustle past. Somewhere in the distance, a tram rumbled.

"Send me a postcard, will you?" I asked, unsure of what else to say.

She smiled. "I will. And don't spend too much time trying to remember. Take a walk, get outside. Just focus on something other than your memories."

"I'll try," I said.

"Please do," she replied. Then she paused awkwardly. "Well, I have to go, Max. I'm late."

We sat there for a moment longer before she stood and, without another word, flagged a taxi at the curb.

And just like that, she was gone.

———

I rented a small apartment—a small apartment I didn't really want. Not anymore. It was a cheap flat in London, overlooking the sort of street more overrun with cats than people. The wallpaper had aged beyond its years, damp at the corners. The bed, at least, was nice. And I had room to keep my attaché case with the radio Hawthorne had spoken through. The flat was old, falling apart, and cramped.

And it was perfect.

I put the attaché case on the table, the way you would put a photograph where you can see it. Just so I could remember. Sometimes I slept in my bed; other times I slept in my chair. And I always tried to remember.

I would write Alicia letters, one after another, until I had stacks of them on my desk. I simply told her about my daily life. They were nonsense, mostly. I would write about the smell outside right after the cold night rain had stopped and was down to a patter. I would write about my whiskey and about the views from the apartment. And I would write about my memories and how they were still broken. But I didn't send any of the letters. I didn't want her to worry. She was busy on her own, and I had enough to worry about.

Because some nights, the other Max came back—SL-042—his face leering at me in my dreams. I would wake when the sun was still solidly beneath the horizon, sweating and panting as I sat up, feeling the spot where the 6F badge had burned a hole in my wrist. Sometimes, I would feel his memories—memories I wasn't sure were his anymore.

Memories that might have been mine.

I took walks, as Alicia told me to. It seemed foolish at first, but it helped me focus and helped my mind quiet itself. So I continued this routine as the New Year drew ever closer.

Less than a week before the New Year, I received an invitation to a small party for old Bureau agents, hosted by a Bureau contact. There would be men and women I knew —old Gerald from the Codes Section—and even some who used to work at MI6, as I once had. Naturally, I went.

I had nothing better to do with my time. I stood in a corner for the most part, people-watching, as it had once amused me. I didn't want to talk to anyone, so I simply let the room pass me by, examining everyone and trying to remember how it had once felt. I enjoyed it, in my own quiet way.

I drank, too. There was plenty of drink to go around—there always was at Bureau parties. At a quarter to midnight, someone began the countdown a bit too early, which made me chuckle to myself. Eventually, however, that heavy silence fell on my mind again, and I excused myself to the balcony.

Out here, it was peaceful and silent. London was dark now. The sun had set beneath the horizon, and I could see the river off in the distance. As I exhaled, my breath fogged, and the cigarette smoke drifted lazily into the air. I knew Big Ben would begin to chime soon.

"It's cold out here, isn't it?" said a voice behind me, and I spun around, not believing my own ears.

She stood there in a wool coat, different from any I'd seen her wear, but her hair and red scarf were unmistakable.

"I thought you were in Montevideo," I said.

"I was," Alicia replied. "My mother finally let me go, on the condition that I bring her back a proper English scarf. But the shops around here just aren't good enough."

"Well, I should hope not." I smiled.

She smiled back at me. "I got in yesterday, heard about the

party, and thought I'd try to come, just in case you came," she said.

I nodded, appreciating her, and we leaned on the railing together, watching the city below. The lights reflecting off the water, the traffic bustling through the streets even at night, and everything else.

"How's your mother?" I asked finally.

"She told me stories," she replied. "I'm not sure if they were right, or if they were true, but I enjoyed them."

We stood there, not talking about the Mirror, or Philby, or anything else—just small talk. She told me about a storm off the Argentinian coast, and I told her about my apartment. She laughed, saying it sounded like a classic place I would have enjoyed, and I nodded in agreement.

Somewhere inside, I heard a man boisterously shout, and the crowd began to count down.

"Ten, nine, eight..."

"Max," she said suddenly.

"Yes?"

"You're here," she said, as if her words could anchor me.

"Only if you are," I replied, and I wasn't lying. For the first time in months, I felt anchored.

As midnight struck, I leaned forward and kissed her. She kissed back, and we pulled apart just far enough to breathe.

"Happy New Year," she said quietly.

"Let's hope this one is better," I replied softly.

As we turned to go inside, however, I saw a man step out of a patch of shadow at the far end of the balcony.

"Congratulations," he said, though it was directed at neither of us specifically. He was well-dressed, and a foreign accent played on his tongue. He held out a small cedar box, and the smell hit me instantly.

"A gift," he said. "For luck. From Havana, with compliments."

He lifted the lid. The cigars were the color of expensive

tanned leather, elegantly arranged in the box, as if they were worth more than anything I'd ever smoked.

I wasn't sure what to do—fight, run, or take a cigar.

"You are Max Calder, are you not?" he continued. "I've heard your work is very... interesting."

"Have we met?" I asked.

He ignored me, his eyes sliding to Alicia. "Señora? Or should I say Señorita? Forgive me... English confuses me."

She didn't respond.

"Who sent you?" I asked.

He laughed and closed the lid. "Cuba is very beautiful this time of year," he said. "You should visit. I think you'll find the mirrors there are very... different."

And just like that, he pressed the box into my hands and stepped backward into the darkness. Before I could follow, he was gone.

"Do you know him?" Alicia asked.

"No," I replied. "No clue who he is. But he seems to know me."

She glanced down at the cigar box and tapped it with one finger. "Cuban," she said. "That's new."

"New Year, new mystery," I replied, tucking the box under my arm.

CHAPTER 28
GHOSTLINES

Later that night, as I made my way back to my small apartment that overlooked London, I examined one of the cigars. The leaf was a beautiful color with a rich scent, displaying all the markings of being foreign, exotic, and rich. I rolled it between my fingers—it had weight. The man had said Cuba.

Outside the window, London's air grew colder, and the New Year set in with a flurry of snowflakes that fell softly to the ground. The radio on the table remained silent, and I sighed, glancing at it with remorse. Hawthorne—how I missed his insights now.

I glanced back down at the cigar I held. I shouldn't have, but I did anyway.

I lit it, and the first draw tasted elegant and classy—as if a single breath from it were more than I could afford. Smoke floated into the air, dissipating. Whatever it was for, I thought while taking another puff, the cigar was of excellent quality.

———

Northbound, Alicia glanced at her reflection in the window, staring at her own face. She glanced at her eyes, sadness hidden within them, and thought back to Max Calder, whom she now knew was in London… likely alone. She missed him.

Still, she had a mission now—a mission in Edinburgh, and a sealed envelope in her pocket with a Bureau stamp. She wound her red scarf more tightly around her neck, sighed, and blew into her gloved hands to warm her fingers.

Though she missed him, The Nine had given her a job, and she planned to finish it—no matter what it took.

———

Vienna was cold, wearing winter like a draped shawl on its shoulders. Philby leaned back in his chair, stirring his coffee in a small café that was better left unnamed. He listened to Modin carefully as the man spoke.

"Washington," Modin said, taking a sip of his black coffee. "When you go, listen more than you speak. The last thing we need is the CIA on our tail. Move carefully, Philby. Russia is counting on you."

"Don't worry," Philby replied with a smile, his face glowing with happiness. "I'm always careful."

Modin nodded and stood to leave. He didn't glance back, but Philby's smile faded as the man walked away. Philby was pleased with his results, but he wasn't pleased with the system he had built, which was beginning to crumble around him. He could sense it.

———

Deep within one of the Bureau's sublevels, Moreau held a report at arm's length, reading it intently. ANGUS was quiet, Kingsway was cold and decommissioned. Yet, the temporal war had only just begun. If Calder was right, as she suspected he was, she knew that they had only scratched the surface of the corruption surrounding them.

And Cuba—the country began to surface in her reports almost daily now, and she closed her eyes, collecting her memories. "Not yet," she said aloud, her voice meant for none other than herself. "Not yet, but soon."

———

I finished smoking, glancing out my window at the night sky. It had been a good smoke, and my head was heavy now—the bed looked inviting, and I accepted the invite. I lay down, and sleep took me.

I dreamed that I was back in Lisbon, happy in my apartment. Except the apartment was not mine; it was a safehouse, and in the very center sat the Mirror. It didn't hum or pulse but screamed, and a dark, black door opened in the very center of it. Lisbon faded away, and my fingers tingled as I ventured through the open vortex at the center of the Mirror.

Then I was in Montevideo—a beautiful place, watching a child run along the beach, holding a kite in her hand. The air was fresh and smelled of beaches and good food.

I blinked, and suddenly, I was in Havana, watching a man stand a yard or so away from me, a white lab coat draped around his shoulders. I I leaned in closer, trying to see his face— and then darkness enveloped me.

I closed my eyes within the dream, and the floor became smooth. The Mirror stood in front of me, and I was back there— back where I had fought SL-042. The panes of glass went up forever, each one holding a version of Calder that could replace me. Each one whispering secrets I had already forgotten.

In that moment, I understood, even in my dream, that my story wasn't over yet.

And neither was the Mirror.

AFTERWORDS

PEOPLE AND PLACES

VIRGINIA HALL - ARTEMIS

Alicia Rayes has the code name Artemis in *Angus Sliders*, in honor of and in remembrance of a World War II heroine, Virginia Hall Goillot (1906–1982). She was awarded the Distinguished Service Cross (DSC), Croix de Guerre, and was a Member of the Most Excellent Order of the British Empire (MBE). She was an American who worked with the United Kingdom's clandestine Special Operations Executive (SOE) and the American Office of Strategic Services (OSS) in France during World War II.

After the war, Hall worked for the CIA's Special Activities Division. The Germans nicknamed her Artemis (the Greek huntress, goddess of the moon and guardian of secrets), and the Gestapo reportedly considered her "the most dangerous of all Allied spies."

Virginia Hall did not leave a memoir, give interviews, or talk much about her overseas experiences—even with her family. She received the United States' Distinguished Service Cross, becoming the only civilian woman during World War II to earn this honor.

THE CAMBRIDGE FIVE

The Cambridge Five was a ring of spies in the United Kingdom that passed information to the Soviet Union during World War II and the Cold War. Active from the 1930s until at least the early 1950s, none of the known members was ever prosecuted for spying. The number and membership of the ring emerged gradually, starting in the early 1950s.

The NKVD recruited the group during their time at the University of Cambridge in the 1930s, although the exact timing is debated. The five believed that Marxism–Leninism, as represented by Soviet communism, was the best political system and the most vigorous defense against fascism. They all provided large amounts of intelligence to the Soviets, to the point that the KGB became suspicious that some of it might have been false.

Yuri Modin later stated that Soviet intelligence doubted the Cambridge double agents during World War II and found it hard to trust that they had access to top-secret documents. They were especially suspicious of Philby, questioning how he could have become a British intelligence officer given his communist background.

Kim Philby is fictionalized in *Angus Sliders* as the story's primary antagonist, bringing both MI6 and the Soviets into the Mirror story.

KIM PHILBY

Harold Adrian Russell "Kim" Philby (1912–1988) was a British intelligence officer and a double agent for the Soviet Union. In 1963, he was exposed as a member of the Cambridge Five, a spy ring that had leaked British secrets to the Soviets during World War II and the early Cold War years. Among the five, Philby is believed to have been the most successful in passing secret information to the Soviets. Suspicion of his activities began in 1951.

Nicknamed "Kim" after the boy-spy in Rudyard Kipling's

novel, he was born in British India and educated at Westminster School and Trinity College, Cambridge. He was recruited by Soviet intelligence in 1934. After leaving Cambridge, Philby worked as a journalist, covering the Spanish Civil War and the Battle of France. In 1940, he started working for the United Kingdom's Secret Intelligence Service (SIS, also known as MI6). By the end of World War II, he had risen to a high-ranking position.

In 1949, Philby was appointed First Secretary at the British Embassy in Washington, serving as the main British contact with American intelligence agencies. Throughout his career as an intelligence officer, he sent large amounts of intelligence to the Soviet Union.

Philby was suspected of warning two other spies accused of Soviet espionage, Donald Maclean and Guy Burgess, both of whom fled to Moscow in May 1951. William Harvey of the FBI was convinced Philby was a Russian spy. Under suspicion, Philby resigned from MI6 in July 1951 but was publicly cleared by then-Foreign Secretary Harold Macmillan in 1955. He went back to working as a journalist and a spy for MI6 in Beirut but was ultimately forced to defect to Moscow after finally being exposed as a Soviet agent in 1963. Philby lived in Moscow until his death in 1988.

Kim Philby's fictionalized involvement in *Angus Sliders* is detailed in "Kim Philby and The Mirror".

YURI MODIN

Yuri Ivanovich Modin (1922–2007) was born in Russia. He joined the NKVD and, in 1947, was sent to London, where he became the primary contact for Kim Philby, Donald Maclean, Guy Burgess, Anthony Blunt, and John Cairncross. He served as an officer of the Ministry for State Security (MGB), the immediate predecessor of the KGB, after initially working as the desk officer for the Cambridge Five at Moscow Center during World War II.

By spring 1951, the situation was beginning to unravel as American codebreakers closed in on Maclean after finally deciphering secret messages he had sent while stationed in Washington during the war. Modin arranged the defections of Maclean and Burgess to Moscow after receiving a tip from Philby and eventually facilitated Philby's own defection in 1963 after he was also finally confirmed as a Soviet agent.

In 1951, Modin told Philby that "his position was becoming increasingly endangered through an intensification of the Security Service's inquiries about him." Initially, Modin feared Philby still worked for British intelligence. "He was so completely, psychologically and physically, the British intelligence officer that I could never quite accept that he was one of us, a Marxist in the clandestine service of the Soviet Union."

Yuri Modin is fictionalized in the *Angus Sliders* story as Kim Philby's involvement with the Mirror is exposed and issues arise between Modin, Philby, and the Russians concerning the acquisition of Mirror technology.

NICHOLAS ELLIOTT

John Nicholas Rede Elliott (1916–1994), the son of an Eton headmaster, was admitted to Trinity College, Cambridge, to study history—the same college his father had attended. Sir Robert Vansittart, the permanent under-secretary at the Foreign Office who worked very closely with the head of MI6, Hugh Sinclair, arranged for Elliott to join MI6. During World War II, he served as an acting lieutenant in the Intelligence Corps. Stationed in Istanbul, he played a key role in recruiting Erich Vermehren, who provided the British with detailed, confidential information on German intelligence operations.

After the war, in 1945, Elliott became head of station for the Secret Intelligence Service at the British Embassy in Bern and later served in the same role in Vienna in 1953. He was a close friend of Kim Philby during their early years at MI6. The two had worked together in Beirut, and Elliott felt Philby's betrayal deeply. Although Philby confessed to Elliott, he delayed signing a confession and fled to Moscow, where he was granted Soviet citizenship.

Nicholas Elliott is fictionalized in the *Angus Sliders* storyline, particularly in Istanbul during World War II and post-war as a supportive colleague of Kim Philby in MI6.

JAMES ANGLETON

James Jesus Angleton (1917–1987) previously worked in the Office of Strategic Services, the wartime predecessor to the CIA, in Italy and London during World War II. While in London, Angleton met Kim Philby and formed a close relationship. After the war, he returned to Washington, D.C., and became one of the CIA's founding officers. Initially, he was responsible for gathering foreign intelligence and coordinating with allied organizations.

As head of Staff A, Angleton worked closely with Kim Philby, who was also in Washington and was expected to become the future head of MI6. Philby called Angleton "a brilliant opponent" and a "fascinating" friend who seemed to be "catching on" before Philby's defection. In the 1950s, Angleton was recognized as the leading counterintelligence expert in the non-communist world.

Angleton served as the CIA's chief of counterintelligence from 1954 to 1975. He became increasingly convinced that the KGB had compromised the CIA and was the Agency's top mole hunter after Kim Philby's betrayal was initially exposed in the early 1950s.

James Angleton is fictionalized in *Angus Sliders* as the primary CIA contact and connection for MI6 and a primary cross-agency colleague of Kim Philby, particularly in Washington, D.C. He is increasingly convinced that Kim is a

Soviet agent, with that belief bolstered by evidence provided by Max Calder.

CHARLES FRASER-SMITH

Charles Fraser-Smith (1904–1992) was an author and former missionary best known as the inspiration for the quartermaster 'Q' in the James Bond films. This reputation comes from his World War II work on what became known as "Q Devices" for SOE agents operating across Europe, named after World War I Q-Ships.

Fraser-Smith was a temporary civil servant at the Ministry of Supply, but in reality, he worked under MI6, developing and supplying equipment for Section XV of Britain's WWII intelligence agency, the Special Operations Executive. He designed a wide variety of spy and escape devices, including miniature cameras hidden in cigarette lighters, shaving brushes with film, hairbrushes with maps and a saw, pencils with maps, and pens with hidden compasses. Fraser-Smith also participated in the intelligence operation codenamed Operation Mincemeat, which involved dropping a body carrying false papers off the Spanish coast to deceive the Nazis and cover up the invasion of Sicily.

Charles Fraser-Smith is fictionalized in *Angus Sliders* as one of the scientists on the MI6 team, further developing Mirror technology at both the Kingsway Tunnels and Invershiel.

TENDINHA DO ROSSIO, LISBON

If there is one true example of Lisbon's tavern culture, with all its simplicity and charm, A Tendinha do Rossio is it. It is the city's oldest running taberna, dating back to 1840. Nestled in the bustling heart of Rossio, right downtown, it offers passersby a window into a bygone era. A Tendinha do Rossio is such an iconic establishment that there is even a fado song from 1930 called "Velha Tendinha," which sings about the good 'ol bohemian days of Lisbon, which often involved downing one too many drinks. Fado literally says "a shabby and ordinary-looking little shop." Today, those in Lisbon take every single one of these words as a compliment.

HOTEL AVENIDA PALACE, LISBON

With the rise in rail traffic in Lisbon, Wagons-Lits, a railway-linked company, proposed to the Royal Portuguese Railway Company that its administrative building and restaurant be transformed into a grand station hotel, similar to the palaces of other European capitals. It was classified as a Second French Empire boulevardier-style building, and in 1890, two bronze fountains manufactured in France were installed in the square.

The interior decor featured an exquisite Belle Époque style. The rugs, portieres, and ottoman upholstery were of the finest quality. The furniture was purchased directly from Maple, one of London's most elegant stores. Almost all the rooms were distinguished by their silk linings or leather wall coverings. The dining room walls were decorated with leafy velvet, alternating with oak wainscoting.

Recognized by nobility and favored by diplomats and secret agents from all over the world, the hotel also served as a hub for knowledge and contacts—a recommended calling card. The hotel met expectations: a private orchestra filled the room with music during their famous Saturday balls, and while pairs danced around, spies from everywhere looked for conspiracies.

THE PARK HOTEL, ISTANBUL

The Park Hotel was one of Istanbul's most prominent European-style hotels during the first half of the twentieth century. Located near Taksim Square on the northern side of the city, it occupied a central position in the Pera/Beyoğlu district, the area historically known for its embassies, consulates, and foreign communities.

By 1948, the hotel had maintained much of its early prestige, although the wartime and postwar years had begun to leave signs of wear.

The building reflected a late-19th-century European design sensibility, with a stone façade, wrought-iron balconies, and large street-facing windows. The interior featured high ceilings, polished wood paneling, marble floors, and imported European chandeliers. The public spaces included a main lobby, reception desk, lounge areas, a dining room, and a modest bar. A manually operated elevator served the upper floors, though many guests used the staircase due to its slower speed.

During the late 1940s, the Park Hotel attracted a mixture of international travelers, business representatives, journalists, and diplomatic personnel. Owing to its proximity to embassies and government offices, it was commonly used for informal meetings and stopovers by foreign service officers and commercial delegations. The hotel was regarded as respectable and centrally located, though no longer considered luxurious by postwar standards.

KINGSWAY TUNNELS, LONDON

The Kingsway Tunnels were constructed in the early 1940s as a deep-level shelter beneath Chancery Lane tube station. Comprising two east–west aligned tunnels—one on each side of the Central Line—they were originally intended to provide air-raid shelter. However, like many deep-level shelters, they were not used for their intended purpose. The government instead used them as a hardened government communications center and a crucial Cold War communications hub.

Eventually, in 1956, it became the UK termination point for TAT-1, the first transatlantic telephone cable. The tunnels had odd entrances: one is next to a shopfront at 32 High Holborn, while the other is a goods lift on Furnival Street. A third access point, a combination of ventilation towers and a passenger lift at Tooks Court, was demolished in 2001.

The Kingsway Tunnels were once home to MI6's Special Operations Executive. They were referenced by Ian Fleming (who worked as an SOE liaison officer) in his first James Bond book, Casino Royale, as the location of M's Q Branch laboratories, which also has a connection with Charles Fraser-Smith.

The fictionalized Kingsway Tunnels in *Angus Sliders* serve as a secret MI6 location where Mirror technology was stored, having been stolen from the Bureau's Rosyth location under Kim Philby's direction.

ROYAL NAVAL DOCKYARD ROSYTH, SCOTLAND

Rosyth Dockyard is located on the north side of the Firth of Forth in Scotland and is one of the largest waterside manufacturing facilities in the UK. Babcock Marine currently operates it for the UK government, primarily for refitting or dismantling decommissioned nuclear submarines and serving as an integration site for the Royal Navy's aircraft carriers. Formerly known as the Royal Naval Dockyard Rosyth, it was under direct Royal Navy control and played a crucial role in both World Wars as a ship-repair and dry-dock facility.

During World War II, the dockyard underwent significant expansion, and over 3,000 warships were repaired or refitted there under the supervision of Rear Admiral Henry Bovell. In 1948, the name HMS Cochrane was restored, re-establishing the facility as an active Royal Navy base. In 2023, Rosyth was returned to the Royal Navy as HMS Caledonia, maintaining the historic connection between the Royal Navy and the local communities in Rosyth.

In the *Angus Sliders* story, the fictionalized Rosyth is the secret location where the Bureau develops the Mirror without the

Royal Navy's knowledge. This Bureau location was incorporated into the World War II expansion of the dockyard in secret.

54 BROADWAY, LONDON

54 Broadway in London's Westminster served as the primary operational base for the Secret Intelligence Service (SIS), also known as MI6, from 1924 onward. MI6 was managed by Hugh Sinclair, who became the second 'C,' taking over from Mansfield Cumming, the original 'C,' in 1923. Broadway also housed the Government Code and Cypher School (GC&CS), although the two organizations operated independently. During World War II, the building displayed a brass plaque outside that read "Minimax Fire Extinguisher Company," though many people knew exactly who was really based there. GC&CS eventually moved to Bletchley Park in 1939. It's alleged that a later MI6 head, Sir Stewart Menzies, had a tunnel from 54 Broadway to his home in Queen Anne's Gate.

THE GORBALS, GLASGOW

The Gorbals is a neighborhood in Glasgow, Scotland, originally known as Bridgend, located on the south bank of the River Clyde. It dates back to at least 1285 AD, when it was a small village near a bridge over the river. The name might mean either 'rough village' (referring to the rough landscape) or 'wide, spacious place.' By the late 19th century, the Gorbals had become a thriving industrial suburb, attracting many Protestant and Catholic immigrants from Ireland—especially from Ulster, notably County Donegal—as well as Italians and Jewish immigrants from the Russian Empire and Eastern Europe.

In the 1920s, the Gorbals gained a reputation as a notorious district characterized by extreme poverty, overcrowded tenements, poor health conditions, and a culture of violence. Despite these hardships, residents built strong communities. During this period, efforts to combat overcrowding began through local authority housing; however, the challenges of slum conditions and social issues persisted for decades.

By 1948, the Gorbals was still marked by dilapidated tenements, severe public health problems, and terrible living conditions. Overcrowding was widespread, with many families sharing a single room, and sanitation facilities were inadequate, resulting in high disease rates in what was considered one of Europe's worst slums.

Despite the challenging environment, a strong community spirit persisted, with residents finding ways to connect and support one another. However, poverty and overcrowding contributed to a culture of violence and gangs, making the area infamous for razor gangs.

In *Angus Sliders*, Max Calder's background growing up in the Gorbals explains many of his capabilities and personal characteristics, including a possible chip on his shoulder.

THE GRAND CENTRAL HOTEL, GLASGOW

The Grand Central Hotel was built into the eastern façade of Glasgow Central Station. The hotel's exterior—sandstone the color of old coins—rose directly above Gordon Street, crowned with turrets and dormers. The copper roof had a dull greenish hue, and the carved stone figures above the archway looked weathered from the elements. It was one of Glasgow's most prestigious hotels in its heyday, hosting residents such as John F. Kennedy, Frank Sinatra, Winston Churchill, Gene Kelly, Bing Crosby, Charlie Chaplin, and Laurel and Hardy.

The hotel was built by the Caledonian Railway and opened in 1883 as the Central Station Hotel. It was expanded along with the station from 1901 to 1906 and later renamed the Central Hotel. The world's first long-distance television images were transmitted to the hotel on May 24, 1927, by John Logie Baird.

By 1948, the rooms were spacious yet weary, with iron-framed beds and thin, starched sheets. The sound of passing trains below vibrated through the floorboards like a distant heartbeat. The Grand Central wasn't just a hotel; it was a listening post in marble. It had heard everything—departures, returns, affairs, farewells, lies rehearsed and forgotten. In Angus Sliders, Bureau men met here under the cover of commerce, exchanging envelopes in plain sight. Its corridors possessed the acoustics of confidence—just loud enough to drown out what truly mattered.

RMS QUEEN MARY

From the start of her construction in 1930 in Clydebank, Scotland, the Queen Mary was destined to stand out as a one-of-a-kind transatlantic liner. In 1948, she returned to passenger service after serving as a troop transport during the war, resuming her prestigious transatlantic voyages between Europe and North America.

Having set a new standard for luxury and opulence with lavish Art Deco interiors and amenities, she carried notable passengers during her post-war period of elegance. She featured five dining areas and lounges, two cocktail bars, swimming pools, a grand ballroom, a squash court, and even a hospital.

The Queen Mary established a new benchmark in transatlantic travel, which the wealthy and famous, including Elizabeth Taylor, Clark Gable, and Bob Hope, considered the only civilized way to cross the Atlantic. She captured the hearts and imaginations of the public on both sides of the Atlantic, embodying the spirit of an era known for its elegance, class, and style.

OPERATION MINCEMEAT

Operation Mincemeat was a successful British deception operation during World War II, aimed at disguising the 1943 Allied invasion of Sicily.

Two members of British intelligence obtained the body of Glyndwr Michael, a homeless man who died from ingesting rat poison. They dressed him as an officer of the Royal Marines and placed personal items on him, identifying him as the fictitious Captain (Acting Major) William Martin. Also placed on the body were forged letters between two British generals, suggesting that the Allies planned to invade Greece and Sardinia—with Sicily serving only as a decoy.

Mincemeat was based on the 1939 Trout memo, written by Rear Admiral John Godfrey, the director of the Naval Intelligence Division, and his personal assistant, Lieutenant Commander Ian Fleming—yes, the same Ian Fleming who later created James Bond. The plan involved transporting the body to the southern coast of Spain by submarine and releasing it near shore, where Spanish fishermen picked it up the next morning. Ultra decrypts of German messages revealed that the Germans bought the ruse.

Charles Fraser-Smith created the container that carried the body, preserving it until it was dropped into the ocean.

ACKNOWLEDGEMENT

BOO BOO BABY, I'M A SPY!

In Chapter 3 of *Angus Sliders*, the storyline draws on material from the award-winning journalist and author Ben MacIntyre's book "A Spy Among Friends: Kim Philby and The Great Betrayal" and the autobiography of Nicholas Elliot.

The splendid description of Istanbul during World War II is derived from Ben's book and from the MI6 official historian's description:

"Intelligence agencies could mix and mingle here in Istanbul, allowed to bribe, seduce, and betray, each agency with a vast network of agents, double agents, blackmailers, arms dealers, pimps, forgers, hookers, and con artists."

The quote *"a ferocious dry martini with the kick of a horse"* served at Ellie's Bar comes from Nicholas Elliot's autobiography.

It was also wonderful to quote the song *"Boo Boo Baby, I'm a Spy,"* adding an element of humor to a city crawling with risks.

Apple Music has a version of it at:

https://music.apple.com/us/album/boo-boo-baby-im-a-spy-single/1772235039

THE MIRROR
AND RECURSION

Recursion is when a function, process, or system calls itself to solve a problem or build a structure, like the pattern of a fern leaf. It involves a loop of self-reference where solving a problem depends on solving smaller versions of the same problem.

In Simple Terms:

Recursion is when something is defined in terms of itself.

In the Mirror universe, recursion is not just a computational or mathematical principle—it becomes ontological: a condition of reality where events, identities, and timelines refer back to themselves. For example, in the Bureau Archives Trilogy, Calder might relive events altered by previous versions of himself. Each loop is defined by the one before it, like recursive function calls. It can create echoes. Recursive anomalies are outputs from partial loops that never fully collapse—"fragments" of identity or memory.

The Mirror acts like a recursion engine, feeding emotional data (such as regret, choice) back into the system to reshape reality (as seen with Max and Alicia's slides). A Mirror recursion loop isn't a mistake. It's the system asking the same question repeatedly until it gets the answer it seeks. Recursion isn't time travel. It's time remembering itself.

KIM PHILBY AND
THE MIRROR

Kim Philby's involvement with *Angus Sliders* and the Mirror is entirely fictional. However, this fictional involvement provides a significant storyline thread throughout the book. Philby stands out as one of MI6's most skilled officers—charming, meticulous, and exceptionally proficient in the secretive world of espionage. By 1948, Philby held a senior liaison role connecting MI6 with the newly formed CIA, granting him direct access to classified Anglo-American intelligence exchanges, atomic research summaries, and inter-agency operations. Beneath his polished, trustworthy exterior, however, Philby's true allegiance was with the Soviet Union and its intelligence agencies—initially the NKVD and later the KGB.

Philby's duplicity enabled him to pass vast amounts of sensitive intelligence to the Soviets. This included critical information from Allied cryptographic programs and early nuclear research. He excelled in ambiguity, both personally and professionally—his mastery of concealment and deception became vital to his role in *Angus Sliders*.

Within *Angus Sliders*, the Mirror is depicted as a classified temporal technology developed under the Bureau's supervision and tested at Rosyth Naval Dockyard from 1943 to 1945. After the disastrous "Rosyth Incident" in 1945, much of the research was believed lost, and the remaining files were locked away under Bureau control. Yet, unbeknownst to the Bureau, a secret faction within MI6, led by a fictionalized Philby and associates in Section IX, had already infiltrated the project's edges.

Philby's role as a counter-operations officer gave him direct access to postwar recovery efforts at the site of the Rosyth explosion. Disguised as area security measure, he orchestrated the discreet extraction of Mirror components and a series of experimental field notes written by Dr. Emil Krane. These documents laid the foundation for MI6's own secret project, codenamed Project Oracle, at a black site called ANGUS in Invershiel, Scotland, where attempts were made to recreate the Mirror. Philby also moved components from Version Zero of the Mirror from Rosyth to the Kingsway Tunnels in London.

The fictionalized Philby's true motives in *Angus Sliders* were twofold: first, to deliver the Mirror technology to Moscow, giving the Soviets a technological edge over MI6 and the Americans; second, to manipulate the narrative within MI6 by using disinformation to mislead the Bureau's investigation and divert suspicion onto others.

In *Angus Sliders*, Philby serves as both a human mirror and a thematic counterpoint to Max Calder. Calder is fractured by time; Philby, by loyalty. Both men lead double lives marked by secrecy and deception, but their duplicity differs: Calder's is existential, while Philby's is ideological.

Philby's theft of Mirror technology ignites a covert Cold War arms race—fought not just with weapons but with time itself, blending political and temporal espionage. His historical treachery becomes, in the *Angus Sliders* universe, the catalyst for a new kind of covert warfare: the weaponization of time. His theft of the Mirror's technology and data at Rosyth isn't just an act of treason—it marks the first incident of temporal espionage.

QUANTUM MECHANICS AND THE MIRROR

The Mirror is, of course, entirely fictional. But the idea of an inanimate object having consciousness or even becoming sentient is no longer regarded as outrageous, especially within the realms of quantum mechanics and panpsychism. This concept forms the foundation of the Mirror in *Angus Sliders* and the *Bureau Archives Trilogy*. Over time, its level of consciousness and sentience increases, and the dangers associated with it grow exponentially.

There are two elements of quantum mechanics that play into the story of the Mirror. The first is quantum entanglement, which posits that what happens in one place can affect what happens in another place instantaneously over any distance, including across the universe. It happens at a subatomic level. When two particles, such as a pair of photons or electrons, become entangled, they remain connected even when separated by vast distances.

A common misconception about entanglement is that the particles are communicating with each other faster than the speed of light, which would go against Einstein's special theory of relativity. Experiments have shown that this is not true, nor can quantum physics be used to send faster-than-light communications. Though scientists still debate how the seemingly bizarre phenomenon of entanglement arises, they know it is a real principle that passes test after test. In fact, while Einstein famously described entanglement as "spooky action at a distance," today's quantum scientists say there is nothing spooky about it.

While all of this is happening at an atomic and subatomic level, *Angus Sliders* proposes that it is happening at a human level. Could a human be in two places at once, yet be interconnected in such a way that what happens to one incarnation happens to the other? And what happens when you have multiple incarnations?

This brings in the second element of quantum mechanics: superposition. The concept of quantum superposition might be difficult to understand or visualize. Many descriptions have been used to try to describe it. One is the analogy of a coin that is both heads up and tails up at the same time—a blended state where the coin is in multiple states until observed at which time it becomes one or the other. Another illustration is the famous Schrödinger's cat thought experiment, in which physicist Erwin Schrödinger imagined placing a cat in a sealed box along with a poisonous substance that has an equal chance of killing the cat— or not—within an hour. Schrödinger proposed that, at the end of the hour, the cat could be said to be both alive and dead, in a superposition of states, until the box is opened, and that the act of observation randomly determines whether the cat is alive or dead. Schrödinger intended this example to demonstrate what he saw as the absurdity of quantum science. But superposition is a major characteristic of quantum mechanics. In the quantum world, particles can exist in a superposition of multiple states simultaneously until they are observed or measured, at which point they "collapse" into one specific state.

When applied to the Mirror, the concept of superposition explains how the device manipulates time and reality in a way that seems impossible under normal conditions. The Mirror exploits the principles of superposition to create multiple potential timelines or temporal realities that exist in parallel, allowing it to influence or access multiple points in time without being constrained to a single path. The temporal slides that Sliders experience are influenced by superposition, where the Mirror creates multiple potential pathways in time for them to travel along. These temporal states are not fixed but exist as overlapping possibilities until the moment of the slide occurs. Sliders experience this as moving through layers of time, each one with its own set of events, people, and circumstances.

This explains the fluidity of time that Sliders experience when using the Mirror—why sometimes events seem to shift unpredictably, or why the temporal landscape feels fragmented, as the Mirror weaves together different temporal threads before settling on a final one.

One of the most fascinating implications of applying superposition to the Mirror is the idea that it could access multiple realities at once. With superposition in play, the Mirror's function extends beyond simple temporal navigation. Instead of following a single, fixed timeline, the Mirror can manipulate a quantum field of time, where countless potential futures and past events exist in parallel. By using the principles of superposition, the Mirror can travel through this quantum time field, collapsing reality into a single path but with endless possibilities before it does so. The Mirror can calculate, adjust, and collapse multiple realities simultaneously, allowing it to manipulate time in a way that traditional technology cannot. The parallel realities and multiple possible futures that arise from this concept make the Mirror not just a time machine but a device capable of accessing and altering the quantum fabric of time, with far-reaching consequences for those who interact with it.

QUANTUM MECHANICS AND PANPSYCHISM

Panpsychism argues that consciousness is not limited to peoples' brains or to living organisms but extends to all aspects of the universe. The word itself was coined by the Italian philosopher Francesco Patrizi in the sixteenth century, and derives from the two Greek words pan (all) and psyche (soul or mind). Panpsychism is a philosophical view that posits consciousness, or a mind-like aspect, as a fundamental and ubiquitous feature of all reality. It suggests that everything, from humans to rocks and even subatomic particles (or Mirrors!), possesses some level of consciousness. This idea challenges the traditional belief that only living beings have consciousness.

Philosophers like Plato have been associated with panpsychistic ideas. Recent interest in panpsychism has been fueled by the hard problem of understanding consciousness, by developments in neuroscience, by quantum mechanics, and a growing dissatisfaction with physicalist and classic approaches to consciousness.

It can be shown that a conscious being can distinguish definite perceptions and their quantum superpositions, while a physical measuring system without consciousness cannot distinguish such states. In particular, it suggests that consciousness is not emergent but a fundamental feature of the universe.

There are many objections to the idea of panpsychism. Mostly around the lack of empirical proof. However, the following academic paper does explore the whole idea of quantum providing a basis for panpsychism.

A Quantum Physical Argument for Panpsychism
Shan Gao
History & Philosophy of Science & Centre for Time,
University of Sydney,
NSW 2006, Australia.
Institute for the History of Natural Sciences,
Chinese Academy of Sciences,
Beijing 100190, P. R. China.

WITH THANKS

I owe a huge debt of gratitude to everyone around me who has put up with the disruption caused by my journey as an author. This is my second novel, which combines espionage and science fiction with a heavy dose of film noir. There is a massive amount of research to get even minute details right, such as the popular bars frequented by suspicious characters or details of locations from specific years. These days, it is slightly easier to check some of the facts; nevertheless, it is time-consuming. The research notes end up being bigger than the final book!

My wife, Lucinda, has been extremely encouraging, especially as I have added "author" to tech entrepreneur, company founder, and advisor to tech company CEOs. However, it has been a long-held desire to take stories and ideas I have had for a long time and translate them into novels, particularly those based around my fascination with computing and quantum mechanics.

For any book, proofreaders and editors play a major role in making sure the novel hangs together and reads well. A big thank you to those who helped in this regard, including Hannah and especially Carson from the great state of Texas.

ABOUT THE AUTHOR

Alexander Bentley is an award-winning author and serial entrepreneur living in California, with experience founding and leading technology companies in both the UK and the USA. He has held senior roles, including CEO, in both public and private enterprises. Over the years, he has had numerous interactions with the government, including the UK Ministry of Defence and the US Department of Defense, as well as various aerospace and defense companies. His own technology companies have included those that address the secure communications and networking markets. Additionally, with a physics background, he is well-versed in the principles of quantum mechanics and quantum computing.

Writing under the name Alexander Bentley, he is married to Lucinda and has two grown children, Alexander (Lex) and Virginia (Ginny).

Angus Sliders is Alexander's second Spy-Fi novel, which entangles the world of espionage with science fiction, bringing a new approach to post-World War II noir writing.

To keep up-to-date with Alexander Bentley:
www.AlexanderBentley.com
and
www.facebook.com/AuthorAlexanderBentley